Leaving the World

Douglas Kennedy's eight previous novels include the critically acclaimed bestsellers *The Big Picture*, *The Pursuit of Happiness*, *A Special Relationship*, *State of the Union* and *The Woman in the Fifth*. He is also the author of three highly praised travel books. His work has been translated into twenty-two languages. In 2006 he was awarded the French decoration of Chevalier de l'Ordre des Arts et des Lettres. Born in Manhattan in 1955, he has two children and currently divides his time between London, Paris and Maine.

Praise for *Leaving the World* and Douglas Kennedy

'An emotionally intense and totally compelling read' *Woman & Home*

'Kennedy is a complete genius when it comes to understanding the minds of stylish but troubled women. What's more, he does so enthrallingly and movingly' *Daily Mirror*

'Kennedy cannot help but write grippingly' *Observer*

'Douglas Kennedy is back with another of his intriguing, beautifully written page-turners' *Elle*

'Kennedy is a fantastic, feisty writer' *Independent on Sunday*

ALSO BY DOUGLAS KENNEDY

Fiction
The Woman in the Fifth
Temptation
State of the Union
A Special Relationship
The Pursuit of Happiness
The Job
The Big Picture
The Dead Heart

Non-fiction
Chasing Mammon
In God's Country
Beyond the Pyramids

DOUGLAS KENNEDY

Leaving the World

arrow books

Published by Arrow Books 2010

6 8 10 9 7

First published in Great Britain in 2009 by
Hutchinson
Random House, 20 Vauxhall Bridge Road,
London SW1V 2SA

www.rbooks.co.uk

Addresses for companies within The Random House Group Limited can be found at:
www.randomhouse.co.uk/offices.htm

The Random House Group Limited Reg. No. 954009

A CIP catalogue record for this book is available from the British Library

ISBN 9780099509684

The Random House Group Limited supports The Forest Stewardship
Council (FSC), the leading international forest certification organisation. All our
titles that are printed on Greenpeace approved FSC certified paper carry the FSC logo.
Our paper procurement policy can be found at www.rbooks.co.uk/environment

Mixed Sources
Product group from well-managed
forests and other controlled sources
www.fsc.org Cert no. TT-COC-2139
© 1996 Forest Stewardship Council

Typeset by SX Composing DTP, Rayleigh, Essex
Printed and bound in Great Britain by
CPI Bookmarque Ltd, Croydon, CR0 4TD

for my daughter Amelia

'The question of authority is always with us. Who is responsible for the triggers pulled, buttons pressed, the gas, the fire?'

– Leonard Michaels

'Fate is not an eagle, it creeps like a rat.'

– Elizabeth Bowen

ON THE NIGHT of my thirteenth birthday, I made an announcement.

'I am never getting married and I am never having children.'

I can remember exactly the time and the place where this proclamation was delivered. It was around six p.m. in a restaurant on West 63rd Street and Broadway. The day in question was January 1st 1987, and I blurted out this statement shortly after my parents had started fighting with each other. Fuelled by alcohol and an impressive array of deeply held resentments, it was a dispute which ended with my mother shouting out loud that my dad was a shit and storming off in tears to what she always called 'the little girls' room'. Though the other patrons in the restaurant gawked at this loud scene of marital discontent, their fight came as no great shock to me. My parents were always fighting – and they had this habit of really combusting at those junctures in the calendar (Christmas, Thanksgiving, the anniversary of their only child's arrival in the world) when family values allegedly ruled supreme and we were supposed to feel 'all warm and cuddly' towards each other.

But my parents never did warm and cuddly. They needed shared belligerence the way a certain kind of drunk needs his daily eye-opening shot of whiskey. Without it they felt destabilized, isolated, even a little lost. Once they started baiting and taunting each other, they were in a place they called home. Unhappiness isn't simply a state of mind; it is also a habit . . . and one which my parents could never shake.

But I digress. New Year's Day, 1987. We'd driven in from

1

our home in Old Greenwich, Connecticut for my birthday. We'd gone to see the New York City Ballet perform the famous Balanchine production of *The Nutcracker*. After the matinee, we adjourned to a restaurant called O'Neill's opposite Lincoln Center. My dad had ordered a vodka Martini, then downed a second, then raised his hand for a third. Mom started berating him for drinking too much. Dad, being Dad, informed Mom that she wasn't his mother and if he wanted a goddamn third Martini, he'd drink a goddamn third Martini. Mom hissed at him to lower his voice. Dad said he was not going to be infantilized. Mom retorted, telling him he deserved to be infantilized because he was nothing more than a little baby who, when reprimanded, threw all his toys out of the crib. Dad, going in for the kill, called her a failed nobody who—

At which point she screamed – in her most actressy voice – 'You pathetic shit!' and made a dash for 'the little girls' room', leaving me staring down into my Shirley Temple. Dad motioned to the waiter for his third vodka Martini. There was a long awkward silence between us. Dad broke it with a non-sequitur.

'So how's school?'

I answered just as obliquely.

'I am never getting married and I am never having children.'

My father's response to this was to light up one of the thirty Chesterfields he smoked every day and laugh one of his deep bronchial laughs.

'Like hell you won't,' he said. 'You think you're gonna dodge all this, you've got another think coming.'

One thing I've got to say about my dad: he never spared me the truth. Nor did he think much about cosseting me from life's manifold disappointments. Like my mom he also operated according to the principle: after a vituperative exchange, act as if nothing has happened – for a moment or two anyway. So when Mom returned from 'the little girls' room' with a fixed smile on her face, Dad returned it.

'Jane here was just telling me about her future,' Dad said, swizzling the swizzle stick in his vodka Martini.

'Jane's going to have a great future,' she said. 'What did you tell Dad, dear?'

Dad answered for me.

'Our daughter informed me that she is never going to get married and never have children.'

Dad looked right at Mom as he said this, enjoying her discomfort.

'Surely you don't mean that, dear,' she said to me.

'I do,' I said.

'But a lot of people we know are very happily married . . .' she answered. Dad cackled and threw back vodka Martini number three. Mom blanched, realizing that she had spoken without thinking. ('My mouth always reacts before my brain,' she once admitted to me after blurting out that she hadn't had sex with my father for four years.)

An awkward silence followed, which I broke.

'No one's actually happy,' I said.

'Jane, *really* . . .' Mom said, 'you're far too young for such negativity.'

'No, she's not,' said Dad. 'In fact, if Jane's figured that little salient detail out already, she's a lot smarter than the two of us. And you're right, kid – you want to live a happy life, don't get married and don't have kids. But you will . . .'

'Don, *really* . . .'

'*Really* what?' he said, half shouting in that way he did when he was drunk. 'You expect me to *lie* to her . . . even though she's already articulated the fucking *truth*?'

3

Several people at adjoining tables glared again at us. Dad smiled that little-boy smile which always crossed his lips whenever he misbehaved. He ordered a fourth Martini. Mom strangled a napkin in her hands and said nothing except: 'I'll drive tonight.'

'Fine by me,' Dad said. Martini number four arrived. He toasted me with it.

'Happy birthday, sweetheart. And here's to you never living a lie . . .'

I glanced over at my mother. She was in tears. I glanced back at my father. His smile had grown even wider.

We finished dinner. We drove home in silence. Later that night, my mom came into my room as I was reading in bed. She kneeled down by me and took my hand and told me I was to ignore everything my father had said.

'You will be happy, dear,' she told me. 'I just know it.'

I said nothing. I simply shut my eyes and surrendered to sleep.

When I woke the next morning, my father had gone.

I discovered this when I came downstairs around eleven. School wasn't starting for another three days – and, as a new-fangled teenager, I had already started to embrace twelve-hour zone-outs as a way of coping with that prevalent adolescent belief: *life sucks*. As I walked into the kitchen I discovered my mother seated at the breakfast bar, her head lowered, her make-up streaked, her eyes red. There was a lit cigarette in an ashtray in front of her. There was another one between her fingers. And in her other hand was a letter.

'Your father has left us,' she said. Her tone was flat, stripped of emotion.

'What?' I asked, not taking this news in.

'He's gone and he's not coming back. It's all here.'

She held up the letter.

'He can't do that,' I said.

'Oh, yes, he can – and he has. It's all here.'

'But this morning . . . he was here when you got up.'

She stared into the ashtray as she spoke.

'I cooked him his breakfast. I drove him to the station. I talked about going to some barn sale in Westport this Saturday. He said he'd be home on the 7:03. I asked him if he wanted lamb chops for dinner. He said: "Sure . . . but no broccoli." He gave me a peck on the cheek. I drove to A&P. I bought the lamb chops. I came home. I found this.'

'So he left it before you went to the station?'

'When we were walking to the car, he said he forgot that Parker pen of his and dashed back inside. That's when he must have left the note.'

'Can I see it?'

'No. It's private. It says stuff that—'

She stopped herself and took a long drag off her cigarette. Then suddenly she looked up at me with something approaching rage.

'If only you hadn't said . . .'

'*What?*' I whispered.

She raised the letter to her face. And read out loud:

'*When Jane announced last night that "no one's actually happy", the decision I had been pondering – and postponing – for years suddenly seemed no longer inconceivable. And after you went to bed I sat up in the living room, considering the fact that, at best, I will be alive for another thirty-five years – probably less the way I smoke. So I couldn't help but think: enough of you, enough of this. Our daughter got it right: happiness doesn't exist. But at least if I was out of this marriage, I'd be less aggrieved than I am now.*'

She tossed the letter onto the counter. There was a long silence. I felt for the very first time that strange traumatic sensation of the ground giving way beneath my feet.

5

'Why did you tell him that?' she asked. '*Why?* He'd still be here now if only . . .'

That's when I ran upstairs and into my room, slamming the door behind me as I collapsed onto the bed. But I didn't burst into tears. I simply found myself in freefall. Words matter. Words count. Words have lasting import. And my words had sent my dad packing. It was all my fault.

An hour or so later, Mom came upstairs and knocked on my door and asked if I could ever forgive her for what she had said. I didn't reply. She came in and found me on my bed, curled up in a tight little ball, a pillow clutched against my mid-section.

'Jane, dear . . . I'm so sorry.'

I pulled the pillow even closer to me and refused to look at her.

'My mouth always reacts before my brain.'

As you've told me so many times before.

'And I was so stunned, so distraught . . .'

Words matter. Words count. Words have lasting import.

'We all say things we don't mean . . .'

But you meant exactly what you said.

'Please, Jane, *please* . . .'

That was the moment I put my hands over my ears, in an attempt to block her out. That was the moment when she suddenly screamed: 'All right, all right, be calculating and cruel . . . just like your father . . .'

And she stormed out of the room.

The truth of the matter was: I wanted to be calculating and cruel and pay her back for that comment and for all her attendant narcissism (not that I even knew that word at the time). The problem was: I've never really had it in me to be calculating and cruel. Petulant, yes. Irritable, yes . . . and definitely withdrawn whenever I felt hurt or simply overwhelmed by life's frequent inequities. But even at thirteen, acts of unkindness already struck me as abhorrent. So when I heard my mother sitting on the stairs, weeping, I forced myself up out of my defensive fetal position and onto the landing. Sitting down on the step next to her, I put my arm around her and lay my head on her shoulder. It took her ten minutes to bring her weeping under control. When she finally calmed down, she disappeared into the bathroom for a few minutes, re-emerging with a look of enforced cheerfulness on her face.

'How about I make us BLTs for lunch?' she asked.

We both went downstairs and, yet again, pretended that nothing had happened.

My father made good on his word: he never returned home, even sending a moving company to gather up his belongings and bring them to the small apartment he rented on the Upper East Side of Manhattan. Within two years the divorce came through. After that I saw my dad sporadically over the ensuing years (he was usually out of the country, working). Mom never remarried and never left Old Greenwich. She found a job in the local library which kept the bills paid and gave her something to do with the day. She also rarely spoke much about my father once he vanished from her life – even though it was so painfully clear to me that, as unhappy as the marriage was, she always mourned his absence. But the Mom Code of Conduct – *never articulate that which is pulling you apart* – was clung to without fail, even though I could constantly sense the sadness that coursed through her life. After Dad left, Mom started drinking herself to sleep most nights, becoming increasingly reliant on vodka as a way of keeping at bay the low-lying pain that so defined her. But the few times that I danced around the subject, she would politely but firmly tell me that she was most aware of her alcohol intake – and she was well able to control it.

'Anyway, as we used to say in French class: "*À chacun son destin*."'

Everyone to their own destiny.

Mom would always point out that this was one of the few phrases she remembered from her college classes – 'and I was a French minor'. But I'm not surprised that she kept that expression close to mind. As someone who hated conflict – and who went out of her way to avoid observations about the mess we all make of things – it's clear why she so embraced that French maxim. To her, we were all alone in a hostile universe and never really knew what life had in store for us. All we could do was muddle through. So why worry about drinking three vodkas too many every evening, or articulating the lasting grief and loneliness that underscores everything in daily life? *À chacun son destin.*

Certainly, Mom put up little resistance some years later when, at the age of sixty-one, the oncologist to whom she had been referred told her she had terminal cancer.

'It's liver cancer,' she said calmly when I rushed down to Connecticut after she was admitted to the big regional hospital in Stamford. 'And the problem with liver cancer is that it's ninety-nine percent incurable. But maybe that's its blessing as well.'

'How can you say that, Mom?'

'Because there is something reassuring about knowing *nothing* can be done to save you. It negates hope – and also stops you from submitting to horrible life-prolonging treatments which will corrode your body and destroy your will to survive, yet still won't save you. Best to bow to the inevitable, dear.'

For Mom, the inevitable arrived shortly after her diagnosis. She was very pragmatic and systematic about her own death. Having refused all temporary stop-gap measures – which might have bought her another six months – she opted for palliative care: a steady supply of intravenous morphine to keep the pain and the fear at bay.

'You think I should maybe get religion?' she asked me in one of her more lucid moments towards the end.

'Whatever makes things easier for you,' I said.

'Jessie – the nurse who looks after me most mornings – is some sort of Pentecostalist. I never knew they had people like that in Fairfield County. Anyway, she keeps talking about how if I was willing to accept Jesus as my Lord and Savior, I'd be granted life ever after. "Just think, Mrs Howard," she said yesterday, "you could be in heaven next week!"'

Mom flashed me a mischievous smile which then faded quickly as she asked me: 'But say she turns out to be right? Say I *did* accept Jesus? Would it be such a bad thing? I mean, I always had comprehensive automobile insurance when I was still alive . . .'

I lowered my head and bit my lip and failed to control the sob that had just welled up in my throat.

'You're still alive, Mom,' I whispered. 'And you could be alive for even longer if only you'd allow Dr Phillips—'

'Now let's not go there again, dear. My mind is made up. *À chacun son destin.*'

But then she suddenly turned away from me and started to cry. I held onto her hand. She finally said: 'You know what still gets to me? What still haunts my thoughts so damn often . . . ?'

'What?'

'Remember what you said to your father on the night of your thirteenth birthday?'

'Mom . . .'

'Now don't take this the wrong way, but you did say—'

'I know what I said, but that was years ago and—'

'You said: "I'm never getting married and I'm never having

children," and followed it up with the observation that "nobody's actually happy" . . .'

I couldn't believe what I was hearing – and found myself thinking: *She's dying, she's on severe painkillers, ignore what she's saying*, even though I knew that she was having one of her rare moments of perfect lucidity right now. We had spent years sidestepping this issue. But in her mind I was still to blame for my father's departure.

'You did say those things, didn't you, dear?'

'Yes, I said them.'

'And the next morning, what happened?'

'You know what happened, Mom.'

'I don't blame you, dear. It's just . . . well, cause and effect. And maybe . . . just maybe . . . if those things hadn't been said at that specific moment . . . well, who knows? Maybe your father wouldn't have packed his bags. Maybe the bad feelings he was having about the marriage might have passed. We're so often on the verge of walking out or giving up or saying that it's all not worth it. But without a trigger . . . that *something* which sends us over the edge . . .'

I hung my head. I said nothing. Mom didn't finish the sentence, as she was racked with one of the small convulsions that seized her whenever the pain reasserted itself. She tried to reach for the morphine plunger that was attached to the IV bag by the side of her bed. But her hand was shaking so badly that I had to take it myself and press the trigger and watch her ease into the semi-catatonic euphoria which the morphine induced. As she drifted into this chemical stupor, I could only think: *Now you can fade away from what you just said . . . but I have to live on with it.*

Words matter. Words count. Words have lasting import.

We never spoke again. I did take some comfort in the knowledge that my parents could never stand each other and

10

that my long-vanished father would have ended it with Mom no matter what.

But – as I've come to discover – there is a profound, vast gulf between *understanding* something that completely changes the contours of your life and *accepting* the terrible reality of that situation. The rational side of your brain – the part that tells you: 'This is what happened, it can't be rectified, and you must now somehow grapple with the aftermath' – is always trumped by an angry, overwrought voice. It's a voice railing at the unfairness of life, at the awful things we do to ourselves and each other; a voice which then insidiously whispers: *And maybe it's all your fault.*

Recently, on one of the many nights when sleep is impossible – and when the ultra-potent knockout pills to which I am addicted proved defenceless against the insomnia which now dominates my life – I found myself somehow thinking back to an Introductory Physics course I took during my freshman year in college. We spent two lectures learning about a German mathematical physicist named Werner Heisenberg. In the late 1920s, he developed a theorem known as the Uncertainty Principle, the details of which I'd so forgotten that I turned to Google (at 4:27 in the morning) to refresh my memory. Lo and behold, I found the following definition: '*In particle physics, the Uncertainty Principle states that it is not possible to know both the position and the momentum of a particle at the same time, because the act of measuring would disturb the system.*'

So far so theoretical. But a little further digging and I discovered that Einstein abhorred the Uncertainty Principle, commenting: '*Of course we can know where something is; we can know the position of a moving particle if we know every possible detail, and thereby by extension we can predict where it will go.*'

He also noted, rather incisively, that the principle flew in

11

the face of a sort of divine empiricism, saying: '*I cannot believe that God would choose to play dice with the universe.*'

But Heisenberg – and his Danish theoretical collaborator, Niels Bohr (the father of quantum mechanics) – countered Einstein with the belief that: '*There is no way of knowing where a moving particle is given its detail, and thereby, by extension, we can never predict where it will go.*'

Bohr also added a little sardonic retort at the end, instructing his rival: '*Einstein, don't tell God what to do.*'

Reading about all this (as the sun came up on another *nuit blanche*), I found myself siding with Heisenberg and Bohr. Though everything in life is, physically speaking, composed of elementary particles, how can we ever really know where a certain particle – or that combination of particles known as an action, an event, another person – will bring us? *Einstein, don't tell God what to do* . . . because in a wholly random universe, He has no control.

But what struck me so forcibly about the Uncertainty Principle was the way it also made me trawl back to that New Year's Day in 1987 – and how, in my mother's mind, Heisenberg was right. One launched particle – my dismissive comments about marriage – results in a logical, terrible outcome: divorce. No wonder that she embraced this empirical doctrine. Without it, she would have had to face up to her own role in the breakdown of her marriage.

But she was spot on about one thing: had that particle not been launched on that given night, the result might have been a dissimilar one . . . and both our lives might have turned out differently because of that.

I think about that a lot these days – the idea of destiny as nothing more than a random dispatch of particles which brings you to places you never imagined finding yourself. Just as I also now understand that uncertainty governs every moment of human existence.

And when it comes to thinking that life works according to linear principles . . .

Well, another physicist back in the twenties, Felix Bloch, proposed the idea that space was a field of linear operations. Heisenberg would have none of it.

'Nonsense,' he said. 'Space is blue and birds fly through it.'

But stories work best when told in a sequential, linear way. And this story – *my* story – needs to be told sequentially, as life can only be lived forwards and understood backwards. And the only way I can make sense of what has happened to me recently is by trying to find some sort of significance lurking behind the haphazardness of it all. Even though, having just written that, I know that I am articulating a contradiction.

Because there is no meaning to be found in the arbitrary nature of things. It's all random. Just as space is blue. And birds fly through it.

Part One

One

WHERE TO START? Where to begin? That's the big question looming over all narrative structures, and something we analyzed ceaselessly in graduate school. *What is the point of departure for a story?* Unless you're writing a big cradle-to-grave saga – '*To begin my life at the beginning of my life*' – a story usually commences at a moment well into the life of the central character. As such, from the outset you're traveling forward with this individual through his tale, yet are simultaneously discovering, bit by bit, the forces and events that shaped him in the past. As David Henry, my doctoral advisor, was fond of reminding his students in his lectures on literary theory: 'All novels are about a crisis and how an individual – or a set of individuals – negotiates said crises. More than that, when we first meet a character in a narrative, we are dealing with him in the present moment. But he has a back story, just like the rest of us. Whether it's in real life or on the page, you never understand somebody until you understand their back story.'

David Henry. Maybe that's a good point of departure. Because the accidental set of circumstances that landed David Henry in my life sent it down a path I would never have thought possible. Then again, *we can never predict where a particle will go . . .*

David Henry. Back at the start of the 1970s, when he was a young professor at the university, he'd written a study of the American Novel, *Towards a New World*, that was noted immediately for its accessibility and its critical originality. Around the same time, he also published a novel about growing up in a Minnesota backwater that immediately saw

17

him acclaimed as a modern-day Sherwood Anderson, alive to the contradictions of small-town American life.

'Alive' was the word everyone used about David Henry back then. *Towards a New World* won the 1972 National Book Award for Non-Fiction. His novel had been shortlisted that same year for the NBA in Fiction (a rare double honor) and was a finalist for the Pulitzer. The photos of him around that time show just why he was such a media star, as he had (to use a line from an *Esquire* profile of him) 'classic square-jawed American good looks and a serious sense of cool: Clark Gable Goes to Harvard.'

He was everywhere back then: appearing on talk shows; writing learned, witty essays for the *New York Review of Books*; debating right-wing hawks in public forums. What's more, though he dressed with a certain Lou Reed élan (black T-shirts, black jeans), he never jumped on the radical-chic bandwagon. Yes, he did publicly denounce 'the Babbitt-like conformism that so dominates one corner of the American psyche', but he also wrote articles in defense of America's cultural complexity. One of them, 'Our Necessary Contradictions', became something of a talking point when published in the *Atlantic* in 1976, as it was one of the first critical explications of what David called 'the two facets of the American psyche that rub up against each other like tectonic plates'. I first discovered this essay while a freshman in college when a friend recommended David Henry's collection of journalist pieces, *Left-Handed Writing*. And I was so taken with it that I must have foisted it on half a dozen friends, telling them that it explained, with brilliant clarity, what it meant to be an American who doubted so much about the state of the country today.

So I was in love with David Henry before I was in love with David Henry. When I applied to enter the doctoral program at Harvard, the essay which accompanied my application talked among other things about how much his approach to American Literature and Thought had influenced my own nascent academic work, and how the thesis I was hoping to write – *The Infernal Duality: Obedience and Defiance in American Literature* – was *so* David Henry.

Granted, I knew I was taking a risk in letting it be known – even before I had been accepted by Harvard – that I already had a preferred thesis advisor in my sights. But I was so determined to work with him. As I was coming out of Smith *summa cum laude* with very strong recommendations from my English professors there, I was willing to be assertive.

It worked. I was called down to Cambridge for an interview with the department chairman. At the last minute I was told by his secretary that the interview would be handled by someone else in the department.

And that's how I found myself face to face with David Henry.

The year was 1995. He was now in his early fifties, but still retained the craggy movie-star aura – though I immediately noticed that his eyes were marked by dark crescent moons hinting at a certain sadness within. I knew that he had continued to write essays for publications like *Harper's* and the *New York Review of Books*, though not with such prolific regularity. From a piece I read about him in the *Boston Globe* I also found out that there had been no second novel and that his long-commissioned biography of Melville remained unfinished. But the article did say that, though his profile as a writer and a public intellectual had faded, he was still a hugely respected teacher whose undergraduate classes were always over-subscribed and who was one of the most sought-after doctoral advisors in the university.

I liked him immediately because he saw how hard I was trying to mask my nervousness and he quickly put me at my ease.

'Now why on earth would you want to go into something as archaic and badly paid as university teaching when you could be out there cashing in on all the material bounty being offered in this, our new Gilded Age?'

'Not everyone wants to be a robber baron,' I said.

David smiled. ' "Robber baron." Very Theodore Dreiser.'

'I remember your chapter on Dreiser in *The American Novel* and a piece you wrote on the seventieth anniversary of the publication of *Sister Carrie* in the *Atlantic*.'

'So you said in your application essay. But let me ask you something: do you rate *Sister Carrie*?'

'More than you do. I do take your point that there is a terrible leadenness to much of Dreiser's prose. But that's something he shares with Zola – a need to sledgehammer a point home and a certain psychological primitivism. And yes, I do like the point you make about Dreiser's prolixity being bound up with the fact that he was one of the first novelists to use a typewriter. But to dismiss Dreiser as – what was the phrase you used? – "*a portentous purveyor of penny dreadfuls*" ... With respect, you missed the point – and also used a lot of Ps in one sentence.'

As soon as I heard that line come out of my mouth, I thought: *What the hell are you saying here?* But David wasn't offended or put off by my directness. On the contrary, he liked it.

'Well, Ms Howard, it's good to see that you are anything but a brown-nose.'

'I'm sorry,' I said. 'I'm sure I've really overstepped the mark.'

'Why think that? I mean, you're going to be in the doctoral English program at Harvard, which means that you are going to be expected to display a considerable amount of independent thinking. And as I won't work with anyone who's a suck-up ...'

David didn't finish the sentence. Instead he just smiled, enjoying the bemused look which had fixed itself on my face.

'Professor, you said: "You're going to be in the doctoral English program at Harvard." But my application hasn't been approved as yet.'

'Take it from me – you're in.'

'But you do know that I will be applying for financial aid?'

'Yes, I saw that – and I spoke with our department chairman about utilizing a fund we have. It was set up by one of the Rockefellers and is granted to one incoming doctoral candidate every year. Now, I see on your application that your father is a mining executive, based in Chile.'

'*Was* a mining executive,' I said. 'He lost his job around five years ago.'

He nodded, as if to say: So that's why money is so tight.

I could have added how I could never, ever rely on my father for anything. But I always worried about burdening anybody (even my boyfriend) with the more unpleasant facets of my childhood. And I certainly wasn't going to start gabbing about them during my interview with David Henry. So I simply said: 'My father told his last boss to go have sex with himself. And since he refused to accept any job below that of the president of a company – and was also known as something of a hothead in his industry – his employment prospects dried up. He's been "consulting" since then but makes hardly enough to keep himself going. So . . .'

And I'd just revealed more than I intended to. David must have sensed this, as he simply smiled and nodded his head and said: 'Well, your winning a full postgraduate scholarship to Harvard will surely please him.'

'I doubt it,' I said quietly.

I was wrong about that. I wrote my dad a letter two months before my graduation from Smith, telling him how much I'd like him to be at the ceremony and also informing him about my all-expenses-paid scholarship to Harvard. Usually it took him around a month to write back to me – but this time a letter arrived within ten days. Clipped to it was a hundred-dollar bill. The letter was twenty-one words long:

> *I am so proud of you!*
> *Sorry I can't be at your graduation.*
> *Buy yourself something nice with this.*
> *Love*
> *Dad*

Within moments of opening it, I was in floods of tears. I had never cried when Dad left us. I had never cried when he had to cancel so many of our planned weekends in the city after he'd relocated down there. I had never cried when he moved to Chile and kept telling me that, next year, he'd fly me down for a few weeks and never got around to it. I had never cried when his response to my straight As at Smith, my election to Phi Beta Kappa – all that damn striving to please him – was silence. And in an attempt to get some sort of recognition from him I wrote that letter. All it did was make me face the looming truth I never wanted to confront: my father always distanced himself from me. *Buy yourself something nice*. A hundred bucks and a five-line note to assuage his guilt . . . that is, if he even had any guilt. Yet again, he was brushing me aside – but this time, I couldn't respond by trying to shrug off his detachment. This time all I could do was cry.

Tom tried to console me. He kept telling me that my father didn't deserve such a great daughter, that he would come to regret his dismissal of me, that my success undoubtedly unnerved him, because he himself had failed so badly in everything he had ever undertaken.

'Of course he's going to push you away,' Tom said. 'How else is he going to handle your brilliance?'

'Stop flattering me,' I told him.

'You're resistant to flattery,' he said.

'Because I don't merit it.'

'No – because you have convinced yourself that your idiot father is right: why should you merit your success?'

But my sadness wasn't just bound up in my father's brush-off of me. It was also rooted in the fact that Tom and I were about to part. The terrible thing about this split was, we didn't want to break up. But I was heading to Harvard and Tom was off to Trinity College Dublin for postgraduate work. Though neither of us wanted to admit it, we knew that once we were separated by the Atlantic, we'd be finished. What made this knowledge even more agonizing was the fact that Tom had been accepted by Harvard to do his Masters in History. But he had decided to take the offer of a place in Dublin – reassuring me that it would only be a year and then he'd join me at Harvard for his doctorate.

'You can come over for Thanksgiving,' he said. 'I'll come back for Christmas, we'll spend Easter together knocking around Europe . . . and the year will pass before we both know it.'

I wanted to believe his protestations. Just as I decided that I wouldn't force his hand or use the sort of emotional blackmail ('If you really loved me, you wouldn't leave me') that I had heard my mother use against my father in the years leading up to his departure.

'Of course I don't want you to go,' I told him after he informed me that he was putting Harvard on hold and heading to Dublin. 'Of course I'm not going to stop you.'

That's when the reassurances began. The more he uttered them, the more I knew he wanted to cut and run. On the day that my dad's five-line letter arrived – and Tom tried so hard to comfort me – I blurted out the uncomfortable truth: 'As soon as you get to Dublin, we're finished.'

'Don't be absurd,' he said. 'I've never intimated that—'

'But it's going to happen, because—'

'It is not going to happen,' Tom said, getting vehement. 'I value you – *us* – far too much. And I understand exactly why you're feeling so vulnerable right now, but . . .'

But what you don't understand is what I understand: men vanish when threatened.

Well, he did head off to Dublin – and we did promise each other that love would see us through and all the other usual romantic clichés. The rupture happened right before Thanksgiving. He was due to come back to the States, with me then meeting him in Paris for Christmas. Fair play to Tom – he didn't feed me a lie or keep me dangling while he said that, due to unforeseen circumstances, he wouldn't be landing in Boston on November 21st. Instead he phoned me and came straight out with: 'I've met somebody else.'

I didn't ask for much in the way of details – I'm no masochist – and he didn't supply too many, except to say that she was Irish, a medical student at Trinity, and that it was 'serious'. When he started saying: 'It really did take me completely by surprise,' I just said: 'I'm sure it did.'

A long silence followed.

'I'm sorry,' he said.

'So am I.'

And that was that. The big central relationship of my life to date was suddenly no more. I took the news badly, withdrawing from everyone for around a week, cutting the lectures and thesis meetings I had at Harvard, and basically moping in my tiny studio flat in Somerville. It surprised me how deeply upset I was. We seemed so right for each other.

24

But timing is everything and ours simply didn't work out.

Tom never returned to the States. He married his Irish medical student. He stayed on to get his doctorate at Trinity and eventually got a job at the university in Galway. We never saw each other after we broke up. Though I presumed he came home regularly to visit his parents, he didn't look me up during the years I was living in Cambridge. There was only one communiqué from him: a Christmas card that arrived just a few years later, showing Tom and his wife Mairéad and their three very young sons – Conor, Fintan and Sean. They were standing in front of what looked like a suburban bungalow. The photo amazed me, as Tom was so adamant – like me – about never wanting children and always vowed never to live in the 'burbs. I didn't feel a residual stab of sadness when I saw this photograph. Rather, all I could do was marvel at the way the narrative of life inexorably moves on – and how, having been so intensely involved with someone else, you can then simply vanish from each other's lives. We lose things and then we choose things. Wasn't that a fragment of a song I heard somewhere? Perhaps with Tom? Or maybe with David? And didn't David tell me – shortly after we became lovers – that everything is just one big continual coming-and-going?

I did reply to Tom's Christmas card by sending one of my own. I kept the message short:

You have a lovely family. I wish you every happiness for the coming year. All best . . .

Of course I wanted to ask him dozens of things: Are you happy? Do you like your work, your new country, your life? And do you ever sometimes think of me, *us*, and how the narrative of our now very separate lives would have been so profoundly different if . . . ?

'*If.*' The most charged word in the English language . . . especially when coupled with '*only*'.

As in: if only you hadn't moved to Ireland, I wouldn't have ended up for a while with David.

But I wanted to end up with David . . . even if I knew from the outset that it had no long-term future. Because ending up with David helped me end things with you.

Or, at least, that's what I told myself at the time.

Two

'THIS IS DANGEROUS,' David said.

'Only if we allow it to be dangerous,' I said.

'If anyone else finds out . . .'

'Is this your usual style of post-coital conversation . . .?'

'I don't make a habit of—'

'Sleeping with your students?'

'That's right.'

'Never before?'

Pause. Then: 'Once. Back in the early seventies when things weren't so—'

'Politically correct?'

'I'm not totally self-destructive,' he said.

'Is this self-destructive?'

'I hope not.'

'Have a little faith in me, David. I know what I'm getting into here.'

'You sure about that?'

'So besides the one student back in the still-swinging seventies,' I said, changing the subject, 'you've been completely faithful to Beth?'

'Hardly . . . considering that she stopped having sex with me back when Reagan was first elected president.'

'And the longest affair went on for . . .?'

'You ask a lot of questions.'

'I simply want to know everything about the man with whom I'm getting involved.'

'You know a lot about me already.'

That was true – as I had been working with David on my thesis for the last six months. At the outset of my time at

Harvard, he showed himself to be a terrific advisor: sympathetic, but not touchy-feely; intellectually rigorous, but never pedantic; very clever, but someone who always avoided playing the bravura card. From the start, I was smitten. From the start I also knew that there was no way I would land myself in an involvement with my advisor. Nor, for that matter, did David flirt with me during those early months in Cambridge. In fact, up until Thanksgiving, our relationship was strictly student/teacher. Then I got the news from Dublin that Tom and I were no more. I vanished for a week, skipping classes, canceling my tutorials, venturing out only to buy food, and generally feeling miserable and sorry for myself. I found myself frequently bursting into tears in inappropriate places like the supermarket or while returning library books. I've never been someone who has been comfortable with the idea of becoming emotional in public. Call it a reaction to that morning after my thirteenth birthday, when Mom blamed me for Dad's departure. Though I ran upstairs and hid in my room, I couldn't bring myself to cry at the unfairness of her accusation. Was that the moment I started thinking that to cry was to lose control? Certainly, Dad preached a doctrine of always keeping everything that was eating at you under wraps, 'otherwise people will see your vulnerabilities and prey on them'. I heeded that advice – especially when it came to all ongoing emotional transactions with Mom – but still privately grappled with a huge sense of vulnerability. In the face of a setback or a loss I would always try to constrain my feelings – fearing what others might think if they saw me in such a weakened state. But inside, the wounds never really cauterized – which meant that, when Tom broke it off with me, the sense of loss was all the more acute. If your father is absent and your mother finds you wanting, you search for some sort of personal ballast in the world. And when that's taken away . . .

Well, all I could do was hide for a while.

So when I left a message calling off a third consecutive meeting with David, he rang me at home and asked if there was anything wrong.

'Bad flu,' I said.

'Have you seen a doctor?' he asked.

'It's not that sort of flu,' I heard myself saying.

I did make our next scheduled tutorial, in which we spent an hour discussing Frank Norris's *McTeague* – which, as David noted, was an indictment not just of American cupidity, but also of early twentieth-century dentistry.

'But you didn't need a dentist last week, did you?' he asked.

'Just sleep.'

'You sure you're over it?'

That's when I lowered my head and bit my lip and felt my eyes well up. David opened a drawer under his desk and pulled out a bottle of Scotch and two glasses.

'When I was in graduate school,' he said, 'my advisor told me that when I became a professor, I should always keep a bottle of whiskey in a filing cabinet . . . exactly for moments like this one.'

He poured us each two fingers of Scotch and handed me a glass.

'If you want to talk about it . . .' he said.

I did so want to talk about it – and the story came out in a rush that took me by surprise, given my refusal to speak to anybody about such things, let alone my thesis advisor. At the end of it I heard myself saying: '. . . and I don't really know why I'm taking it so hard, as I knew six months ago that this is how it would turn out. In fact I told him this last spring, when he decided that Dublin was his destiny. But he kept telling me—'

'Let me guess: "The last thing I want to do is leave you. It

29

will only be eight months and then I'll be back in your arms"?'

'Yes, words to that effect. And the thing is, I wanted to believe them.'

'That's pretty damn understandable. If we don't want to lose something . . . *someone* . . . we always want to believe the declarations of others, even if we privately doubt them. We all talk about how much we hate lies. Yet we prefer, so often, to be lied to . . . because it allows us to dodge all those painful truths we'd rather not hear.'

'I certainly didn't want it to end.'

'Then why didn't you follow him to Dublin?'

'Because I wanted to come here. And because I didn't want to live in Dublin.'

'Or be tethered to his career?'

I felt myself tighten. David noticed this.

'Hey, there's hardly anything wrong with not wanting to be in the shadow of someone . . . though have you ever thought about the fact that perhaps your fellow didn't want to live in your shadow? Take it from me, men are very uncomfortable when they realize a woman is more accomplished than they are.'

I felt a blush spread across my face. 'Please . . . I don't take flattery very well.'

'I'm not trying to flatter you. I'm just pointing up the reality of the situation. Maybe everything was commensurate between you when you were both at college. But graduate school is another matter, because everyone's looking ahead to their careers and the atmosphere gets just a little competitive and cut-throat. Though, of course, at Harvard we really disdain competitiveness . . .'

He shot me a mischievous smile, then added: 'The hardest thing about a break-up is being the one who's been left. It's always better to do the leaving.'

He then directed the conversation back to the work at hand. In the coming weeks he made a point of *not* asking me anything more about the situation. Rather he simply opened our tutorials with the question: 'How are things?' Though I could have told him I was still feeling extremely fragile about everything, I chose to say nothing. Because there was nothing more to say about it and I always hate sounding sorry for myself – even though it took several months before the sense of loss began to diminish.

And the very fact that my involvement with David only began around six months after Tom sent me his kiss-off letter meant that . . .

Well, what exactly *did* it mean? That David wasn't an opportunistic sleaze who hit on me when I was feeling vulnerable and alone? That ours quickly became a serious relationship, as we had known each other for almost a year when we crossed that frontier between camaraderie and intimacy? Or that we both played a very long game with each other – as it was clear early on (to me anyway) that we were more than attracted to each other.

But he was my professor, he was married – and I couldn't even contemplate entering that realm of clandestine adulterous mess, or assuming the grim role of the Other Woman. Bar that one moment when he got me talking about the break-up with Tom, we stayed on neutral ground with each other.

Until one late afternoon in mid-May – when we were in the middle of a tutorial discussion on Sherwood Anderson, and the phone rang. If the telephone started buzzing during one of our weekly sessions David would always ignore it. That day he tensed as soon as it began to ring, then reached for it, saying: 'Have to take this . . .'

'Would you like me to leave?' I asked.

'No need . . .'

He reached for the phone, swiveled around in his chair so his back was to me, and started to talk in an agitated whisper.

'. . . Yeah, hi . . . look, I've got someone here . . . so what did the doctor say? . . . Well, he's right, of course he's right . . . don't tell me I'm bullying you when I'm just . . . this is all down to you not taking the meds and then having these episodes . . . there's no need to . . . all right, all right, I'm sorry, I'm . . . oh, Jesus, will you please . . . yes, I am getting angry, fucking angry . . . and I can't take this, you . . .'

Suddenly he stopped talking – as if the conversation had been cut off. He sat in his chair, immobile, trying hard to keep his anger and upset in check. A good minute passed – during which David simply stared out the window. Finally I said: 'Professor, maybe it's best if I—'

'I'm sorry. You shouldn't have heard that.'

'I'll go.'

He didn't turn back towards me.

'OK,' he said.

When I saw him again the following week, he was all business – continuing our discussion of Sherwood Anderson. But at the end of the hour, he asked me if I was free for a beer.

Actually the 'beer' turned out to be a Martini in the bar of the Charles Hotel off Harvard Square. He drank his – gin, straight up, three olives – in around three gulps, and fished out a pack of cigarettes.

'Yes, I know it's a disgusting habit – and yes, Gitanes are about as smelly and pretentious as they get – but I keep it down to ten a day maximum.'

'Professor, I'm not a health fascist. Smoke away, please.'

'You must stop calling me Professor.'

'But it's what you are.'

'No, it's simply my title. David is my name – and I insist that you use that in the future.'

'Fine,' I said, slightly surprised by the vehemence in his voice. So was David, as he immediately flagged down the waitress for a second Martini and lit up another Gitane, even though he already had one balanced on the lip of the ashtray.

'Sorry, sorry,' he said. 'Sometimes these days I find myself—'

He stopped, then started again: 'Have you ever been through a time when you found yourself so consumed with rage that—?'

Another pull on his Gitane.

'I shouldn't be talking about all this,' he said.

'It's OK, Professor . . . sorry, *David*. Talk away.'

Another long drag on his cigarette.

'My wife tried to kill herself two weeks ago. It's the third time she's tried to end it all this year.'

That's when I first found out that – for all his professional accomplishment and high academic standing – David Henry had his own private hell. Her name was Polly Cooper. They'd been married over twenty years, and from the 1970s photographs of her I'd seen in his office, she'd been the quintessential thin, willowy beauty back then. When he met her, she'd just published a collection of short stories with Knopf *and* had also done a big Avedon photo shoot for *Vogue*. Back in 1971, the *New York Times* profiled her, calling her '*impossibly beautiful and impossibly smart*'. When David hooked up with her – fresh off his National Book Award triumph and fantastic reviews for his first novel, and his appointment, at the age of thirty, to a full Harvard professorship – they were deemed a golden couple, destined for further greatness.

'When I met Polly, it was such an instant *coup de foudre* for both of us that we were married within six months. A year after that, our son Charlie was born – and Polly went into this real tailspin within a few weeks of his arrival. She stopped sleeping, stopped eating and eventually refused to even touch him, saying that she was certain she was going to mangle the child if she picked him up. It got so bad that, at one point, she went four straight days without sleep. That's when I found her one night in the kitchen, prostrate on the floor, banging her head on the side of the stove.

'When the ambulance arrived, the guys on duty took one look at her and brought her straight to the psychiatric wing at Mass General. She was there for the next four months. What first seemed to be a serious case of post-natal depression was eventually diagnosed as a major bipolar disorder.'

Since then her mental health had been, at best, patchy. There was at least one major breakdown per year, followed by a period of relative calm. But she could never find the necessary creative energy to write another story and the years of being medicated had taken their toll on her physical health and her looks.

'If it's been that awful,' I asked, 'why didn't you hit the self-preservation button and leave her?'

'I tried to do that over a decade ago. I'd met this other woman, Anne, a violinist with the Boston Symphony Orchestra. It got serious very fast. Polly – for all her manic moments – still could whiff a lie. When I seemed to be spending several afternoons a week away from the university, she hired a detective . . . who got photographs of me going in and out of the violinist's apartment in Back Bay and the two of us holding hands in some nearby restaurant. God, clandestine details are so banal.'

'Was it love with you and the violinist?'

'I certainly thought so. And so did Anne. But then I came

home one evening to discover the detective's eight-by-tens of me flung around the living room and Polly in the bathtub, her wrists slashed. She barely had a pulse.'

The medics had to give her over five pints of blood to stabilize her.

She spent another three months in the psychiatric wing.

'Our son Charlie – who was ten at the time – told me I couldn't leave. You see, he came home from school around a minute after I had found his mother. I tried to stop him from coming into the bathroom, but he burst in anyway and saw his mother naked, floating in bloody water. After that . . .'

After that, Charlie closed down for a very long time, becoming withdrawn and gloomy. He crashed and burned at a series of schools. As he stumbled deeper into adolescence, he also discovered hallucinogenic drugs – and was ejected from one school for that perennial 'bad trip' stunt: trying to set fire to his bed. They tried a more progressive school, they tried a tough-love military academy, they even tried having him tutored at home (he trashed his room). Eventually, the son of two rather brilliant people ran away on the eve of his seventeenth birthday. He wasn't found for another two years – during which time David went through over a quarter of a million dollars ('my entire inheritance from my father') trying to find him. He was eventually discovered living in a hostel for the destitute off Pioneer Square in Seattle.

'The good news was that he wasn't HIV positive and hadn't drifted into anything horrible like prostitution. The bad news was that he was quickly diagnosed as schizophrenic.'

For the last three years, he'd been living in a 'managed care' facility near Worcester. 'It's depressing, but at least he's in a place where he can't harm himself.'

Meanwhile his mother had somehow managed to find a way back to a reasonably sane place. So much so that – after a fifteen-year silence – a slender book of stories was published by a small university press.

'They probably sold no more than five hundred copies – but, for her, it was a huge victory. And what was wonderful was the way Polly seemed to rally and become, once again, the smart and beautiful woman I married. But these interludes were just that – momentary respites from the full onslaught of her craziness.'

The ongoing fragility of his wife and son had a knock-on effect, as David found it difficult to get back to his own books. The first novel had cascaded out of him 'like a geyser – once I started I simply couldn't stop. The story was *my* story, even though it was all heavily disguised. Every day that I sat down to write, it all came without hesitation, without a moment of doubt. It was as if I was on some sort of auto-pilot – and it was, without question, a six-month period when I sensed what real happiness is about.'

'What is it actually about?' I asked.

'Believing that you have been spirited away – for even just a few short hours every day – from all the crap of life, all that quotidian shit which clogs up everything and sends you hurtling towards despair.'

'Remind me not to bump into you with a hangover.'

'You can bump into me any time.'

There was a long, uncomfortable silence after this comment was uttered. I stared down into my Martini, my cheeks reddening. David realized that his comment could be interpreted as provocative, and immediately tried to cover his tracks.

'What I meant by that was . . .' he said.

I covered his hand with mine.

'Shut up,' I whispered.

I left my hand there for the next half-hour – as he talked more about 'the Gordian Knot' that was his second novel –

how it simply wouldn't flow the way the debut book did; how he knew from the outset it was overwrought and overworked. So he turned his attention to the big Melville biography for which he had received a considerable advance from Knopf. But again, he couldn't find the mental space needed to get on with the work.

I listened to all this with a growing sense of amazement and privilege. After all, this was *David Henry* confiding in me. Not just confiding in me, but also letting me keep my hand on his. I felt like an idiotic schoolgirl – yet one who didn't want to pull back and play by the rules of propriety. A wildly cerebral and attractive man in pain is – I was discovering – such an aphrodisiac.

'Had I been a proper novelist,' he said, 'I would have found a way, despite all the domestic chaos, of still writing. Because real writers write. They find a way of somehow shoving aside all the other detritus and getting on with it. Whereas I was always trying to be the great polymath: academic, novelist, biographer, media darling, talk-show bullshit artist, crap husband, crap father . . .'

'David . . . *stop*,' I said, now grasping his hand tightly.

'This is what happens when I drink. I become Pagliacci – the sad, pathetic clown.'

He suddenly stood up and threw some money on the table and said he had to go. I reached again for his hand, but he pulled it away.

'Don't you know there are rules against such things these days?' he hissed. 'Don't you know the trouble you could land me in?'

He sat down. He put his face in his hands. He said: 'I'm so sorry . . .'

'Let's get you home.'

I guided him out of the bar towards the front entrance of

the hotel. He was very subdued and said nothing as he got into the cab and muttered his address. When it drove off, I returned to the bar and finished my half-drunk Martini and tried to mull over what had just happened. What surprised me was that I wasn't horrified or offended by the show that David had just put on. If anything I suddenly saw all the contradictions he was living with – the private grief behind the public face – and how it had so changed the contours of his own life. We always admire people from afar, especially those who have accomplished so much with their lives. But listening to David vent his anger and frustration also got me thinking: nobody gets away lightly in life. And the moment you think you've arrived is the moment that it all goes wrong.

As I downed the last drops of the Martini, another thought struck me: David was everything I was looking for in a man. Brilliant, original, seductive, vulnerable. I wanted him – even though I also knew I was stupidly smitten and straying into dangerous terrain. But though I was more than willing to give in to intoxication, I was also determined not to create havoc. Just as I also knew that this would not start between us until David let it be known he wanted it to start between us.

I didn't have to wait long for that signal. Around nine the next morning, the phone rang at my little apartment in Somerville.

'This is your shamefaced professor,' he said quietly.

'You mean you've decided I can no longer call you David?'

'I've decided I'm a horse's ass – and I hope you won't think I was being—'

'I thought you were just being human, David.'

That comment gave him pause.

'And I also appreciated the fact that you decided to confide in me.'

'So you're not going to approach the head of the department—'

'And report you for harassment? You didn't harass me, David. And I was the one who took your hand.'

'I was thinking more that you might not want to work with me again.'

'Now you do sound hungover.'

'Guilty as charged. Could I buy you a cup of coffee?'

'Why not? But as I'm finishing up some work, could you maybe stop by here?'

And I gave him the address.

When he arrived half an hour later, the cup of coffee was quickly forgotten. As soon as he was inside the door we were all over each other.

Afterwards he turned to me and said: 'This is dangerous.'

'Only if we allow it to be dangerous,' I said.

'If anyone else finds out . . .'

'Is this your usual style of post-coital conversation . . . ?'

'I don't make a habit of—'

'Sleeping with your students?'

'That's right.'

And that's when we had our little conversation about his past flings, culminating in him telling me that I asked a lot of questions.

'There's one thing you have to know from the outset – that is, if this thing between us is to carry on beyond today. There is no future for this as anything more than an arrangement, a little adventure. So I'm never going to play the clichéd other woman who becomes increasingly possessive and psychotic. But I will demand that you're always straight with me. If you ever want to hit the escape button, tell me. You're not to string me along.'

'You've evidently thought this out beforehand,' he said.

'So have you.'

'Are you always so rational?'

'If I was rational I wouldn't be in this bed right now.'

'Good point,' he said.

That's how it started. And yes, from the outset, I did take an ultra-rational approach to our 'adventure'. I knew that, by remaining rational, I could insulate myself against any disappointment or heartache that might attend our involvement. The thing was, I knew I'd fallen in love with David Henry and that elated and scared me. Because the central problem with falling in love with a married man is . . .

Well, you can fill in the blank.

Of course I knew I was playing the other woman. Just as we both knew that if word ever got out about our little arrangement, it would be the end of David's career and would possibly also result in my expulsion from the doctoral program. ('They'd probably see you as the victim,' David once noted, 'and would still let you go for getting preferential treatment from your thesis advisor.') What this meant was that I couldn't – *wouldn't* – tell anybody. Not Sara Crowe – a very patrician, somewhat grand, but witty New Englander who was working on a doctorate on American Puritanism. Sara was someone who was massively well connected. She held a salon every Sunday night at her apartment off Brattle Street where a Who's Who of Harvard (or anyone of importance visiting Cambridge that weekend) always seemed to be in attendance, and after we met at an on-campus symposium on Emily Dickinson she decided I was interesting enough to be asked over for dinner occasionally. But she was certainly not someone to whom I would have confided anything.

Nor did I even say anything to Christy Naylor – and she was the one truly close friend I'd made during my first year at graduate school.

Christy was from Maine – and had so goofed off in high school that she had ended up at the State University in Orono. While there she suddenly turned into this academic star

40

('Largely because the men were so boring'), graduating *summa cum laude* in English and, like me, getting the all-expenses-paid package to Harvard. Her specialty was American modernist poetry, especially Wallace Stevens, whom she considered a near-deity. She herself had also begun to get the occasional poem published in small magazines and journals. A self-proclaimed 'backwoods girl' from Lewiston, Maine – 'the shithole of New England' – she was someone who thought nothing about smoking forty cigarettes a day and getting drunk on cheap beer. But start her talking about the metric intricacies of one of Pound's *Cantos* or the use of pentameter in Williams's 'Thirteen Ways of Looking at a Blackbird', and she demonstrated an intellectual acuity that was nothing short of dazzling. Her own work also mirrored the high modernism of the poets she so admired.

'The problem with me,' she said one night when we were out drinking, 'is that, when it comes to art and men, I always go after the most complicated, difficult person in the room.'

The fact that she was somewhat overweight – and that exercise or even the most marginally healthy diet were anathema to her – lent her an added allure: the redneck intellectual who looked as though she'd just walked out of a trailer park, but nevertheless managed to always have some preppy guy named Winthrop Holmes III chasing after her.

'I think they see me as rough trade, whereas the fact is: I like rough trade. Or crazies. Whereas you – the Patron Saint of Self-Restraint with your damnable inability to put on weight . . .'

'It's not for want of trying.'

'Yeah, you're just some goddamn ectomorph – and pretty to boot.'

'I'm hardly pretty.'

'You would say that, given your talent for self-deprecation. But take it from me, guys find you easy on the eye.'

David told me the same thing on several occasions, commenting how he often saw me frown when I looked in the mirror, as if I didn't like what I saw there.

'I've always had a thing against mirrors,' I said.

'Well, you're hardly a plain Jane,' he said. 'More from the Audrey Hepburn school of—'

'Oh, please . . .'

'Even Professor Hawthorden – the chairman of the Harvard English Department – noted the resemblance.'

'My hair is longer than hers.'

'And you have the same patrician cheekbones and radiant skin and—'

'Stop, now,' I said.

'You can't take a compliment, can you?' David said with a small smile.

I don't trust them, I felt like telling him, but instead said: 'You're simply biased.'

'That I am. And what's wrong with that?'

Take it from me, guys find you easy on the eye.

I looked back up at Christy and just shook my head.

'One of these days you're going to actually start liking yourself,' she continued. 'Maybe then you'll start putting on just a little make-up and stop dressing like some tour guide in the Rockies.'

'Maybe I don't care about style.'

'Maybe you should stop playing the rigid, self-protective card at all times. I mean, shit, Jane . . . it's graduate school. You're supposed to drink too much and start dressing like an intellectual slut, and be sleeping with a lot of unappetizing and inappropriate guys.'

'I wish I had your epicurean attitude to such things,' I said.

'*Epicurean?* I'm just a slob and a nympho. But come on, you've got to have some guy stashed somewhere.'

I shook my head.

'Why don't I believe you?' she asked.

'You tell me,' I said.

'Maybe because – one – I sense you have a secret lover, but – two – you're so damn controlled and disciplined that you're keeping his identity secret, because – three – he's somebody you don't want anyone to know you're involved with.'

I worked hard at putting on my best poker face – and concealing the fact that I was quietly terrified that she might know something about David and myself.

'You have a very vivid imagination,' I said.

'You're seeing someone on the side.'

'But as I'm not married . . .'

'You're the *thing on the side*, sweetheart.'

'Again, I admire your ability to conjure up—'

'Goddamn it, Jane – I am your friend, right? And as your friend, I think I deserve to know all the salacious details . . . just as you know all of mine.'

'But if there aren't any salacious details to report . . .'

'You are impossible.'

'So I've been told.'

Told, in fact, by my very own mother on many occasions during adolescence when I wouldn't share details of my own life with her. As Mom didn't have much life outside of our own life she was frequently bothered by the way I didn't tell her things, and seemed to keep so much to myself. Part of this was a reaction to her need to be all-interested in everything about me – to the point where she was downright overbearing. Now, of course, I see the very personal despair – the loneliness and isolation and sense of having been cast off by my father – that made her turn her energies on to me as her very own Grand Project, who would achieve in life everything that had been denied to her. So, back in high school, every homework assignment, every book I read, every movie I saw, every mark I received on an exam, every guy who ever asked me out on a date (not that there were many of them) became something for her to scrutinize.

It all became too much. My mother had turned into a micro-manager – trying desperately to make certain I side-stepped as many potential pitfalls and mistakes as possible. By the time I reached college, I had became so much more private, so guarded, that the landscape between us had changed irrevocably. She enquired less about my life and checked herself whenever she was about to veer into the meddlesome. On the surface, we were still pleasant enough with each other – and I did let her in on the basic superficial stuff in my life. But she knew that we were no longer close.

Yes, I felt terrible about this – especially as I knew that, for Mom, it was further proof that she could 'do nothing right'.

But perhaps the most telling exchange we ever had about all this was after the break-up with Tom. It was Christmas. I was back home in Connecticut, and I hadn't mentioned anything yet to her about the phonecall I had received from him before Thanksgiving. Naturally, on my first night back, she asked me if 'my future son-in-law' would be arriving on December 26th (as he always had done in the past).

'I'm afraid Tom will be spending Christmas with his future in-laws in Ireland.'

Mom looked at me as if I had just spoken to her in Serbo-Croat.

'What did you just say?'

'Tom met someone in Ireland – a medical student. They're an item now . . . and we're not.'

'And when did this happen?'

I told her. She turned white.

'And you waited this long to tell me.'

'I needed time.'

'Time to do *what*, Jane? If you haven't forgotten, I'm your mother – and though you may have pushed me to one side—'

'I call twice, three times a week, I show up for every major holiday—'

'And you keep all the big stuff in your life hidden from me.'

Silence. Then I said: 'This is the way I have to do things.'

'But why? *Why?*'

We can rarely tell others what we really think about them – not just because it would so wound them, but also because it would so wound ourselves. The gentle lie is often preferable to the bleak truth. So in answer to her demand, 'But why? *Why?*', I simply met my mother's maimed gaze and said: 'It's my problem, Mom . . . not yours.'

'You're just saying that to keep me quiet, to let yourself off the hook.'

'Let myself off the hook for *what?*'

'For being such a closed book. Just like your father.'

Dad. I so wanted his approval, his interest. But he always remained elusive, distant, beyond my reach. He was now living full-time in South America – and, from the sporadic, quarterly phone calls I received from him, I knew he was shacked up with a much younger woman, and little else beyond that. But I still adopted his closed-book way of dealing with the world. Maybe I was subliminally trying to please him – '*See, Dad, I can be just like you* . . .' Or maybe the distance I kept between myself and others was simply a modus vivendi, because it kept so much chaos at bay and because it meant I knew how to guard against intrusion or prying eyes or even a cross-examination by my best friend.

'You are impossible,' Christy Naylor said.

'So I've been told.'

45

'You know what the big difference between us is?'

'Enlighten me.'

'I reveal everything, you reveal nothing.'

'A secret remains a secret until you tell somebody. From that moment on, it's in the public domain.'

'If you don't trust anyone, don't you end up feeling lonely?'

Ouch. That was a direct hit – a real right-to-the-jaw. But I tried not to show it and instead said: 'Everything has a price.'

But the harboring of secrets also has its virtues. Not a single person ever knew of my involvement with David Henry . . . and we were together for four years. We would have probably been together longer – in fact, I often think that we might still be together right now – had he not died.

Three

FOUR YEARS with David Henry.

Considered now, it all seemed to pass in a fast heady rush. That's the tricky thing about time. When you're living it on a daily basis, it can seem impossibly slow – the routine grind making you believe that the distance between Monday and the weekend is a vast one, riddled with longueurs. But regarded retrospectively, it always appears hyper-charged. A click of two fingers and you have left childhood and are trying to negotiate adolescence. Click – and you're in college, pretending to be a grown-up and yet still so wildly unsure of yourself. Click – and you're doing a doctorate and meeting your professor three afternoons a week to make love in your apartment. Click – and forty-eight months have passed. Click – and David dies. Suddenly, randomly, without premonition. A man of fifty-six, without what is known as 'medical issues', goes out for a bike ride and . . .

As David so often noted, the prosaic always forces its way into everything we do. We fool ourselves into thinking we are extraordinary. Even if we are one of the lucky ones who do extraordinary things, commonplace realities inevitably barge in. 'And the most commonplace reality,' David once said, 'is the one we fear the most: death.'

Four years. And because we were 'operating in the arena of the clandestine' (another of my favorite David quotes), we were able to sidestep so many banalities. When you set up house with somebody you're bound to find yourself falling into the usual petty disputes about domestic minutiae and personal idiosyncrasies. But when you're meeting the man you love from four to seven, three times a week – and are denied access to him at all other times – the hours you spend together take on a heightened reality . . . because, of course, they're so unreal to begin with.

'If we lived together,' I said to David a few months after it all started, 'the let-down would be huge.'

'That's a decidedly unromantic thing to say.'

'Actually, it's a decidedly *romantic* thing to say. I don't have to find out whether or not you floss your teeth, or kick dirty underwear under the bed, or only take out the garbage when cockroaches start to crawl out of—'

' "No" to all of the above.'

'Delighted to know that. Mind you, judging from your near-perfect personal hygiene when you're over here—'

'Ah, but maybe I'm just on my best behavior during our afternoons together.'

'And if you were with me all the time . . .?'

Pause. I could see how that question made him instantly uncomfortable.

'The thing is . . .' he finally said.

'Yes?'

'I pine for a life with you.'

'I wish you hadn't said that.'

'But it's the truth. I want to be with you every damn hour of the day.'

'But you can't, for all sorts of evident reasons. So why, *why*? Tell me that.'

'Because I find it very difficult leaving you, leaving here, and returning to . . .'

'All that you don't want, but refuse to walk away from. Isn't that known as a paradox? Especially as I handle the situation. That's my pragmatism. And it bothers you, because I make no demands on you. Would you rather an insane harpy who lies in wait for you outside your house, who threatens to report you to the Dean of the Faculty if you fail to meet a liaison or decide to end things?'

'I'd never end things.'

'That's nice to hear. But *I* might if you keep on talking about this – *us* – and how painful it is to say goodbye to me after our afternoons together. It simply makes me think you're doing the usual male thing of trying to explain away your guilt and your need to vacillate. And David, the thing is: you're smarter than that.'

To his credit, he never brought up the subject again. Perhaps the reason why I got so harsh with him for talking about it in the first place was because I was so damn crazy about him. And knew if he continued to hint about wanting to end things with his wife and set up house with me . . .

Well, the sense of expectation would have been unbearable, coupled with the knowledge that, at the fifty-ninth minute of the eleventh hour, he would have found a way of backing out of our life together. Because David could never come to terms with that which he wanted and that which he felt he couldn't abandon.

Four years with David Henry.

We were very adept at divorcing our life outside Harvard from the one we had within the university. Whenever I came to David's office for our weekly thesis meetings, it was business as usual between us. Though a knowing smile would occasionally pass between us, we both made it a point to treat these professional meetings as just that – and never even bring up the next rendezvous *chez moi*. Similarly, if I ever saw David at a campus event, I would always call him 'Professor' and behave in a relatively formal manner. Just as I was rigorous about getting him to cover his own tracks, so his wife wouldn't get suspicious about all his absences. That's when I suggested he tell her that he was writing in his office during our afternoons together – and invest in an answerphone that he would turn on before leaving for my place, but which he could access remotely. Having told Polly that he would be working for these hours – and that the answerphone was on – he had his alibi.

This ruse worked. After plaguing him for a couple of weeks, Polly bought the lie. He was 'moving forward' on the novel he'd been threatening to write for the past decade . . .

But, on one level, he was telling the truth. In order to cover his hours with me – and to prove to Polly that he was writing – he started getting to his office most mornings by eight and turning out a page of his book (he was a very slow writer) before his first class at eleven.

It took him over two years to finish it. He never talked about its contents – except to say that it was set in the 1960s and had a somewhat experimental structure. He wouldn't show it to me for several months after finishing the first draft. Even then, he seemed hesitant, especially as his agent was getting quite a number of passes from the major New York publishing houses to which it had been submitted.

'They're all saying it's too damn out-there,' he told me after the sixth rejection rolled in.

'Well, any time you want an outside opinion . . .' I said.

'I'll let you read it after it's accepted.'

'You know, David, it doesn't matter to me whether some publisher has given it the thumbs-down.'

'Let's just see what happens,' he said, sounding very much as though he didn't want to be pressed further about it.

Finally, after months of thumbs-down, a small but highly respected publisher, the Pentameter Press, gave David's novel the thumbs-up. He showed up at my apartment that day with champagne and a wonderful gift: a first edition of H.L. Mencken's *A Little Book in C Major*, which contained one of my favorite of his aphorisms: '*Conscience is the inner voice which warns us that somebody may be looking.*'

'That edition must have cost you a fortune,' I said to David, after telling him just what a fantastic surprise it was.

'That's my worry.'

'You're far too generous.'

'No, you're far too generous – on all levels.'

'So . . . this novel of yours. Do I get to read the damn thing now?' I asked.

He hesitated for a moment, then said: 'All right . . . but you must take the whole thing with a Lot's wife-sized grain of salt.'

He wouldn't elaborate on this point, but it did raise my suspicions that he'd been writing some sort of a *roman-à-clef*, in which our relationship played a certain role. The very fact that he had been so tight-lipped about it heightened my concerns, as did the way he gave me the manuscript during our next afternoon together: literally pulling it out of his shoulder bag just before leaving, placing it on a kitchen counter and saying nothing more about it except: 'See you Friday.'

The novel was entitled *Forty-Nine Parallels*. It was quite a short book – two hundred and six pages of double-spaced manuscript – and quite a long read. Ostensibly it was the story of a man in late middle age – simply referred to as 'the Writer' – who is driving across Canada (hence the play on the 49th Parallel) to see a brother who's had a nervous breakdown while doing some property deal in Vancouver. The brother is rich. The Writer teaches in a middling university in Montreal. He has a wife – referred to always as 'Wife' (no definite article) – whom he no longer loves, and who keeps talking about seeing 'Visions of the Divine'. The Writer has been having an affair with a younger writer, known only as 'She'. *She* is a young professor at McGill – brilliant, self-contained, willing to be his

51

mistress, but unwilling to handle his 'emotional dynamite'. The Writer adores her because he knows that, though he can 'have' her, he still can't *have* her . . .

Though the basis of the story might sound linear and conventional (adultery and disaffection among the intelligentsia), David's narrative – or perhaps his anti-narrative – completely obliterated all accessible elements in the story. Instead what we had was a sort of extended interior monologue as the Writer points his 'venerable, but fading' VW Karmen Ghia in a westerly direction and negotiates the 'Great Elongated Nowhere' that is the Canadian Prairies. The Writer – suffering from guilt, depression, 'the nihilism of the everyday, the illusory exhilaration of escape' – drives and thinks about the two women in his life in an extended stream-of-consciousness way. There was a lot of tortured imagery, not to mention three-page-long sentences describing the 'mesmeric nothingness of the plains', and (now this was interesting) 'the peach-compote tang of the cunt of She'.

Working my way through it – and it was most definitely *work* – I didn't have the shock of recognition that I feared. David did not reinvent our relationship per se. No, what surprised me the most about *Forty-Nine Parallels* was its inherent badness. It was deliberately obscurantist, making the reader struggle to maintain some sort of comprehension of the Writer's stream-of-consciousness; his wild shifts in cognitive direction; his endless digressions on everything from Wittgenstein to Tim Horton doughnuts.

To say that it was a curious experience reading David's novel would be to engage in understatement. I was genuinely thrown by it. You think you know someone so well. Through all your conversations about life and art and the stuff that matters and the stuff that doesn't matter – and through the intimacies of love – you think you're pretty damn certain what is churning around in his head; how he reacts to things and sees the world. And then . . . *then* . . . he turns around and writes something so defiantly weird and unsettling . . . though, at least, it was somewhat of a relief to discover that *She* bore little relation to *me*.

And now I was dreading our next rendezvous. Because he would ask what I thought – and there was no way that I was going to tiptoe around this one. It was too big, too primal to avoid. I had to tell him the truth.

But when he showed up that Friday, he didn't mention the book at all. Instead, we fell into bed. My ardor was even more intense than usual, perhaps due to the guilt I was feeling about so hating his novel. We lounged in bed afterwards and he talked at length about a new biography of Emily Dickinson which he had been asked to review for *Harper's*, and how Dickinson's rigorous virginity so informed her world-view, and how 'After Great Pain' remained one of the benchmark poems of American literature and . . .

'Don't you want to know what I thought of the book, David?' I asked.

'I know that already. In fact, I knew what you were going to think of it before you even read the first page. That's why I was so reluctant to give it to you.'

'So you wrote it knowing I would hate it?'

'Do I detect a hostile tone in your voice, Jane?'

'I'm just baffled by it, that's all.'

'I never knew you were such a creative conservative.'

'Oh, *please*. Give me credit for a little more literary sophistication than that. Mickey Spillane's *I, the Jury* is easy to read. James Joyce's *Ulysses* is hard to read. The thing that binds them together is *engagement*. It doesn't matter how facile or taxing a novel is – as long as it engages the reader.'

'Which mine obviously didn't for you.'

'Its density is overwhelming; its intentional ellipticism maddening. And then, when you write a line like *'the peach-compote tang of the cunt of She'* . . . I mean, David, *really* . . .'

'You know, Polly thinks it's a masterpiece.'

That comment landed like a slap on the face. He went on.

'And, for some time, she'd been pushing me to make a radical break with traditional narrative structure.'

'So, to her, it's a phenomenal novel.'

'Her praise bothers you, doesn't it?'

That's because I didn't trust it and because I sensed that Polly exerted pressure on David to go all hyper-modern as a way of curbing his success, holding back his once-brilliant career being one of her major preoccupations. Just as I sensed that David – guilty about her depression and about having a long-standing affair with yours truly – wanted to do something to please her. Since he was telling her that he was writing this book while actually making love to me three afternoons a week, well, why not assuage the guilt by doing her bidding and by scaling the thorny edifice of high literary modernism? The wife wins on all fronts. She's gotten her man to reject popular success for aesthetic marginality. She can call herself David's amanuensis. Best of all, she can damage him – because I knew that, once the book came out and vanished without a trace, David would have another crisis of creative confidence and wonder if he ever had it in him to write fiction again.

This entire train of thought swirled in and out of my head in a matter of seconds. Even though I could see the ultimate denouement of this story, I felt powerless to articulate anything. To speak my mind would be to lose him. So instead I said: 'David . . . as you predicted, it's not my sort of novel. I'm pleased that Polly so rates it. And let's face facts – I could be wrong about it.'

That was the closest we ever came to a moment of real

conflict – and, typical me, I defused it before it could blow up into something terrible and honest. He left that afternoon with the manuscript. Months passed. We continued to have our three afternoons a week. As the late-January publication date approached, David finally did start communicating his nervousness about the novel's possible reception.

'Well, one thing you must know already,' I said, 'is that high modernism has always divided people. So you will undoubtedly get wildly divisive reactions to it. And there's nothing wrong with that.'

As it turned out, my worst-case scenario came true. Because it was David Henry's first novel after such a long period of silence – and because Pentameter Press was such a respected publisher – it received an extensive amount of critical attention. And with one or two exceptions, he was slaughtered. The *Atlantic* was the first review out – and their critic (who was a self-confessed David admirer) pronounced himself baffled as to why he had '*slammed the door on his talent as a hip comic novelist with such shrewd compassion*' to write such '*nonsensical contortions*'. The *New Yorker* limited its appraisal to a paragraph on its 'New and Noteworthy' page: '*A campus novelist decides he's going to out-Finnegan Joyce – on a Canadian highway no less! The result is a novel that reads like a parody of the French* nouveau roman . . . *though it's dubious whether any French* nouveau roman *had so many references to pudenda and maple-glazed doughnuts . . . which, we think, is something of a fictional first . . .*'

But it was the *New York Times* which really trashed him. Their critic – I won't even mention her name, I am still so enraged by her thoroughgoing vindictiveness – wasn't simply content to damn the novel for its obvious flaws. Instead she had to use it as a platform to trawl through David's two previous novels and proclaim that his once-touted brilliance was merely *a 'shabby veneer which allowed him to con a willing public into believing that he was the pumped pectoral polymath of every Radcliffe girl's dreams . . . whereas close scrutiny of his limited and limiting oeuvre show him to be a second-rate intellect who, in true American huckster style, has conned his way into the upper echelons of the academy . . . and now has the arrogance to think that he can play anti-narrative games and not get found out. If this absurd enterprise of a novel demonstrates anything, it's that David Henry deserves to be finally found out.'*

There are moments when the cruelty of others is simply breathtaking. I read the review in a little café on Brattle Street. As I worked my way through it, I found it difficult to fathom its all-out sadism. All right, David had written a bad book. But to totally decimate his reputation; to call him a fraud in all departments . . .

After putting the review down, I broke one of the long-standing rules I had with David – showing up at his office any time but the arranged hour for our weekly advisory meeting on my thesis. When I got there, the door was closed and there was a notice taped to the door in his own scrawly handwriting:

I Will be Unavailable Today.

He was due to come by my apartment that afternoon. It was the first time he missed a rendezvous – and he left no message on my answering machine. I couldn't ring him at home, but I did leave a very neutral, correct message for him on his office voicemail: 'Professor, it's Jane Howard. I need to speak with you about a scheduling problem this week. If you could please call me . . .' I got no reply.

Two, three days went by. His office remained shuttered, the note – *I Will be Unavailable Today* – still undisturbed on his door. I was growing increasingly worried and frantic, especially as another hammer-blow had landed on David in the days after the *Times* review. A writer with *New York* working for their 'Intelligencer' sector, their upscale gossip pages, had been tracking the acidic reception of *Forty-Nine Parallels* and decided to see if there were any antecedents to David's novel. Lo and behold, he discovered that one of the benchmark works of the French *nouveau roman*, Michel Butor's *La Modification,* was a stream-of-consciousness account of a writer traveling between Paris and Rome on some trans-Europe express and musing at length about his wife and his mistress.

'*Yes, Professor Henry does make a passing reference to* La Modification *in his exceedingly obscurantist tome,*' wrote the uncredited *New York* journalist, '*as his narrator does talk about writing a book that "would out-Butor Butor". But this one buried reference does not really exempt Henry from the charge of essentially transposing the entire structural and thematic idea of someone else's novel on to his own. Or perhaps the good Professor has a deconstructionist theory about this case of High Modernist Reappropriation . . . also known in plainer English as Plagiarism.*'

As soon as I read this, I rushed out to the Harvard Coop to buy an English translation of Butor's novel. Like *Forty-Nine Parallels*, it was dense, elliptical and very much an 'in-his-head' form of narration. But beyond the basic premise, the two books couldn't have been more disparate. So what if they had obvious similarities in terms of the man-on-a-journey-caught-between-two-women set-up. Every piece of literature is, in some form or another, a reinvention of someone else's previous work. Only a vindictive hack journalist – out to debase and wound a talented man – would equate an evident *homage* with plagiarism.

I tried ringing David again at his office. I even called the department secretary, Mrs Cathcart. Again using very neutral language I said that, if she was speaking to Professor Henry, would she please tell him that I felt the plagiarism charge was completely preposterous.

Mrs Cathcart – who was around sixty and had been the department's secretary since the early 1970s – cut me off.

'I'm afraid the university doesn't think it preposterous, as Professor Henry was suspended today while a faculty committee examines the charges against—'

'But that's ridiculous. I've read the other novel and there is no plagiarism charge to answer.'

'That is your interpretation, Miss Howard,' Mrs Cathcart said. 'The Faculty Affairs Committee will—'

'Crucify him, because he has so many enemies on that—'

Again she cut me off. 'If you want to help Professor Henry, I wouldn't make such statements public. It might cause people to speculate.'

'Speculate what?' I asked.

But she didn't answer that, except to say: 'I gather Professor Henry has gone to ground and left Cambridge. You could call his wife, if you so wish.'

Was there an undercurrent of malice to that comment? Was she letting me know, *I'm on to you*? But we had been so damn careful, so completely circumspect. Surely she was just being her usual devious self – as she was notorious in the department for always making others feel uncomfortable.

'Do you have his home number?' Mrs Cathcart asked.

'No.'

'I'm surprised you don't know it, having worked so closely with the Professor for the past four years.'

'I never call him at home.'

'I see,' she said with a hint of ice. And I ended the call.

I immediately rang David's home number. There was no reply and the answerphone wasn't on. Had Polly gone with

58

him to Maine? He had a little cottage there outside of Bath in which we never stayed, as it was in a very small village with 'all-seeing, all-knowing neighbors'. If Polly had gone there with him and if I showed up . . .

But if he was alone in Maine . . .

Part of me wanted to rent a car and drive straight up there. But the cautious side of me counseled against such rash action – not just because Polly might be up there with him, but also because I sensed (or, at least, hoped) that David would make contact with me when he needed me.

But there was no contact, no sign from him of his where-abouts or his state of mind. A day went by, then two, then three. I called his home number three times a day. No answer. I checked in again with Mrs Cathcart. 'No one knows his whereabouts,' was all that she would say. I called Christy and met her for more than several drinks, a night out with Christy always being an excuse to get hammered. She had lots of inside departmental gossip, and told me that at least three of David's colleagues (she had their names) had approached the Dean of the Faculty, demanding that David be dismissed for professional misconduct, and had been assured that, if the plagiarism charges were authenticated, the Dean would be backing them.

'There is a group of very bitter shits in the department,' Christy said, 'who have always wanted to bring the guy down. This resentment goes back to the seventies when they were all starting out together and Professor Henry was perceived to be too flashy and celebrated by these already-gray assholes. And they've also always hated his popularity with just about every student he's worked with. So now they're having their *schadenfreude* moment and are just delighted to see him fighting for his professional life.'

'I'm pretty certain he's gone to his place in Maine.'

'If that's the case, he's on his own up there.'

'How do you know that?' I said, sounding just a little surprised.

'Because Mrs Cathcart told me that, when the shit hit the fan, Henry'd had a big blow-up with his wife – accused her of talking him into writing such a drecky novel, told her she'd always been doing her best to sabotage his career.'

Oh, Jesus.

'How did Cathcart hear all this?'

'*Madame* Henry told her. It seems that Crazy Polly frequently calls that crusty old bitch to vent about her wayward husband. And Cathcart encourages her – because, hey, information is power, right?'

'Well, why did that "bitch" then tell me that I should call David's wife to find his whereabouts?'

'Because she likes to play head games, that's why. And because – like everyone else in the department – she suspects that you and the Professor have been romantically involved for quite a long time.'

The news made me flinch. *They knew. Everyone knew.*

'That's total nonsense,' I said.

'I figured that would be your response,' replied Christy. 'That's why, as much as I like you, I can't really call you a friend. And that's not just the booze talking. But you know this—'

'I know there's a lot of stupid innuendo that simply isn't true.'

'And I know that I'm outta here,' she said, throwing some money down on the table, 'because I'm not going to sit here and be lied to.'

'I am *not* lying,' I slurred, all that vodka and beer elongating my words and emboldening me to trumpet my innocence.

'This conversation is over,' Christy said. 'But do your man

a favor. As soon as you wake up tomorrow, get a car and get up to him in Maine. He needs you.'

I don't remember giving the cab driver my address, or paying him or negotiating the stairs up to my apartment, or getting out of my clothes and collapsing onto the bed. What I do remember is waking with a start around eight and cursing myself for having gotten so smashed. I didn't even want to get into the ramifications of what Christy said last night – not just about my untruthfulness with her (guilty as charged), but about the appalling realization that there had been much departmental speculation regarding my non-professional relationship with David.

I got out of the arctic shower. I put on some clothes. I made a pot of coffee and called Avis and arranged to pick up a car at their Cambridge location in half an hour. I downed two Alka-Seltzer followed by two scalding mugs of coffee. I was about to start throwing some things in an overnight bag when the intercom began to buzz.

David!

I went running downstairs. But when I yanked open the door, Christy was standing there. From the way she looked at me – a mixture of distress and fear – I could tell immediately that something was terribly wrong.

'Can we go upstairs?' she asked.

We climbed the stairs and entered my apartment. I switched off the coffee maker, then turned back to the door-way. Christy was standing there, five fingers wrapped around the door handle, as if she was preparing to make a break for it.

That's when I knew. From the moment her frightened face was revealed outside my front door . . . *I knew*.

'David?' I asked in a near-whisper.

She nodded slowly. Then: 'He was knocked down and killed by a car yesterday.'

It took a moment or two to register. I found myself gripping the side of the stove. The world grew very quiet, very small. Christy continued talking, but I wasn't aware of her anymore.

'He was on a bicycle down by a beach near his house in Maine. It was late in the afternoon. A lot of glare and shadows. He was pedaling along this back road, a truck came by, and . . .'

She paused. Then: 'They think it was an accident.'

Now I was very cognizant of her again.

'What did you just say?'

'The driver of the truck—'

She broke off.

'Tell me,' I whispered.

'According to Mrs Cathcart, the driver of the truck was on the opposite side of the road from David. He could see him cycling towards him. But then, suddenly, David seemed to swerve right into his path. And . . .'

I let go of the stove. I sank down into one of the kitchen chairs. I put the palms of my hands against my eyes and pressed hard. But the world wouldn't black out.

Christy came over and put her arms around me. But I didn't want to be consoled. I didn't want someone to *share* my loss. In the moments of aftershock that accompanied the news, a little voice in my head cautioned me to be careful how I played all this. *Get hysterical and they'll realize the truth.*

I shrugged Christy off. I said to her: 'I think I need to be by myself now.'

'That's the last thing you need,' she said.

I stood up and started heading for the bedroom.

'Thank you for coming here and telling me.'

'Jane, you don't have to pretend.'

'Pretend *what*? There's nothing to pretend here.'

'For fuck's sake, your lover just died.'

'We'll talk tomorrow.'

'Not if you can't even bring yourself to—'

I closed the bedroom door. I sat down on the bed. I half-expected Christy to barge in and confront me with all of my manifold shortcomings – especially the way I couldn't even talk to her at the worst moment in my life.

But there was no such dramatic confrontation. Instead I heard the front door open and close and the apartment go silent.

What happened next surprised me. I felt as if I was operating on some sort of autopilot. I got up. I grabbed the overnight bag and threw some clothes into it. I called a cab. I went to Avis, I picked up the rental car I had reserved. I drove out of Cambridge, headed north to Route 1, branched onto Interstate 95 and sped up to Maine.

Why was I doing this? I had no idea. All I knew was that I had to see where he died.

I was in the town of Bath by one o'clock that afternoon. I stopped in a gas station and got directions to Popham Beach. The road east to the ocean passed through expansive New England terrain – green rolling fields, white clapboard houses, old red barns, a salty inlet from the ocean. I focused on every feature, every characteristic of that road which he biked down towards his death. I reached Popham around thirty minutes after leaving Bath. The parking lot was empty. I was the only beachcomber on this bleak May day, the sky the color of dirty chalk. I walked down a little pathway through some dunes and reached the water. Everything David had told me about Popham – and he often talked about it – was spot-on correct.

'Three miles of unbroken sand, unspoiled, often empty, with the best ocean vista in New England. Any time I'm up in

Maine and out of sorts with the world, I take a walk on Popham and stare out at the sheer vastness of the Atlantic . . . and somehow, it always makes me feel that possibilities still exist beyond the confines of my little life, that there's always a way out.'

I stood on the beach and gazed out at the Atlantic and heard David's voice telling me all that. And I couldn't help but wonder if, two days ago, he was finding things so unbearable, so beyond consolation, that the sight of Popham tipped him over the edge. Not only was it just too beautiful to bear, but say it didn't do its restorative magic? Say its raw epic grandeur didn't console, but rather heightened his sense of having been trounced. Say he was at such a low point – so defeated by everything – that the beauty of the water was simply too hard to bear. Say he shut his eyes to its metronomic surf, its shimmering surface, and began to think: *If I can't bear this . . .*

Personally I couldn't bear looking at the water and simultaneously thinking about what David might have been going through in the final hour of his life. So I returned to the car and drove out of the parking lot and turned right, following the road towards the direction of a signposted summer colony of houses. Halfway there, the road narrowed, owing to traffic cones with police tape stretched between them. I stopped the car and got out. The police cones and tape were shaped into an elongated rectangle – like a long coffin, perhaps fifteen feet by four. I swallowed hard and stared down at the blacktopped road. There were noticeable skid marks across it, the wide imprint of the tire tread indicating that it was a substantial vehicle which hit him. I walked over to the police tape and peered down. The side of the road here was marked by dirt and scruffy grass. I peered closer at its surface and could see the dried remnants of blood at that frontier between the blacktop and the earth. There was one significant stain – a large blotch that seemed to have oozed out in a long thin trickle.

I shut my eyes, unable to look at it any longer. *But you came here to look at it in the first place*. I straightened myself up and stood in the middle of the road and noted the narrowness of the blacktop at this point. I checked its surface, walking forwards beyond the police cones, looking downwards, hoping to find . . .

Yes! There, beneath my feet, was a pothole. Not a particularly big pothole – maybe a foot or so in diameter – but located in a telling spot, perhaps twelve feet or so before the skid marks and the police cones. A narrative assembled in my mind. David left the beach and was coming along the road at speed. He saw the truck moving towards him. He prudently steered himself to the edge of the blacktop. But then his front wheel hit the pothole, he lost control of his bicycle and was thrown into the path of . . .

That was it. That's how it happened. An accident. So random, so arbitrary – an unlinked set of circumstances coming together to create disaster.

I could now tell myself that it wasn't suicide; that, truly, David had simply been in the wrong place at the wrong time.

I walked back to the car, feeling no relief, no lightening of my sadness, no sense that this personal confirmation of his accident had made his loss easier to bear. All I could think was: *Why are you here? OK, you've confirmed what you wanted to confirm. Now what?*

Now . . . nothing. Except the drive back to Boston. And then . . .?

But before I headed back I decided I should see his house. I'd passed it on my way out to Popham – knowing it immediately because he had talked so often about its exact location in the village of Winnegance.

65

Now, upon reaching it, I first stopped at the end of his driveway and got out, looking up its winding path to ascertain that no car was parked there. Then I drove the rest of the way to his house. It was exactly as he had described it – a small saltbox structure, situated on an elevated prospect looking right out on the water. I walked around the house and stopped when I saw the room that was obviously David's study: a small simple space, with a desk, a bookshelf and one of the several Remington typewriters that he owned (he refused to write anything but academic stuff on a computer). The desk faced a wall, just like his office at Harvard – 'Otherwise I'd look out the window and get distracted by everything that's going on outside.' I found myself getting shaky. But I forced myself back into the car and returned to the main road, parking at the little general store just opposite David's place to buy a bottle of water.

Or, at least, that's what I told myself I was doing there. Once inside, the elderly, flinty-looking woman behind the counter gave me the skeptical once-over that she probably reserved for anyone who wasn't a local during the off-season.

'Hey,' she said tonelessly. 'Get you anything?'

I asked for some sparkling water and a copy of the local paper.

As I paid for them, I said: 'I was just taking a walk down on Popham Beach and saw the police tape. Did something happen there?'

'A guy steered his bicycle into a truck,' she said, making change for me.

'An accident?'

'If a guy deliberately steers his bike into the direct path of a truck, it's no accident.'

'Did you know the guy?'

'Sure did. Professor from Boston, had a place just across the road. Pleasant enough guy. Never would have thought . . .'

'But how can they be sure that it was—?'

She gave me a long, cold look.

'You're not some kind of reporter, are you?' she asked.

'Just interested,' I said, sounding nervous.

'You know the Professor?'

I shook my head.

'You know Gus?'

'Who's Gus?'

'Gus is my second cousin – and the fella who was driving the truck. The man's completely devastated about what happened. Been driving the same fish truck 'round here for over twenty years. Never hit anything or anyone. Poor guy's in total shock, won't get behind the wheel again. Says he saw the Professor biking towards him and, then, right when he was almost alongside him, the Professor swerved right into his path. Completely deliberate . . . like he wanted to get hit.'

'But maybe he ran into a pothole on his bike and—'

'If Gus says he swerved into him, he swerved into him. Gus is a little slow in the head, but if there's one thing I know about him, he never lies.'

I left. I got into my car, drove off and hit the highway. Somewhere south of Portland I had to pull off the road because I was crying so hard.

If Gus says he swerved into him, he swerved into him.

I wanted to believe my own version – the one I created after seeing the site of the accident. But here now was contradictory information – from the one authoritative source at the scene.

Maybe that was why I was crying so hard – not just because David's loss was finally hitting me with full-frontal force, but also because the manner of his death was so ambiguous.

When I returned to my Cambridge apartment that night, I discovered, in my mailbox, a plain white postcard. On one side, in David's scratchy handwriting, was my address, and a Bath, Maine postmark. On the other side were three words:

> *I'm sorry*
> *David*

I went up to my studio and sat down at my little dining table. I put the card down and stared at those three words for a very long time. My head was swimming. His last message to me. But what was he telling me? *I'm sorry . . . and I'm going to kill myself*? Or: *I'm sorry for the mess I've caused*? Or: *I'm sorry I didn't listen to you about the book*? Or: *I'm sorry I've disappeared*? *Or . . .*

Nothing definitive. No answers. Just more ambiguity.

I'm sorry.

With the door slammed on the outside world, I broke down again, crying like an idiot. But this time my tears weren't just a response to my sense of loss – a loss I couldn't share with anyone. Rather, they were also bound up with real anger. I was furious with David – not just for dying, but also for trying to salve his conscience with that fucking postcard and a message which simply added another enigmatic wrinkle to an already ambiguous situation.

I'm sorry.

In the days that followed, my anger ebbed a bit, replaced by a sadness that was hard to shake. I received a call from Mrs Cathcart – all quiet and conciliatory, telling me how everyone in the department was so distressed by Professor Henry's death (a lie); how there was now a general backlash against the *New York* journalist who penned the accusations of plagiarism (another lie); and how she was thinking about me during this difficult time because 'I know how close you were to the Professor'.

'That's right,' I said, trying to sound controlled. 'He was a brilliant thesis advisor and a good friend.'

But before I added 'Nothing more', I stopped myself. When you protest too much you incriminate yourself.

'You should know that the Maine police ruled the whole thing an accident,' she said. 'Just in case you were wondering.'

'I wasn't wondering anything,' I said, while simultaneously wondering: Did they decide not to believe the testimony of Gus the Driver? Or maybe Gus was talked into a narrative explanation – 'The bike hit the pothole and the next thing I knew he was thrown directly in front of my vehicle' – as a way of simplifying matters, ending ambiguity and quashing all difficult questions. As I later heard on the departmental grapevine, the very fact that David's death was ruled an accident meant that his wife would receive his life-insurance payout. Maybe the cops – wanting to minimize the pain suffered by the driver and by David's family – stuck with the accident scenario.

But I knew the truth. And the truth was: *There is no truth here*. It's like that line of Eliot's from 'The Hollow Men': '*Between the motion/And the act/Falls the Shadow*.'

I'm sorry.

I'm sure you were, David. But it doesn't lessen the questions, doesn't diminish the shadows.

His funeral was private. He was cremated and his ashes sprinkled on the water fronting his cottage. When I learned of this – from Mrs Cathcart, naturally – I couldn't help but think of something David once said to me about the transient nature of everything.

'We try so hard to put our mark on things, we like to tell ourselves that what we do has import or will last. But the truth is, we're all just passing through. So little survives us. And when we're gone, it's simply the memory of others that keeps our time here alive. And when they're gone . . .

'That's why – when I go – I'm asking that my dust gets tossed on the water. Because everything ends up floating away.'

Everyone in the department was very solicitous towards me. The chairman, Professor Hawthorden, rang me personally and asked if I would drop by his office for a chat. I steeled myself for the third degree. As it turned out, he was the very model of tact. He talked about the 'accidental tragedy' of David's death, and how the plagiarism charges were nothing more than 'trial by hack journalism'. He also wanted me to know that David always spoke very highly of me as a student, and that he himself would like to take charge of my dissertation, if I was 'comfortable' with this offer.

Why did the department head want to be my advisor – especially as his specialty was Early American Literature? Was he trying to silence any gossip about my relationship with David? Was he keeping me 'on side'? I had no idea. If Professor Hawthorden preferred to keep things nice and ambiguous, I was not going to argue. As I had come to discover, ambiguity had its virtues.

I threw myself into work, writing two pages of my dissertation per day, six days per week. I kept a low profile, seeing Hawthorden twice a month for an hour-long conference, but otherwise spending most of my time at the library or at my apartment. I vanished for the next nine months. Bar Christy, my life at Harvard had been David. And with David gone . . .

But I liked the solitude. Check that: I *needed* the solitude . . . needed the time to . . . grieve, I suppose. But also to somehow reorder my brain and put David's death in a box that I had already marked '*Off Limits*'. Though I might quietly mourn him, I had to accept the cold brutality of his demise. Just as I was determined that no one would ever be privy to the grief I actually felt.

There was a considerable amount of public hand-wringing at Harvard and in the press about whether David had been unfairly victimized by certain English department colleagues. Fair play to the *Harvard Crimson* – they outed the bastards who had been calling for his head. But what did it matter now? David was still dead. There was also a memorial service held at the college chapel three months after his 'accident'. Naturally I attended. Afterwards, as everyone spilled out of the church and Polly found herself shaking a lot of hands, I stood by the chapel door surveying the scene. At that very moment, Polly glanced around and her eyes happened to land on me. Her gaze was cold, yet level – and followed by a very fast nod of acknowledgement. Then she turned back to a group of mourners who had gathered around her. That look haunted me for a very long time. Was she telling me that she knew exactly who I was? But why follow such an arctic stare with a gesture that almost seemed to acknowledge the connection – and loss – that we both shared? Maybe I was simply trying to impose far too much interpretation on five seconds of eye contact. Perhaps the cold gaze was just the look of a woman trying to stay in control of things during a difficult public juncture, the nod nothing more than a simple 'Hello to you . . . whoever you are.'

We can never really determine the truth behind the unspoken. A gesture can have any meaning you wish to impose on it. Just as the truth behind an accident will never be fully understood. Just as embracing ambiguity can shield you from so much.

That's something David's death taught me. If you confess to nothing, you provide those around you only with sup-position . . . and no proof. That which remains hidden does, indeed, *remain hidden*. I took some comfort in this realization – not just because I saw it as a way of constructing the defensive shield I needed to get through the subsequent months at Harvard, but also because it somehow allowed me to compartmentalize all the rage and sadness; to control the demons within. So I went to ground. I did my work. I allowed myself little latitude when it came to a life outside of my thesis. Professor Hawthorden – who read each chapter as it came 'off the press' – seemed pleased with its progress. When I completed it, he expressed his amazement that I had managed to deliver it six months before its provisional due date.

'I've just had an extended burst of . . . concentration,' I said.

Usually there is a four-month gap between the delivery of the thesis and your defense of it. But Hawthorden – evidently wanting to speed things along – informed me that he would be arranging the defense before all faculty members disappeared for the summer break. As it turned out, there were only three other members of the department quizzing me on the finer points of *The Infernal Duality: Obedience and Defiance in American Literature*. There were questions about whether there was any real Zola-esque leitmotif in Dreiser, and about the uses of progressive political thought in Upton Sinclair's *The Jungle*. One professor got rather tetchy about my need to find a socio-economic subtext in every novel under discussion (I fielded that one handily), someone else queried my own need to be 'novelistic' in an academic thesis . . . and I left my defense doubting whether I was in any way credible.

Within a week I received an official letter from Hawthorden, informing me that my thesis had been approved and that I would be granted the degree of Doctor of Philosophy from Harvard. At the bottom of the letter were two handwritten lines:

It has been a pleasure working with you. I wish you well.

And Hawthorden initialed this.

Was he telling me, in as polite a way as he was able: 'Now please get lost'? Was this the reason he gave my thesis express service – to dispatch me from their lives as quickly as possible? Or, again, was this simply one of many interpretations that could be applied to twelve words? Was everything always so riddled with multiple meanings?

A few days after I received my letter from Hawthorden, I was also contacted by the Harvard Placement Office, asking me to drop by for a chat. The woman who saw me – an all-business type in her forties named Ms Steele – told me that there was a last-minute job opening for an assistant professor at the University of Wisconsin in Madison.

'It is a tenure-track appointment – and Wisconsin is pretty first rate as state universities go.'

'I'll take the interview.'

Two days later I was flown out to Madison. The chairman of the department – a rather harried, exhausted man named Wilson – picked me up at the airport and unburdened himself to me on the drive to the university: how this position had opened up when an assistant professor developed an unhealthy interest in one of his students and was let go; and how he was also having to fill another post, in medieval literature, as the woman who had held it for the past twenty years had finally drunk herself into the local intensive care unit, and . . .

'Well, what can I say?' Wilson told me. 'It's just your average dysfunctional English department.'

When I sat around the conference table that afternoon in some administrative building, being interviewed by Wilson and four other department members, I looked at the drabness of my future colleagues – their air of enervation and tetchiness; the way they undercut each other as they sized me up, finding out just how smart I thought myself, whether I'd be a threat to them or someone they could manage, and asking what I thought about the scandal that had engulfed one of their colleagues.

Careful here, I told myself, then said: 'As I really don't know the details of the case—'

'But what do you think in general about the rules against intimate student–faculty relationships?' this woman asked.

Does she know about me and . . . ?

'I can't condone them,' I said, meeting her gaze. The subject wasn't raised again.

I flew back to Boston that evening, remembering something that David once told me: 'Anytime you ever think about taking a teaching post, always remember that most time-honored of clichés: the reason everyone is so bitchy in academia is because the stakes are so low.'

David. My poor wonderful David.

And the idea of now embracing the world that had helped to kill him . . .

So when the call came three days later from Wisconsin, informing me I had the job, I told the department chairman I wasn't taking it.

'But why?' he asked, sounding genuinely shocked.

'I've decided to make money,' I said. 'Serious money.'

Part Two

One

MONEY. I NEVER gave it much thought. Until I started making real, proper grown-up money, its existence was something that I largely ignored. As I now realize, how you deal with money – how you control it and how it controls you (and it inevitably ends up doing that) – is something you learn very early on. My adolescence was a frugal one, as Dad paid Mom a very nominal amount of alimony and child support. At high school I was always known as 'the librarian's daughter'. Unlike most other teenagers in Old Greenwich, I didn't have my own personal car, let alone membership of a country club – Old Greenwich being the sort of place where boys get their first set of golf clubs on their eleventh birthday. As I began to understand, *not* having a car and *not* spending the weekends at some white-bread enclave was no bad thing. But I still wished I could have had some of their fringe benefits – most of all, not having to worry about asking Mom for certain things, as she was constantly embarrassed about her small salary and the fact that she couldn't do more for me, even though I kept reassuring her that I needed no more than I had.

It's extraordinary how patterns of behavior develop without either you or those closest to you ever realizing that they are being formed. Mom felt guilty about not having much money. I felt guilty about Mom feeling guilty, and also felt hurt and confused about my father being so parsimonious. Simultaneously I wanted to win scholarships (and hold down assorted part-time jobs) to relieve my mom of certain financial burdens and show my father that I could hold my own in the world.

So while at college, I did work fifteen hours a week in the library to earn basic pocket money. During grad school at Harvard, I taught an introductory freshman course in English composition to augment the fellowship stipend. And because everything had to be so carefully budgeted in my life, I became very adept at living on very little. After my tuition and books, the fellowship paid me $700 per month. My studio apartment cost me just over $500 – and once the fee I received for teaching that freshman composition course was factored in, I was left with just under $400 a month for everything to do with the business of day-to-day life. I cooked most of my meals at home. I bought clothes at discount outlets. I could easily afford to see two movies a week. The T got me around Cambridge and into Boston. I never felt I wanted for anything . . . because I wasn't really longing for anything.

That's the thing about not having a great deal of money. You learn that you actually require very little to keep things interesting. It's only when you begin to make money that you find yourself thinking you need things you never dreamed of needing before. And once you get those things, you start ruminating about everything else that you don't have. Then aspirational despair sets in. You find yourself wondering how the hell you got so bound up in the desire to acquire. Because you know that, in feeding the consumerist urge, you're simultaneously papering over the large fissures in your own life; bluffing yourself into believing all this stuff would quell the doubts and melancholy within.

Money. The trickiest substance in life – as it's the way we keep score, measure our worth, and think we can control our destinies. Money: the essential lie.

But in those first crazy months when I started working at Freedom Mutual, money seemed like a great new crazy lover who was determined to show me a fresh way of looking at the world. Out with the drab, narrow economies of a frugal life. In with the pleasures of living well and not having to pay a vast amount of attention to the price tag attached.

Money. Much to my continued surprise, I found myself becoming a fast convert to its heady pleasures and the sense of possibility that it engendered.

Money. It was also a game.

Or, at least, that was how Brad Pullman looked upon it.

Brad Pullman was the CEO of Freedom Mutual. He was in his late thirties – a dentist's son from Long Island and a self-described 'one-time geek' who had been settling scores with the world from the moment he discovered Money. He went to Middlebury, then to Harvard Business School, after which he found his way into the 'secure, low-stress world of mutual funds'.

'Everything I did in the first thirty years of my life was predicated on risk aversion. I tell you, Jane, fear is Life's Big Roadblock.' (Those were his caps, by the way.) ' It's the one and only thing that will keep you from achieving all that you want to achieve, or living the life you deserve. And the truly insidious thing about fear is – it's completely self-perpetuated. We create the dread that clogs up our lives.'

Yes, Brad Pullman did often talk in such self-help-guru outbursts. It was 'part of the package', as he put it. He saw himself as a living testament to the 'Necessity of Overcoming the Negatives'. This doctrine was christened by everyone around the company as NON. 'I like it,' Brad said, when he first heard the acronym, 'except that it's French – and like any reasonable American, I hate the fucking French.' Brad himself had applied the NON doctrine to just about everything in his life. He jettisoned his first wife ('the classic starter marriage') when her 'dull negativity' finally wore out his patience. He jettisoned his trapped suburban-man image, not to mention his fleshy physique. Fifty pounds were stripped from his frame courtesy of a savage diet and an equally savage personal trainer. With his new-found sleekness came his new-found need to play the sartorial dandy.

'I am happy to admit that, in my 5.4 million-dollar townhouse on Beacon Hill, I have fifty designer suits. Does any man need fifty suits and one hundred and fifty shirts? Don't be absurd. Fifty suits and one hundred and fifty shirts in a 5.4 million-dollar townhouse is a sign of futile over-consumption . . . until, of course, you do the math. Fifty suits and one hundred and fifty shirts – let's say the outlay was around 100k over a five-year period, so 20k per annum. Now if you are some mid-level exec pulling down one hundred and 50k per annum before taxes, 20k a year on suits . . . well, it's virtually a crack-cocaine habit, right? But if you're pulling down eight million per annum, as I did last year . . .'

That was another thing about Brad Pullman. He not only announced the cost of everything – 'Like my new watch? Jaeger LeCoultre. Bought at European Watches on Newbury Street. Fifty-four hundred dollars – actually a steal' – but also let it be known – all the time – how much he was making, how much the firm was making, how much you, his minion, *should* be making, but aren't because . . . well, 'Do you have the juice to Overcome the Negatives and score the big bucks?'

I met Brad Pullman at my interview. I'd found out about the job courtesy of the Harvard Placement Office. After turning down the post in Wisconsin I asked Ms Steele if there were any openings in the world of Big Bucks.

'Plenty, of course – but you have a Ph.D. in English, so why would you want to—?'

'It's a career change,' I said.

'Even before your career has started,' she said.

'I've decided I don't want to be an academic. So if I'm rejecting university life I might as well go after the best-paid work possible.'

'Professor Henry wouldn't have approved,' she said drily. I managed to stay cool.

'Professor Henry hated everything about the pettiness of Harvard life – so, in fact, he definitely *would* have approved.'

'Well, you certainly knew him better than I did.'

'That's right,' I said. 'I did.'

Then I asked her about 'money jobs'.

'Well, hedge funds are the big thing now,' she said. 'And Boston has become a real hub for them over the past few years. These companies are always looking for entry-level traders, especially from Harvard. The fact that you have a doctorate in literature might baffle them a bit. However, it might also make you more interesting than the other candidates.'

Brad Pullman certainly thought that. Initially I was surprised to find myself being interviewed by the company head honcho for a mere trainee job. But Brad let it be known that, given Freedom Mutual's deliberately small size (only thirty employees), he was 'totally hands-on about every aspect of the company. So yeah, I am in on *everything* from the start. And I like your smarts, so why the hell shouldn't we have an expert on Dreiser working on the trading floor? The starting salary is one hundred thousand per annum and a twenty-thousand-dollar joining bonus, payable immediately. No problem with that?'

'None at all.'

'But it could end up being ten, twenty times that if you turn out to be profitable. You play your cards right with us, you could be set up for life by the time you're thirty. But before you start here, I'm giving you two thousand bucks and sending you out tomorrow afternoon with Trish Rosenstein –

who, with a name like that, doesn't "summer" at Kennebunkport with the fucking Bushes, but is one ace fund manager and knows how to dress. She's going to help you buy a new office wardrobe. Conservative, but classy. Right now, you look like you've just walked out of the Student Union and are about to eat some organic cookies with a mug of elderflower tea. It might get you hit on at the local health-food shop, but it will compete with the wallpaper here. So, if you want the job, you accept the wardrobe upgrade.'

There was a part of me which listened to this spiel and thought: *This is an actor, brilliantly impersonating a sexist dick.* The thing was, Brad *knew* that he was playing this role – and was testing you to see whether you took offense (at which point you'd be out on your ass, because he'd write you off as a prig) or could adapt to his machine-gun repartee, his delight in excessive bullshit. As I listened to him, the English Department drabbie in me found herself being curiously subverted by his patter. I'd never met anyone like Brad Pullman before – though, of course, I knew that the type existed. But what surprised me was that his bullshit came across – especially after my interview with the walking mummies at the University of Wisconsin – as both engaging and in touch with the realpolitik of the way we lived now. Yes, it was crass, but there was something weirdly refreshing about such blatant mercantilism. He was an updated version of the sort of swaggering capitalist buccaneer who peopled so many of the naturalist novels I'd studied: a wholly American construct, with a ferocious energy for the combustive engine that was pure capitalism.

'Are you ready to get into bed with the free market?' Brad asked me at the end of the interview.

At $100,000 per annum, with another 20 grand up front? Damn right I was.

82

'I think so,' I said, trying to sound demure.

'That's the last hesitant statement you make around here. Our world is defined by either a definite "yes" or "no", with absolutely no ambiguity in between.'

Trish Rosenstein was the definitive embodiment of this Manichean world-view. Though her primary objective was my sartorial reorganization – and Brad had told us both to take the following afternoon off to 'get the job done' – once we finished shopping we naturally ended up in the bar of the Four Seasons, trading life stories.

Brad had been spot on about Trish. She had a voice which combined the vowels of Brooklyn with the gaseous honk of a foghorn, a voice designed to turn heads in restaurants, to scare young children and cower domesticated animals. As we set off down Newbury Street, and she escorted me into assorted emporiums of fashion, I found myself thinking: *I'm not going to last more than ten minutes with this woman.*

'You don't wanna try that on,' she yelled to me as I was looking at a business suit in Banana Republic. 'Gonna make you look like some anorexic twat.'

Everyone on the floor spun around after she made that pronouncement. And she immediately stared everyone down, shouting: 'Something I say bother you?' That silenced the store. Then she turned to me and said: 'C'mon, let's find you something classy elsewhere.'

Once we were out on the street, I did say: 'You know, there was no real need to—'

'Say what I think? Why the hell not? I didn't insult anyone back there. I just made a comment.'

'A very loud comment.'

'So? I talk loud. It's how I deal with the world.'

She insisted on dragging me into Armani. 'The sale's on,

and we might find you something to help you lose the Crunchy Granola look.'

By the end of the afternoon, I had acquired three suits, two pairs of shoes and assorted separates – all stylish, yet simple – and even had $200 left over to blow on underwear. Trish might have had the manners of a stevedore, but she did have an eye for clothes and she certainly knew how to shop – which, as she correctly surmised, was an activity that held little interest for me.

'Brad circulated your résumé, like he does everybody's he's thinking of hiring,' she told me after directing us into the bar of the Four Seasons Hotel and ordering Martinis – two for herself, the first of which she downed almost at once. 'We all had you sized up pretty quickly: the smart girl raised in strained circumstances. Your father must be some class of creep, by the way.'

'What makes you say that?' I asked.

'Stop sounding tetchy. It is just a simple *deduction*. Daddy's in the copper business, but has jettisoned you and your mother for a new life with a string of South American *bimbas*, right?'

'There've only been two—'

'To the best of your knowledge. All men are putzes at heart – even the good ones. But you know that by now, don't you?'

I looked at her carefully.

'What do you mean by that?' I asked.

'Oh, come on, you don't think Brad – Mr Micro-Manager – didn't dig a little bit into your past and find out about you and the Professor?'

I looked at her, appalled.

'When I applied for a job as a trainee, I didn't think my past private life would be vetted.'

'There are three of us in the company who form the vetting committee to make certain we hire someone who will fit into the Freedom Mutual culture. Do you know what we all liked about you – besides the Harvard doctorate and pulling yourself up by your bootstraps and not being a snot . . . ?'

'Enlighten me.'

'The fact that you had a four-year thing with your thesis advisor and kept it completely out of the public view.'

'Who told you this?'

'Do you honestly think I'd reveal our sources? I mean, *puleeze*. But, between ourselves, Brad was also super-impressed about how you never showed your hand, never stirred the pot, and kept a dignified silence in the wake of his death. What a business, by the way. I really felt for you . . . especially with all the ambiguity surrounding—'

'I'm leaving now,' I heard myself saying.

'Have I said the wrong thing?'

'Actually you have. Just as I find it completely abhorrent that you and your colleagues have dug into my past and—'

'We all know each other's stuff in the office,' she said. 'I'm aware that Brad is cheating on his wife with a bond dealer named Samantha who has a nasty temper and frequently scratches his back during sex, causing him to wear a T-shirt in bed with his wife for a few days. Everyone knows that Brad should break it off with her, but he's addicted to trouble. Just as Brad knows that I've been in a relationship with a cop named Pauline for the past two years.'

'I see,' I said, trying to sound nonplussed.

'Go on, act all blasé and inclusive. Pretend you're not shocked to discover I'm a dyke . . .'

'It really is your own business.'

'Not at Freedom Mutual. Brad insists on total transparency. No secrets, no hidden baggage. Everything out in the open. So . . . go on, ask me any question about myself. *Anything*. You ask, I'll tell.'

'I'd rather not.'

'Loosen up.'

'All right. Why do you talk so loud?'

'Good question. And here's the answer: Because I had a mother who was always screaming at everybody and complained a lot about how life had been one big let-down, and how: "If you want to be really disappointed by things, then you should definitely have children."'

'Charming.'

'That she wasn't.'

'She's dead?'

'They're all dead. My dad, my mom, my brother Phil . . .'

'How old was he when he died?'

'Nineteen.'

'Had he been sick?'

'It was suicide, so, yeah, he'd been sick.'

'Why did he—?'

'Hang himself in his bedroom on Christmas Eve 1979 . . .?'

'Oh, my word.'

'Can't you be American and use "fuck"?'

'That is just horrible.'

'Fucking horrible. I was twelve at the time and my big brother was just home from his sophomore year at the University of Pennsylvania. It was a big deal in my family, the first-born – *the guy* – getting accepted into an Ivy League university, being pre-Med and all that. What my parents didn't know is that, after a brilliant first year, near straight As, he had some kind of breakdown and suddenly got a C in Biochemistry. Now for anyone who's pre-Med, a C in Biochemistry is a huge setback. And Mom gets his report card on December 23rd. Having nothing better to do – and being fucking Mom – she begins to do this vast big number on him, saying how he's a huge disappointment, how she'd given up everything to raise him, and this is how he repaid her. My mom ruined everything – and everyone – she touched. And if I'm sounding like a shrink, well . . . I did do nine years of the talking cure after finding my brother hanging from the clothes rail in his closet.'

'You found him?'

'That's what I said.'

She paused and downed the Martini, then put her hand up for a third one.

'Not for me,' I said when she tried to order two.

'You're having one – like it or not. Because if there's one thing I know about life, it's the fact that everyone needs to get drunk from time to time – even you, Miss Propriety.'

'Your parents must have been devastated after—'

'Dad died about six months after Phil. Throat cancer – the payback for forty years of non-stop cigarettes. He was only fifty-six and I'm pretty damn sure that everything started metastasizing after Phil killed himself.'

Trish said she never wavered in dealing with her mother after that. When her mother tried to make phone contact Trish changed her number. When she had an uncle and a second cousin show up at her office to make entreaties, she refused to see them.

' "Surely you'll feel terrible if she suddenly dies on you," they all told me on the phone, to which I could only say: "No, I won't feel a single iota of guilt." '

'And when it finally happened . . . ?' I asked.

'That was around three years after my dad went. Mom was driving to the mall near our house in Morristown and had a mild coronary. The car went out of control and crossed over into the oncoming lane, and there was this motherfucker of a truck barreling down the highway – and *splat*. I was an orphan.'

She downed the dregs of the Martini. Like anyone who was staring down into the bottom of a third Martini, she was seriously smashed. So, for that matter, was I. The difference between us was that, when I spoke, I wasn't shouting at the top of my lungs.

'You want to know if I felt guilt afterwards?' she asked, sounding like she was talking through a megaphone. 'Of course I felt fucking guilt. The cunt was my fucking mother and even if she was a total scumbag who drove my poor screwed-up brother to lynch himself with a fucking Boy Scout's belt . . .'

That's when a guy in a tux showed up at our table, informed us that he was the hotel's duty manager, and that we were to settle the check and leave the premises immediately.

'Listen, asshole, you're gonna have to get every fucking Mick in the Boston PD to get me out of here,' Trish said.

'Please do not force my hand,' the duty manager said.

I stood up and threw a considerable amount of money on the table.

'We're going,' I told him.

'No, we are fucking not,' Trish said.

'I'm getting you home.'

'You are not my cunt of a maiden aunt.'

'That's it,' the duty manager said and stormed off.

Trish sank deeper into the armchair and smiled.

'See, I won.'

'If he calls the cops you'll be arrested. And if you're arrested—'

'I'll give the arresting cop a hummer on the way to the station – and I'll be let go with a thank-you.'

I could tell that every eye in the Four Seasons bar was now upon us. Just as I also knew that I had to act fast. So I hoisted Trish up by the scruff of her jacket and before she had a chance to protest too much, I yanked her left arm behind her in half-nelson style.

'You say a word,' I hissed in her ear, 'and I'll break your fucking arm.'

I frogmarched her out of the bar and into one of the cabs lined up in front of the Four Seasons, the duty manager acknowledging my avoidance of a police incident with a curt nod as we walked out. Trish once tried to struggle against my grip – letting out a torrent of invective until I yanked her arm up higher, to the point where I knew she was in real pain. She shut up then – and said nothing until we were inside the taxi.

'Give the man your address,' I told her.

She did so. The cab pulled away from the hotel. Falling to one side of the seat, she suddenly began to weep. But this was no ordinary booze-fuelled crying jag. Rather, this was a full-scale lament – loud, primal, agonized. Up front the driver – a Sikh – kept glancing at us in his rear-view mirror, his eyes widening. Like me, he was thrown by the desperate sorrow that was emerging from some point deep within her psyche. When I tried to reach out and steady her, she batted me away. So I simply sat there, watching helplessly as this woman fell apart.

Trish lived in that corner of the city, near South Station, which had been gentrified into a quarter for the monied classes. The cab pulled up in front of a renovated warehouse. As soon as she saw the front door, she brought herself under momentary control.

'Do you want me to come up with you?' I asked.

'Go fuck yourself,' she said, then threw open the door and staggered inside.

There was a moment of shocked silence in the cab – the driver and myself trying to absorb all that had happened here over the past ten minutes.

'Do you think she'll be all right?' he asked.

'I have no idea,' I said and then gave him my address in Somerville.

When I awoke early the next morning, I was pretty damn sure that, as soon as I walked into Freedom Mutual, I'd be told to vamoose – as Trish would have to get me fired to hide the events of the previous night.

Another thought also hit me: I'd left all my assorted shopping bags at the Four Seasons and no doubt the duty manager had ordered them to be thrown out, as payback for creating a scene in the bar.

But when I entered the office that morning, all the shopping bags were piled behind the reception desk. I grabbed them and entered the trading room – where Trish and eight of her colleagues were shouting into phones – and dumped them on my desk. There was an envelope on my chair, with my name written on the front. I opened it. Inside were two $100 bills and a note:

To cover the damages. Trish.

I put the money back in a new envelope and grabbed a sheet of paper and wrote:

I was happy to pick up the tab. Jane.

Then I walked over and dropped the envelope on Trish's desk. She didn't even look up to acknowledge me. I returned to my desk, picked up several of the shopping bags, disappeared into the ladies for a few minutes and changed. When I turned to face myself in the mirror, the individual staring back surprised me. You put on a simple but beautifully cut black suit with a simple black silk blouse and stylish shoes, and you suddenly think: *There's a grown-up in the mirror.* As I had so rarely dressed up for anything, the transformation surprised me.

90

Clothes have a language, reflecting your sense of self, your class and education, your aspirations and the image you wish to present to the world. Maybe Trish was right: I always saw myself as something of an eternal student in hiking boots and chunky sweaters. But now, having changed into that suit, I appeared to be someone with responsibility and money. Much to my surprise, I liked the way I looked . . . even if I knew I had neither the responsibility nor the salary that the suit signified.

I returned to the desk at the far end of the trading floor. An hour passed, in which I sat there wondering what happened next. When the first hour of being ignored morphed into a second one, I stood up and crossed the floor, approaching Trish at her workstation. She was screaming into the headset at someone. After ending the call with 'and fuck you too' (what I came to know as a Trish Term of Endearment), she looked up at me with undistilled contempt.

'What do you want?' she asked.

'I'd like to go to work.'

'That's the smartest thing you've said all day.'

I could have pointed out that this was the first thing I had said to her since walking in this morning, but thought that such pedantry mightn't play well. She pointed to the empty chair next to hers and said: 'Sit down, shut up and try to learn something.'

Two

MONEY. I STARTED to make it. And – best of all – I discovered I was good at making it.

Hedge fund managers claim that they operate according to a very simple principle: they invest in stocks and hedge their position in such a way that they cannot but make money.

Rule number one of hedge fund management: position your trade to cover your downside, and always take advantage of a company's inefficiencies when trading its stock. By this I mean: if you buy a stock always buy, at the same time, an option on selling a stock short. How do you learn such a craft? Practice – and a gambler's instinct when it comes to working out how to cover your downside. If you play the game shrewdly, the only loss you will accrue is the cost of buying the option. As soon as the stock goes up, you gain. Big time.

Other stuff you need to know: hedge fund companies are always investing in all sorts of publicly traded securities: stocks and commodities and foreign currencies. And managers are always talking strategies, along the lines of: *There's a British info-tech company that's about to do an IPO in three months. Market indices show a strengthening pound – but not until the next quarter. So let's put an option on sterling and clean up when it moves three cents upwards come September.*

'Two basic caveats,' Trish told me on that first day as her trainee. 'Number one is: always have a nose for the next big opportunity, and number two: always work out strategies to lessen risk and maximize profit.'

A company like Freedom Mutual had, I learned, investment capital of over $1 billion to play with. Brad might have been something of a loose (or, perhaps, *louche*) cannon in private, but he certainly knew how to make big-time investors want to do business with him. The cool billion consisted of such diverse investors as Harvard University ($120 million), Wellesley College ($25 million), a consortium of German and Swedish venture capitalists ($165 million), and . . .

Well, the list was a long one – and Brad told me that he was rather choosy about whom he would get into bed with as investors.

'No Russian *shtarkers*. No snake-oil salesmen. No chophouse shitheads who have the SEC inspecting their sphincter every ten minutes. And definitely no goombahs who go greaseball when you don't get them a minimum of fifteen percent return. Think what you like about that tip-off artist . . . when it comes to my investor pool, it's strictly blue chip. Low-renters need not apply.'

Two for twenty. This was the other great rule of hedge fund life. As in: we take a 2-percent fee of everything you invest with us to cover our overheads. And then we also take another 20 percent of everything we make for you as our remuneration for generating such a big return on your investment. So say we make $200 million for you (on your initial investment of $150 million) in a given year. Are you really going to begrudge us the $40 million we keep as our fee?

Two for twenty. I quickly understood why Brad lived in a very large townhouse on Beacon Hill and why Trish had a 3,000-foot loft in the so-called Leather District near South Station. The company made absurd sums of money yet shrewdly kept its intense profitability out of the public eye.

'Do yourself a favor,' Trish said on my third day under her command. 'Don't go buying yourself a Maserati or start flashing big diamonds around the office.'

'Do you really think I'd engage in such conspicuous consumption?' I said.

'Trust you to use the big expression.'

'I'm not into "stuff".'

'So you say – but once you start getting handed a cool million in bonuses every Christmas . . .'

'Is that what you've been getting?'

'At the very minimum.'

'And what do you do with it?'

'Well, I used to put a significant amount of it up my nose. But ever since I made the acquaintance of Jesus—'

'You serious?'

'You've just failed a vital test. In this business, people are going to relentlessly sell you a bill of goods. *I'm gonna be straight with you. I'm gonna cut you the most fantastic deal since . . . I am really a very moral guy who takes communion twice a week and never goes down on my wife.* Your job – besides becoming a very big profit zone – is knowing how to detect bullshit at one hundred yards. You detect it at fifty yards, you're screwed – because you've already engaged with it, which means you've either committed something to it or you've wasted valuable time getting seduced by a lie. In this business, everyone's a liar. You want to make it here, you learn to lie. You learn how to compartmentalize, how to hide what you're thinking, how to bluff. And – this is all-important – you call somebody when they're bluffing. I talk to you about my personal relationship with J.C. and you tell me: "How nice." The fuck is your problem? You go stupid like that with me again and you're outta here, get that? Around here we can tolerate mistakes – and, believe me, you'll make plenty of them. But we can't tolerate naivety. Bambi does not make it as a hedge fund manager. Nor does the Big Bad Wolf, because the putz was outsmarted by a bunch of pigs. We want hardened realists here. Read Hobbes, read Machiavelli and follow the bottom line.'

Being assigned to Trish was something akin to being

dispatched to Marine Corp boot camp and handed over to a particularly vindictive drill sergeant who operated according to the principle that you build character through humiliation. Trish – like all the other managers – was wired to a desk. Her computer screen was awash with numbers. CNBC and Bloomberg played non-stop on two nearby plasma televisions. She wore a headset and speed-dialed numbers (all from memory) at breakneck pace. And she yelled. She yelled at her other colleagues. She yelled at the people on the other end of the phone. She yelled at me whenever I got something wrong or didn't pick up on one of her riffs. But, most of all, she yelled at herself.

'*Stupid fucking cunt cow.*'

This was a typical Trish self-criticism – and one which she would blurt out if she missed a 'sell' opportunity, if she was thirty seconds late on a trade and lost one-quarter of 1 percent, if she hadn't been able to gauge the momentum of a currency, if she didn't know that a major pharmaceutical company was about to release a hot new anti-depressant that allegedly didn't play havoc with the libido, if she wasn't up to date with German car-manufacturing statistics, with Spanish inflation figures, with the state of the Norwegian krone, with the interior monologues of the Chairman of the Federal Reserve, with . . .

'*Dumb! Dumb! Dumb!* Look at this clown, everybody? Harvard Ph.D. and can't figure out a simple trading differential. Should be off teaching Jane Austen to future cheesehead housewives.'

My sin, in this instance, was to be unable to calculate – in ten seconds flat – 20 percent of $2.34.

'You moron, you loser, you baby,' she screamed at me. '*Forty-six-point-eight cents*. You know how you calculate that in your head?'

'Double the sum and move the decimal point one number to the left?'

'The bitch has got talent, ladies and gentlemen. Too bad she hasn't figured out how to use it yet.'

No one in the trading room was quite as appalling as Trish. There were just twelve managers, three of whom – Cheryl, Suzy and Trish – were yellers. The men also yelled, but never with the insane vitriol of the women. Ted Franklin always had a box of pencils on his desk and seemed to chew through six of them a day. When he messed up an option purchase on some new Swiss foodstuffs company that had just beat out Nestlé for the Unicef dried-milk concession, he actually snapped the pencil in two with his teeth. Anatoli Navransky – Tony the Russian as he was known on the floor – also had a 'wooden substance in the mouth' addiction. His thing was interdental toothpicks, minted, which he bought by the case. His dexterity when it came to conducting multi-million-dollar trades while picking his teeth was mesmerizing – especially as he always shoved the interdental so deep into the gum line that blood would begin to leak out, forcing him to spit it into a mug on his desk. Tony the Russian was thirty-one, but appeared to be crowding the big five-o, largely owing to his habit (as I learned from Trish) of downing at least one bottle of Stoli every night. He worked sixteen-hour days, never took a vacation, needed serious pharmaceuticals to sleep, consistently maintained a three-day growth of beard and always looked as though he'd sat up in some damn basement all night drinking potato hooch from a still. He also had a habit of screaming (for no more than five seconds) in an amalgamation of Russian and Hebrew whenever things didn't play his way.

At least Tony the Russian wasn't one of the smokers. There were three of these: Phil Ballensweig, overweight, bald, notoriously flatulent and the biggest 'rainmaker' – Brad's expression – in the company, with over $18 million net profit tagged to him last year; Morrie Glutman, Orthodox Jewish, seven kids, ultra-serious, ultra-straight, no excessive habits bar a two-pack-a-day cigarette addiction; and Ken Botros, Egyptian-American, little goatee, lots of bling – a huge gold Rolex, pharaonic cufflinks – and a habit of wearing sunglasses indoors. Between the three of them, they got through seventy or so cigarettes a day. Smoking indoors in Massachusetts was definitely against the law. Considering how tar and nicotine were essential to the trading skills of Ballensweig, Glutman and Botros, Freedom Mutual had decided they needed an 'environment' in which to maintain their toxic habit, as it fueled their ridiculous profitability. According to Trish, Brad actually paid over $300,000 to build a small air-filtration plant in a custom-built cupboard next to the glassed-in room where they congregated. The filtration system sucked the tobacco cloud out of the room, managed to clean it of impurities and then voided it through the usual outdoor vent without it giving off telltale smoke signals. Of course, this was all highly illegal. But Freedom Mutual paid out an additional $50,000 in bribes every year to keep building staff and local health inspectors on side.

'Fifty grand, just to let a couple of guys smoke?' I said when Trish first told me about the smoking-room set-up.

'Fifty minimum,' Trish said. 'From what I heard, one of the health guys – a short little Irish fuck – strong-armed Brad last year, demanding a fifty percent increase. Brad told the guy to go down on himself. The guy ratted us out to his superior. The superior called Brad – who offered him the same sweetener that he'd been paying the cheezy Irish fuck. The superior accepted it and then fired the cheezy Irish fuck on the pretext that he'd never reported such illicit goings-on. And Ballensweig, Glutman and Botros continue to smoke and make us a lot of money.'

Trish didn't like Ballensweig, Glutman and Botros. She didn't like Tony the Russian. She found Ted Franklin 'nothing less than depressing'. And she despised Cheryl and Suzy, whom she considered her arch-competitors.

Cheryl was from Jersey, with big hair and claw-like fingernails. Suzy, a woman in her late thirties from the San Fernando Valley, was mousey and highly strung. Her dad was a mortician. Accordingly, she'd been dubbed by Trish and the others 'the Stiff'. This also had something to do with her legendary rigidity when it came to her personal decorum. Though she was brilliantly hyper-analytical when it came to tracking a market movement, she went ballistic and abusive whenever there was a setback or if an underling displayed any human fragility. If you wanted to throw her into a rage, the worst thing you could do was to leave a document, a newspaper, even a paperclip on her desk. I made this mistake my second day as a trainee manager. Trish told me to deposit some company report on Suzy's stand. So I placed it on her keyboard, first making certain that her computer terminal was off. Cheryl noticed this – she was at the adjoining station – but said nothing. Ten minutes later, Suzy came storming over to where I was sitting and proceeded to fling the report at me.

'You never, *never* interfere with my space again,' she said, her voice low, controlled, spooky.

'Having one of those bad mornings, psycho?' Trish asked.

'You put her up to this,' Suzy screamed. 'You knew – *knew* – what would happen if she put the report directly on my desk.'

'Know what I just *love* about you, Suzy?' Trish said. 'The fact that you make me feel relatively sane.'

'The *in-tray*,' she said to me, her eyes alive with danger. 'You want to walk out of here alive, you leave everything in my in-tray.'

'She's my bitch, not yours,' Trish said. 'And if you can't control your temper-tantrums—'

'You don't think I can have you fired? You don't think—'

'I know what Brad thinks – that you are certifiable. The sort of control freak who gives anal retentives a bad name. But hey, go on and make trouble, Princess Mischkin. See how our boss decides that you aren't the most profitable zone in the organization.'

'You cross me, you're going to find out.'

It was like watching two kids in a playground, engrossed in that game called 'I dare you to cross that line'. What I discovered very quickly was that everyone at Freedom Mutual acted out a variation on this theme. Just as everyone was also, in some way, either damaged or perennially the outsider. After a few days on the trading floor I began to understand that Brad's employment policies were largely based on finding unhappy or awkward people with something to prove, training them into the laws of the marketplace and then turning them loose in an unapologetically Darwinian environment. Brad himself encouraged such survival-of-the-fittest antics, just as he also had a natural sense of corporate combustion. Competitiveness wasn't the only driving force behind all the aggression on the trading floor. Rather, it was also rooted in our boss's instinctive eye for the troubled idiosyncrasies of others.

'You don't get a job here,' Trish told me over the late-evening drink she insisted on every night after work, 'unless you're super-bright *and* super-damaged; someone with a score to settle in the world.'

'But not everyone here—' I heard myself saying.

'Is as screwed up as me?' Trish said.

'That's not what I was about to say.'

'No – what you were about to say was: "Not everyone here is screwy", the implication being that you're Little Miss Nice and Sane. Allow me to let you in on a little secret, kiddo. Brad was onto your inadequacies, your sense of being abandoned by your asshole father and having to fend for yourself courtesy of your ineffectual mother, and still mourning the one-time big-deal professor whom you still consider the love of your life, even though he'd never leave his dreadful wife and treated you as a convenience, especially as you were happy to spread your legs for Daddy—'

That's when I threw my drink in her face: a twelve-dollar gin and tonic that completely drenched her. Before pausing for thought, I tossed some money down on the table and said: 'That's for the drink and your dry cleaning.'

Then I stormed out.

I must have walked around for about two hours after this incident, feeling desperate and alone and very angry. The anger, I knew, was bound up in grief. David. My David. I still couldn't wrap my brain around the brutal reality that he was no more – and no amount of pleading or cajoling could change that monolithic fact. Though the grief was constant and would catch me unawares at odd moments, I largely kept it out of the public eye. But that sense of 'if only' constantly haunted my thoughts about him. *If only he'd sought me out when the press started to crucify him . . . If only I'd been more upfront about how much I really cared for him, maybe he would have left his dreadful wife . . . If only I'd driven straight up to Maine after he'd been suspended from the university . . .*

Is life so often about desperate missed opportunities?

So yes, the grief kicked me hard in the stomach yet again –

until I fought it off with rage. Rage at the vindictiveness of Trish's comment. Rage against the hazing to which I had been subjected all week. All right, maybe this was all a big test to see if I could cut it in their highly idiosyncratic world. But two conflicting thoughts kept gnawing at me: (a) I had turned down a safe but steady job to enter this Darwinian construct called Freedom Mutual, and (b) I really wanted to survive this baptism by bile.

This second realization surprised me because everything about Freedom Mutual continued to strike me as anathema to all that I valued in my life. The place was belligerently anti-intellectual, even though Brad would occasionally drop a literary reference in my company – just to remind me that, once upon a time, he had read books. Everyone looked on the world as nothing less than a jungle to be clawed through. Why the hell did I want to jump into such a feral playpen?

We all want to get even with the parent who has, in some way, found us wanting . . .

The thing is: getting even is so sad.

It took me two hours to walk back to Somerville. When I got inside my apartment I made two phone calls. The first was to my old friend Christy Naylor – with whom I was in occasional email contact. After finishing her doctorate a year earlier than me she'd landed a teaching post at the University of Oregon and had just published her second collection of poems. '*It was a finalist for the Pulitzer and sold eleven hundred copies,*' she told me in an earlier email. She still didn't have a guy in her life, though '*when I need sex there are several reasonable redneck bars in town – and as long as you have a taste for bikers (which I have reluctantly developed), there is action aplenty.*'

Good old Christy – she was still unapologetically incorrect. And when I rang her at her house and said that I needed some advice and told her about turning down the Wisconsin job for Freedom Mutual, her first comment to me was: 'Well, of course you are *conflicted* – because you know all those mad people you now work with have figured you out as well . . . that is, if they can even look beyond their own insanities for a moment or two.'

'I'm only doing it for the money.'

'That's bullshit – and you know it. But I'm sure as hell *not* criticizing you. If I had my way, I'd hit the eject button and parachute right out of this fucking job. The thing is, I'm too damn comfortable in the interminable self-importance and mediocrity that is college life.'

'Safety has its virtues.'

'But you've never played it safe, Jane – despite all your protestations otherwise. You need this job – because you need to punch the lights out of everyone who's ever fucked you over. So make my night and call your asshole father and rub his nose into the fact that you're going to be making more money than he ever even touched.'

Shortly afterwards Christy ended our call, heading out to meet the Hell's Angel of her dreams. That's when I phoned my father. The line to Santiago was all static and when Dad answered he sounded as if he was on the far side of the moon – and just a little drunk.

'To what do I owe this honor?' he asked.

'How are you, Dad?'

'Why would that interest you?'

'For all the usual reasons.'

'I'm breathing.'

Long pause. I should have hung up on the spot as Dad was playing his usual head games with me. Turning his own guilt about everything to do with me into a display of petulance and chilly distance.

'And besides breathing, Dad?'

'Are you calling just to bug me about something?'

'Can't I just call you to say hello?'

As I said this I heard him drop ice into a glass, followed by a cascade of some liquid being poured over it. Then he said: 'So . . . what? . . . you want me to make conversation?'

'You doing OK?'

'You've asked that question already. But yeah, everything's just fine. Consuela moved out two weeks ago.'

'Oh God, that's terrible.'

'It's not great, yeah.'

'Do you mind me asking what happened?'

'I do mind. But I'll tell you anyway. She says I slugged her.'

I took that in.

'Well, did you?'

'Not that I can remember, but I was a bit loaded at the time.'

'If she said you hit her—'

'You taking her side or what?'

'Hardly. I'm just—'

'You know anyone who can loan me ten thousand bucks in a hurry?'

'Why do you need ten thousand dollars, Dad?'

'That's none of your damn business.'

'I certainly would want to have at least a hint of what you need it for before giving it to you.'

'*You* give me ten Gs? That's funny.'

'I've got the money, Dad.'

'You've got shit – unless you've been running some illegal Girl Scout cookie scam.'

'I've got the money, Dad,' I said again.

'I don't understand.'

When have you ever understood anything?

103

'I've got a job.'

'Yeah, that teaching thing at Wisconsin. Your mom told me.'

'You've been talking to Mom?'

'Hardly. She's got no money, I've got no money. So we've not exactly been burning up the phone lines between Santiago and Old-fucking-Greenwich. Anyway, I have nothing to say to her. But she keeps insisting on sending me these chatty goddamn emails. Keeps thinking we're going to somehow patch it all up, let bygones be bygones, and all that other forgiveness stuff.'

'Well, Mom doesn't know this yet, but . . .'

That's when I told him about the job at Freedom Mutual. He didn't interrupt me, though I did hear more ice hit the glass after I reached the part about the $100,000 starting salary and the joining bonus. I was nervous as I spoke, because – well, I was always nervous when I talked to my father. When I finished there was a long silence. Then: 'Don't take the job,' he said.

'I've taken it.'

'Call Wisconsin back, tell them you still want the teaching thing.'

'I've already informed them I'm not coming.'

'You call them first thing tomorrow, tell them you've had a change of heart, you really want the job.'

'But the thing is, I really *don't* want the teaching job.'

'You take the Freedom Mutual thing, you're gonna be out on your ass in six months. I know how those hedge fund assholes work. Once they figure out you're a lightweight who can't cut it—'

'What makes you think I can't cut it?' I said, suddenly angry.

'You kidding me? Thirty years punching my weight in the

104

metals business and you think I can't spot someone who won't make it to the end of round two?'

'My boss thinks otherwise.'

'Your boss is probably some sadistic sonofabitch who's decided to strip the hide off some Harvard broad who—'

I put down the phone. I walked over to the kitchen, in great need of a drink. But as soon as I picked up a wineglass, I smashed it into the sink and cursed myself for calling Dad with the foreknowledge that he would respond exactly the way he had responded.

The phone started ringing again. I ignored it. It kept ringing. I let it switch on to voicemail. I picked up another glass and decided I needed the instant kick that only vodka could provide. So I poured myself two fingers of Smirnoff. The phone sprang into life again. Against my better judgement I answered it.

'Look, you're right to hate me,' Dad said.

I didn't reply.

'And when I drink . . .'

He didn't finish that sentence – and again, I maintained a very large silence.

'I'm sorry, OK?' he said.

Silence.

'Please tell me you accept my apology.'

Silence. Then I asked: 'So why do you need ten thousand dollars?'

'I'm not asking you for it.'

'Why do you need it?'

My voice remained calm, but firm. On the other end of the line the clink of ice cubes returned.

'Because . . . I'm out of money, that's why.'

'I thought you had that consulting thing.'

'I did . . . but it ended.'

'When?'

'Four years ago.'

'Four *years*?'

'That's what I said.'

'And since then . . .?'

'Nothing.'

'So how have you lived then?'

'Bit of Social Security back home – and Consuela. But as she's a hairdresser . . .'

'So the big house with the pool and the butler and the staff and the three stallions you kept telling me I'd one day ride . . .?'

'That all went years ago.'

And he never let on for a minute – always turning down my requests to visit him, always spinning this line about his Chilean hacienda, always getting me to write him care of a post-office box in Santiago.

'And now that Consuela's left you . . .'

'I've got six hundred bucks a month to live on, courtesy of the federal government.'

'And where are you living now?'

'The same place I've lived for the past three years.'

'A house, an apartment?'

'Yeah, kind of an apartment . . .'

'By which you mean?'

'A studio. Nothing much, maybe two hundred square feet.'

'Jesus, Dad . . .'

'Hey, it's just a temporary thing. Like I'm about to get into something very surefire. Young American guy – Creighton Crowley – working down here and doing this dot.com thing for Latin America. Wants to hire me as a business consultant.'

'Is he going to pay you?'

'Not exactly. He's promised me shares in the company.

Says once it goes to an IPO it will treble everything I've invested in twelve months.'

'Everything *you've* invested? You've given this guy money?'

'Not yet – because I've got none. But he definitely wants me to put some money into the company.'

'How much?'

'He suggested fifty grand.'

'Fifty thousand dollars? Jesus, Dad.'

'Look, if he can triple it . . .'

'And you actually believe him?'

'He's a smart guy. Virginia Law, a couple of years with a big firm in DC.'

'Where he evidently didn't make partner, as he's hustling some shoddy business proposition in South America.'

'What the hell do you know about business?'

'I know how to smell a fraudster.'

'Unlike you, I've been in business for thirty-five years. Unlike you, I am a fucking professional with a first-rate bullshit detector when it comes to knowing someone who's trying to con me and someone who is legitimately exploiting a gap in the marketplace.'

His anger level rose as he said this and I could hear him become flustered in the face of his own building rage.

'There I go again,' he said, catching himself.

'Yes,' I said quietly. 'There you go again.'

'I need ten grand in a real hurry, Jane.'

'To "invest" in this "operator's" company?'

'To pay someone back.'

'This Crowley crook?'

'Will you stop acting all goddamn superior here, Jane.'

'To whom do you owe the money, Dad?'

'Some guy.'

'What guy?'

'A guy I borrowed money from.'

'A friend?'

'I wish. He's just a guy who lends money.'

'Oh, Jesus, you didn't borrow money from a loan shark, did you?'

'I was desperate. I literally couldn't pay the rent. That six grand's kept me afloat for almost two years . . .'

'You've been living on one hundred and fifty bucks a month?'

'More like three hundred. Social security pays me six, but I was handing over four-fifty to another guy who helped me out . . .'

'You're in hock to a second loan shark?'

'No, I've just about paid him off.'

'Jesus Christ, Dad.'

'Go on, tell me I'm a fuck-up. You've been wanting to do that for years. And now that you're the big-deal hedge fund manager—'

I'm a big deal nothing, *Dad – as you've never tired of telling me. I'm the kid who worked every damn summer and held down every kind of part-time job to keep myself afloat in college and grad school, because you were off squandering all the money you once had south of the border. But in your more sober, rueful moments, you know all that and hate me for making you feel guilty about your own inability to be responsible.*

Or, perhaps, like so many people, you've managed to filter the truth through the sort of distorted lens which allows you to perceive your own bad behavior as other people's problems. After all, why accept responsibility for your own actions when it can so easily be foisted upon others?

'Will the ten grand settle the matter?'

'Yeah, it will definitely get the guy off my ass.'

'So he's threatening you?'

'Well, what do you think?'

I think you're a sad, angry, little man.

'And once you pay off the loan shark, then what?'

'If I can come up with fifty grand, Crowley will hire me.'

And then disappear with your money.

'Tell you what. I'll wire you the ten grand tomorrow.'

'This dot.com thing is a surefire winner, Jane. And Crowley
. . . the guy's credentials are impeccable.'

'I don't have a spare fifty thousand. But why don't you send
me the company documents anyway.'

'I don't need your due diligence. And it gives me no fucking
pleasure to beg you for—'

'Send me your bank details and I'll transfer the money
tomorrow. Once I get the documents, we'll talk.'

I put down the phone. I poured out that much-needed
vodka. I flopped into my broken-down armchair, still covered
with the cheap Indian-print covers I made for it years ago. The
Harvard broad needed to upgrade her furniture, not to
mention her apartment. The Harvard broad should have
never agreed to bail out her father – but would have hated
herself for leaving him dangling in the wind. Just as she was
also trying to absorb something she had suspected for years,
but always sidestepped: the fact that her father had so failed at
everything he'd put his hand to.

I woke the next morning feeling strangely lucid. I dressed in
one of my new suits and even put on some make-up. Then I
reported for work, fully expecting again to discover my
termination notice on my desk. Instead, I found Trish sitting
at her terminal, staring straight ahead at the raft of figures on
her screen. Without looking over at me, she motioned for me
to take the chair next to her.

'Find out everything you can for me about Australian zinc
futures,' she said.

I did as ordered and had a report on her desk by midday. She read it in ten minutes, pronounced herself pleased with it, and then proceeded to school me in the business of following the movement of a currency – in this case, the euro versus the yen – and how to gauge the range of its current upper and lower limits. As always, Trish dazzled with her range of knowledge about everything – from German GDP figures to fluctuation in All-Nippon Airways shares. When she ordered me to work out a 7 percent commission from a $3.875 million trade and I didn't have my calculator exactly to hand, the abuse was once again fast and robust.

'Fucking idiot, you learn nothing, do you?'

I said nothing. I simply reached for the calculator (which happened to be on the adjoining terminal), tapped in the appropriate figures and informed her that the answer was $287,000.

'Next time, don't keep me waiting thirty seconds,' she said.

I said nothing. I just got on with the next thing Trish asked me to do. Sometime during the course of the late morning I received an email from my father with his bank details, nothing more. No: *Dear Jane*. No: *I do appreciate this*. No: *I would like us to try to patch up things between us*. Just his account number, the IBAN and the SWIFT code for his bank. I called my bank and arranged for $10,000 to be sent to his account in Santiago by next-day transfer. Then I sent him an email:

Dear Dad
The money has been sent. Please let me know when it is received.
And please send me the investment documents as soon as possible.
As always I wish you well.
Your daughter,
Jane

I reread the email several times over, making certain that it had the desired effect – detached, cool, yet pointed. Knowing my dad, he'd choose to ignore it. Just as he'd choose never to thank me for this bail-out.

Five minutes after I sent this email, another one bounced back at me from him:

Will be in touch.

But Dad never got in touch with me after this. Five days after the money was transferred I called my bank who confirmed that, yes, the funds had been lodged in the designated account in Santiago. I sent him a follow-up email, asking him to confirm arrival of the money. No response. Five further days passed. I sent two more emails. Still no response. I called his apartment in Santiago and got an operator recording in Spanish. Ken Botros spoke the language fluently ('cause I was stupid enough once to marry a "Rican"'). I asked him to listen to it.

'The babe's saying this number no longer works,' he said. 'Says it's been cut off. Your dad must be elsewhere.'

Another week went by. I sent an email:

I am still waiting to hear from you.

But I now knew that there would be no reply.

That same afternoon Trish was called into Brad's office for a ten-minute meeting.

'Keep an eye on things,' she told me.

This directive terrified me, but I remained glued to the swirling numbers on the screen, trying to find order amidst this statistical bombardment. Literally a minute after she had left, a notice flashed up on the MSNBC screen:

SWISS GENFEN GROUP WANTS $7 BILLION STAKE IN NIPPON TECH

A little alarm bell went off in my head. Trish had mentioned something to me earlier that morning about how Brad was in talks with a Mumbai-based financial consortium. They were trying to purchase a controlling interest in Nippon Tech – one of Japan's leading manufacturers of optic fibers – and Brad was just waiting for the moment when another financial group started pursuing Nippon to stage a big move on them. 'We want the Jap motherfuckers to shit curry,' was the way she artfully put it, tossing out this information in typical rat-tat-tat Trish style. Then she grabbed a phone and started berating a currency dealer who'd let her down on an Aussie dollar move.

And now, three hours later, here was a flash news item in a corner of the MSNBC screen about Nippon Tech being pursued by . . .

I picked up the phone and punched in the number of Trish's cell.

She answered on the first ring.

'What?' she barked.

'Nippon Tech—' I said.

'What about them?'

'Some Swiss group are making a move on them.'

'You making this up?'

'It was on the television.'

'Holy fuck,' she said, then hung up.

What happened next was the stuff of pure theater. Trish came racing back to her workstation, shouting orders at everyone in her path, the gist of which was: 'The Jap motherfuckers are shitting Swiss cheese.'

Everyone on the floor seemed to understand the metaphoric significance of this comment as all the traders dived to the phones and began dealing like mad. Brad showed up a few moments later, all smiles.

'We need to close this sucker by the sound of the bell on Wall Street,' he shouted above the din. Then turning to me he said: 'Good call, Jane.'

What was going on was a long-planned attack on Nippon Tech. Orchestrated by Freedom Mutual and financed by some very wealthy Indian and Russian plutocrats, Nippon Tech became the target of a leveraged buyout, in which Genfen – the Swiss consortium who were putting together that $7 billion offer – were outgunned at the last minute by Brad and Company.

'This is General Patton territory,' he bragged to me as the afternoon wore on. Through dense, precisely executed trading maneuvers, the Freedom Mutual team managed to drive Genfen's stock price down, thereby creating uncertainty about their ability to pony up the $7 billion offer; in turn, opening up the way for the Mumbai consortium to snap up Nippon Tech for $7.1 billion.

In the midst of all this free-market frenzy, Brad disappeared into his office for three hours. When he emerged back on the floor, he called for silence. And then, with a showman's flourish, he quietly said: 'The deal is done. And Freedom Mutual is 142 million dollars richer this afternoon.'

The place erupted. Within five minutes three cases of chilled champagne were wheeled out by some caterers. And everyone seemed to be drinking a bottle by the neck.

'I promise not to call you a cunt for at least three days,' Trish told me after vanishing into the ladies for around ten minutes and then emerging with white crystal still adhering to both her nostrils.

'I was just the messenger,' I said.

'No, you were fucking smart. Had you not seen that news flash—'

'Someone else here would have.'

'But you saw it first, and that's what counts.'

Actually, this era of good feeling between myself and Trish lasted all of two days. When I was ten minutes late – due to a mechanical breakdown on the T – she threatened to fire me on the spot if I was ever tardy again. I simply apologized and assured her it was a one-off mistake. Then it was business as usual. The triumph of the leveraged buyout was quickly forgotten. At Freedom Mutual there was always more money to be made.

Months passed. I got on with my job. I was still under Trish's direct control (no one at the company was allowed to start trading independently until after half a year minimum), but her abuse seemed to be directed at me only 25 percent of our working hours together and I took that to be a sign that I was making reasonable progress. I spoke with my mother on a regular bi-monthly basis. After being initially shocked about my change in career direction ('Well, finance is the last place I ever expected to see you end up'), she told me that 'making good money can't be a bad thing . . . and I know your father's so proud of you.'

'Oh, have you heard from him recently?'

'No, not recently. And you?'

'Not for months.'

'Maybe he's on an extended business trip somewhere,' Mom said.

'Maybe that's the truth,' I said, not wanting to upset her but also not knowing the truth myself.

Until, that is, two days later. It was early afternoon and I was trying to gauge derivative futures (don't ask). The phone rang on my desk. It was Brad. I immediately tensed, as Brad never called me.

'Could you come to the boardroom straight away.'

The line went dead. I stood up and headed down the long

corridor to the boardroom. I knocked on the door and heard Brad tell me to come in. As I walked inside the first thing I saw was the strain on Brad's face – discomfort mixed with a look of real anger that he shot me as soon as I was within his field of vision. There were two men seated next to Brad at the boardroom table – one stocky, one thin. Bland features, bad suits, hard faces. They both regarded me with cold professional interest. In front of them were assorted open dossiers. Among the papers spread out on the table, I saw a file with my father's photograph stapled to the left-hand corner.

'This is Agent Ames from the FBI,' Brad said, pointing to the thin man, 'and Mr Fletcher, an investigating officer from the Securities and Exchange Commission. And they have been asking me a lot of questions about you for the past half an hour. Because it seems that you've helped your father flee from justice.'

'I *what*?' I said.

'You sent him ten thousand dollars,' Agent Ames said, 'which allowed him to vanish from view.'

'What's he done?' I asked.

Mr Fletcher pointed me into a chair.

'Lots,' he said.

Three

OVER THE NEXT hour I learned a great deal about my father. I learned that, for the past five years, he had been living off a small pension that had been arranged for him by the regime of Augusto Pinochet. And the reason why the Chilean dictator's cohorts had been slipping him the equivalent of $10,000 per annum?

'Well, back in the seventies,' Agent Ames told me, 'before the coup took place, your father was well regarded within highly conservative circles in Chile: captains of industry, fellow mining guys, the military. The fact is – and I can mention this because it's now declassified information – he was an operative for Langley—'

'My father was a spook?' I said, sounding far too shocked and far too loud.

'The term Langley likes to use is "operative", especially as, at first, he wasn't a paid operative for the Agency. I'm sure you remember when your father was setting up that mine in Iquique . . .'

'That was before I was born.'

'Well, I'm sure your mother might have talked about him being away at the time.'

'My father was always away, all the time.'

'As you might remember – even from just a passing acquaintance with Chilean history – the government of Salvator Allende nationalized all the copper mines in 1969, your father's included. At that point he was approached by the Agency – knowing that he was still active, business-wise, in Chile – asking him if he would supply them with information about anyone and everyone he was meeting in the country, as he had first-hand contact with the Allende regime. They had employed him to stay on for an additional twenty-four months as a consultant, advising them on how to run the mine.

'As you can imagine, your father was an important conduit of information for Langley. He knew everyone in the Allende cabinet and was considered a "good" gringo. He came home to the States for a considerable amount of time in 1972. His cover had been blown when some secret-police types tortured a Chilean operative whom they caught trying to photograph top-secret documents on Soviet plans for military installations. Your father basically made it to Santiago Airport and onto the last flight out of the country around thirty minutes before Allende's goons raided his apartment.

'His mistress of that era – a certain Isabelle Fernandez – was the daughter of Allende's Minister for Mines. She was also informing on him to Allende's secret police. After the Pinochet coup her father fled to East Germany. It was not the most appealing of destinations, but it was a way of avoiding being "suicided" – the fate that befell Allende and so many of his comrades. Señorita Fernandez, on the other hand, found a different sort of escape route. Though it's not documented, it's been surmised that she met the same fate as so many of the thousands of "Disappeared" during that era. She was packed into a military plane with around a dozen other prisoners and heavily armed soldiers. The plane took off and headed in the direction of the Pacific Ocean. Once over water, the soldiers would open a hatch and systematically toss each prisoner out – from a height of around three thousand feet. Considering that they were a good hour's flying time from Santiago, the chances of a body being washed up onshore were virtually non-existent. So there was no evidence of any malfeasance on the part of the junta. Dissidents were arrested, rounded up, and then – *splash*. They simply disappeared.

117

'Now all this has only come to light in the past few years, when Chile's new socialist president ordered that all the old records be opened up – those that weren't shredded, that is. It's taken a long time for their people to dig up the dirt, but around three weeks ago, they uncovered an interesting nugget of evidence: your father worked as a paid informer to the Pinochet regime.'

'By "informer",' I said, 'you mean—'

'I mean exactly what is *meant* by the term "informer". In the early weeks after the coup, your father returned to Chile and offered his services to the Pinochet regime. They hired him immediately as a consultant on the re-privatization of the mining industry. But they also asked him for names: names of people he'd met during his years as an advisor to Allende and Company. According to the documents found a few months ago, your father readily informed on people he knew to be leftists, dissidents and/or potential troublemakers for the dictatorship. One of them happened to be his ex-lover, Isabelle Fernandez.'

'I don't believe this . . .'

'Believe it, Miss Howard. Not only was your father paid five thousand dollars for every known enemy he named, he was also rewarded with that consulting job, which he held for ten years, and with the pension I mentioned earlier. He even got an apartment out of the junta as well.'

I stared down at the table and said nothing.

'From your silence, I presume this is all new to you,' Ames said.

'Of course it's new. If I had known—'

'You would never have helped him flee?'

'Like I told you before, I didn't think I was helping him flee.'

'What did he tell you exactly?'

I took him through the entire conversation about the loan shark to whom he owed money – and how Dad was allegedly being threatened with grievous bodily harm. Just as I also mentioned his alleged employment prospects with Creighton Crowley. Mr Fletcher looked up from the papers in front of him when I mentioned that name.

'Did you have any prior knowledge of this Creighton Crowley?' he asked.

'None whatsoever – though I did tell my dad that being asked to invest fifty thousand dollars in this dot.com company he was touting—'

'Yeah, we know all about Creighton Crowley and his dot.com scam. Just as we also know that your dad was part of the entire thing . . .'

'In what way?'

'He sold shares in this company to twelve very foolish people who should have known better. Blocks of shares at fifty to one hundred grand a go. Your dad pocketed twenty percent of each sale.'

'Then why was he badgering me for money?'

'We estimate his net profit was around one hundred thousand dollars,' Fletcher said. 'That's what he lived on for around three years. Divided by three, it's not exactly big bucks. But because several of the investors he tapped were in the States, it did bring him to our attention. We've been after Creighton Crowley for some time now. The guy's got a history of insider trading and creating bogus investment schemes. The problem is, he's always slipped through our radar – and eventually ended up in Chile. Your father met him through "mutual business associates" and, professionally speaking, it was love at first sight.'

Ames came in here: 'The only reason I mentioned your father's colorful political past in Chile,' he continued, 'is for

119

you to understand that the man you helped flee – even *if* it was unwitting on your part – is nothing short of a crook. He sold shares in a company that was non-existent. He informed his investors that he was buying shares on their behalf, even though he was "gifted" these shares in his "contract" with the company.'

'Not that there was a "contract" of any sort between Mr Crowley and your father,' Mr Fletcher said. 'More of a simple letter of agreement, in which Crowley gave him fifty thousand shares in this sham of a company. Your dad could have had fifty million shares. It didn't matter. It was all a big con job. He'd been gifted the shares as part of his employment contract and he'd then sold them on. Crowley was, of course, doing the exact same thing.

'Want to hear a real lulu? Ever remember a family friend named Don Keller?'

Of course I remembered Don Keller. He worked with my dad – a geologist who dealt with all the technical stuff in the mining operations and a world-class boozer who was always going out on binges with my father.

'They were professional associates,' I said.

'According to Mr Keller,' Fletcher said, 'they were very close friends. Keller had "alcohol issues" and lost his career and his marriage around ten years ago. He's been living a very modest life in a very modest house on the outskirts of Phoenix. His entire life savings amounted to one hundred and fifty thousand dollars – and late last year, your father convinced him to invest it in his company, promising him – *in writing* – that he could double it in twelve months.'

'Don Keller is now a ruined man, thanks to your father,' Agent Ames said. 'He's completely penniless – and his rage is vast. So vast that he contacted us about your father's business activities. As it turned out our friends at the SEC were also interested in Mr Crowley's investment scheme. As we were monitoring all movements of money to your father, we were naturally interested when we saw your ten-thousand-dollar transfer to him.'

Again I was about to protest my innocence, but it struck me as best to say nothing further for the moment. I did look up and made eye contact with Brad. His displeasure was massive.

'We have naturally been investigating your own bank records,' Mr Fletcher said, 'and noticed a deposit of twenty thousand dollars from Freedom Mutual in the past few weeks. Mr Pullman here informed us that this was your "joining bonus" for starting work here.'

'That's right,' I said. 'That was the deal Brad offered me.'

'Why did he offer you, a graduate student in literature, such a large sum of money?' Mr Fletcher asked.

Brad came in here.

'I'm a talent spotter – and, as I told you, it was clear that Jane had talent and that if I was going to tempt her away from academia, I had to cough up some serious money.'

'Knowing your company's considerable turnover,' Ames said, 'I don't think twenty grand could be classified as serious money.'

'Well, do you really think I'd be paying a mere rookie more?'

Long silence.

'We're still not entirely convinced that Miss Howard acted unknowingly when giving her father the money,' Ames said.

'Sir, my father has never been – in any way – a responsible man. Dig back into my personal history – if you haven't done so already – and you'll see that he never paid my tuition at college or grad school, that I had to rely on financial aid and scholarships to get through. Call my high-school principal, Mr Merritt, and get him to tell you how hard up my mother and I were. The only reason – the *only damn reason* – I sent that bastard ten thousand dollars was because I wanted to let him know that, unlike him, I wasn't going to let members of my family dangle in the financial wind. So how dare you think that I was in any way in cahoots with that awful man.'

I was yelling – and judging from the alarmed looks on the faces of Ames and Fletcher, my vehemence had been noted. Brad, on the other hand, remained impassive, staring at me with chilly detachment.

There was a moment of awkward silence after I ended my rant. Then Ames and Fletcher exchanged a glance before Ames spoke.

'Be that as it may, Miss Howard – and my instinct tells me you're being straight with us – the fact remains that the money you sent your father allowed a wanted criminal to vanish. My superiors in the Bureau will need a full accounting of your financial position, to see whether this is a one-off or a pattern of pay-offs.'

'I have never, *ever* given him money before.'

'Then this assertion will be borne out by a thorough inspection of your bank records and all other financial transactions over the past five years.'

He reached into his briefcase and pulled out a legal form.

'We could, naturally, get a court order to run a thorough investigation on your accounts,' he said. 'But I'm certain you'd prefer it if your record showed that you fully cooperated with the Bureau and the SEC in their investigations.'

'I have nothing to hide,' I said.

'Then you will not object to signing this form, which authorizes us complete access to all your accounts.'

He pushed the document towards me, laying a Bic pen on top of the page. I stole a fast glance at Brad. He gave me a very discreet but rapid nod. I picked up the pen and read quickly through the document, which essentially gave the Federal Bureau of Investigation and 'any other government agency' the right to poke everywhere in my financial affairs. I picked up the pen and signed it, then pushed the document back to Agent Ames. He accepted it with a severe nod, then said: 'Do you have a passport, Miss Howard?'

'Of course,' I said, thinking: *He probably knows that already*.

'We'd like you to surrender it to us,' he said, 'just until our investigation is terminated.'

'How long will that be?' I asked.

'Three to four weeks . . . as long as there are no further queries about your involvement in the case. You weren't planning to travel overseas in the coming weeks, were you?'

'Hardly.'

'Then I'm certain you wouldn't mind – as another act of goodwill – surrendering your passport to us. If your boss doesn't mind, one of our agents will drive you to your apartment in Somerville to retrieve it now.'

They know where I live.

'I have no problem with that,' Brad said.

'Glad to hear it.'

Ames reached into his pocket, pulled out a cellphone and dialed a number, then talked quickly for a few seconds before closing it with a decisive snap.

'An Agent Maduro is waiting outside in a blue unmarked Pontiac. He will bring you home and back here within an hour, traffic permitting. He'll also give you a receipt for the passport. Once we've finished our investigations we'll be in touch and will return the document to you.'

Ames stood up, followed by Fletcher. They proffered their hands. I took them, hating the fact that I had to engage in such politesse. But I had no choice here, and I knew it. Brad, meanwhile, stayed seated, staring at his fingernails, refusing to look over at me.

I went downstairs. Agent Maduro was standing by the car.

'Miss Howard?' he asked.

I nodded.

'Thirty-two Beverly Road in Somerville?'

'You've done your homework,' I said.

He smiled a tight smile and opened the back door for me. Once I was settled inside he climbed into the driver's seat and we were off. He said nothing to me all the way into Cambridge. Not that I minded – as I was now seething with unadulterated rage at the monster that was my father. I'd read somewhere once that embezzlers operated in a parallel universe where they justified their malfeasance by never considering the harm they were doing to others. My dad obviously cloaked himself in a similar sort of amorality. Everything to do with that man had been predicated on falsehoods and dirty dealings. Though I had been trying to tell myself otherwise for years, I now knew what I'd never dare admit: he never loved me and I'd grown up knowing that I could count on him for nothing. My welfare, my well-being, had never interested him and I could no longer pretend otherwise. Any more than I could turn to Mom for the unconditional love I always craved. Hell, she was still telling herself that, one fine day, Dad would come back to her. Just as she would also let me know – when I revealed all that the FBI and the SEC just told me – that my father was incapable of such wrongdoing; that she knew he was the honest person she had deluded herself into believing him to be.

Out of nowhere I slammed a fist into the upholstered back seat and found myself gulping down the scream that so wanted to leap out of my mouth. In the front seat Agent Maduro studied me in the rear-view mirror.

'You all right, ma'am?' he asked.

'I'm fine,' I said, my teeth gritted.

When we reached my apartment Agent Maduro got out and opened the car door for me, then said: 'If you don't mind I'll come upstairs with you.'

'No problem.'

Upstairs I found my passport and handed it over to him. Maduro acknowledged its receipt with a nod and spent several minutes copying details from it onto a form. Then he handed it to me and asked me to fill in my home address, phone and work numbers, and sign below the printed declaration that I was giving this passport up without coercion; that I granted the Federal Bureau of Investigation the right to hold it 'for an indefinite period', and that I waived my rights to demand it back before the Bureau saw fit to return it to me. I pursed my lips as I read this.

Agent Maduro saw this and said: 'Generally, if everything checks out, you should have the passport returned within a few weeks but, of course, that depends on whether . . .'

He let the sentence die there – because he knew he didn't need to finish it. I took the pen and scribbled my signature. He pulled off a duplicate copy and handed it to me.

'Here's your receipt,' he said. Then we returned to the car and said nothing to each other all the way back to Boston.

When I entered the foyer of Freedom Mutual, the temporary receptionist stopped me dead with: 'Mr Pullman wants to see you immediately.'

I'm sure he does.

'Please wait here until I call him,' she said.

She picked up the phone and whispered something into it, then looked up at me and said: 'He's waiting for you in his office.'

I had never been in Brad's office before. As I was walked

down the corridor to the big wood-paneled doors, I sensed this might be my one and only glimpse of his sanctum sanctorum. I was strangely calm as my heels rapped percussively on the parquet floor – the sort of calmness that arrives in the face of the stoic acceptance of one's fate.

I knocked on the door. I heard Brad shout: 'Come in.'

I opened the door and entered a room that had been done up to look like something out of a London gentlemen's club – all heavy mahogany and oversized distressed burgundy armchairs, and Federalist art, and a massive fireplace currently ablaze with logs, and a huge nineteenth-century globe, and Brad sitting behind the sort of vast wooden desk that looked like the place where Admiral Nelson once plotted naval strategy. Knowing Brad's ability to buy anything he wanted, it probably *was* Nelson's original damn desk.

Brad was staring into a computer monitor as I came in, a pair of glasses (never seen in public) on the edge of his nose.

'Sit down, please,' he said, not turning away from the computer monitor.

I did as ordered, sinking into the armchair in front of his desk and doing my best to sit up straight in it. He turned away from the computer, pulled off his glasses, drummed his fingers on the desk and said: 'There is dumb and there is stupid – and you are guilty of the latter. I don't care if the guy was your father and you've been spending your entire damn life trying to impress the son of a bitch. You never, *never*, hand over any sum over five thousand dollars to anybody if there is the slightest doubt in your mind about the probity of the individual. Courtesy of the SEC and Homeland Security, all foreign wire transactions over five grand are immediately scrutinized by assorted spooks and financial regulators. The fact that you transferred money over to a shyster—'

'I never knew.'

'In our game – and at the level we play our game – that is not a satisfactory answer. The problem here is—'

'I know what the problem is,' I said, cutting him off. 'I've brought heat to this company and you don't want – or need – that sort of heat. So I'm very willing to take responsibility for my actions and resign on the spot.'

'Your resignation is accepted. Your future here is finished. In fact, your future in any financial-sector industry is finished because no other company will ever touch you after this business – and also because you will now trigger a red flag whenever the SEC or the Feds are running one of their standard security sweeps of the business.

'As far as the world of money goes, you're dead.'

I stared down into my hands and thought: *My father has gotten his wish. I've finally followed in his footsteps and failed at something.*

Brad continued talking.

'There will be a termination payment. Our lawyers will be in touch with you in the next few days to discuss this.'

'I don't want your money.'

'Don't be noble about this,' he said, turning back to his computer. 'People get fired all the time in our world. If they are as junior as you they rarely get sent off with a golden parachute.'

'Then why are you giving me one?'

'That big deal you scored for us. It was a lucrative piece of work and it showed you had smarts. You made us money. We now have to let you go. But you will still get some compensation for that one piece of good work. End of story. Take the money or don't take the money. The choice is yours.'

There was much I wanted to say right now. But I knew that I had betrayed an unspoken corporate code of conduct by bringing unwanted heat across the office threshold. It didn't matter that I had been duped. According to the Brad Pullman Rules of Engagement I had screwed up royally and now had to pay the price of banishment – albeit one with a golden parachute to keep me afloat.

So I did what was expected of me. I stood up and left. As I reached the door I said two words: 'Thank you.'

Brad Pullman looked up from his figures and replied with two final words: 'You're welcome.'

As soon as I was outside Brad's office, I was greeted by Reuben Julia. He was Freedom Mutual's 'office manager' – though everyone in the firm knew that he was the de facto head of security and the man whom Brad counted on to keep all shit at bay. As I was now in the 'shit' category, Reuben was here to sweep me away. He was a man in his mid-fifties, small, dapper.

'Miss Howard,' he said, with not a hint of menace to his voice, 'I'm going to escort you out of the building now.'

'Fine,' I answered.

We said nothing to each other as he tapped a few numbers into a keypad next to a side door. It clicked open and I followed Mr Julia down a series of long corridors to a back elevator. As we rode downstairs he said: 'I'll get someone to clear your desk today.'

'There's not much there anyway.'

We reached the first floor. A Lincoln Town Car was waiting outside.

'Max here will be taking you home,' Mr Julia said. 'As Mr Pullman told you, our lawyers will be in touch in a couple of days.'

With a quick nod of the head he said goodbye. The car took me home. A few minutes after I crossed the threshold the phone rang. A gentleman named Dwight Hale was on the line, informing me that he was from the firm of Bevan, Franklin and Huntington and acted as Freedom Mutual's legal counsel. He asked me to drop by his office near Government Center tomorrow to discuss 'the settlement'.

I did as ordered, showing up at ten the next morning. Dwight Hale was in his late thirties – slightly chubby, very 'time is money'.

'Freedom Mutual is planning to offer you three hundred thousand dollars as part of a termination agreement,' he said.

This information took a moment or two to register.

'I see,' I finally said.

'Is that acceptable?'

'Absolutely.'

'There is one small condition to the settlement – that you sign a confidentiality agreement, stating you will never talk to anyone about your time at Freedom Mutual.'

You mean, just in case the Securities and Exchange Commission begins to nose around their books and decides to interview all employees past and present?

'I know so very little about the inner workings of the company.'

'I'm sure that's true. This is a mere formality.'

Better known as an oath of *omertà* . . . yet one which was worth a cool three hundred thousand dollars.

'I need to have my own attorney look over the agreement before I sign it.'

'We have no problem with that. But if we don't have an answer from you in forty-eight hours the settlement offer will be rescinded.'

'You're not trying to pressure me in any way, are you?'

'We just want to get the matter settled as quickly as possible.'

'Of course you do.'

I didn't have a lawyer but I did know how to use a

phonebook. And when I got home to Somerville an hour later, I picked the first name under 'Attorneys' in the local *Yellow Pages*. It was a guy named Milton Alkan. He answered the phone himself with the voice of an ageing and inveterate chain-smoker. When I explained what I needed done – and preferably before the end of the day – he informed me that he charged $200 per hour (a bargain by Boston standards) and if I could get the documents to him in the next fifteen minutes . . .

Milton Alkan was in his late sixties – diminutive, gnarly, with thick coke-bottle glasses and an emphysemic cough. His office was a storefront off of Davis Square. Though he sounded as if he'd been working his way through two packs of cigarettes a day for the past fifty years, his manners were courtly and avuncular.

'So you worked for Freedom Mutual,' he said, scanning the first page of the confidentiality agreement. 'I'm surprised you didn't go to some white-shoe law firm downtown.'

'I'm certain you can tell me what I need to know for around a quarter of the cost.'

'That, young lady, I can do. So why don't you go get yourself a cup of coffee somewhere and I'll have this all done for you within an hour tops.'

Mr Alkan kept his word. When I returned sixty minutes later he favored me with a wry smile and said: 'If I'd known the size of the pay-off you were getting I'd have charged you double. But feel free to go ahead and sign the papers. There's nothing tricky or sinister contained herein. They are just covering their *tukkas,* like all business types. But if you don't mind me asking you something: Why did they let you go?'

It's curious, isn't it, how we sometimes unburden ourselves to strangers. But Mr Alkan had the demeanor of a Jewish Father Confessor and the story came tumbling out of me in a matter of minutes. He listened impassively, shaking his head a few times when I told him about my conversation with my dad and the revelations I learned about him from the FBI. When I finished he went silent for a few moments, then said: 'Under the circumstances I think three hundred thousand dollars is the very minimum you should have received. What you did for your father by giving him the money was a mitzvah. And though he may have hated you for it, he must also feel a deep abiding shame. You did something honorable – and even though it backfired on you, you still behaved ethically. In my book, that counts for a lot.'

Christy told me the same thing when I called her late that night in Oregon and brought her up to date on everything.

'You were conned by a con man – who also happened to be your father. And that, my friend, is awful.'

'The thing is, I helped fund his con. I looked stupid as a result of his con. But naivety is just that: naivety.'

'Stop berating yourself – even though I know you are genetically programed to do so. When you've been duped by your own father, you have to start pondering the larger question: Is anyone ever really worthy of trust?'

'And the answer to that is . . .'

'Hey, I write poetry. I have no answers, just a lot of unsolvable questions. Meanwhile, take their money and do something interesting for a while. A new perspective or two wouldn't hurt you.'

The only perspective I had right now was the belief that life was so often a series of major and minor betrayals. Dad had been betraying everyone close to him for years. Just as my beloved David had betrayed his wife for years – and I had played a key role in this betrayal. And though the pay-off from Freedom Mutual could be considered a termination agreement, I also knew that it was a way of buying my silence.

But Christy was right: I should still take their cash. After all, life so rarely pays you for actually trying to do the right thing. So I called Dwight Hale the next day and said that the signed documents were ready for collection. He informed me that he would send a courier for them straight away and I could expect the money in my account within a week. He also asked me to phone him should the FBI be in touch with me 'about any further matters'.

'I have nothing to tell them,' I said.

'That's good to hear.'

I found myself becoming guilty about my immediate lack of occupation or industry. So I set myself up at a desk in the Wiedner Library at Harvard and forced myself to start working. My project was a straightforward one: to turn my thesis into a book which, if published, might just help me land a teaching job somewhere. I put in fourteen-hour days for a full month. The writing all came easier than I expected – perhaps because I was simply reshaping an existing manuscript and also because work, for me, was always a form of escape; a way of subsuming the furies within.

Halfway through the month-long writing marathon, I took two days off and headed to my mother's house in Connecticut. Did I want to be doing this? Hardly. But after not paying her a visit in four months it was a duty I could no longer dodge. So I showed up with champagne and expensive truffles and insisted on taking her out to an expensive restaurant in Greenwich for dinner. Mom repeatedly worried out loud about all the money I was spending. Though I kept trying to reassure her that I was making serious money – for all sorts of obvious reasons I couldn't tell her I had lost my job at Freedom Mutual – she kept saying that I shouldn't be making a fuss of her, that she was doing 'just fine' on the librarian's salary she was holding down.

'So that's why you're driving a fifteen-year-old car and haven't had the furnace overhauled since Reagan was president.'

'I get by.'

'"Getting by" isn't good enough. "Getting by" is half a life.'

'I'm fine, Jane. Just hunky-dory.'

'And I'm buying you a new car tomorrow.'

'You're not to go squandering your money on me, young lady.'

'And you're to stop sounding like a Thornton Wilder character and let me indulge you a little.'

'I've never been indulged in my life and I'm not going to start now.'

I didn't point up the sad irony of that comment to her, but on the day after Thanksgiving I did drive her arthritic Toyota Corolla to a VW dealership on the Old Post Road and spent $8,000 on a new Rabbit for her. She put up a huge fuss but the salesman – a total smoothie, like all car dealers – immediately grasped the dynamic of the situation and played to her anxiety about having her only child buy her a car.

'Now when I am your age, ma'am,' he said, his Chicklet-like teeth fixed in a game-show-host grin, 'I will hope two things: the first is that I am as young and lovely as you are. The second is that my daughter will think so much of me as your lovely daughter so evidently does of you – that she too will want to buy me a spanking new VW Rabbit.'

Mom, starved of overt male flattery, bought right into his shtick. Within half an hour, he'd convinced her to choose a Rabbit 'in patriotic Liberty Red' (Is there such a color – and do Germans manufacture it?) and to treat herself to air conditioning as well.

'I don't know what to say,' Mom told me as we drove away in her new vehicle.

133

'Say nothing. You need – deserve – a good reliable car.'

'You're really making that much money in this financial job?'

'I wouldn't be spending it like this if I didn't have it, Mom.'

'Your father would be so proud of you.'

I said nothing.

'Anything wrong, dear?' she asked me.

'No, nothing at all.'

'Heard from Dad recently?' she asked, trying to make this question sound as nonchalant as possible and not pulling it off.

I shook my head.

'He must be working very hard then.'

'No doubt about it,' I said and the matter was dropped.

Later that day I called a local heating contractor. He was having a slow afternoon and dropped by the house. Again my mother made a big fuss about having perfectly adequate heating. Again she was silenced by a man of commerce, as the heating contractor told her (after an hour-long inspection of her home's furnace) that her system was on the brink of implosion and if she didn't replace the furnace next week he could guarantee her burst pipes and assorted other horrors.

'How much do you think this will all cost?' I asked him.

'I can't give you anything more than a ballpark figure,' he said.

'So what's the ballpark?'

'Around ten thousand.'

'That's obscene,' my mother said.

'No,' said the heating contractor, 'that's what it costs.'

I told him to call me on my cellphone after the weekend to give me a precise figure – and said I would pay eight grand if he could guarantee that he could start work on Tuesday.

When he rang me promptly on Monday morning, he said he'd do it for nine grand, tax included, if I could pay him half of it by the next day.

'No problem,' I said and got my bank to transfer $4,500 that afternoon to his account. At the same time I also dispatched an additional $10,000 to Mom's checking account. On the day it reached her I was back in Cambridge. Mom called me, sounding deeply distressed.

'What on earth do you think you're doing?' she asked.

'Making certain you have enough money to keep yourself in a reasonable style.'

'I've told you before: I do just fine.'

Which is why you've been largely subsisting on canned goods for the past couple of years.

'Mom, I'm in the money right now.'

'You can't buy me, you know. It's what your father always said: You can never buy somebody's affections—'

I snapped my phone shut and kicked a waste basket across the room and put my palms flat against my eyes in an attempt to block out everything to do with my two parents.

Mom called back three minutes later.

'Did we get cut off?' she asked.

'No, I hung up.'

'Oh,' she said. 'Did I say the wrong thing?'

'I'll talk to you next week, Mom.'

'You really shouldn't take what I say seriously, Jane.'

But I do, I do. Because you mean exactly what you say.

I returned to the Harvard Library and buried myself again in the book. Some weeks later – at 10:47 on a Friday evening – I typed the final sentence. I sat back in my desk chair, reeling with that mixture of elation and depression that every writer I've ever read about usually experiences when they have finally reached the last word . . . and with the knowledge that, with a book, writing the final word was only the beginning of the real work. But then a security guard came by and informed me that the library was closing in a few minutes, and could I please pack up and vacate the building. I bundled everything into a couple of backpacks and staggered out into Harvard Yard, awkwardly trying to balance my bundles. As I reached the street and flagged down a cab, the thought struck me: *I'll never finish another book again because I never want to write another book again.*

When I got home, I emptied a bottle of red wine while printing up the manuscript. Then, around one in the morning, when I'd downed three-quarters of a litre of rot-gut red, I started getting Boston-Irish maudlin, thinking: *You are all alone in the world.* My mother would naturally dispute this statement – but I knew it to be true. I could rely on nobody but myself. Bar a friend three thousand miles away in Oregon, who else did I have in my life? Since David's death, I had completely closed down – removing myself entirely from any personal involvement, even one simply based on friendship. And after being duped by Dad . . .

Well, I'm certain a good Freudian would have much to say about all that and about the tears I was shedding now for my loneliness.

But then night woke up and I vowed two things: *No more cheap red wine . . . and no more self-pity.* Instead, I would confront my unhappiness in a predictably American way: I would go shopping.

I went out and bought a car. Nothing too fancy or extravagant. I could never see the point of dropping excessive amounts of money on four wheels and a motor. But given that I did have all that money in the bank, I decided that I could splurge in a modest sort of way and dropped $19,000 on a Mazda Miata. I'd always secretly wanted a sports car – but one that didn't mark you out as an exponent of conspicuous consumption. The Miata was stylish, but relatively sensible (will you listen to me, always justifying, *justifying*). Its color was muted British Racing Green with a hood that you had to lower and hoist by hand. I loved it from the moment I got it out on I-93 with the salesman and revved it up to ninety in about eight seconds.

'You always drive this way?' the salesman asked, just a little shocked when I put the pedal to the metal and the car took off.

'Hey, it's a test drive,' I said.

I insisted on taking the car right down to Providence, Rhode Island and back again, breaking speed limits with impunity, knowing that this would be the last time I engaged in such a bad-girl habit (but hey, it's a test drive). When we returned to his office, I undercut the car's sticker price by two thousand.

'My margins are too small to accept that.'

'That's what every salesman says,' I told him and stood up, thanking him for his time.

'I could give you a grand off . . .'

'Two grand or no sale,' I said, adding: 'and I'll pay you cash on Monday morning.'

'Fifteen hundred.'

'Thanks again for the test drive,' I said and walked out. He was behind me five seconds later.

'OK, OK. Nineteen thousand and you've got the car.'

As we were later signing the paperwork he said: 'You're some tough operator. What are you, a hedge fund honcho?'

'I'm looking for a job teaching English.'

'I pity your students.'

That Monday afternoon I drove out the door of the Mazda dealership with my first-ever new car.

As I sat in my apartment that night, contemplating my next

move, the phone rang. It was Agent Ames. He asked if he could drop by and see me tomorrow morning.

He arrived promptly the next day at eleven. As I opened the door and let him inside I could see him taking in the grad-student style of my little studio – and being surprised by its modestness.

'I was expecting something a little more in keeping with your salary,' he said, simultaneously letting me know that he knew what I'd earned.

'I was just a trainee, sir – and tried to save most of what I made while at Freedom Mutual.'

'That's very admirable. Then again, you did have to learn thrift early on, didn't you? Though that's a rather flashy car you just bought yourself.'

I smiled tightly and asked: 'How can I help you, Agent Ames?'

'Here's your passport,' he said, reaching into his briefcase and handing the document over to me. 'As far as the Bureau is concerned you are no longer under suspicion – but if your father does happen to get in touch with you—'

'I promise, you will be the first to know.'

'That's good to hear,' he said. 'What are you up to right now?'

'I've been hiding in the Harvard Library, trying to turn my doctoral thesis into a book.'

'That's also very admirable. Most people would have taken the Freedom Mutual pay-off and headed for Mexico.'

'I couldn't do that, because you had my passport.'

'How right you are. And we're returning it to you now, not just because you've been cleared of any wrongdoing vis-à-vis your father, but also because we know you didn't engage in any of the insider-trading scams that Freedom Mutual have been suspected of running for the past four years.'

'I wasn't aware of such activity.'

'As I said, I believe that. But if you were willing, we'd still like to have one of our colleagues at the SEC interview you.'

'I honestly don't know anything, sir.'

'Let the SEC be the judge of that.'

'I was just a trainee.'

'But I'm certain you saw and heard things that could be useful to their investigation.'

Play for time, play for time.

'I really need to talk to my lawyer about this.'

'People only talk to their lawyers when they are guilty of something.'

'I'm guilty of nothing, sir.'

'Then you don't need to talk to your lawyer.'

I met his challenging gaze.

'I'm talking to my lawyer first, sir.'

'You might soon find yourself being subpoenaed, Ms Howard.'

As soon as Ames left I was on the phone to Dwight Hale.

'You did the right thing,' Hale said after listening to me recount my conversation with the FBI man. 'You know nothing – and I will make certain the Bureau understands that you are not to be bothered again.'

'How can you ensure that?'

'I have my methods. The thing is, it's no longer your problem. On the contrary, it's my problem now – and I'll take care of it.'

'But say he approaches me again?'

'He won't.'

'He said he would.'

'Trust me, that won't happen.'

'How can you be so sure?'

'Because I'm a lawyer. My advice to you now is this: as you

have gotten your passport back why don't you take a vacation somewhere outside the country, and preferably for a couple of weeks.'

'Are you telling me to go on the run?'

'I'm just telling you to take a foreign vacation.'

'Do I have to leave today?'

'I'd make yourself scarce as soon as possible. But do understand – all they can do is subpoena you to testify. Since you know nothing, there's nothing to worry about. However, if you do happen to be out of the country they can't easily serve you with the necessary papers. So the choice is yours: stay and find yourself being given the third degree and being put under a cloud of suspicion . . .'

'Even though I am entirely innocent of—'

'Clouds of suspicion often envelop innocent people. I'm just trying to save you some grief. Anyway, you probably have forty-eight hours before a process server shows up on your doorstep. So over to you now.'

Forty-eight hours. I went straight to work, packing a suitcase, packing up my laptop, dumping all perishables out of the refrigerator, paying some bills and collating my manuscript and research papers. Then I carted everything down to my car and managed to squeeze my bags into the small trunk, with my books and manuscript ending up on the empty passenger seat. Climbing in behind the wheel I put the key in the ignition and heard the engine fire into life.

As I pulled away from my front door and steered the car in the direction of the highway, a thought struck me: *So this is what they mean by going on the run.*

But this was quickly supplanted by another thought: *My romance with money is over.*

Part Three

One

Within an hour of leaving town I crossed the border into Maine. Forty minutes after that I came to that junction on the interstate where you could turn off to coastal 295 and then on to Route 1. A quick exit at Bath, a right turn on Route 209 and I'd be at David's cottage in Winnegance in no time, whereupon I'd tell myself that, one of these days, the constant low-level agony would abate . . . maybe when I fell in love again . . . if that were ever to come to pass . . .

Common sense kicked in as the exit to I-295 loomed. I signaled left, pulled into the fast lane and kept zooming north-east, passing Lewiston, then Waterville, then Bangor, before veering east on a lonely stretch of road for around three hours. It traversed nothing but dense woodlands. Finally there was a clearing in the distance – an outpost called Calais (and pronounced – as I discovered in a local gas station – the same way as the hardened skin on your foot). I drove on to a narrow bridge, passing a small patch of no-man's-land, after which was a customs post festooned with a Maple Leaf flag. There was a large woman in an olive-green uniform standing inside the booth, wearing a peaked hat that seemed more suited to the forestry service than immigration control. Courtesy of my Saskatchewan-born father I'd always had a Canadian passport (the Feds didn't seem to know this) in addition to my American one. Not that I'd ever had an opportunity to use it before now. The immigration officer quickly scrutinized my passport, asking me where I lived in Canada. When I explained that I had never been in Canada before now and would only now be visiting for a few weeks, she said: 'Well, if you decide you like the place, you'll need to get yourself a social insurance number.'

'Thanks for the tip,' I said.

'You bringing in any liquor?'

I shook my head.

'Well, welcome home . . . I guess.'

I stayed that night in St Andrews. It was a curious town – imitation English, with a slightly down-at-heel air. Like the guesthouse in which I was billeted, there was a fustiness to everything – what I imagined early-sixties Britain to have once been. It was ferociously cold outside – minus ten degrees centigrade. As I drank a cup of weak coffee the next morning in the ridiculously over-the-top dining room of the B&B – red velour wallpaper and one of those Axminster carpets that look like a faded Rorschach test – I found myself thinking: *Only you, with a couple of hundred thousand in the bank, could decide to hide out in Atlantic Canada during the perma-frost season.*

An hour after leaving St Andrews I stopped in Saint John, an old port and mill town, now ossified. Run-down red-brick buildings, depressing shops, gray people in gray clothes, an air of shabby listlessness hanging over the downtown. I grabbed a bad sandwich and pushed on further east, stopping for the night in the town of Sackville, right on the Nova Scotian border. It was a college town – one of Canada's best univer-sities, Mount Allison, was located here – and I immediately felt at home amidst its faux-Gothic architecture, its used bookshops, its student cafés and bars, even an old-style fifties cinema where they were screening a Kubrick festival that week. Funny, isn't it, how we always respond to that which is cozy and familiar and fits into the way we want to look at the world. Before heading here I had this image of New Brunswick as a chocolate-boxy vision of Anglophilia in the New World. Instead, with the one small exception of

Sackville, it was all blimpish, down-at-heel. Even the little hotel which I found on the main drag of Sackville reminded me of something out of an Edward Hopper painting – that low-rent 1940s world of the cheap and the sad, the sort of place where I could easily have imagined a retired showgirl – all peroxide hair and running mascara and wildly rouged lips – smoking filterless Chesterfields while downing her nightly fifth of Canadian Club. When I sipped my coffee the next morning in some local café I realized that I would go mad teaching in a small college town like this one. My brief flirtation with money had truly contaminated my once clearly defined world-view.

I left Sackville that morning and headed further east, stopping for two nights in Halifax. I'd read somewhere that the city had a trendy caché. The downtown seemed chewed up by new buildings from the reinforced-concrete school of seventies brutalism. Yes, I did find a quarter-mile stretch of shops and boutiques and 'we're trying to be New York' restaurants which gave the appearance of being vaguely hip – but I wasn't buying it. Like Saint John, Halifax dispirited me – and I would have turned tail and headed north towards Quebec if I hadn't, by chance, discovered a beach with the very un-Canadian name of Martinique.

The discovery came courtesy of a concierge in the little hotel where I was staying. I mentioned that I might be leaving town the next morning.

'That's earlier than expected,' he said, noting that I had booked myself in here for another three days.

'I don't think Halifax in January was the best of ideas,' I said.

'Well, before you go, you really should take a drive out to Martinique Beach and have a walk – that is, if you don't mind taking a hike when it's minus fifteen.'

'I'm from New England. We all take hikes in idiotic conditions.'

Martinique Beach was a forty-five-minute drive from Halifax. I negotiated my way through a series of ugly suburbs, punctuated by gasoline alleys and the usual strip malls, until the road narrowed and I passed through little nondescript towns, most of which lacked much in the way of rustic charm. But just when I was about to write off this stretch of road as charm-free, the route narrowed. I turned a corner and, suddenly, there was water. A patch of forest, then a glimpse of the Atlantic. A small town, a bridge, another fast sighting of the sea. A house, a meadow, another patch of aquatic blue. Driving this road was like being visually teased all the time – just the most transitory sightings of sand and surf.

I followed the signs to Martinique Beach, cruising down a back road with the occasional barn or house breaking up the empty wooded landscape. Then I was suddenly driving alongside dunes, with scrubby vegetation pockmarking the sand. Though I had both windows closed up against the cold, I could still hear the roaring of the surf on the nearby beach. There was a little parking lot up ahead – absolutely empty, as only a masochist would venture out here on a January morning like this one. I parked the car and, zipping up my parka and pulling a wool hat down over my ears, I stepped out into the cold.

And, by Christ, it was *cold*. Though the temperature back in Halifax had been minus fifteen, here there was a boreal wind that must have lowered it by another ten degrees. But I hadn't driven all the way here to suddenly turn tail and head back to shelter. I was going to walk the damn beach. Plunging my gloved hands into my pockets, I followed the little wooden walkway over the dune, then found myself staring straight out at the Atlantic. The beach was vast. It stretched for miles – and on this sub-arctic day, it could have passed for an outpost of the Mongolian steppe or the furthest reaches of Patagonia: the ends of the earth. The tide was out. The wind emitted a low-level but persistent howl, beyond which the percussive thump of the surf was more than discernible. That's because the breakers were ferocious, primal – slamming down against the sand with an Old Testament vehemence. The sky was slate-gray, the world drained of color. Martinique Beach, with its harsh monochromaticism, had an elemental grandeur.

I started to walk. Fortunately the wind was to my back – but that, of course, meant that I would be facing into it on my return. The breeze propelled me forward. I held my head up, my eyes wide to the cold, my nostrils frozen, but still imbibing the deeply salted air. I was the only person on this beach – and it struck me that, were I to twist an ankle and become immobilized, I mightn't be found here for days. By which point . . .

But this thought didn't trouble me. Maybe it was the endorphin rush of walking in sub-zero temperatures on an empty, limitless shingle of sand. Maybe I was having a major pantheistic moment, in which the sheer overwhelming power of the natural world gave me a sense of larger forces at work on this strangely benighted planet of ours. Or maybe it was the simple brutality of the cold – and the dark, angry majesty of this seascape – that suddenly released me from all thoughts about any life beyond here, or any of the baggage I always carried with me. Whatever the reason, for an instant or two, all external considerations melted away and I actually felt a sort of happiness. A pure, undistilled sense of just living in the here and now; of being liberated from the complex narrative that was my life. Was that all that happiness amounted to? A moment, here and there, when you could run away from yourself? When you fled the stuff that haunted your thoughts and ruined your sleep and remembered that temporal existence was pretty damn wondrous? Did it take the extremities of cold and wind – and the detonation of surf on an empty beach – to remind me that simply being here was a cause for happiness itself?

I walked on for another mile and then it began to snow. Lightly at first – a gentle cascade of hesitant flakes. But within a minute or so, it transformed itself into a minor blizzard; the downfall so dense that all visibility was curtailed and all I could see in front of me was a white void. It caught me unawares and the silent serenity of it all was instantly superseded by a larger consideration: getting off this damn beach right now.

But with limited visibility this was no simple task. I kept my head down and pushed forward, trying to retrace my steps as best I could. My progress was slow, my eyes stinging with the wind-whipped snow, my hands beginning to stiffen. The moment of clean, absolute happiness had turned into a grim trudge.

But then, out of nowhere, the snow stopped. It was as if someone had flipped a celestial switch and turned off the blizzard. The beach – now frosted by this sudden storm – was returned to me. I moved as quickly as possible back to the car. Once there, I turned the heater on full blast and stared at myself in the rear-view mirror. My face was a deep shade of crimson, my lashes and eyebrows iced up. But as hot air started returning my body temperature to something approaching normal, I felt that weird exhilaration of someone who had stumbled into physical danger and then managed to stumble their way out of it again.

That's the greatest relief in the world – knowing that you have got away with something you really shouldn't have.

I sat in the car for a good ten minutes, waiting for myself to thoroughly thaw out. Then I stripped off my parka and gloves – it was now that warm inside – and began to drive back to Halifax. But just at the end of the beach road, I saw a sign on a mailbox, flapping in the wind. It read:

FOR RENT. CALL SUE AT: 555.3438.

The mailbox was at the end of a driveway. Intrigued, I turned into it – and drove the hundred yards up to a modern Scandinavian-style A-frame house. It was shuttered and dark. The door wasn't boarded up, however. Peering inside I could see a simple sitting room, nicely furnished in a country style, with an old pot-bellied stove in one corner.

An image passed through my head of me sitting in the rocking chair by the stove, reading Melville or Flaubert and listening to classical music on the radio. I returned to the car, drove back to the mailbox and, using my cellphone, called the woman listed on the sign.

Luck was with me. Sue Macdonald lived around five minutes away and happened to be at home.

'You really want to rent the place?' she said, sounding genuinely surprised and also wheezing that wheeze which hinted at a lifetime's involvement with cigarettes.

'If it's not taken,' I said.

'Not taken? It's January in Nova Scotia – of course it's goddamn available. Hang on, be down there in a tick.'

She showed up a few minutes later – a woman in her late fifties with short, stiff gray hair, dressed haphazardly in jeans and a mothy cardigan underneath an old army greatcoat. A cigarette was hanging out the side of her mouth. I liked her immediately, even if she did size me up with suspicion.

'So if you don't mind me asking,' she said while opening the front door, 'are you on the run or something?'

'Nothing that glamorous,' I lied. 'I got fired from a job, I got a nice pay-off, and I decided to hide out somewhere for a while, think things through . . .'

'Well, you sure as hell have come to the right place for being alone with your thoughts. Martinique Beach is so dead during the winter we actually had to shoot someone a couple of years ago to start a cemetery.'

The house was – as expected – simple, but with a certain degree of ascetic charm. The furnishings veered towards the Shaker. There was a very comfortable armchair, a traditional rocker, a nice four-poster double bed in the one upstairs room, a functional kitchen with pine cabinets, a large shortwave radio on a coffee table near the stove, no TV.

'Now I suppose the two biggest questions you have are: How do I heat the damn place, and how much is it going to set me back? Well, there's an oil-fired boiler which I currently turn on once a day to make certain the pipes don't freeze. If you decide to take the place I'll turn it on now full-time and you'll move into a warm house by this time tomorrow. In the utility room off the back, there's a whole cord of chopped wood, which you can also use in the stove. And everything else is electric, so it's not like you'll have to stoke a fire in order to cook. What the hell did you say you did down south?'

'I didn't say . . . but I used to work in finance. Now I'm trying to finish a book based on my doctoral dissertation.'

She looked at me warily.

'You got a Ph.D.?'

I nodded.

'From where?'

'Harvard.'

'Heard of it. And what's the thesis on?'

I told her. She lit up a new cigarette.

'I once started a Ph.D. in English literature, just like you. "Jane Austen and the English Blah Blah Blah . . ."'

'You never finished it?'

'Came back from McGill one summer, hooked up with a local fisherman and was stupid enough to kiss Montreal goodbye and live with the guy for the next twenty years.'

'After which . . . ?'

'After which he had the nerve to die of a sudden heart attack – and break my heart at the same time.'

'I'm sorry.'

'Not as sorry as me.'

'When did he die?'

'Eleven years ago – and the thing is, it still feels like yesterday. Will ya listen to me, getting all self-pitying. The rent is one hundred per week and for that I'll change the bedclothes twice a week and also get the local girl to come in here and clean the place for you every Tuesday. How long would you be thinking of hiding out here?'

'A couple of weeks, I guess, maybe three.'

'You really don't have much of a plan, do you?'

'You mean, beyond getting this book finished? No, none at all.'

Considered now, the three weeks that followed were among the happiest of my life. What was that oft-quoted *pensée* of Pascal about man's unhappiness all coming down to his inability to sit alone in a small room and do nothing? Well, I didn't do nothing during those three weeks but I did spend most of my time alone in a small room. And it suited me.

I moved in the afternoon after seeing the place. Not only had it been scrubbed clean of all the accumulated dust, but there was a fire roaring in the pot-bellied stove and fresh flowers in jugs on the dining table and on the bedside table. The fridge was full of milk and cheese. There were even two bottles of local Nova Scotian red wine on the table by the rocking chair. And there was a note:

151

*Hope you're comfy. I'm getting out of Dodge this afternoon
to sunnier climes – as in that Yankee dump, Florida.
Marge – she's the cleaner – will be in twice a week to
change your sheets and tidy up. If you plan to stay longer
than three weeks, no sweat. Just give Marge the dough.
Hope you get done what you want to get done . . .*

I settled in, blaring CBC Radio 2 – their classical service –
as I unpacked. I used one end of the long dining table as a
desk. I set the manuscript of the book to one side of my
laptop, putting several well-sharpened pencils on top of it.

The next morning I was up at six. I made oatmeal and
coffee. I left the house at first light and walked forty minutes
up the beach, forty minutes back. It was minus five outside,
according to the thermometer posted by the front door of the
cottage, with no wind whatsoever: perfect walking weather. By
the time I returned home it was just eight-fifteen. All residual
grogginess had been blown away by the morning cold, the sea
air. My head was open. I was ready to work.

And work I did – five hours every morning. I ripped
through the manuscript with relish, excising all digressions,
sharpening up the arguments, and injecting what I hoped was
a necessary vein of wit to a very academic book. The work
went rapidly – especially as I maintained a diligent schedule.
Up every morning before dawn. Breakfast. The eighty-minute
walk on the beach (why eighty? I've no idea – it just worked
out that way), then five hours on the book, then lunch, then
another two hours grinding through the manuscript, then a
further eighty-minute beach hike, then reading, then dinner,
then more reading. And I was in bed every night by ten.

Why this need for such a rigid schedule? Discipline is all
about the imposition of control – the belief that, by following
a precise regime and avoiding distractions, you can somehow

keep the disorder of life at bay. Maybe that was the reason why I was up so early every morning. The discipline allowed me to keep my mind off the worry that the Feds might now be enquiring about my whereabouts. And it also allowed me to dodge the belief that no one would ever read the book I was rewriting. But I still had to finish it – because it was the one thing in my life right now that gave me some sort of focus, some *raison d'être*. Was it guilt that was keeping me going? Every time I did my twice-daily walks on Martinique Beach I thought of David: how much I missed him every hour of the day; how he so loved walking the sand at Popham; how I kept seeing his body on that road, a look – I imagined – of bemusement on his face, as if to say: *So this is it?* And how I kept trying to tell myself that he so wanted to live; that he could never have fallen into such despair as to . . .

The lover for whom you wrote your thesis dies opposite a beach . . . and then you rent a cottage on a beach to finish the transformation of said thesis into a book.

God, how we are all prisoners of our own baggage. Why can we never really free ourselves from its malignant weight, and the way it so dictates the way our lives map out?

I had no answers to such questions. I just kept working. I had no outside contact, no intrusive stimuli bar the news on the radio. Reduce everything down to certain essentials and you can live a very agreeable existence – as long as you also choose not to risk anything.

However, guilt made me phone my mother once during my time away. I began the call by breaking the news about my departure from Freedom Mutual. Her reaction was classic: 'Your father will be so disappointed. He would so have liked you to have succeeded for a change.'

As per usual, I said nothing, swallowing my rage, and instead told her what I was doing up here.

'I suppose that fills the days, dear,' she said. 'You will send our library a copy if it gets published?'

'You can count on that, Mom.'

A silence. Then: 'I'm very cross at you about something, Jane.'

'What might that be?'

'I had two gentlemen from the FBI stop by the library asking to see me. It seems your father has been wrongly accused in some financial swindle thing . . .'

'Wrongly accused?' I heard myself saying.

'Don't sound so suspicious. Your father is a brilliant businessman.'

'My father is a crook.'

'So you believed everything the FBI told you.'

'How did you know that—'

'An Agent Ames informed me that they interviewed you – and that you filled them in on everything you knew about your father's business dealings.'

'Which wasn't very much.'

'You still cooperated.'

'They were the FBI, Mom. I mean, the man cheated his friends and then cheated me out of ten thousand dollars—'

'I'm not listening to this.'

'Of course not. That would be too goddamn painful – to admit the truth. Because that would mean admitting—'

'I'm hanging up now.'

'Dad's dishonesty cost me my job.'

'Don't you go trying to blame him for—'

'*Blame him! Blame him?* Didn't the Feds tell you—?'

'They told me a lot of half-truths – and asked if I had heard from him. Now it seems he's on the run because of your—'

That's when I clicked my phone shut. I did what I only could do when furious with the world. I went back to work.

For the next four days I upped my daily writing hours to eight, continuing to be ruthless with the text, relentlessly working my way towards the end.

I tried to keep focused on the task in hand but, as much as I also kept trying to blank him from my mind's eye, my father's image continued to plague me. Since his disappearance, I had often speculated on where he might be now. Was he living under an assumed name in some South American beach dive? Might he have changed his physical identity, bought himself a Uruguayan passport and found himself some twenty-year-old *puta* with whom he could hide out? Or maybe he had snuck himself back into the States and – using a bogus social security number – was now eking out a living in some faceless sprawl of a city.

How I wanted to kill all thoughts of him. But can you ever excise a bad parent? Though you might come to terms with all that they have psychologically bequeathed you, they can never really be expunged. They're the stubborn, permanent stain that will never entirely vanish in the wash.

However, rage can have its benefits if you can use its toxicity to propel you forward. So the eight-hour writing days extended to ten and I also found myself working half the night when insomnia started snapping me awake at three in the morning. For the rest of the week, I slept no more than five hours a night. Barring my two daily walks on the beach – and the very occasional trip to the local shop for supplies – I ground on with the rewrite.

The end came at six in the evening on the third Sunday. I typed the last sentence and stared at the laptop screen for a few dazed minutes, thinking: *And after all that, it will never find its way between hard covers.* But at least it was done.

The next morning, after breakfast and the usual sunset beach hike, I climbed into my car and drove into Halifax. My first port of call was an internet café on the Spring Garden Road. My email inbox was pretty damn empty – a three-line communiqué from my mother: *'I do hope you have stopped holding a grudge against me. You seem to fly off the handle at everything I say. I would appreciate a call . . .'* Not likely. A reassuring email from Dwight Hale: *'The Bureau does not seem interested in questioning you any further about your time at Freedom Mutual, so return home whenever you feel like it.'* A fast hello from Christy: *'What's with the disappearing act? A word or two about your whereabouts and well-being would be appreciated.'* And the following from the Harvard Placement Office:

> *Dear Ms Howard*
> *We notice that you have recently re-registered with us as a*
> *candidate for an academic posting. Could you please call*
> *us as soon as possible to discuss a position that has just*
> *opened at the last minute in the English department at*
> *New England State University.*
> *Sincerely yours*
> *Margaret Noonan*

I gnawed on my lip when I read the words *New England State University*, as it was a third-tier place, favored by the sort of kids who either goofed off entirely in high school and/or were determined to do so in college. But . . . it was a job opening. Despite all that money in the bank, I kept telling myself I needed a job, which is why I had sent an email to Harvard a week earlier, saying I was in the market for an academic post. Because how could I do anything risky like take a year off to live in Paris – or bum my way around South America – when a job at a minor league university (albeit in Boston) was up for grabs?

Sitting there in that internet café on a gray morning in

156

Halifax I could see, laid out in front of me, the course of action I shouldn't take: making the call to Margaret Noonan, arriving back in Boston, doing the interview, starting straight away as a full-time professor, and repenting at leisure for having steered myself into a professional cul-de-sac.

Don't make that phone call to Harvard, I told myself in that Halifax café. But I made the call. And I got the job. And as I accepted the job, I thought: *The lure of safety drags us into lives we'd prefer to dodge.*

Two

MY OFFICE AT New England State University was in the basement of a dull concrete building. It was around eight by nine feet and had one half-window that was always streaked with dirt. Whatever low-level natural light entered the office was therefore always refracted through a prism of smudged glass. When it snowed – and it snowed a lot in Boston that winter – the window disappeared, and I was reduced to making do with the fluorescent tubes that provided most of the interior light.

'I'm afraid the new member of the department always gets the Black Hole,' Daniel Sanders told me after offering me the job.

The job was an assistant professorship in English. It had fallen open when its previous holder – a specialist in early-twentieth-century American literature named Deborah Holder – had died of a fast-acting stomach cancer that had killed her just three months after its initial diagnosis.

'Debbie was genuinely loved by everyone in the department,' Sanders told me during our post-interview lunch. 'She was just thirty-one, married with a young son, hugely popular with her students, and someone who genuinely had a major academic future ahead of her. She was a star – and nice on top of it. I am probably being very impolitic here by telling you all this, but I'd rather you be aware of the size of the shoes you are about to fill than find out through all the usual interdepartmental whispers just how loved she was.'

'I appreciate your directness.'

'That's my style. That's why I'm also going to be very direct with you right now about several other things. As you know this is a tenure-track job. But you definitely won't be granted tenure unless you get a book published within the next four years – and with a reasonably high-level academic press. So you really must get the book between hard covers as quickly as possible.

'The second thing I have to tell you is this: everyone in this department knows that you were romantically involved with David Henry.'

'I see,' I finally said, telling myself that I was a fool to think that nobody at New England would have been tipped off about this most gossip-worthy part of my past history.

'I am not telling you this to make you feel uncomfortable, nor to pass any judgment on you. You should know that, in the course of the assessment process, I did speak to Professor Hawthorden at Harvard. He only had excellent things to say about you – but I did ask him directly if your involvement with David Henry caused problems for him or other members of the department. He informed me that you were very discreet about it.'

'It's in the past, Professor,' I said, interrupting him. 'And I hope I will not be defined within this department by something that was very private, that was never discussed with *anyone*, and that had no bearing whatsoever on my doctoral thesis—'

'Which was considered a first-rate piece of work,' he said, completing the sentence. 'I wouldn't be offering you this job if I didn't know that, or if I wasn't also aware that you consider this "relationship" now historical and not to be repeated in the future.'

'What happened with Professor Henry would never be repeated again, sir.'

Yet again I was finding out one of the most fundamental rules of life: the repercussions of the past always rumble underneath everything. If you're lucky the rumblings are only heard by yourself in that most private of realms, your conscience. But if your private life tips into the public domain, you will always be reminded of its shadow and the suspicions it tosses up about you.

Professor Sanders decided that my assurances were worth the gamble. Once I offered them, he told me I had the job – as long as I could start four days from now on Monday.

'No problem, but I do need to see everything that Professor Holder was lecturing on.'

That afternoon I was ushered into Deborah Holder's office. It looked as though it was still fully occupied. Standing in the doorway with Professor Sanders I took in its crammed bookcases and noticed what seemed to be first editions of Emily Dickinson and Sinclair Lewis, stacks of papers, a framed poster of the Paris Métro system, and a bulletin board crammed with photographs. They were all family snaps. Deborah Holder had been a pretty woman with pulled-back black hair and an easy smile. Judging from the photos her sartorial style was Shetland sweaters and blue jeans, as was that of the bearded thirty-something man who shared so many of the photographs with her. Then there was her little boy, seen in these snaps at various stages of early development, the last of these showing him around the age of four, his arms draped around a mother now drawn and pale, her hairless head part-covered by a scarf.

I took in all the incidental office details. Everything here hinted at a life still in full swing. It was as if Deborah Holder had just stepped away from it all for a few minutes and fully expected to return to it any moment. Professor Sanders must have been reading my thoughts as he said: 'She'd checked herself out of Mass General after the last course of chemo-therapy, insisting that she was well enough to teach. As it

160

turned out, she'd only left the hospital when she was told there was nothing more they could do for her. But she was determined to go back to her students and kept the diagnosis from everyone.

'Now, we could have her husband clear everything out of here for you, I suppose, if you really didn't want to work in the Black Hole . . . That office is not as spacious. In fact, it's downright poky. But—'

'I'll take it.'

Sanders nodded his approval, then motioned me to follow him out of there and into his own office. It was a large room with floor-to-ceiling bookshelves, a venerable oak desk, framed Hogarth prints of eighteenth-century London (his area of expertise was Swift and his contemporaries), a worn Persian rug covering the institutional linoleum on the floor. He motioned for me to take the wing-chair that fronted his desk.

'I don't know about you, but I could definitely use a stiff whisky. Going into Deborah's office . . .'

He let the sentence drop.

'I wouldn't say no to one,' I told him.

Sanders opened a filing cabinet and pulled out a bottle of Teacher's and two glasses.

'Very Philip Marlowe, *n'est-ce pas*?' he said, pouring me two fingers.

'I didn't know Raymond Chandler was one of your specialties,' I said, accepting the glass.

'He isn't. I made the mistake of getting locked into the epoch of George III,' he said. 'At least you are dealing with something more concrete, more recent, more about what we grapple with in this country.'

'Does everything have to have immediate contemporary relevance?' I asked, clinking glasses with him.

'According to the philistinic fools who sit on the board of this university . . . well, they don't see any point in finding additional funding for the humanities, let alone those that address times past. But, sorry, I'm starting to rant.'

'There's nothing to apologize about. Your anger sounds very justified.'

'You went to Smith and Harvard, so you must understand that your undergraduate students at New England State will largely have been C students in high school, and will not dazzle you with their insights into *Sister Carrie*. Having said that, given the insane competition for places in the Ivy League and the better liberal-arts colleges, we are getting a somewhat improved level of undergraduate – by which I mean uninspired, but not altogether stupid – and I think I'm starting to rant again . . .'

He opened a desk drawer and pulled out three hefty files.

'Here are Debbie Holder's lecture notes. You are going to have quite a long weekend ahead of you if you want to be ready to face your students Monday morning.'

He was completely right about that. I went straight home after the meeting and spent the following two days burrowing into Professor Holder's lectures. Part of me felt like a poacher as I was reading through these notes to discover the shape of her courses and the take she had on the Naturalists and Dickinson. There were times when I vehemently disagreed with her – especially when she tried to discern leitmotifs in Dreiser. But her analyses of Dickinson's internal metric rhythms – and the metaphysic of her poetry – hugely impressed me. The passion she had for the work she was discussing was both remarkable and intimidating. I couldn't help but feel that she was several cognitive notches above me; a true natural when it came to engaging with the flow of literary ideas. Of course I felt a stab of envy – but it was the sort of envy that arises out of seeing someone in your field raising their game and playing at a higher level. Reading her notes was both sobering and sad because, by the end of the weekend, I realized just what a major loss Deborah Holder had been.

When I returned to New England State early Monday morning I was in an advanced state of anxiety. My first day as a professor – and as I strode into the classroom, a firm smile on my face, a voice in my head kept telling me: *They're all thinking, 'You're not Deborah Holder.'*

The first class was a course in American Originals, encompassing new movements in twentieth-century American poetry from Ezra Pound to Allen Ginsberg. According to her notes, Deborah Holder was about to start discussing Wallace Stevens's 'Thirteen Ways of Looking at a Blackbird'. When I reached the combined desk and lectern at the front of the hall, I found myself staring at seventeen students (I'd made a point of learning all their names over the weekend). They all looked bored, half-awake, wishing to be anywhere but here. I wrote my name on the blackboard, and under that my office hours and the number of my telephone extension. As I scrawled this information across the board I could feel my clammy fingers failing to gain purchase on the chalk.

This was stage fright. Like all such manic jitters, it was bound up in that most commonplace of horrors: being found out. More than anything this dread permeates so much of adult life: the very private belief that a few ill-chosen words will show the world what a total fraud you know yourself to be.

As I finished writing my extension number, I shut my eyes for a nanosecond and told myself that the show must go on. Then I turned around and faced the class.

'OK,' I said, 'let's make a start.'

I took another fast steadying breath. I started to talk – a long exhalation which lasted for the next hour and during which the self-doubt was replaced by an ever-growing sense that I was pulling this off. After explaining my awkwardness about taking over Professor Holder's classes – and my realization that I would be replacing someone who was irreplaceable – I started speaking about 'Thirteen Ways of Looking at a Blackbird' and how, as the title implied, the poem dealt with a simultaneously simplex and complex idea.

'How you interpret all that arrives in life determines so much about how the narrative of your life is dictated. Perception *is* everything. We choose to see the world in a certain way. This perception can – and most certainly *does* – change as we grow older. But we are always conscious of the fact that, as Stevens so lucidly notes, there are thirteen ways of looking at a blackbird – and that, like so many things outside the range of empiricism, there is no one defining point of view. Like everything in life, it's all subjective.'

I sensed I lost them a little bit with the reference to empiricism, but I was still pleased overall with this first outing and did seem to have engaged them . . . for a moment or two anyway.

The class in American Naturalism was a little shakier. It had over seventy students, many of whom seemed to be members of the jock brigade and had chosen it as a means of getting one of their English requirements out of the way. The football players – loud, show-off types – sat together in a pack and made a point of whispering loudly as I lectured, slipping notes back and forth and generally trumpeting their team-player ignorance for all to see. Interspersed among them were several cheerleader types, the sort of blonde, clean-limbed women who all had names like Babs and Bobbi, probably came from white-bread suburbs, and would end up marrying the same sort of blocky men who were now showing off to them at my expense.

I was trying to talk about the trial scene in *An American Tragedy* where Clyde admits to 'thinking' about killing his pregnant girlfriend, and how Dreiser plays with notions of culpability and the way we all want to confess something, even if it means orchestrating our own self-destruction. But as I was warming to this theme, the biggest and blockiest of the football clique turned around and started chatting loudly with one of the giggly cheerleaders. I stumbled over a sentence and then snapped.

'You . . .' I said.

The guy continued talking.

'You . . .' I said again.

The guy ignored me.

I threw down my pen and stormed right up the aisle to where he was talking. He kept chatting to the bimbette.

'You . . .'

He finally looked at me.

'You want something?' he asked.

'What's your name?'

'What's it to you?'

'This is my course, my classroom, and you are behaving in a rude, disruptive manner.'

He turned to his jocky cohorts and pulled a face – one which essentially said: *Do you believe this nobody?* My rage turned cold.

'Your name.'

He continued to pull a face. That's when I slammed a fist on his desk.

'Your name *now*.'

There was shocked silence as Mr Football realized that he had just crossed that line of scrimmage marked Danger Zone.

'Michaels,' he finally said.

'Well, Mr Michaels, gather up your things and get out. You're now officially on Dean's Report.'

He looked wide-eyed at me.

'You can't do that,' he said, suddenly little-boyish.

'Oh, yes, I can. You're on Dean's Report and you're to leave this classroom now.'

'But if you put me on Dean's Report—'

'It's not an "if", Mr Michaels. You're there already.'

I turned and walked back to the lectern. Michaels didn't move, but he did look to his pack for support. Everyone was suddenly averting their eyes from his and generally zoning him out.

'We are all waiting for you to go, Mr Michaels,' I said. 'Or do I have to call Security – a call that will result in your immediate suspension from this university.'

Another long silence. Michaels again looked to his cohort, beseeching them to back him up here. But they all stared down at their desks.

'Mr Michaels, I am not going to say this again. There is the door. Use it.'

His face was now full of rage. He grabbed his books and his backpack and stormed out, slamming the door behind him. I let the silence in the classroom hold for a good fifteen seconds. Then, in as mild a voice as possible, I asked: 'Now where were we?'

And I resumed the lecture.

After class I returned to my office and typed up a Dean's Report which detailed the event in the classroom and the reason why Michaels was evicted. A Dean's Report was a reasonably big deal at New England State. I had read about it in the hefty Faculty Rules book that I had received from Professor Sanders last week and noted that it was 'only to be used when a student breaches all rules of classroom etiquette and/or engages in actions that are disruptive and detrimental'. I read this statement again before writing up the report and actually incorporated it into my comments on Mr Michaels's rude and ignorant behavior. Then I sent one copy to Alma Carew, the Dean of Students, and another to Professor Sanders. An hour after I had dropped them off, Sanders was knocking on the door of my office.

'You've had an eventful first day,' he said.

'I'm not going to be bullied by a student, Professor.'

'Word has it that you engaged in an act of physical force.'

'Did Michaels tell you that?'

'No, Michaels told his coach that. Just as he also told his coach that he was on Dean's Report for the second time this term, which means an automatic suspension until next autumn.'

'So he won't miss the start of the football season.'

'He's a hockey player, Jane. The captain of the team – and a complete moron. The first Dean's Report was for setting off firecrackers in the toilets of one of the girls' dorms. Really classy.'

'Well, I didn't engage in an act of physical violence.'

'But you did slam your fist down on his desk.'

'That's right. I did just that, in an attempt to get his attention as he refused to acknowledge me when—'

'Yes, I heard all that from one of my spies in the class.'

'I didn't know I was under surveillance, Professor.'

'Be glad that you are. This student backed you up and told me that Michaels deserved being tossed out.'

'And this student's name is . . .?'

'You don't expect me to reveal my informants, now, do you? What I will say is that she . . .'

So it was a 'she'.

'. . . was very impressed with the way you didn't let him push you around. Michaels is the sort of oaf who's always getting his own way because he understands the uses of intimidation. You called his bluff and I congratulate you for it. But there is nonetheless a problem now. Not only is Michaels the captain of the hockey team, but he is also "the lynchpin in their entire offensive structure" – and yes, that's a direct quote from his coach. They have a big game against U. Mass this weekend. If the university has no choice but to enforce the second Dean's Report then he is effectively suspended for the rest of the semester. Which means he can't play in the game on Saturday. And if New England State lose because of this . . .'

'I will look like the villain in the piece.'

'Absolutely – and the English Department will also take the rap. According to the very jock-oriented trustees, we will have cost the university a big game, upon which hinges their ability to hoist some goddamn trophy that I don't give two shits about. But it could be the stick they beat us with when we ask for nothing more than the maintenance of our current departmental budget next year.'

'So you want me to rescind the Dean's Report.'

'No, that's not what I want. That's what the Dean of Students, the Director of Athletics, the Director of Giving and the university President want. Personally, I only care about this in so far as it has an impact on my – *our* – department.'

'If I refuse . . .?'

'You won't be doing me any favors. You will also be getting yourself off to a shaky start. However, I cannot influence your decision except to say that, quite frankly, I'd prefer it if you'd let the idiot off this time.'

'I'll need an apology from Michaels,' I said. 'An apology in writing.'

'I'm certain that's possible.'

'I'll also need an assurance that he won't pull this sort of stunt again.'

'That won't be a problem either. I'm very grateful for this, Jane. It saves me a huge headache.'

The apology arrived the next morning – a hastily scribbled letter, written on a half-torn piece of notebook paper and scrawled in such a way as to emphasize Michaels's desire not to make amends. The penmanship was deliberately hard to read, but I still managed to decipher:

Dear Professor Howard
I apologize for my rude behavior in class yesterday.
It won't happen again, OK?

Then he signed his name. I wanted to call in on Professor Sanders and toss the letter on his desk and tell him that this was the sort of payback you received when you let louts off the hook. But I decided it was best to let the entire matter drop.

The next day my course in American Moderns went smoothly, as we dissected Stevens's 'Notes Toward a Supreme Fiction', honing in on the lines: 'You must become an ignorant man again / And see the sun again with an ignorant eye / And see it clearly in the idea of it.'

'Stevens focused his attention on that most American of beliefs,' I said. 'Reinvention. Yet here he's tempering it with the perception that, once again, how you look at something determines how it is for you. Or perhaps he is saying: the only way we can escape our given realities is by accepting that we have to somehow try to reinterpret that which we see every day.'

The students in this class remained relatively animated and asked reasonable questions. But there was one student who immediately struck me as well above the intelligence quotient for New England State. She had remained quiet during my first lecture, but when I asked for questions at the end of my talk on 'Notes Toward a Supreme Fiction', she raised her hand cautiously and asked me in a shaky voice: 'Do you think that Stevens's ultra-conservative professional life forced him into such experimental language?'

Hey, a thinking student . . .

'That's an excellent question, Ms . . .'

'Quastoff. Lorrie Quastoff.'

She stared down at the floor as she said this.

'Well, Lorrie, why don't you tell me – and everyone else – what you think about that.'

'No thanks,' she said.

'I know that's throwing the ball back at you but that's kind of what I'm paid to do. Just as Stevens was paid to . . .'

Lorrie Quastoff continued regarding the floor, then looked up in horror at me when she realized I was waiting for her to supply me with the answer. I gave her a nod of what I hoped was encouragement, and she finally said: 'Sell insurance. Wallace Stevens sold insurance. Actually, he didn't do the selling. He was an executive in a big insurance firm in Hartford, Connecticut – and he kept his poetry very much to himself. When he won the Pulitzer Prize for "Notes Toward a Supreme Fiction" it came as a total surprise to all his fellow executives. They had no idea that he did this in his spare time – just as, I guess, no one at the Charles Raymond and Co. insurance agency knew that Charles Ives also wrote music.'

Good God, the kid is knowledgeable. But why does she keep staring at the floor and rocking to and fro when she speaks?

'Does anyone here know who Charles Ives was?' I asked the class.

A big vacuous silence.

'Lorrie, would you mind . . . ?'

'Charles Ives – 1874–1954,' she said in a loud demonstrative voice, standing up to speak. 'American composer noted for his use of polyrhythms, polytonality, quarter-tones and aleatorical technique. Notable works include "The Unanswered Question" (1906) and "Three Places in New England" (1903–1914). Was awarded the Pulitzer Prize for Music in 1947.'

It was like listening to a talking dictionary, but I was immediately intrigued. When one member of the class – a very preppy guy, dressed in a cream crew-necked Ralph Lauren jumper – snickered at the automaton style of her delivery, I shot him such an angry look that he immediately blurted out 'Sorry' in her direction. Lorrie seemed oblivious to this.

'That's incredibly impressive, Lorrie,' I said. 'But besides making the connection between the fact that they both worked as insurance executives and both won the Pulitzer Prize, are there any other points in common between Stevens and Ives?'

Come on, kiddo . . . show your classmates just how smart you are and knock this one out of the park.

Again she wouldn't make eye contact with me. Again she engaged in this swaying motion as she spoke, like an Orthodox rabbi at prayer.

'They both were responsible for extending the possibilities of language. In Ives's case, a musical language. With Stevens, a reductive abstractionism . . .'

Reductive abstractionism! Way to go!

'. . . which allowed him to speak of large metaphysical matters in a style that, though rich in metaphors, never tempts lushness.'

Then she sat down.

'That's really brilliant, Lorrie – and you've really got it in one when it comes to Stevens's language. But I'd like to return

171

to your first question: whether you think that Stevens's ultra-conservative business life made him even more experimental in his poetry.'

She stood up again.

'It's not what I think,' she said. 'It's what *you* think, Professor.'

'But I'm throwing the question back at you again – which may be unfair, but so it goes.'

'What do *I* think?' she asked, sounding so automaton.

'Yes, please.'

A long pause.

'I think . . . I think . . . well, I *really* think that if you work at something *really* boring like insurance, you *really* need an escape hatch.'

That got a big laugh from her fellow classmates – and Lorrie Quastoff, taken aback by such support, momentarily smiled. Then she sat right down again.

I was hoping I could catch her attention at the end of class but she was gone out the door before I could motion her over for a chat. When I ran into Professor Sanders in the English Department corridor that afternoon, I mentioned how extraordinary Lorrie Quastoff was.

'Yes, I meant to talk to you about her,' he said. 'She is rather special. As you can gather she is something of a savant—'

'But not an idiot savant?'

'*We* certainly don't see her that way – but other people may do. You see, Lorrie Quastoff is something of a "special case" for us. Because she is a very high-functioning autistic woman.'

Everything suddenly made sense: the monotone delivery, the inability to make eye contact, the rocking back and forth when she spoke.

'We accepted her after much deliberation, not so much to do with her intelligence – which, as you have seen, is formidable –

but about whether she could function socially in the university environment. So far she's done reasonably well, though some of the jock brigade have engaged in a degree of mockery from time to time, and she doesn't really have much in the way of friends. We've assigned one of the proctors in her hall of residence to be her minder and make certain she's coping. As it turns out, she's ferociously well-organized – the proctor told me her room is immaculate – and she has a capacity for pedagogy that is simply remarkable. She's still just a freshman, but I have recommended her for a transfer to that place across the river in Cambridge . . . and I think Harvard would be mad not to take her.'

'If there's anything I can do to help with that, let me know. I do know the Harvard English Department inside out.'

As soon as that comment was out of my mouth, I regretted it. Professor Sanders worked hard at suppressing a smile.

'I've no doubt of that, Jane. No doubt at all.'

When I returned to my office and ran through the list of seventy-three students in my American Naturalism class, lo and behold Lorrie Quastoff was there. The course was so big – and held in such a large lecture theater – that I hadn't seen her in the crowd. But when I arrived at the hall that afternoon, I scanned the rows of students and noted that she was sitting way in the back, off to the right, on her own. As I searched for her, I also saw Michaels sitting with his beefy acolytes and their blonde squeezes. As I caught his eye he made a face at me, mimicking a naughty schoolboy caught by the teacher. Then the bastard actually winked at me, as if to say: '*Think you could get me suspended, did you?*'

I coughed to bring the class to attention, then wished everyone a good afternoon and returned to *An American Tragedy*, discussing the grim scene leading up to Clyde's execution for a crime he didn't commit. Having gotten their attention with the details of the electrocution I asked the class if anyone had considered which major work of fiction had influenced Drieser's novel. No one answered. At the back of the class I could see Lorrie Quastoff wanting to raise her hand, but feeling intimidated.

'Ms Quastoff,' I said, 'you seem to want to say something.'

The moment I mentioned 'Ms Quastoff' I saw Michaels pull a monkey face at one of his chums. As he did this, Lorrie suddenly stood up. And in a far-too-loud voice she said: 'Dostoevesky. That's the answer. Dreiser loved *Crime and Punishment* and he used the same theme of self-recrim . . . crim . . . crim . . .'

She'd gotten stuck on that syllable and kept repeating it. The titters from Michaels and Company got louder. And when I heard him distinctly mimic her – '*Crim . . . crim . . . crim . . .*' he said in a loud whisper to the guy behind him – I pounced.

'Mr Michaels,' I shouted. 'On your feet right now.'

There was a long shocked silence – and Michaels was suddenly looking very worried.

'I said: on your feet *now*.'

Michaels rose to his feet, his eyes boring into me – a stare meant to intimidate but which I saw off with a caustic shake of the head.

'What were you just saying?' I asked.

'I was saying nothing.'

'That's not the truth and you know it. You were mocking Ms Quastoff.'

'No, I wasn't . . .'

'I heard you very distinctly, Mr Michaels. You went "*crim, crim, crim*" when Ms Quastoff had trouble with the word. Did anyone else hear Mr Michaels mock Ms Quastoff?'

'I did,' Lorrie Quastoff said. 'And he's always doing that to me. Always calling me "spaz" or "Rain Man". He's a big bully and he always does it to show off to his friends.'

'I'm really sorry if—' Michaels said.

'You were sorry the other day as well when you insulted me during my lecture,' I said, 'and I let you off with an apology, which is why you are back in this classroom today. But to then go and mock a student with developmental challenges . . . there is no way that a simple apology is going to get you out of this one. You're back on Dean's Report, Mr Michaels, and this time the automatic suspension will stick. Now get the hell out of my class.'

He didn't look to his buddies this time for support. He simply bolted for the exit, then turned and shouted at me: 'You think you're going to get away with this, you're wrong,' and slammed the door behind him.

After the class I asked Lorrie Quastoff to stay behind. Once everyone else had left the lecture theater, she stood by my desk, rocking back and forth, her agitation showing.

'They're gonna get me now. Really get me. Make me pay. You shouldn't have called on me . . .'

Her rocking became so repetitive that I had to put a steadying hand on her shoulder.

'Lorrie, I promise you, they will not get you if you do exactly what I say.'

'And if I don't do what you say?'

'Well, that won't be the end of the world. But it might not put an end to the teasing. This will, trust me.'

'He's going to be suspended?'

'And more – if I have my way.'

'You want me to write something?'

'You're ahead of me.'

'Like Dostoevsky was ahead of Dreiser.'

I went back to my office and wrote up my Dean's Report. True to her word – as I told her I needed it within an hour –

Lorrie slipped her own signed affidavit underneath my office door and was gone immediately. I stuck my head out the office door but before I could say her name she had turned a corner and vanished. I picked up her report. It was written with amazing fluidity and accomplishment and it detailed, at great length, the hectoring and intimidation she had received over the past term and a half from Michaels and Company. Immediately I revised the final paragraph of my report. It read:

> *It is clear from Lorrie Quastoff's signed statement that New England State University has allowed a coordinated and lengthy series of intimidations to be perpetrated on a young woman with learning difficulties. The very fact that Mr Michaels is a star athlete, and has been allowed to get away with his campaign of intimidation against a brilliant student who also happens to be on the autistic spectrum could be interpreted in the wider arena of general public opinion as an indication that the university is more concerned with athletic success than protecting the rights and dignity of a student who is so admirably overcoming the disability with which she was born. I am certain that the university would not want to stand accused of such a charge, as I am also certain that this runs contrary to all university policy.*

I knew these last couple of lines would provide the knockout punch I wanted to land, as they were veiled with the idea that this incident might turn into a media cause célèbre that could cost them dearly. I finished the report, read it through, signed it, and then called Professor Sanders to brief him.

'Oh, *merde*,' was his initial reply, followed by: 'But if what you say in the report can't be refuted—'

'It can't be refuted.'

'Others will be the judge of that, because this whole business is going to end up on the desk of Ted Stevens.' He was the President of the university. 'If my instincts prove me right, he will move to close the whole thing down within twenty-four hours. I doubt they're going to side with Michaels because they don't want reporters from the *Boston Globe* or the *New York Times* crawling around the campus. Do understand, though, after this you're going to be regarded as Typhoid Mary around here. The administration will side with you publicly while at the same time privately despising you for costing them dearly. Hockey's a big sport in this school.'

And the university President, Ted Stevens, was a very big hockey fan. He told me that himself when he called me into his office the next day to 'discuss' the situation. He was a man in his mid-fifties, hyper-fit, wearing a very conservative suit and rep tie, with pictures of himself and the first George Bush on a wall near his desk. He looked very much like a high-powered executive (and as a quick glance at his bookshelf informed me, he was very much an exponent of applied corporate management principles). Seated in his office were the Dean of Students, Alma Carew (African-American, late thirties, wiry, intense); the Head of Sports, Budd Hollander (short, hefty, wearing an ill-fitting brown blazer and a check shirt); and Professor Sanders.

'Now, according to Mr Michaels's very high-powered and expensive attorney,' Ted Stevens said, 'you provoked him into mimicking Ms Quastoff.'

'With respect, sir, that's nonsense.'

'With respect, Professor, several other members of the class have corroborated this.'

'Were they members of Michaels's little clique?' I asked.

Ted Stevens didn't like this question one bit.

'Not all of them,' he said.

'Well, I'm certain if you were to interview Ms Quastoff—'

'We have interviewed Ms Quastoff. Or, I should say, Dean Carew has.'

Alma Carew came in here.

'Lorrie told me she didn't have her hand in the air, but you still called on her.'

'I called on her because I had posed a question to the class and no one was offering an answer. Lorrie Quastoff had spoken brilliantly that morning in my course on American Moderns and I could see that she knew the answer to my question.'

'How could you see that?' Alma Carew asked.

'She was on the verge of raising her hand.'

'Lorrie Quastoff denies that she even moved her hand. She said you sought her out.'

'Does it really matter whether Ms Quastoff did or did not raise her hand?' Professor Sanders asked. 'The fact is, Professor Howard was perfectly within her rights to call on any student she wanted to. As she wasn't getting a response to a general question thrown out to the class, she called on a student she knew to be bright and knowledgeable—'

'And who she also knew was on the autistic spectrum and had been subjected to alleged bullying by Michaels.'

Budd Hollander came in here: 'Joey told me he never, *never* bullied Lorrie Quastoff.'

'Her signed statement says otherwise,' said Professor Sanders.

'But she doesn't have witnesses.' This was Hollander.

'Are you saying that she lied about being harassed by Michaels?' I asked, sounding angry.

Ted Stevens came in at this point: 'All Coach Hollander is saying . . .'

Coach?

'. . . is that it's his word against hers.'

'And mine,' Professor Sanders said. 'Because Ms Quastoff came to the late Professor Holder last term and complained to her that Michaels and his cronies were teasing her – and Professor Holder, in turn, informed me of this.'

'Did she write this down, file a report, anything like that?' Alma Carew asked.

'No,' Professor Sanders said. 'But, to repeat, she did tell me that Lorrie Quastoff was being bullied by Joseph Michaels. And if that little creep didn't happen to be the captain of the hockey team, we wouldn't be here now, trying to see if there's a way out of suspending him.'

'With respect, Professor,' Alma Carew said, 'the issue here is whether Michaels was provoked into saying what he said in Professor Howard's class. We know already that she had issues with Michaels.'

'*Issues*,' I said, sounding outraged. 'The creep was deliberately rude and obstreperous in my class two days ago and was put on report for that. I rescinded the report because I was told that if he missed the big championship game on Saturday night it would be disastrous. So I decided to give him a second chance. What does he do? He winks at me at the start of the lecture and then viciously mocks a student with developmental challenges—'

'You didn't mention the wink in your report,' Alma Carew said.

'I felt it was irrelevant.'

'But it got you angry, didn't it?' Budd Hollander said. 'So angry that you decided to call on Lorrie Quastoff in the hope that Joey Michaels would—'

'I did nothing of the sort,' I said, now sounding very angry, 'and I find it extraordinary that you are turning this discussion into a cross-examination.'

'This is not a trial, Professor,' said Ted Stevens.

'Well, it's certainly starting to smell like one. I genuinely resent being made to feel as if I am at fault here. The fact is, this kid is a nasty piece of work and he does not play by the rules when it comes to his comportment, let alone showing decency to a young woman who has overcome so much to simply gain admission to this university.'

'Do you truly understand what you're perpetrating if you insist on keeping him on Dean's Report?' asked Budd Hollander. 'This university hasn't won a major national hockey tournament in over twenty years. The team is on the brink of doing this, going into the game against U. Mass heavily favored to win. But Joey Michaels is the lynchpin of the team. Without him . . . well, it will be something of an uphill struggle. He's the highest-scoring forward in our division, the NHL are already scouting him—'

'And having been let off the hook less than thirty-six hours ago, he then plays on his "above the law" perspective by belittling an autistic student. Sorry – but you can't excuse that. His arrogance landed him in this situation.'

'I don't think he's the only arrogant person in this situation,' Alma Carew said.

'For the life of me I don't know why you're defending this kid,' I said to her. 'I mean, if he had uttered a racial epithet against a person of color, would you still—'

'That is so way out of line.' Carew was suddenly furious.

'Sounds like a perfectly reasonable question to me,' Professor Sanders said.

'And that is absolutely *enough* from all of you,' answered Ted Stevens.

He let the silence that followed hang in the air for a good minute – no doubt a strategy he had learned from one of his management books about defusing verbal fisticuffs among his underlings.

Finally he said: 'Could I have a word with Professor Howard in private? I'll be in touch with all of you by the end of the day to inform you what course of action I plan to take next.'

They all stood up, Alma Carew and Budd Hollander saying nothing to me as they walked out the door. Professor Sanders raised his eyes slightly in my direction. Was he indicating that I should proceed with prudence or was he telling me he'd stand by me, whatever came out of this mess? Certainly the tone of his comments during this 'discussion' hinted that he was in my corner, but in the ever-shifty world of university politics there was no such thing as ongoing loyalty. The default position always was public support but private subversion.

So I was suddenly alone with Ted Stevens. Having been sitting with the four of us around a conference table in one corner of his capacious office, he now stood up and moved to the equally capacious desk that covered one substantial corner of the room. As he motioned me to sit down in the narrow straight-backed chair fronting his desk, I wondered if he had picked up this tactic from another of those management guides in a chapter titled 'How to Intimidate'. But I had decided that I wouldn't be intimidated – and in the back of my mind was the idea that if he fired me now, he'd be letting himself in for a very public fight. No doubt he'd already worked this one out, as his first comment to me was: 'Do you realize what this university stands to gain if we win the ECAC championship on Saturday night? Ken Malamut . . . ever heard of him?'

'The big hedge fund guy.'

'I forgot that you did a brief stint in high finance,' he said. 'Very brief, in fact.'

'I decided that I wanted to return to academic life.'

'Of course you did,' he said, tingeing the comment with just the slightest hint of sarcasm. 'Which is why you left Freedom Mutual in such a hurry.'

I said nothing.

'We actually thought you were quite a catch when you were recruited to fill Deborah Holder's post. But given the eventful first week you've had here—'

'Now you listen to me, sir,' I said, cutting him off. 'The only damn reason I've had an eventful first week here is because of the antics of your star hockey player. I refuse to be made the scapegoat for his obnoxious—'

He held up his hand like a traffic cop forcing a driver into an immediate stop.

'Personally, I think Joseph Michaels is an odious little shit,' he said, 'and one with a vast entitlement complex. So yes, I am in full agreement with you and have no doubt that the little bastard did everything you say he did. And as for the deliberate disrespect underscoring his alleged apology to you—'

'But here's the thing, Professor. I may concur with you, but I am, at heart, a manager, not an academic. I was brought in here to manage a third-tier university that is trying to become second-tier and simultaneously to up its national profile and its endowment base. So far, I've increased our overall endowment by twenty-seven million dollars in just under nineteen months. And here I have, in my sights, Ken Malamut: one of Wall Street's major league players, a New England State alumnus and a genuine college hockey fanatic. And he has promised me – *us* – a one-off gift of ten million dollars – nothing to a guy who's worth close to one billion dollars – but a definitive ten million dollars if we win that hockey trophy on Saturday night.'

'So I'm going to cost New England State ten million dollars if I keep Michaels on Dean's Report?'

'Well, I wouldn't put it so bluntly . . .'

'Yes, you would.'

'All right, straight talking, no BS – yes, you would do just that.'

I lowered my head. I tried to shift around in the narrow seat, but realized it was designed for making the occupant feel very restricted and cowed by the big man in the big chair behind the big desk. Maybe it was the realization that this 'management tool' chair was deliberately restricting me – and that Ted Stevens struck me as exactly the sort of smarmy executive type I so hated in American life – which made me look up at him and say: 'I'm not rescinding the Dean's Report.'

He flinched, then tried to hide the fact that he had flinched.

'That's a foolish decision, Professor,' he said.

'Perhaps,' I said, 'but it's also the decision I can live with.'

'I want you to think very carefully about—'

I stood up.

'Nice meeting you, sir,' I said.

'You think you're clever, occupying the emotional high ground and all that. You also think that a guaranteed cause célèbre around Lorrie Quastoff will shield you from retaliatory action from the university. Perhaps it will . . . in the short term. And no, I'm not so stupid as to fire you on the spot. But your four-year contract with us . . . it may allegedly be "tenure track". But know this: if you cost us this ten million dollars, I can unequivocally promise you that you will never, *ever* get tenure. I'll see to that.'

'I'm sure you will,' I said, then headed to the door.

'Professor – *Jane* – why make life difficult for yourself?'

I wanted to say: '*I hate all bullies, that's why*' and make certain he understood that, by implication, I was including him. But I stopped myself. All justifications are defensive –

183

and this afternoon, I had decided not to be defensive, even though I knew it was going to cost me big time.

So my only response was a shrug and a polite reiteration of, 'Very nice meeting you, sir,' as I left the room.

The Dean's Report on Joseph Michaels was therefore not rescinded and he was suspended for the rest of the term. When, two days later, I walked into my class on American Originals, I scanned the students and caught sight of Lorrie Quastoff. She looked away and wouldn't make eye contact with me. That afternoon, I steeled myself for dirty looks from the Michaels clique in my Naturalism course. Like everyone else in the lecture theater, they hushed themselves as soon as I entered the hall and behaved immaculately throughout my one-hour lecture. Had I earned their respect? Had my refusal to give in to popular sentiment won me a certain hard-ass reputation? It was difficult to say – though I did make a point of knocking on Professor Sanders's office door later that day to hear him say that Stevens would definitely make good on his threat to eventually deny me tenure.

'Maybe that's no bad thing from your standpoint, Jane. You know now things are finite here for you.'

'Even though you think I've made a huge mistake.'

'You decided to adhere to a point of principle – and that's admirable. But do understand that no one is going to like you for it. We all need scapegoats. And when the team loses the Big Game, you are going to be cast in that role.'

As it happened, the Big Game turned out a little different than everyone expected. I went online at eleven on Saturday night, fully expecting to see that U. Mass had emerged victorious. But on the Boston.com website, there was a short item in the Breaking Sports News department, heralding the '*Sudden Death Goal*' which won New England State its first ECAC Championship: '*a goal scored by a certain Pete O'Mara* [one of Michaels's cohorts in my class] *at 3:37 in the second overtime period'.*

> *Playing without their star forward, Joseph Michaels, who had been controversially suspended from New England State less than forty-eight hours before the big game, New England State trailed 1–0 before leveling the score with less than ninety seconds to go in normal time. And then, out of nowhere, in the second overtime period . . .*

So there are such things as happy endings – though when I ran into Ted Stevens while crossing the main campus quadrangle on Monday and wished him a good morning, he simply smiled thinly at me. It was a smile which said: *You're dead here.*

On the Monday afternoon after the Big Game, I received a phone call from Professor Sanders, asking me to drop by his office.

As I walked in, he asked: 'Scotch?' and poured it before settling into the chair opposite his desk.

'Is the news that bad?' I asked.

'Nothing you don't already know. My advice to you is: get that book of yours published, write as much as you can for as many journals and magazines as possible, and hopefully find a new teaching post by sheer force of your output and ambition. Because once your contract is up here you will be packing your bags.'

After this drink Professor Sanders began to distance himself from me. He was never arctic in public – he was too smart to play that game – and he did make a point of asking for my take on things in departmental meetings. But he always referred to me as 'Professor Howard' while calling all my other colleagues by their first names. The other members of the department noted this, just as they also noted the way he had dispatched me to his own genteel version of Coventry. Or as Marty Melcher put it: 'Sanders is *subtextually* telling us you are one dangerous babe . . . And go on and report me for using the word "babe".'

'Now why would I do a thing like that, Professor?' I asked.

'So you're not PC, a crypto-feminist or even an uber-feminist?'

'*Über* with an umlaut?' I asked.

'Sanders said you're fast. So fast that you refused to be threatened by Our Beloved Leader, President Stevens.'

'Might I have a vodka, please?' I asked. We were in a bar and Melcher's smarmy banter now had me regretting the fact that I had accepted his offer of an after-work cocktail – especially as another departmental colleague, Stephanie Peltz, had warned me he was a lech (just as Marty had warned me that Stephanie was *the* departmental gossip. 'And believe me, there's quite a competition for the number one spot in that field').

Marty Melcher. Fifty-something. Fleshy, messy, but with a full head of gray-black curly hair and a walrus moustache that made him look like an American Günter Grass (*with* the umlaut). A specialist in twentieth-century American fiction ('Not those second-tier imitation Zolas you like, but the Big Guns: Hemingway, Fitzgerald, Faulkner'). A man whose face could ostensibly have been described as 'lived in', though 'lived through' might be closer to the truth. Certainly, Melcher had lived through a considerable amount (according to Stephanie Peltz): three divorces, a lengthy battle with painkillers, and a near career-destroying affair with a senior colleague, Victoria Mattingly, which ended when she suffered a nervous breakdown and confessed all to her husband. He then hired two goons from Southie to kick the crap out of Melcher in the driveway of his house in Brookline.

'Might I have a vodka, please?'

'Grey Goose on the rocks?' he asked.

I nodded and he gave our order to a passing waiter.

'I've been trying to figure you out, Jane. From afar, that is. The mistress of the late great David Henry – I actually did rate him, even that last crazy book of his. A brilliant thesis at Harvard. Turning down a position at Wisconsin, the sort of teaching gig most newcomers to the university game would kill to obtain. A flop in the big money game – or was there more to it than you not being able to cut it there? And then, *then*, after being hired as a last-minute replacement for our beloved Professor Holder – and yes, I did once hit on her, just to keep the record straight – *shazam*, you are responsible for the suspension of a leading knucklehead jock.

'So what I think is: you're good, sweetheart. The original tough cookie. And you've kicked ass in a way that most of us lifers here can only dream about.'

'I'm glad I've won myself a fan.'

'You've got yourself a boyfriend now?'

'What a personal question.'

'Just curious.'

'No, I'm flying solo.'

'You interested in one? On a part-time basis, of course.'

I laughed. 'You really do hit on everyone, don't you.'

'Absolutely.'

'Thanks for the drink, Professor.'

Back at the apartment, I called Christy in Oregon and explained how I had squandered all chances of promotion at New England State.

'Personal morality – how to play things – is an ongoing dilemma and often agonizing,' she said. 'Do the right thing and you get punished for it. Don't do the right thing and you get punished for it – especially by yourself. Not that you'd ever engage in such self-flagellation.'

'Why is everything in my life so damn contradictory?'

'"*We do not what we ought/What we ought not, we do/And lean upon the thought/That chance will bring us through*" . . .'

'Browning?' I asked.

'Close, but no cigar. Matthew Arnold.'

'Who the hell quotes Matthew Arnold these days?'

'I do,' she said. 'And my advice to you, madame, is to consider yourself in a form of internal exile. You go to the university, you teach your classes, you do brilliantly with – and by – your students. You make certain you're there for anyone who needs you. You keep long office hours if students need to drop by. You get your book published. Unless called upon to attend a meeting or give an opinion, you politely ignore your departmental colleagues and the honchos in the administration. You're there, but you're not there – if you catch my drift.

'And the other thing I would do if I was in your position and with all that funny money in the bank – is to spend some of it. Preferably not on anything sensible.'

I took Christy's advice. When I returned to New England State on Monday, I took my classes, did my office hours and vanished from view. I maintained this narrow-focused approach for the rest of the week – concentrating my efforts on being accessible to my students, doing my best as a lecturer, and acknowledging my colleagues in assorted corners of the campus with a polite but distant nod.

As I was consolidating this professional modus vivendi, I was also dealt a lucky card. My book *The Infernal Duality* was accepted for publication by – wait for it – the University of Wisconsin Press. And they say that America is an irony-free zone. I kept quiet about the news. But when I attended the departmental meeting two days later, Professor Sanders kicked off the proceedings with: 'I got a phone call from a colleague

188

at the University of Wisconsin yesterday who informed me that Professor Howard's book will be published by their press this year. I'm certain we all want to congratulate her on this achievement.'

Then he moved on to other business.

Stephanie Peltz came up to me after the meeting ended and said: 'Oh, my God, your book's been accepted! And by Wisconsin! *Wisconsin* . . . Oh, my God, that's one of the top ten university presses in the country.'

Top twenty is closer to the truth. Still . . .

'Oh, this is amazing, Jane. Why on earth did you keep it all to yourself?' she asked.

I said nothing, except to thank her for her good wishes. Then Marty Melcher pulled me aside.

'You really are an operator,' he said. 'Just like everyone who's ever gone to Harvard.'

Yeah, Marty – that's what they teach us over there in Cambridge: how to be a smarty pants.

But I simply replied to his comment with a nod and a smile.

And that was the last time anyone in the department mentioned my book again. Life at New England State carried on. I taught my classes. I met with my students. I left the university as soon as the business of the day was done for me. I lived below the internecine radar.

I also took Christy's second piece of advice and spent some of the money that was gaining interest in my bank account. But I didn't use it frivolously. No, my ultra-sensible side guided me in the direction of several real-estate agents in Somerville. Within four days I had agreed to pay $255,950 for a one-bedroom apartment on a leafy street right off Davis Square. The flat was located on the top two floors of an American Gothic house dating from the 1890s and very Grant Wood in its baroque flourishes. The apartment had been owned by a recently deceased Professor of Philosophy at Tufts, a lifelong bachelor who lived with his books and a long succession of cats (the ingrained smell of feline urine was everywhere). The kitchen was Nixon-era, the bathroom dated back to Eisenhower. But there was a huge living room with a balcony that overlooked the street. The bedroom was spacious and there was an alcove that would make an ideal study. The floorboards – though in need of painting and staining – were solid. And the surveyor who examined every damn crevice of the place let it be known that the walls were damp-free and ready to be replastered.

The entire place needed an overhaul – and one which a local builder estimated would cost me an additional fifty thousand. 'Once you put the money in, the place'll be worth four hundred and fifty K immediately,' he told me with the authority of a man who speculated in Somerville and Cambridge property all the time. I did some fast calculations and knew that I would be able to buy the place outright, but would still need to take out a loan of $75,000 to pay for the renovations and taxes. As someone who always feared debt it made me nervous borrowing this amount, even though the mortgage broker who set up the loan told me that, on my annual salary from New England State, this wasn't an excessive amount. *But say I can't find work again after I'm shown the door in a few years' time?* Still, I comforted myself with the thought that an apartment was always a saleable item and that I would now actually possess that most magical of commodities: *equity.* As Dad always used to say: *You're finally an adult when you're in hock to a bank for the roof over your head.*

So I called Mr Alkan and told him I needed his services again. 'No problem,' he said and took care of all the paperwork. I approved the $50,000 budget with the builder and chose kitchen cabinets and bathroom sinks and wall colors, and then dropped another $15,000 buying a bed and sofas, and a great big turn-of-the-century roll-top desk for myself, and a new stereo and plates and cutlery and . . .

I agreed to teach the summer term at New England State. By the time mid-August came and I'd submitted my grades and even managed a few days at a friend's family place on the Cape, my apartment was ready to be occupied. It looked wonderful – freshly plastered white walls, maple-stained floorboards, a Shaker-style kitchen, a modern bathroom, tasteful light wood furniture, that wonderful desk in the alcove that would be my study, and a huge king-sized bed which suddenly felt very empty and only seemed to emphasize something I had been dodging for a very long time: I was lonely.

When you have a need, you fill it. Within a few weeks of moving into the apartment, I had someone sharing the bed with me. I told myself it was love.

And, perhaps, at the time, it was just that . . . for a little while anyway.

Three

THEO MORGAN LOVED movies. Check that: Theo Morgan was fanatical about movies. 'A certifiable cinephile' as he described himself. Since the age of thirteen – when the movie bug first hit – he'd kept a filing card for every film he'd ever seen. At the last count he had 5,765 cards – 'that's close to three hundred movies per year in the past nineteen years' – each of which contained, on the front side, the name of the film, the director, principal actors, screenwriter, etc., while the back contained his own individual commentary on the movie, all written in a spindly handwriting that only he could decipher.

Theo Morgan grew up in a bland suburb of Indianapolis ('the vanilla ice cream of American cities – anemic'), the son of an insurance executive and a mother who was something of a creative spark at college but ended up re-enacting Sinclair Lewis's *Main Street* by doing what was expected of her: 'marrying a stiff and moving to a dull little midwestern town'. His father was an ex-Marine who preached a doctrine of God and country and tried to stamp down hard on Theo's burgeoning interest in film.

'I spent a lot of my free adolescent time sneaking off to see movies at the Indiana University Film Society,' he told me on our second date. 'In my junior year, there was a big festival of Bergman's films and I had to tell Dad that I had gone out for the school fencing team which trained twice a week from seven to nine. When he found out that I had been seeing "atheistic European crap" – his exact words – he grounded me for three months after punching me in the stomach as a "lesson in the price to be paid for insubordination". My mom

192

– being an impassive resident of the Valley of the Dolls – told me that "your dad only wants the best for you", which is why he also threatened to "rearrange my face" and send me to military school if he caught me watching any more "ungodly pictures".'

Fortunately Theo was a bright kid and he had a powerful ally at school in the form of an English teacher named Mr Turgeon. The teacher was gay, but very closeted.

'He had a boyfriend – one of the librarians at the university – and his life was rather cozy in what he called "a circum-scribed way". Outside of classical music his real passion was film, and though this was the early days of the VCR he had this fantastic film library at his home. When he discovered that I was getting into cinema, he started asking me over to his house after school to give me a crash course in film history. I mean, the guy had something like three thousand VCR tapes and I watched everything from D.W. Griffith to Fritz Lang to Billy Wilder with him. Of course I had to keep all this quiet from my parents and Mr Turgeon told me on more than one occasion that, if it ever got out that we were having these movie sessions at his home, he could lose his job – even though the man never, *ever* came on to me. He simply recognized a fellow sufferer. That's what cinephiles really are: people looking for an escape hatch.'

Theo's father never found out about the afternoons at Mr Turgeon's – watching Truffaut and Rivette and Carl Theodor Dreyer while sipping proper Earl Grey tea that Mr Turgeon bought in bulk during his annual summer pilgrimage to London. But when he was grounded after attending the Bergman festival at the University of Indiana, Theo told all to the one person in Indianapolis who understood him. Turgeon knew that raising the matter with the school authorities might wreak havoc so he counseled Theo to sit tight, bide his time and work his ass off to get the best grades possible in his last three semesters before applying to college.

Theo did as instructed. He was a straight-A student for those three terms, and even impressed his father with his diligence. Then, at Turgeon's urging, he made Columbia University his main choice. Theo's dad would not hear of it – 'over my dead body are you going to that degenerate city' – and refused to write the $75 check for the application fee. So Turgeon paid for it himself and also used inside pull there (he'd done his MA at Columbia) to secure Theo a fully paid scholarship.

'When Dad discovered that I'd applied to Columbia on the quiet, he made good on his threat and actually rearranged my face. After the assault, I went to school with two black eyes. Mr Turgeon insisted on marching me down to the principal. Our principal was one of these flag-hugging idiots and a deacon in the local Presbyterian church. But even he was horrified by my father's assault on me and actually called my father in to school and told him that I had earned a major scholarship to an Ivy League university, so he had absolutely no right to stand in my way of accepting it. And if he ever assaulted me again, he would be turned over to the cops.

'After this meeting, my mother cried for hours, asking me why I had to go running to the authorities and "play tattle-tail". My dad, on the other hand, simply told me to get out of the house and never come back.'

'And you were just eighteen?' I asked.

'It's the right age to cut and run – especially if you've just been handed an all-expenses-paid scholarship. That effectively removes you from the parental sphere of influence.'

I certainly knew a thing or two about that sort of liberation through academic funding. As he spoke with dry irony of his insane family and the pain they visited on him, I also knew that I was falling for him. Don't we often seek out someone who's traveled through the same damaged emotional landscape as ourselves – and, as such, understands us? From the outset I was pretty certain that our shared family misery – and the way we both partially broke free of it – meant that Theo understood me, as I did him.

Once he started at Columbia he effectively cut his ties with his parents. He never returned home again. Within three months of landing in New York, he'd also found a part-time job in the film department of the Museum of Modern Art as an assistant archivist. He held on to that job for his four years at Columbia – where he also ended up as head of the Film Society, movie critic for the campus newspaper and habitué of every small independent cinema in the city.

At twenty-two – with a *magna cum laude* degree in hand and a rent-controlled studio apartment on Amsterdam and 118th Street – he was poised for a big life in the Big City. In fact, Columbia offered him another full scholarship to complete a doctorate in Film Studies. UCLA also contacted him, letting it be known that they too would like him to accept a doctoral scholarship and a teaching position in their cinema department.

'I had all these offers and wanted nothing to do with them,' he said. 'Call it a lack of ambition – as several of my college advisors did – but I just wanted to program movies for a cinema.'

So he accepted a gig being the chief programmer for the Anthology Film Archives in Manhattan. 'One hundred and fifty dollars a week and I was happy as hell, especially as you could get away with anything at the Film Archives. I mean, it was the ultimate cinephile wet dream – a truly "out there" place where I could organize an entire season of East German musicals and get away with it. The work absolutely suited me. I could report to the cinema at noon and work until eight or nine in the evening without hassle. And then I could stay up the rest of the night watching movies.'

For five years he happily kept his zombie hours and created strange 'out there' seasons for the Film Archives: obscure Czech animators, forgotten anti-Communist B-movies from the McCarthy era, the great goofy classics of Japanese science fiction, every James M. Cain adaptation ever made . . .

Theo would reel off his film knowledge with rapid-fire delivery. He was a motor mouth, yet the spiel he spieled was always so spirited and erudite that I quickly came to accept his mile-a-minute repartee. Passionate intensity can be very seductive.

He only stood five foot six – and had a big unruly mop of black curly hair, a Frank Zappa goatee and a slight pot-belly (he abhorred all exercise). He always dressed in size 36 black Levi's 501s, a black T-shirt and an old black leather bomber jacket. Though he wasn't conventionally handsome, the interest he showed in everything to do with me wowed me. Ever since David I'd always dreamed of meeting another verifiable intellectual. So what if Theo tended to eat crap food and never took vitamins and insisted on getting up to watch a movie after we made love . . . He was never less than interesting.

For such a physically unruly person, he was surprisingly fastidious about certain elements in his life. He was fanatical when it came to flossing his teeth, and showered at least three times a day. His apartment in Cambridge was small – maybe 300 square feet – yet it was amazingly orderly. The hundreds of films that dominated all the bookshelves weren't just alphabetized, they were also organized with library-style dividers. His bed was always immaculately made and he insisted on changing the perfectly ironed sheets every other day. Just as his black jeans were always perfectly pressed, as well as the boxer shorts that he would only buy from Brooks Brothers. That was another thing about Theo – he had certain rigid consumerist choices from which he wouldn't deviate. His black T-shirts came from the Gap and once a year, so he told me, he'd rent a car and drive the two and a half hours to Freeport, Maine where there was a Gap outlet. Once there he'd buy thirty size large black T-shirts for $5 a shirt and then go to the Brooks Brothers outlet in the same town and purchase eighteen pairs of boxer shorts for $155 – he was very specific when it came to recalling prices. Finally he'd move on to the Levi's outlet and buy eighteen pairs of black 501s at $25 a pair. Purchases complete he'd drive north to the village of Wiscasset and buy a lobster roll and a root beer at a famous take-away shack called Red's. He'd plonk himself down at a table facing the bay, look at that widescreen vision of coastal Maine at its most bucolic, eat his lobster roll, drink his iced tea, and then turn his car around and head south for Boston, arriving back to catch at least three movies that evening *chez lui.*

'That would take care of both my clothes shopping and my view of the Great Outdoors for another year.'

Now I know all this sounds just a little quirky – because he really didn't buy another shred of clothing for the rest of the year and he resisted all my attempts to get him to spend a weekend somewhere outside of Boston that *didn't* have a cinema. But there was something strangely compelling about his quirks, just as I liked the fact that he was outside the mad consumerist dance that characterized so much of modern life. He got his DVDs free from all the distributors he knew. He ordered any books he needed from publishers or libraries. He did all his own washing and cleaning and cooking – and largely subsisted on a diet of Cheerios and frozen lasagne and instant soups and Ben and Jerry's ice cream. And when he awoke every morning at noon, he'd start the day by writing for two straight hours before heading off to his job at the Harvard Film Archive.

Theo ended up in Cambridge after getting tossed out of the Anthology Film Archives for failing to maintain budgetary control over his programs and running up an annual deficit of over $200,000. One of his old 'film geek' buddies (his term), Ronnie Black, had landed a job running the Harvard Archive and Cinema and was looking for a second-in-command. 'You're the best programmer this side of Paris,' Ronnie told him, 'but you like to be deliberately profligate. So here's the deal: you get the job on the proviso that you cannot spend a penny of our money without me signing off on it. You try to play games with me on this front, you're out on your ass and that will be the end of your career. But if you play by the rules, together we'll be able to run the show in Cambridge and do exactly what we want to do at Harvard . . . within reason.'

I met Theo at a dinner organized by an old Harvard friend named Sara Crowe. She was the very model of a New England Brahman, with one of those lean angular faces that put me in mind of the sort of Massachusetts *grandes dames* painted on commission by Whistler. She combined a certain ascetic *noblesse oblige* with a horror at the tawdriness of most human endeavor. She was considered perhaps the most important colonial historian since Perry Miller. Her book, *American Theocrats: New Journeys into the Puritan Mind*, won her considerable critical attention, not to mention a tenured professorship at Wellesley. Just to augment the manifold accomplishments of her life she had also married disgustingly well. He was a mutual fund star named Frederick Cowett: Princeton, Wharton, a big family compound in Wells, Maine and their very own townhouse on Beacon Hill, where they lived in upholstered elegance with their two young sons.

Sara was a marvel. The woman never put a foot wrong, never seemed to juggernaut down the wrong street, moving steadily from achievement to achievement. When I got the call at New England State to come over for dinner, she was completely warm and upbeat, telling me she'd heard from her spies all about the way I had stood up to Ted Stevens over the jock issue, and how proud she was of me for 'being moral at a time when careerism takes precedent over everything else'.

'Anyway, it's clear that New England State is nothing more than a way-station for you before you find your way to grander things.'

Translation: What's a Harvard smarty like you doing teaching at a third-tier university like that one?

Then she changed the subject by mentioning the dinner party to which she wanted to invite me two weeks from Friday.

Yes, her house was magnificent and decorated in subdued but immaculate good taste. Damn her, Frederick didn't even turn out to be a bore. Instead he came across as charming in a well-bred preppy way, reasonably literate, and not averse to the eclectic group that Sara had assembled for the evening.

That was the other intriguing thing about Sara Crowe – for all her apparent Brahmanism, she did cultivate eccentrics and people who did not dress in Brooks Brothers shirts and bermuda shorts. Which is why, during our Harvard years, she got chummy with Christy – even if '*La Poète*' (as Sara always referred to her) was the antithesis of Sara's button-down style and had this habit of shocking her friends by drinking far too robustly and then launching into a scatalogical stream of consciousness.

I often thought that Sara needed such extreme friends as a way of informing the straightlaced world in which she dwelled that she was not totally one of them; that her circle would include artists and writers and even a mad film archivist like Theo Morgan.

Sara knew Theo because she sat on the board of the Harvard Film Archive, and because she also spotted him early on as a *premier cru* oddball.

'Don't think I'm trying to fix you up by seating him next to you,' Sara told me in a fast whisper in a corner of her living room, before we all entered the very formal dining room to be served by two liveried waiters. 'But I promise you that you'll have a far more entertaining evening with Theo at your side than if I sat you next to Clifford Clayton – who will trace back his lineage to the *Mayflower* for you and also talk at great length about the derivatives market.'

Sara was right. Though I had to readjust my thought processes to tune into his mile-a-minute delivery, Theo Morgan proved to be excellent value.

'Know what this place reminds me of?' he said loudly as he sat down next to me. '*The Magnificent Ambersons.*'

'Didn't know anyone read Booth Tarkington these days,' I said.

'The movie is better than the book – which is upmarket soap opera.'

'It's rare that a movie betters a novel,' I said.

'You mean Mario Puzo's *The Godfather* is a masterpiece and the movie is pulp?'

'Ooops.'

'And how about *The Treasure of the Sierra Madre*? I mean, the B. Traven novel isn't the worst, but Huston's film . . .'

'Remind me never to challenge you on a film question again.'

He shot me a mischievous smile.

'But I like being challenged,' he said.

As I quickly came to discover, I too liked the challenge of

being with Theo. At the end of the dinner – by which time I'd barely spoken to the man on my other side – he asked me to write down my number in a small black notebook that he pulled out of his jacket pocket. I really didn't expect him to call after this evening. But he surprised me and phoned the following Monday.

'Now I do hope that you approve of Howard Hawks.'

And he invited me to a screening of *Only Angels Have Wings* the next evening at the Brattle in Cambridge. We went out for a pizza afterwards – and started that first-date ritual of telling each other about ourselves. So I learned about his less-than-happy childhood in Indianapolis and he heard about my less-than-happy childhood in Connecticut. When I dropped the fact that my father was currently on the run from the law, his eyes actually widened.

'Now that's what I call classy,' he said.

'I never thought of it that way,' I said, sounding just a little defensive.

'Oh, come on,' he said. 'A dad who is a fugitive. You should be writing this story, not telling it. I mean, it's irresistible stuff – especially since he can't have left you feeling all warm and cuddly about him.'

'You know, my mom always used that expression, "warm and cuddly".'

'But not with the emphasis on heavy irony that I bring to it.'

We saw each other again that weekend – a Bogart double-bill, *The Maltese Falcon* and *High Sierra* – and dinner at some cheap hamburger joint. On the third date – two Rohmer talkathons and a cheap Chinese place that was rather good all the same – he invited me back to his apartment. I accepted without hesitation.

Naturally I was nervous. So too was Theo. But when he

finally made the move, we both responded with a fervor that was surprising.

Afterwards he put on a Miles Davis album – 'Great post-coital stuff.' Fetching us a decent bottle of wine he let it be known that he was seriously falling for me.

'Now I know that, strategically, this is a dumb thing to say – because I'm supposed to play diffident and stand-offish and "don't crowd my space". But I'm not going to assume some role I don't want to assume. I'm going to give it to you straight, Jane: you're wonderful – and I'm a tough critic.'

When we have a need, we generally try to fill it. Theo Morgan did just that for me – and his declaration of intention didn't push me away. On the contrary I was ready to be in love again, ready to give up the isolation and solitude that had been so much a part of my life since David's death. For years I couldn't even imagine the embrace of another man. I had shut down in that department (not that there were men flinging themselves in my path). But here was a guy who was singular and different and so comfortable in his own quirky skin. I loved his wit, his mental gymnastics and the fact that he could riff wildly on any subject – from George Bush's ineptness in the English language, to an avant-garde jazzman of the 1950s named Jimmy Giuffre, to Joseph Strick's film versions of Joyce (of which he was a big fan), to a forgotten Miami crime writer named Charles Willeford, whom Theo considered on a par with Chandler.

The range of his interests was dazzling. I sensed he so loved and needed these private passions because they masked a terrible loneliness. A few weeks after we became lovers he admitted to me that he hadn't had a proper girlfriend for years, and that the one big love in his life – a performance artist named Constance van der Plante – had unceremoniously dumped him after he lost his job in New York.

'You know, I almost didn't go to that Sara Crowe dinner,' he said. 'Lucky me that I did.'

Sara was more than surprised when I told her that Theo and I were now an item.

'Well, this was certainly not what I had planned when I put the two of you together.'

'Don't sound so shocked. He's wonderful.'

'Of course he is,' she said, not sounding as though she meant it. 'The thing is, Jane . . . well, I just wouldn't have guessed that the two of you would have hit it off like that.'

'Life is always brimming with surprises.'

'You do sound happy.'

'And you *do* sound genuinely unsettled by this news,' I said.

'It's just taken me unawares.'

That reaction was pure Sara. She 'loved' her eccentric friends, but had this rather Victorian view of love: you can sleep with a mad artist when you're of a certain age . . . but you must settle down with the sort of sober, reasonable man who is going to keep up his end of the conjugal bargain and provide you with an upscale life. So the idea that I was now Theo Morgan's lover . . .

'I really do like Theo,' she said. 'And, of course, he has every opportunity of becoming a rather important writer on film. But – and this is not a heavily emphasized "but" – he really is not the sturdy foundation upon which . . .'

'I get your point,' I said.

'I didn't mean to cause any offense.'

'None taken,' I said.

Christy met Theo a few weeks later when she was back in Boston to give a reading at Eliot House, and thoroughly approved of him. We went out to dinner after the reading which, in that great tradition of most poetry readings, was only attended by around thirty interested people. It didn't matter that Christy had been another Pulitzer finalist the previous year for her second collection of poems. Poetry in our culture didn't have much in the way of commercial legs.

But Theo – much to my amazement – knew his stuff when it came to modern American poetry. Over dinner, he was exchanging critical comments with Christy on everyone from Hart Crane to Howard Nemerov to Auden. When he disappeared off to use the toilet, Christy flashed me a knowing smile and said: 'Well, I'd jump him if I was living here. But I like obsessive compulsives.'

'He's not that obsessive,' I said.

'Oh, yes, he is. But there's nothing wrong with being a brilliant case of arrested development. Like me, you teach writers. In some way or another, all writers are damaged – and believe me, I can spot damage in a nanosecond. But there's "bad damaged", psycho-boy stuff. Then there's "good damaged", out there but interesting. Your fella falls into the second category.'

'So you approve . . . with reservations.'

'I think he's super-smart and super-complicated. If you can handle that, marry the guy. But just know one thing: if you are thinking in any way of changing him, forget about it. He's got his own way of doing things, and he's not going to ever shift away from that.'

Christy was certainly right about Theo's rigidity. He refused to ever get up before midday. He started the day with a pot of extra-strong espresso. He would only use one specific brand of espresso coffee – Lavazza – and would only make it in one of those small old-fashioned stove-top espresso makers. While the coffee was brewing, he'd eat a bowl of a particularly sweet and unhealthy cereal called Captain Crunch – but he refused to do so with milk, as he completely abhorred it. Then he'd install himself at his desk and begin the two hours he passed every day working on his magnum opus, a comprehensive history of American cinema – 'about the most opinionated and idiosyncratic book ever written on the movies in this country' and one which (he was sure) would instantly make him the most renowned critic in the country . . . if he ever got around to finishing the damn thing. It wasn't that Theo lacked discipline or diligence. Rather the problem was that it was so insanely long: 2,130 pages of manuscript and he hadn't yet reached the 1960s. I'd read the section on Orson Welles – he did allow me that privilege, after I'd promised I wouldn't be overly critical – and I was amazed at how lucid and well-written and intelligent it was. Just as I was also dazzled by the scope of his ambition.

But when I asked to read more, he demurred, saying that he really shouldn't have shown me anything in the first place, that I might be opening myself up for disappointment with the rest of the book, and that he could have possibly 'tainted' the writing process by letting me have a glimpse. He got so agitated and downright stressed out as he told me this that I had to mask my shock at the way he talked himself into an obsessive-compulsive corner.

'I can never, *never* let you even touch the manuscript again,' he said, pacing up and down his studio room at a manic pace.

'Theo, there's really no need to get so upset about—'

'No need to get upset! No need to get upset! What do you know about upset? For four years, no one – *no one* – has touched this manuscript.'

'But you *gave* it to me, Theo. You asked *me* to read it. So I don't understand—'

'That's right, you *don't* understand what it means to—'

But before finishing the sentence he had grabbed his leather jacket and was out the door. I thought about following him, but decided it was best simply to let him be – especially as I was so damn thrown by this out-of-body scene that had just been perpetrated. I decided there and then that, if he didn't come back with some sort of explanation for this deeply disturbing act, I'd leave that night.

When he didn't show up after an hour I scribbled him a note:

I waited for you. I hope you are in a better place.

And I went home.

At this point in time we'd been going out together for around six weeks and though we had spent a few evenings at my apartment in Somerville we'd generally stayed at his place in Cambridge, as it was far more convenient for all the cinemas we attended around Harvard Square. Though we were seeing each other two to three nights a week we had an unspoken rule to never show up uninvited at the other person's residence. Until that night . . . when, around midnight, the doorbell rang. I hesitated before answering it, thinking: *Say this evening was the moment when the veneer of normality and romantic bliss finally cracked and from this moment on, I'll be seeing all the spooky, strange stuff he's so far kept from view?*

But another voice said: *And if you push him away now because of one small outburst, you'll be alone. And you don't want to be alone again.*

So I opened the door. He stood there, looking spent, his eyes brimming with fear and shame.

'That was . . . awful,' he said in a low whisper. 'And I'll understand if you slam the door on me. But . . .'

'Is this a little secret habit you've been holding back on me – insane rages over nothing?'

'I'm sorry. You don't know how sorry I am. Can I come inside, please?'

I hesitated. He said: 'Please, Jane . . .'

I nodded for him to follow me upstairs. Once in my living room he put his arms around me and told me that I was the best thing that had ever happened to him, that the last time he got one of these 'rages' was around two years ago. If it ever happened again he'd understand if I dropped him on the spot, and he'd do anything to make it up to me, and . . .

Though I did appreciate his contriteness, neediness is always a bit unnerving – even though I simultaneously found it reassuring. Perhaps because, at this point in time, I also needed him, and the way he made me feel wanted and central to his life. It's that old endless tug-of-war between wanting to feel essential to someone else and concurrently fearing this dependence because of the responsibility it imposes on you.

So I put my arms around him and told him there was nothing more to say about it, except: Let's go to bed.

Which we did. When I woke up the next morning at eight Theo had broken his 'never up before noon' rule and had cooked a huge breakfast for us. When he started singing his contriteness aria I silenced it with a kiss.

'There will never be a repeat performance,' he promised me.

'I'll hold you to that,' I said.

I went off to work, determined to try and put the entire incident behind me.

And Theo kept his word. There was no repeat performance in the months after this one-off incident. It wasn't as if he became ultra-cautious around me, always on his best behavior and never showing me his complexities. On the contrary he reverted to his vampire hours shortly thereafter – continuing to watch movies all night and never rising before noon, and steadfastly refusing my attempts to change his junk-food habits. But I wasn't complaining. If I'd had a particularly bad day at the university – or suddenly got hit with one of those black moods that occasionally overtook me – he instinctually understood how to manage the situation: attentive, but never oppressive. Knowing when not to crowd someone is never the simplest of learned lessons, but we both seemed adept at it. Whenever he was not around I genuinely missed him, just as I also liked the fact that we were never with each other day in, day out.

Eight months passed. One afternoon I arrived home to find a delivery van from Sony outside my door. The driver approached me as I climbed the steps to my front door, asked if I was Jane Howard, and said that he was delivering a 42-inch plasma television to me. When I said: 'There must be some mistake,' he showed me the dispatch order – and there, in fine print, was Theo's name.

'I really don't want such a big television,' I told him.

'Well then, you should have discussed this with the guy who ordered it for you.'

I asked the man to wait for five minutes while I ran upstairs and called Theo at the Harvard Film Archive.

'Are you insane?' I asked him.

'I think you know the answer to that question,' he said.

'Why would I want such a big damn television?'

'I thought we needed one.'

We. It was the first time he had used the first person plural to describe *us.*

'Trying to watch movies on that tiny little set of yours is kind of a sacrilege. So . . .'

'You should have talked this over with me first.'

'But that would have killed the surprise necessary in all surprises.'

'Don't those sets cost a fortune?'

'Isn't that still my problem, not ours?'

Again the use of the plural. Was this his way of telling me he was moving in?

'I don't know what to say . . .'

'Say nothing until I show up tonight with a new DVD transfer of Pressburger and Powell's *A Matter of Life and Death*. You will not believe the hallucinogenic use of early Technicolor . . .'

Theo was right: the television did fit into the corner space near the fireplace – and Pressburger and Powell's expressionistic film on war and the hereafter did seem visually lush when viewed on such an absurdly wide screen.

'I knew you'd love it,' Theo said.

'Just don't make a point of overwhelming me with such grand gestures again.'

'But I like overwhelming you. Anyway, we both know you're far too rational and practical for your own good.'

Ouch – but he was speaking the truth. I did weigh every small financial decision I made, and only indulged myself with something when I was sure that it was not profligate or whimsical. Theo would watch me try on clothes in shops and then reject them because they were 'too expensive' (even if it was just the Gap) or 'more of the same' (my way of saying I didn't need it).

'But you don't have a decent leather jacket,' he said when I saw one I liked in a shop on Newbury Street.

'I can live without one.'

'But you look cool in this one.'

'It's nearly four hundred dollars.'

'Indulge yourself.'

'I'm not comfortable indulging myself.'

'No kidding. But you should learn to do so a little more. Life is too damn short otherwise. And you don't have to continue to prove to the world that you're not your con-artist dad.'

'Remind me not to tell you my secrets again.'

'It's hardly a secret if the FBI knows it. Anyway, I'm just asking you to lighten up on yourself.'

'I don't do "guilt free",' I said. 'I wish I could, but my brain simply can't liberate itself from the idea that there is a price to everything.'

'You should be the one writing about Puritanism, not Grande Dame Sara.'

'But I do, I do. The Naturalists were as obsessed with our Puritan guilt as Hawthorne. Only they saw it from the perspective of our hyper-capitalist obsessions. Money and God and Guilt: the great all-American Trifecta. And none of us can totally shake loose from it.'

But I still bought the leather jacket, and I didn't make any further noises about the extravagant television that now dominated a corner of my living room. Nor did I balk when he suggested we spend a week at a 'groovy little retro hotel' in South Beach 'on my tab'.

'You have a "tab" in Miami?' I asked him.

'It's a turn of phrase.'

'Can you really afford to plump for a week?'

'Will you stop being so damn cautious. If I say I can plump for a week I can plump for a week.'

'Because I'd certainly be happy to plump for half of everything.'

'Thank you for draining my romantic offer of all its inherent romanticism.'

'That wasn't my intention. I was just being – OK, guilty as charged – cautious.'

But on our second night in Miami I did something incautious. After drinking far too many margaritas in some Mexican dive off Lincoln Road, we returned to our Art Deco room in our Art Deco hotel and proceeded to make very drunken love. When night woke up and I staggered into the bathroom and caught sight of the tequila aftershock in my eyes, a desperate thought hit me: I had failed to insert my diaphragm before we had collapsed onto the bed.

Counting backwards on my fingers I calculated (with mounting fear) that I was just three days off the middle of my cycle. I knew that if I articulated such worry to Theo it would cast a large uneasy shadow over the rest of our time in the Floridian sun. Surely the mathematics would work in my favor.

But as the week dragged on – and the thirty-six-hour deadline passed for the use of the morning-after pill – I tried to keep my anxiety out of Theo's sight. Bar one or two awkward moments when he sensed that I was troubled by something, I did keep my fear under wraps.

That is, until a month later, by which time I was two weeks late and vomiting every morning. I went to the local pharmacy and bought one of those home pregnancy tests. Back at my place I peed onto the touch paper. I put it in its accompanying vial. I went into the kitchen and made coffee. I returned five minutes later (even though it said to wait half an hour) to discover that it had turned pink. At this somewhat momentous – and thoroughly unwanted – juncture in my life a completely banal thought popped into my head:

Who decided that pink is the color of new-found maternity?

Another less-banal consideration followed:

Is this how destiny works?

Four

UNWANTED. IT'S SUCH a big bad word when placed in front of *pregnancy*. But I was certain of two things as soon as the home pregnancy test blushed into pink: I didn't want this baby and I couldn't bear the thought of terminating this baby.

Still, if I had been that adamant about not getting pregnant back in Miami, I would have made an excuse to slink off for a couple of hours, and found a doctor, and gulped down the morning-after pills, and then made further excuses as I dealt with two days of being absolutely ill and untouchable. But I didn't follow this course of action. And that begs the question: Was the *unwanted* something that I actually *wanted*?

'Of course you wanted to get pregnant,' Christy said when I called her in Oregon, waking her up at seven her time. This was not a smart move, as she hated early mornings – though when she heard the fear in my voice, she ceased telling me off and said: 'This must be something rather serious.' That's when I blurted out what had happened and how I had mathematically gambled on being just a few days off the middle of my cycle.

'You mean you *actually* relied on the rhythm method?'

'It was just an oversight on my part. A drunken oversight. And then—'

'Bullshit. Of course you wanted to get pregnant. You may not believe that, but it's the absolute total truth.'

'So what do I do now?'

'You either have the baby or you don't.'

'I'm not ready for motherhood.'

'Then find the name of your nearest abortion clinic and—'

'I just can't do that.'

'Then you have a real dilemma on your hands. What's the thing that's scaring you most? The lifetime commitment, the loss of personal freedom, the way this is going to permanently glue you and Theo together?'

'All of the above.'

'Well, you don't have to make a decision today.'

'But once I tell him, he's definitely involved in the decision.'

'Considering the mechanics of how one gets pregnant, the fact is, he's already very much involved in the decision . . . whatever that decision is. But before you go talking to him, you'd better figure out which way you're going to jump.'

The thing was, I'd resolved long ago in my head not to have children. But that resolution was borne out of my long-standing belief that a child would force me into a cul-de-sac of my own construction. And given that my parents had engaged in similar self-entrapment with my arrival in the world . . .

Then there was the all-encompassing question of Theo. Did I love him? I told myself that I did – just as he had made that declaration on several occasions. But underscoring these pronouncements was a deep-rooted worry: could I actually set up house with someone who kept vampire hours and needed a post-coital film fix? Would his hyper-organization make me feel as if I was living with a man whose behavior veered towards the monomaniacal, and for whom the movies were the greatest love of his life?

Rebutting these worries was my knowledge that if Theo committed to something (like his massive, still-growing book), his sense of responsibility was ferocious. Just as I also knew that ever since that bad outburst months earlier his behavior had been exemplary; that he was very conscious of keeping under control all the dark stuff lurking within.

Anyway, his heart was very much in the right place. I was

'the best thing that had ever happened' to him. I was 'the person who really got' him. I made him happy. How can you argue with that?

But I did fear telling him the news because it was bound to toss up so many damn questions, the biggest one being: *Why the hell didn't you tell me you might have screwed up on the contraception front? I mean, didn't I need to know about this as well?*

Theo was amazingly sanguine about all that. 'Accidents do happen – especially after five margaritas. Anyway, it's great news.'

'You sure about that?' I asked.

'I wouldn't say it if I wasn't. I mean, you do want to have a kid with me, yes?'

'Of course, of course,' I heard myself saying. As those words came out of my mouth I thought: *Here it is now. Your mind has been made up for you.*

'You do understand, Theo: this will change so much for us.'

'I'm cool with that.'

'Well, that's . . . wonderful.'

'But are you cool with all this, Jane?' he asked, catching the hesitancy in my voice.

'It's . . . a big step.'

'But we won't exactly be the first people who ever did it. And it's what I want. Because I want a life with you.'

'And I with you,' I said, even though I was still not so sure of that. How can you say such a definitive thing when you're still so tortured with doubt?

When I called Christy back and told her about Theo's enthusiasm for fatherhood – and for a proper everyday life with me – she said: 'Well, that's what you wanted to hear, right? And it speaks volumes for the fact that the guy isn't going to play the slacker dude and throw all the childcare responsibility your way. So this is genuinely good news.'

'I'm not so sure . . .'

'Then stop being a wuss and get a termination. You can always tell Theo that the baby miscarried. It happens all the time. I'm even happy to come back east and hold your hand and all that while you go through with it.'

'That's a big decision . . .'

'Indeed it is. But remember this Blinding Glimpse of the Obvious: once you have the kid, you have the kid.'

As George Orwell once noted, all clichés are fundamentally true, and the one which Christy just articulated made me realize that the decision was based on something I dealt with all the time in literature: *interpretation*. How do you choose to perceive a moral choice? Guilt is all rooted in the interpretation of events. It's predicated on your take on things. How willing are you to twist reality to your own version of events? What can you (or can't you) live with?

This was the deciding factor for me – the realization that if I didn't go through with this, it would bring me untold grief and would remain an open wound that wouldn't cauterize. Simultaneously, I knew that I so wanted to keep this child . . . even though it would bind me to Theo in ways that still made me uneasy.

But Theo's enthusiasm for impending fatherhood proved boundless. The guy acted like a 1950s dad-to-be – all but passing out cigars and telling just about everyone we met that I was pregnant. Unbeknownst to me he even called Sara Crowe to let her in on the good news. I received a rather tart return call from Sara who, in her best Katharine Hepburn voice, expressed bemusement at my news.

'Well, I suppose congratulations are in order.'

'I did mean to call you, but it seems Theo got there first,' I said, trying to disguise just how appalled I was that he was dispersing this news as if it belonged on Reuters.

'Theo was very touching,' she said, failing to mask the irony in her voice. 'He told me that inviting you over that night had changed his life and he wanted me to know that he would be "ever grateful" to me for that.'

'I see,' I said.

'No doubt you're enormously grateful to me too.'

'There's no need for sarcasm, Sara.'

'I didn't realize I was being sarcastic, Jane. Ruminative yes, but . . . well, it is your life.'

'That's right. It *is* my life. Thank you for your good wishes.'

That night, when Theo came over to my apartment, I raised the issue about him informing all comers that I was pregnant.

'You mean, you're embarrassed about this, *us*?'

'Hardly. It's just . . . if something went wrong, if I was to miscarry . . .'

'But that's not going to happen.'

'I hope not.'

'Then what's the big deal? Can I not be publicly pleased about this? And the very fact that Sara was the one who introduced us—'

'That's not the problem.'

'Then what is the problem?'

'I'm just jumpy, that's all.'

'We're going to be fine,' he said, putting his arms around me.

'Of course we are,' I said.

'And we do need to start thinking about when I move in with you.'

This last comment didn't come as a jolt. Once I told him I was pregnant, I knew it was just a matter of time before we began to discuss long-term domestic arrangements. And as I was the possessor of the far-bigger apartment . . .

'Given you've only got one bedroom – and your alcove office will probably double as the nursery – it's going to be a bit hard for me to move all my stuff into your place. So why don't I plan to sleep at your place but keep my apartment for work?'

I was actually relieved that he suggested this arrangement. It would minimize the disruption to my life and would also give us both necessary space. If my parents' marriage had taught me anything it was that a sense of entrapment is the death knell for any long-term relationship. Fair play to Theo for sensing that we'd benefit from the safety valve of time apart.

'I think that's very smart and grown up . . . and thank you for suggesting it,' I said.

A few days after our conversation, Theo borrowed a friend's van and showed up one morning with a few basic essentials: his standard collection of T-shirts and jeans, a leather jacket, two pairs of black Converse Hi-Top sneakers, some underwear and socks. It all fit neatly into the chest of drawers I'd found for him. He also showed up with an espresso maker and a special stainless-steel vacuum-packed jug in which he kept his Lavazza coffee. Then he decided to re-alphabetize my entire library. And rearrange all the shelves in the kitchen. And re-grout a corner of the shower tiles that had never been properly filled in. And decide that the front hallway could benefit from a re-sanding. And . . .

'If you start ironing my underwear,' I said, 'it's over.'

He did laugh at that, just as he also reorganized my closet and sanitized every drain.

'When did this propensity for home improvement hit you?' I asked.

'When I finally had a proper home to improve. But you're not complaining, are you?'

No, I wasn't complaining, as he wasn't one of those mad anal retentives who went berserk when a bathroom towel was out of alignment. And if I happened to forget to sort out the laundry or leave dishes in the sink . . . *hey presto*, Mr Clean rendered them clean.

'Be pleased you are with a guy who actually cares about such stuff,' Christy said when I phoned her from my office. 'It also means he actually cares about you. On which note – are you still having that daily rendezvous with the toilet bowl?'

Actually the chronic morning sickness had finally left me in peace. In its wake came a bout of manic itchiness. My obstetrician told me that it was a not-unusual side effect in pregnancy and gave me a cream that would relieve the sensation of bed bugs crawling beneath my skin. Theo insisted on rubbing it in every night and then we would sit down together and pore through all the baby and childcare books that I'd been able to find. And when I finally went to sleep, he would sit up until dawn, in thrall to one film after another on our big-screen television.

The itchiness disappeared after two weeks. When I hit the three-month mark and was starting to show, I decided that the moment was right to break the news of my pregnancy to the two people I was dreading telling most: my department chairman and my mother.

As I predicted, Professor Sanders was less than pleased to learn that I would be out on maternity leave in five months' time.

'Your timing could not be better,' he said, 'especially given the fact that you yourself were a last-minute replacement. Now I'm having to find a last-minute replacement for the last-minute replacement.'

'Five months' notice is not exactly last-minute.'

'In the academic world it is just that. Still, what must be

done will be done. And I do suppose that congratulations are in order.'

Word naturally got around the department in three nanoseconds. Marty Melcher cornered me in the hallway and said: 'So you're not a virgin after all.'

'You know, Professor – that comment could be considered a form of sexual harassment.'

'Or mere banter. It's all a question of interpretation, isn't it?'

'No, it's a question of civility – which you lack.'

'If you want to report me to the Sexual Ethics officer or whatever the hell she's called, be my guest. And you can further your reputation as a prig.'

'Then I'll do just that.'

'I apologize,' he said as I walked off. I stopped and turned back towards him.

'What is wrong with you?'

No comment from Marty Melcher. Just the uncomfortable look of a bully who'd been caught out.

Stephanie Peltz, meanwhile, had been researching my 'beau' (she'd been at a literature conference with Sara Crowe) and as she came up to me in the university café she said: 'What wonderful news! And what an *interesting* man as the father . . .'

I couldn't wait until I was free of New England State. But one stupendous thing did happen during that spring semester: Lorrie Quastoff was accepted as a transfer student at Harvard. This came about after I took Lorrie out for lunch at the beginning of term and mooted the idea with her.

'Harvard won't want a weirdo like me,' she said.

'My feeling is that they would want you very much. The big question will be: Do you want them?'

'It's kind of brainy, Harvard.'

'But so are you, Lorrie.'

'Don't think so.'

'Well, I do – and so does everyone else in the department here. You're our star and you need a more rigorous intellectual environment to—'

'Harvard won't like my autism.'

'They will like you because you are super-smart and have the grades to prove it. They will like you because I will make the necessary phone calls and write the sort of recommendation that will make them realize they would be insane to turn you down. But most of all they will like you because, once they interview you, they will see just how fantastic you are.'

'Fantastic rhymes with autistic,' she said.

'What's wrong with that?' I asked.

It took two further meetings before I could convince Lorrie to at least put in the application. When Harvard came back, inviting her for an interview, she told me: 'I don't want you putting in a good word for me there.'

'But it's how the world works, Lorrie.'

'Not the way I work. If Harvard wants me it's not because of my autism. I find out you've talked to them beforehand I'm turning them down.'

'Don't worry – I promise they won't hear from me now.'

The truth was, I'd already called the Harvard admissions office and the English Department chairman and raved to them about Lorrie Quastoff, saying they had to accept her. But Lorrie didn't need to know this. And I was very willing to follow her directive and stay silent from this point on, though (when requested by the Harvard admissions office) I did write her a forcefully argued letter of recommendation.

Her acceptance was big news at New England State, yet it was met with a muted response by the administration. Stephanie Peltz informed me that El Presidente was not pleased, stating that it would have been more prestigious for the university to have kept this gifted (read: autistic) student here. And why did that meddling damn woman Howard yet again show us up?

Right after Lorrie was accepted we went out for a celebratory lunch at the Charles Hotel in Cambridge. I couldn't drink for obvious physiological reasons, but I convinced Lorrie to have a glass of champagne. She looked a little fearful when the waiter poured it for her, and ran her finger nervously around the stem of the glass for the better part of a minute before I finally said to her: 'It won't turn you into a pumpkin.'

'But I might get drunk on it.'

'Not unless you're the cheapest date in history.'

'That's a joke, right?'

'Yes, that's a joke – but you really still do merit a glass of champagne. You don't get into Harvard every day. So come on, give it a try.'

With great care she lifted the glass to her lips, closed her eyes tightly as if expecting the liquid to melt her lips, and took the smallest of sips. Her eyes opened again. She seemed surprised that death had not befallen her, so she indulged in another small sip.

'It's not bad,' she said, 'but I think I prefer Diet Coke. You can't drink because of the baby, right?'

I'd only mentioned once to her that I was pregnant. This was some weeks back – and her reaction at the time was to simply nod and move on to the next subject. She said nothing more about it until now.

'That's right,' I said. 'The doctors advise you not to drink during a pregnancy.'

'You happy about having a baby?'

'I think so, yes,' I said.

'So you're not "over the moon" happy?'

'There's no such thing as "over the moon" happy, except in crappy women's magazines.'

'So you don't want to be pregnant?'

At moments like these it was hard to tell if Lorrie's ferocious directness was a byproduct of her autism or simply her inability ever to engage in subtle discourse (except when it came to discussing literature).

'I *am* pregnant,' I said.

'Bad answer.'

'I know I will love this baby when he or she arrives.'

'Everyone says your husband is a weirdo.'

'He's not my husband – and who's been calling him names?'

'I'm not telling.'

'He's not weird. In fact, you'd like him a lot.'

'Is he autistic too?'

'All men are a bit autistic.'

'But is he really autistic?'

Careful here.

'No, he's not.'

'What's love like?'

'Complicated.'

'Really complicated?'

'It depends, I guess . . .'

'You mean, like the professor you were sleeping with at Harvard?' Lorrie's face remained impassive. She didn't register the effect that comment had on me.

'How did you know about that?' I asked.

'Everyone knows about that. Was that love?'

'Yes, that was definitely love.'

'And because he was married it was complicated?'

'Yes, that made it complicated.'

'He died, right?'

222

'Yes, he died.'

'And you were sad?'

'Sadder than I've ever been.'

Again this comment didn't register on Lorrie's face. She simply nodded a lot.

'So Emily Dickinson is right. Love is the "hour of lead".'

'I think she was really talking about loss.'

'But love is loss, right?'

'In many cases, yes, love is just that.'

'So this new guy, the weirdo – you're going to end up losing him too, right?'

'That's not the plan. But you never know . . .'

'Doesn't sound like you love him the way you loved the professor.'

'It's . . . different, that's all.'

' "Different" isn't love.'

My mom did a variation on a similar theme when I brought Theo down to meet her a few weeks later. I had paved the way – correction: I had tried to pave the way – by calling her two weeks earlier and breaking the news that I was pregnant. As anticipated she took this badly – not just because I was 'with child, out of wedlock', but also because I was only telling her three months after I knew that I was to become a mother.

'You had to wait until now to tell me?' she asked, her hurt so evident.

'I wanted to be sure that the pregnancy would take.'

'No – you just didn't want to share this with me.'

Silence.

'And the father . . . ?' she finally asked.

I told her a bit about Theo.

'He sounds . . . different.'

Different. That word again.

'He is very original.'

'Now you have me even more worried.'

'So do you want to meet the guy?'

'Of course I want to meet Theo.'

Two weeks later, when Theo and I got into my Miata (my ever-expanding midsection let it be known that this little sports car would soon be traded in for something that could haul a baby around) I vowed to myself that I would do everything possible to make this weekend *chez* Mom work. But when we arrived at the family home on Pleasant Street in Old Greenwich, I could see Mom's visible shock when she first laid eyes on the man who had fathered her future grandchild. Just as I could see Theo take in the charmless decor, the peeling wallpaper, the furniture that hadn't been recovered in thirty years. Then there was the state of my mother, looking ever more withdrawn and battered by the world's indifference to her. I felt a desperate stab of guilt when I saw how shrunken and sad she seemed – and I did put my arms around her and tell her how wonderful it was to see her. But her reaction was one of detached bemusement. She actually tensed as I held her, then pushed me away with a slight but noticeable tap on the chest, her scolding eyes informing me: '*Don't you dare think that, for the benefit of this guy, you can act like we're close.*' The fissure between us was so deeply established that our relationship had become nothing more than a mass of defensiveness and barely concealed hurt.

'So you're the fella,' my mom said, looking Theo over in a deliberate manner.

'Yes, ma'am,' Theo said, all smiles. 'I'm the fella.'

'Well, lucky you.'

Theo proved very adept at handling such comments and keeping the atmosphere light and free of potential conflict.

'You know, Jane once told her father and me that she would

never get married and never have children,' Mom said over the meatloaf dinner she had made us.

I knew that Mom would bring up this damn story again, waiting for the opportune moment to salt the wound. But I had already prepared Theo by telling him all about it in advance of our arrival. He dealt with it wonderfully. After hearing her out he said: 'That is a sad story, Mrs Howard. But guess what? I told the same thing to my parents – and they didn't break up. So I guess it really comes down to how good or bad the marriage is in the first place. Or how much guilt you want to apportion to someone else for your own problems.'

He said all this with a smile on his face. I could see that Mom was immediately disarmed by the tough talk behind the affable tone. When he excused himself to use the bathroom she leaned over and whispered: 'You briefed him before he came here, didn't you?'

'I don't know what you're talking about, Mom.'

'You let him know I was bound to tell that story.'

'You don't think that what he said had more than a grain of truth to it?'

'He doesn't understand the entire ramifications—'

'Of something that happened sixteen years ago and about which you've made me feel horrible ever since? And nothing, *nothing*, I have ever done for you will ever change your need to continually return to that damn evening and blame me for something that was between you and Dad.'

'We were doing just fine until—'

'Oh, Jesus, will you ever stop? I am so sick of being treated like the greatest mistake in your life.'

'You dare accuse me of hating you.'

'Well, you sure as hell don't—'

Suddenly I saw Theo standing in the doorway.

'Am I interrupting something?' he asked.

There was an embarrassed silence which my mother broke.

'I was just informing Jane that I have so many pressing things to do tomorrow that it's best if you leave in the morning.'

There was another embarrassed silence.

'No problem, ma'am,' Theo said, all smiles.

'Yes, there is a damn problem,' I said. 'We drove all the way down here so I could introduce you to—'

'Jane . . .' Theo said calmly. 'Let it be.'

'You are a very sensible young man,' my mother said, standing up. 'I wish you well.'

And she went upstairs.

I sat at the kitchen table and put my head in my hands. Theo came over and put his arm around me and said: 'Let's vote with our feet and get out of here now.'

Half an hour later we were checked into a Hilton hotel on the outskirts of Stamford. It was modern and sterile, but the bed was huge and the bathtub deep and I sat immersed in very hot water for half an hour, trying to digest what had just happened. At one point Theo came in and sat on the edge of the bath and said: 'Look at it this way: you'll never need to feel guilty about not seeing her again. Being cast out does have its fringe benefits.'

'She didn't even come downstairs and say anything when we were leaving.'

'Because she wanted you to run upstairs and beg her forgiveness and tell her you'd try to be a good little girl again and all that other guilt-trip shit she has probably been pulling on you since the year dot. But you let it be known that you were no longer playing that game – for which I congratulate you. It's long overdue.'

'You're wonderful,' I said, taking his hand.

'Yes,' he said. 'I am.'

When we returned to Cambridge the next day I slipped into a serious funk. We all want to fix things. Just as we all believe that so much in life can be rectified. *Mend fences, build bridges, reach out, engage in mutual healing.* The modern American lexicon is brimming with the language of reconciliation – because, *damn it*, we are the 'can do' nation. Surely we can sidestep tragedy and the insoluble gulfs between people, as there always has to be some solution to life's interpersonal conundrums. The problem with this viewpoint is that it refuses to acknowledge that there are things we simply cannot solve – that, like it or not, we can never make better that which has gone so terribly wrong.

I stayed in that funk for days. It lifted when I received an advance finished copy of my book. I held it in my hand and opened it up and heard the quiet but noticeable crackle of newly bound pages being turned for the first time. As I glanced through the hundred thousand words contained within I thought to myself: *I've actually done all this*, and wondered what it all meant in the great scheme of things.

Theo was even more excited than I was at the sight of the published tome.

'You should be jumping up and down, swigging champagne from the bottle,' he said.

'Not exactly the best thing for a woman in my state.'

'At least be thrilled by the achievement.'

'I am,' I said.

'That's why you sound so damn melancholic right now.'

'It's just . . .'

'Jane, there's nothing you can do to make the woman like you.'

Theo read the book in one sitting and told me it was brilliant.

'I wouldn't go that far,' I said.

'Because you can't handle the idea that anything you've done is in any way good.'

'That's me, Ms Self-Doubt.'

'Well, stop doubting. It's a fantastic piece of scholarship.'

'It's just an academic book.'

'Where did you learn to be so hard on yourself?'

'Where did you learn how to be so nice?'

'I've always been nice.'

I couldn't argue with that. For all his quirks and oddities, Theo remained, fundamentally, a very good guy – and one who, I had come to recognize, could cope with my quirks, my permanent sense of doubt. Perhaps one of the greatest surprises in temporal existence is actually finding yourself outside of the uncertainty and struggle that so characterizes most of our time here. It's a rare interlude – and at least I recognized it as such, and was able, for a while, to keep that nagging voice of inner uncertainty well and truly muzzled.

Even the birth of my daughter didn't turn into the 'Götterdämmerung' that I had always feared. On the contrary, there was something rather textbook about the whole process. On the morning of July 24th I got up to make tea and suddenly felt a telltale stream of liquid cascading down my leg. I didn't panic or fall into a state of advanced fear. I simply walked back into the bedroom and told Theo: 'Time to get up – my waters have just broken.'

Though he'd only fallen into bed two hours earlier after an all-night Fritz Lang marathon, he was wide awake and dressed in about sixty seconds. He grabbed a bathrobe for me and the bag that (true to his hyper-organizational needs) he had packed for me a week earlier. We made it across town to Brigham and Women's Hospital in less than a half-hour. Within sixty minutes I was checked in and wired up and being given an epidural. Four hours later, Emily arrived in the world.

It's strange being told to push and heave when the entire lower half of your body is numb. It's strange to glance upwards at the mirror that has been strategically placed in front of your otherwise covered legs and watch as this blooded thing is slowly yanked out of you. But the strangest of all sensations is the moment after you have been freed of the baby – and the baby of you – and you are handed this tiny shriveled creature to hold for the first time . . . and you feel a mixture of unbelievable instant love and desperate fear. The love is overwhelming – because, simply put, this is your child. But the fear is also immense, vast. Fear of not being up to the task. Fear of not being able to make her happy. Fear of letting her down. Fear – quite simply – of not getting it right.

But then the baby starts to cry and you clutch her to you. Amidst the elation and exhaustion of just having been delivered of a child and having entered that brave new world of being a mother, another thought takes hold: *I will try to do my very best for you.*

Happily, Theo didn't video the birth as he had threatened to do. As I held Emily (we'd chosen this name long before her birth) close to me he crouched down beside us and stroked her head and clutched my hand and whispered to his new daughter: 'Welcome to life.'

Then he told me again just how much he loved me. And I said how much I loved him.

Only much later did I realize that this was the last time we ever said those words to each other.

Five

Snapshots from Emily's first eighteen months.

Bringing her home from the hospital and me standing watch by her crib all the first night, out of fear that something might happen to her.

Discovering that my daughter's toothless gums were made of reinforced steel when they snapped down on my nipple.

Emily discovering the pleasures of ice cream for the first time. When I gave her a small spoonful of vanilla at age eight weeks her reaction – after shock at the cold – was a very noticeable smile.

A bout of colic which kept her awake all night for the better part of two weeks and had me in a state of absolute despair, as I walked the floor with her from midnight to dawn every one of those fourteen days, willing her to sleep and failing miserably.

Finally getting back to work after twelve weeks' maternity leave and having to drop Emily off in a crèche for the first time and expecting her to cry vehemently . . . but my daughter handling the transition with absolute serenity.

Buying Emily a set of classic wooden building blocks, all engraved with letters of the alphabet. 'Can you make a word?' I ask her – and she laughs and throws a block across the room.

Emily crawling across the living room for the first time to where I'm grading papers and picking up a book on the floor, holding it upside down and saying her first word: *Mommy*.

Emily picking up a pen and scrawling lines on a blank pad and saying her second word: *Word*.

Emily coming down with a virulent strain of the flu, her temperature rising to 106 degrees, the pediatrician making a middle-of-the-night house call and warning me that she might have to be admitted to hospital if the fever doesn't break in twenty-four hours, and my daughter wimpering as the fever makes her breathing irregular and she can't yet articulate in language just how horrible she now feels.

The fever finally breaking and Emily taking more than a week to get back to her normal self and my exhaustion manifesting itself when I nod off in a departmental meeting.

Theo – on one of the few evenings he is at home – actually spending time with his daughter and screening for her the original 1937 *Snow White and the Seven Dwarfs*, and giving her a five-minute lecture about the 'contextual importance' (yes, he actually used those words) of the film in the history of cinematic animation.

Emily's first full sentence some weeks later: '*Daddy not here.*'

Because Daddy was hardly ever *here*.

That was the prevailing subtext of Emily's first year and a half: her father's increased absences. It was a gradual yet noticeable disengagement. Within the first week of Emily returning home – and, like all newborn babies, treating us to ongoing sleep disruption – Theo began to retreat to his apartment, saying that he had no choice but to press on with the writing of his book.

'Well, you could do that here,' I said. 'We did set up a small office for you.'

'But I've got all my research stuff back at the apartment.'

'All of your research stuff is on the internet. And since we also installed wireless here for you . . .'

'The vibe isn't right here for the sort of writing I have to do. And the broken nights are killing me.'

'Emily only wakes for around a half-hour. And she's such a wonderful child.'

231

'I need my eight hours.'

'And I don't?'

'Of course you do. But you're not working right now and I am. And if I don't sleep . . .'

Why did I give in to this argument? Possibly because he was the guy going out to a job every day, while I was still staying at home, on maternity leave. So yes, I didn't have to be as mentally alert as Theo did right now. Though I mentioned several times that I would like him to spend more time with us, I also didn't push the issue. I was simply too damn tired to start a fight with him. But I also sensed that – with the tangible arrival of his very tangible daughter – the reality of parenthood had caught him unawares. For all his pre-natal talk about so wanting to play the dad, the very fact that Emily was now omnipresent in our lives had thrown him. Could it be that we say we want something, even if we secretly doubt that we do? As I had been guilty of this same sort of behavioral pattern throughout my life, I couldn't point an angry finger in Theo's direction – not just now anyway, as I was hoping that his need to run away was just a temporary phase.

Once Emily began to embrace the idea of nine uninter-rupted hours of sleep, Theo did return to the apartment. He even started taking Emily for walks in her stroller, to occasionally bathe and change her, to get down on the floor with her and play with her collection of toys, and generally make her laugh. But there was a concurrent detachment in his relationship with me. It was a subtle yet noticeable one. We still chatted, we still shared meals and kept each other abreast of stuff going on in our respective lives. However, a certain chill had crept into our time together – and whenever I asked Theo if anything was troubling him, he always dodged the issue.

'There's no problem,' he said one evening after he had

fallen silent for several minutes over dinner and I had commented that such Pinter-esque pauses were a tad unnerving.

'In the theater Pinter's pauses never last more than five beats,' he countered.

'Which is why the five minutes we just spent in absolute silence strikes me as worrying.'

'I'm not worried about anything,' he said, simultaneously avoiding my gaze.

'Is something wrong, Theo?'

'Why would there be anything wrong?'

'I sense your detachment from this household, from us.'

'That's also news to me. I mean, I'm here every night.'

'But you seem preoccupied.'

'As do you.'

'In what way?'

'Your mind is frequently elsewhere,' he said.

'It's called juggling parenthood with a full-time career.'

'Which I'm doing as well.'

'Not as much as me.'

'Oh, please, we're not going to play the "Who's doing more around here" game.'

'Well, you did leave me completely alone during the first eight weeks of Emily's life.'

'That's not true. I slept elsewhere because we agreed that, as I was the one who was still working—'

'We didn't agree that. You simply decided to absent yourself and I was stupid enough to go along with it.'

'If you were that upset about it, you should have said something at the time.'

Checkmate. He had me on that one. And he damn well knew why I hadn't brought up his absences at the time – because I was terrified of alienating him, because in my postnatal, sleep-deprived zombie state I had this ever-augmenting fear that he would cut us loose if I pushed him too far. Perhaps that's what the smile now told me: *We're not married . . . we don't own anything together . . . I could walk away any time I wanted to . . .*

The smile moved from the supercilious to the reconciliatory.

'If there's a problem between us,' he said, 'don't be shy. Just tell me. I don't want you to feel there's any sort of disconnection between us.'

But the disconnection continued to deepen. When I returned to work, I dropped Emily off every morning at the crèche, as Theo was still never getting up before midday. The thing was, she had to be collected every afternoon at three p.m. As the classes I taught fell on Monday, Wednesday and Friday and continued on until four p.m., it had been agreed that Theo would pick her up from the crèche in Cambridge and bring her back to his office at the Harvard Film Archive until I arrived there at five-thirty.

But after three weeks of this schedule he informed me one evening: 'I can't do the pick-ups any more.'

'Why not?' I said, trying to mask my surprise.

'It's just not working out.'

'In what way is it "not working out"?'

'She demands a lot – which I'm happy to give, but not during work time.'

'Define "demands a lot".'

'"Demands a lot", as in "constant attention", as in "having to feed and change her", as in "crying and disturbing my co-workers", as in "not being able to duck away for the ninety minutes she's at the office".'

'Theo, the deal between us was—'

'I know what the deal *was*. The thing is, deals are there to be renegotiated. I need to renegotiate this one.'

'Well, it's not that simple.'

'It is that simple. You wouldn't bring her into one of your classes, so why should I bring her into the archive?'

'Because I'm bringing her to the crèche five mornings a week and picking her up from the crèche two afternoons a week. Because I look after her every evening, as you work until at least nine or ten, as well as most of the weekend. And I'm happy to have all this time with her – because she is such a fantastic kid. So the only thing I ask of you is those ninety minutes you spend with her on the three afternoons when I'm teaching. It's a pretty good deal, Theo . . .'

'It's unworkable. What we need to find is some nice, competent, responsible childminder who's willing to pick Emily up—'

'That's going to cost us at least one hundred and fifty dollars a week.'

'We can afford that.'

'You mean, *I* can afford that.'

'Well, you do earn more than me – and you must still have some money in the bank.'

'Not that much money.'

'Well, you did blow all that money on an apartment.'

I stared at him, amazed at that last comment.

'Did you hear what you just said to me?' I asked.

He laughed, then walked out the door. He didn't return for two days, during which time I had no choice but to approach a childcare agency and hire a very nice Colombian woman named Julia to help me out. It was decided between us that she would collect Emily from the crèche and look after her until seven p.m. every evening, during which time she'd also cook and deal with laundry. Julia was thirty-five, married with three kids and living in Jamaica Plain; an American resident for ten years who still hadn't thoroughly mastered the English language. She was very determined to do everything possible to please me and to get as many hours from me as she could. As she bluntly told me: 'I need the money.' And I was happy to give her the extra hours – to hell with the cost – because it freed up the entire afternoon portion of my schedule and allowed me more time to deal with student papers and administrative trivia and also start planning the next book: what I hoped would be a major critical study of Sinclair Lewis.

So we agreed a salary of $350 for twenty hours per week and suddenly I was freed of the hassle of having to race across town to collect Emily right after my afternoon classes. In turn, Theo was completely free of any domestic responsibility whatsoever. As soon as I had hired Julia I called him at his apartment, got the answerphone and left the message: 'All right, you win, we have a childminder who will deal with all the afternoons. Whether or not you want to return to us is completely up to you.'

He was back in the apartment that night, bearing flowers, a very cute denim jacket for Emily, a bottle of champagne and no apology for having left two days earlier. This was, I had come to discover, Theo's style. He'd never raise his voice or hector or demand. If he didn't like something or felt cornered by a possible domestic obligation, he'd react by simply vanishing from view or letting it be known through passive-aggressive means that it was pointless to argue with him.

So when I asked him: 'Is this sort of disappearing act going to be a feature of our domestic repertoire?' he let it be known that he wouldn't talk about it. What's more he wasn't going to explain his feelings on the matter. Take it or leave it.

'So why create the hassle, Jane?'

'Because this is supposed to be a partnership – and in a partnership we share responsibility.'

'No partnership is ever based on fifty-fifty shared responsibility. Anyway we had a problem with the afternoon pick-up arrangements and now they're sorted out. And by the way, I'm happy to contribute a hundred and seventy-five bucks towards the cost of Julia. That's fifty-fifty, if my math hasn't failed me.'

'I won't put up with you vanishing like that again.'

'You know, Jane, threats do not become you.'

When I tried to continue the conversation he simply walked out of the room and played with Emily in her nursery. When he returned half an hour later I said: 'I can't live this way.'

'Live what way?'

'You leaving the room every time we—'

He left the room again, returning to Emily's nursery. I stormed in after him and shouted: 'Will you please pay me the minor courtesy of at least engaging with me.'

The result of this angry comment was a squall from Emily. My loud voice had frightened her. Theo said nothing. He just scooped his daughter up in his arms and rocked her and gave me a quiet reproving look. At that moment I sensed that I would never be able to win with this man.

But what exactly was I trying to *win*? All domestic relationships become, in one way or another, exercises in power. Even if you tell yourself you're not trying to control another person, you are, in some way, trying to put your imprint onto the domestic situation. The maddening thing about Theo was that he would never really meet me halfway but would use stratagems that made me seem unreasonable and eventually allowed his way of operating to prevail. If I raised objections he would simply absent himself. He was playing a game similar to the one that my father practiced throughout his life: *My way or the highway.* Only unlike Dad, Theo got what he wanted through silence, stealth and cunning. Though I must admit that the end result in this case – a part-time nanny – was not entirely disagreeable for me.

Once the childcare issue was resolved, Theo was very much around again. He came home most nights about eight. He'd often make dinner and always spent some time with Emily. We'd hang out until midnight and continued to make love at least twice a week. Whether or not we had sex I'd be asleep by twelve-thirty and up with Emily by six-thirty. After she passed the three-month mark she did us a great ongoing service by sleeping soundly for ten hours a night. Theo was very good about dealing with her if she happened to wake up sometime in the middle of the night, and also perfected a way of crawling into bed beside me at four a.m. without stirring me. He would always sleep with earplugs, so he would miss her early-morning wake-up call. All credit to our wonderful daughter, as she never wailed herself awake. Perhaps I'm reading far too much into all this, but what always impressed me from the start with Emily was the way she made her needs known, yet did so in a manner that wasn't whiny or hyper-demanding. She was also a great smiler and greeted me every morning with a big beaming grin. It made all other worldly concerns fall away for a few necessary moments, reminding me that, yes, parenthood was worth all its incumbent pressures and concerns.

Right before her birth I'd traded in my little Mazda for a VW Touareg. I bought a year-old model, but it still meant adding an additional $8,000 to augment the price I was getting for a trade-in. More tellingly it meant accepting that I was now an SUV-driving parent.

Theo didn't try to dissuade me out of buying the car.

'Hey, it's not a station wagon and it doesn't have the "right on" prigginess of one of those Toyota hybrids. Fact is, it's a sharp-looking car – and I sure as hell won't be ashamed to be seen in it.'

But it was me who was driving it every day as it was me who

was bringing Emily to her crèche. Drop-off time eight-thirty a.m. and no earlier – and outside this upscale day-care center off Porter Square, just across the city line into Cambridge, there were always a good two-dozen professional mothers (and no more than three dads), all lined up with the kids in strollers, all dressed for work, all glancing at their watches, all ready to dash as soon as the doors opened and the children could be deposited inside. Then we could race to our respective workplaces and begin the daily well-paid grind – all the while fretting about the dilemma of balancing career and children, and the attendant pressures of sustaining a relationship, and telling yourself that, one of these days, you'll actually feel fulfilled by it all.

But my fretting was more bound up in the realization that I was dodging a basic truth about my relationship with Theo: I was very much out of love with him. Or maybe I should rephrase that sentence as an interrogative one: Was I ever really in love with him, and would I still be with him now if Emily hadn't entered our lives?

Perhaps this question was predicated on another: Was he actually in love with me? As Emily approached her first birthday and I was beginning to think that Theo and I had established a decent rhythm between us, he switched course and began not showing up again for several nights in a row. What made this especially maddening was the fact that he didn't phone me to say where he was and kept his cellphone off just to infuriate me more – or, at least, that's the way it seemed to me. After one particular stint of seventy-two hours he did deign to answer one of my increasingly frantic calls. His reaction was deadpan: 'I'm at home, writing.'

'And you couldn't bother to simply call me and tell me where you were? I mean, I must have left you a dozen messages on your landline and your cell.'

'I turned both off. No distractions, that sort of thing.'

'I'm a distraction?'

'You sound stressed.'

'Of course I'm stressed. You went AWOL.'

'If you had bothered to look at the message I left . . .'

'I saw no message.'

'Maybe you weren't looking in the right place.'

'I tore the house apart, seeing if you left me anything.'

Actually I'd only checked the kitchen counter and the stand in the hallway where we usually left each other notes. I hadn't looked in . . .

'The bedroom,' Theo said. 'Your side table, underneath the lamp.'

I put down the phone and walked briskly into the bedroom. As soon as I hit the doorway I looked directly at my bedside table. There, stuck halfway under the lamp in a way that left it half-hidden, was the note. I pulled it out. It read:

Going to my place to write.

That was it: no name, no signature, no further explanation.

I came back into the living room and picked up the phone again.

'All right, I found it. But is there any reason why you couldn't have put it in a more visible place?'

'Don't blame me for you not seeing it.'

'I blame you for nothing, Theo. I just wish you treated this relationship like a relationship – and not like a convenience station you stop by whenever you need sex or a home-cooked meal.'

But the next night he showed up before I came home from work and organized a small Thai feast from a local restaurant. A few days later, he took Emily off for a long Saturday afternoon at the zoo, then cooked me an Italian dinner while

240

regaling me with amusing anecdotes about Welles and Huston and Ford and Hawks and all the other great directors he so admired. And when, out of nowhere, he put his arms around me and told me I was wonderful . . . well, for the remainder of the evening I had a glimpse of how good things could be between us. Until all my doubts flooded in again.

'When will you ever accept the fact that it's all so damn flawed, and that you will always be hit with doubt?' Christy asked me one evening when she rang close to midnight and admitted that she herself was nursing a bruised heart. ('And no, it's not another dumbshit biker – the guy had some class and some smarts, which makes it all the worse.')

'So what you're saying is: be happy with what you have, despite its flaws.'

'No,' Christy said, 'my thought for the day is: you have an interesting career which will get more interesting once you are liberated from that university. You live with an interesting man who may not be the ideal partner but certainly can't be described as boring. To add the maraschino cherry to the cake, you have a beautiful daughter – and you are managing to walk that tightrope between professional life and motherhood that makes you the envy of the majority of women I know, this one included.'

'Now that's news to me. I mean, you've always been so adamant about not having children.'

'That doesn't mean I'm not in constant conflict about it. I mean, look at you. I know you consider Emily—'

'The best thing that ever happened to me,' I said, finishing her sentence.

'There you go. And I know full well that, fifteen years from now, if I have let the moment pass, I might well rue the fact that my independence was far more important than the gamble which is parenthood.'

241

'You might not rue it.'

'We all end up rueing everything. It's the nature of this thing we call "our condition". *Could, but didn't . . . Wanted to, but stopped myself . . .* All the damn statements of regret we can never dodge.'

Maybe Christy was right. Maybe it was best to embrace the ambivalence that hovered over everything. Maybe that which was flawed was also that which was always interesting.

But, as I told Christy, if there was one thing about which I was never ambivalent it was Emily. No matter how frustrated I would get with Theo, or with the inanity of university politics, my daughter would smile at me or say something completely disarming, or would simply snuggle up against me and lift me out of the pettiness and diffidences that characterize so much of life.

'Mommy . . . Daddy . . . good,' Emily said one evening as Theo and I sat chatting over the remains of our dinner and laughing at some absurdity he'd overheard in a coffee shop that afternoon.

'Yes, you're right,' Theo said. 'Mommy and Daddy *are* good.'

I took his hand. I smiled.

Ten days later, he came home with an announcement: He had just gone into business with a woman named Adrienne Clegg.

After that, Mommy and Daddy were never good again.

Six

ADRIENNE CLEGG. From the moment Theo brought her home, I couldn't stand her. Check that: I loathed her. Because, from the outset, I could see that she would bring us nothing but grief.

To admit that you loathe someone is to admit failure. Hate is such an extreme emotion. Once in its grip, you often find yourself wondering whether it's really worth despising someone that much. My father might have cost me my job at Freedom Mutual and left me feeling betrayed, but I still couldn't bring myself to hate him. That would have been almost like hating myself.

Adrienne Clegg was different. She wasn't family – and in her own insidious way she helped unpick the entire fabric of the life that I had created for myself. So yes, I hated her – and in turn I loathed myself for not blocking, from the outset, her invasive attack on our little family.

Perhaps that remains the hardest thing to stomach – the fact that, as soon as I met her, I knew she was trouble. So why didn't I fight back far earlier? What was it in me that allowed her to visit such damage on us?

But I'm getting ahead of myself here.

Adrienne Clegg. She was in her early forties. Tall. Rail thin. Electric-red curly hair that was worn tightly around her head. Skin that seemed perma-tanned. ('I'm one-quarter Inca Indian,' she once told me.) A woman who always wore leather and huge ostentatious earrings and chunky rings on six of her ten fingers. She came across as a cross between a biker chick and one of those relentlessly ambitious Manhattan women who are constantly on the make.

The thing was, Adrienne Clegg had struck out in Manhattan. Just as she had struck out in LA and in London. But then she landed herself in Boston. In that happenstantial way of things, she met Theo right at the moment when he had connected with a local filmmaker named Stuart Tompkins. And Stuart had just made, for around $10,000, a violent/comic 'Bonnie and Clyde Go Insane' movie set in a college fraternity. It was called *Delta Kappa Gangster* – a terrible title. Stuart was a classic movie geek. Like Theo he was in his early thirties. Like Theo he lived in a tiny apartment and also subsisted on a diet of fast and frozen food. But there all comparisons ended. Stuart was tall. Seriously tall and seriously thin, as in six foot five and one hundred and thirty pounds. He had serious acne. ('His face is like a penicillin culture,' Theo noted.) He also had serious body odor. Fortunately I was never invited over to his apartment. Theo – being his new best friend – did get asked to drop by one evening and informed me later that night that he would never repeat the experience. There were dishes that hadn't been washed in six months, cruddy underwear strewn across the floor, a toilet that hadn't been cleaned since 9/11, and the pervasive stench of someone who didn't take personal hygiene very seriously.

Given Theo's anal obsessions with order and cleanliness, it wasn't at all surprising that he returned from his first – and only – visit to *chez* Stuart looking as though he was in an advanced state of toxic shock.

'Never doing that again,' he said, actually opening a bottle of my eau de cologne – my only bottle of eau de cologne – and holding it under his nose to sniff in its cleansing floral scent. 'It was like walking into a septic tank. But the guy has made a great little movie which is going to make me a considerable amount of money.'

'*Make* me *a considerable amount of money*.' As I reflected back on all this much later on, I realized that, from the outset, Theo saw this potential windfall as benefiting him and him alone.

Full credit to Theo – I would never have thought that more than ten people would ever dream of watching *Delta Kappa Gangster*. But he immediately saw its big potential and also considered Stuart to be a major talent, 'if I can ever get him to wash'.

He'd met Stuart at the archive where he had a part-time job in the film library and, like Theo, thought nothing of watching movies for ten hours a day. As it turned out, Stuart had used a very small inheritance from 'a crazy aunt' ('I mean, she had to be crazy to leave me anything') to finance this eighty-minute horror fest. He'd shot it on HDV on the campus of a local community college in Marblehead. All the actors were locals, everyone worked for a $300 fee and Stuart shot the entire movie in ten days. He also knew a couple of budding special-effects guys who looked upon this film as a chance to try out, on a minuscule budget, some of their more outlandish ideas.

That was the first thing that struck me about *Delta Kappa Gangster*: its absolute outlandishness and crudity. Theo insisted on screening it for me at home. He even made a massive bowl of popcorn for us to munch while we watched the damn thing. It was, in its own strange way, riveting stuff. Behind the primitivism of much of the acting and the low-budget effects was a noticeable flair when it came to grabbing the audience by certain soft parts of the anatomy and forcing them to pay attention.

The story was a straightforward horror-cheapie idea: a homecoming weekend at a particularly moronic fraternity turns most gory when a geek and his goth girlfriend wreak havoc on the jocks who once hounded him. The geek and the goth become avenging angels and devise horrible deaths for the football-playing, beer-swigging stooges: electrocution, eye-gouging, defenestration onto a spiked fence, impromptu brain surgery with an electric drill, even yanking out a tongue with a handy pair of pliers . . .

And then they start robbing banks.

The film's violence, though utterly extreme, was also executed with a maniacally black wit. Stuart and his colleagues poured on the gore but they did so with such brio and subversive anarchy that you couldn't help but be amused by it all – while simultaneously feeling uncomfortable about being so taken in by such slasher stuff.

What intrigued me even more was the film's overall subtext: how it could be viewed as an attack on the sort of rabid anti-intellectualism that has always been a component of American life. It was the ultimate Geek's Revenge movie – the kid who had always been ridiculed and picked on turning the tables against the arrogant, vapid morons who found his bookishness a threat. As much as I was appalled by the rabid violence, the part of me which had always loathed bullies was cheering the madman on.

'Well, that certainly got my attention,' I said as the final credits rolled. 'Now all I need is three steadying vodkas and a cleansing hot shower.'

'It's a masterpiece,' Theo said.

'I wouldn't go that far.'

'I would. You just don't run into this sort of talent every day.'

'It's a pretty unrefined talent.'

'Yeah, that's what makes him so interesting. He's a primitive – with the body odor to match.'

'Yes, it does have a decided stench to it.'

'What you also need to know is that this kind of movie sells.

Properly distributed it will be a huge hit in every college town in the country. Even the fraternity types will dig it. And when it gets released on DVD . . . I'll be driving a Porsche.'

'I can't exactly see you in a Porsche, Theo.'

'I was being metaphoric. I promise you, this film will do gangbusters. All I need to get things rolling is about fifty grand.'

'And where do you propose to find that?'

'Well, I was hoping that you might like to invest in the project . . .'

I knew this pitch was coming, but it still made me feel desperately uneasy.

'I don't really have fifty thousand to spend on something like that.'

'Yes, you do.'

'How can you say that?'

'Because I've seen your bank statements.'

'You've been going through my papers?'

'Hey, lose the accusatory tone. Of course I haven't been rifling through your papers. But last month, when you were doing your accounts, you did have all the bank statements on your desk . . .'

'And you just had to look them over.'

'If you leave stuff on a desk for all to see, it will get seen.'

'Only if someone decides to take a look themselves – which is what you did, Theo. I mean, you leave your journal on your desk all the time and I have never, *ever* opened it.'

'Well, why would you? It's a closed book. But paperwork scattered on a desk . . .'

'Are we really going to get into a semantical debate here about what constitutes a breach of privacy?'

'The thing is, I know you have around sixty-eight thousand left in the bank.'

'That's money I've saved over the years, month by month.'

'Well, it's just sitting in some account. And if you were to go into partnership with me and Adrienne . . .'

That was the first time he ever mentioned her name.

'Who's Adrienne?'

'Adrienne Clegg. This absolutely brilliant film distributor I'm planning to work with.'

'I see,' I said, my tone chilly. 'And when exactly did you meet this "absolutely brilliant film distributor"?'

'Don't worry – I'm not fucking her.'

'Well, that makes my day.'

'I met her through Stuart. He met her at this big horror festival in Bratislava last year—'

'Bratislava, New York?'

'Very funny. Stuart was in Slovakia covering the Bratislava Horror Festival for some fanzine he writes for. And the only reason he was able to get to Bratislava is because the festival agreed to fly over one fanzine journalist to cover it – all the horror distributors know that they shift a hell of a lot of DVDs through these magazines. As Stuart is considered the most knowledgeable horror-film journalist out there these days—'

'So he's the Pauline Kael for the "Driller Killer" set, right?'

'Very witty.'

'I don't like the set-up, Theo.'

'Look, Adrienne is this amazingly knowledgeable woman—'

'Whom you met during an intimate dinner at Stuart's hovel?'

'You actually sound jealous . . .'

'I'm just surprised you didn't mention her before now.'

'Do I ask you for a detailed rundown on everyone you're meeting, day in, day out?'

'No, but I haven't suddenly announced that I'm going

248

into business with someone . . .'

'Adrienne came by last week to the archive after I first saw the final cut of Stuart's movie and told him that I wanted to distribute it. He told me he was up for that but only if I'd work with Adrienne, as he thought we'd be a great team. Which, as it turns out, is the truth. She's got the business clout and I've got the passion. She figures we should do fifteen million dollars minimum, which, given that the distribution agency takes thirty-five percent, is—'

'Five hundred and something . . .'

'Five twenty-five. Your fast math is impressive.'

'You really think it can make that sort of return?'

'I don't *think* . . . I *know* it will surpass that. And if you invest fifty grand, I can assure you that the first fifty thousand we make will be immediately refunded to you, and then you'll receive twenty percent of our commission. So you could easily make back the principal and double your money in less than a year.'

'If the project is so sure-fire wouldn't it be better to approach a bank or a finance house?'

'Banks and big-deal investors don't touch no-budget splatter movies. It's not exactly the sort of thing that's in their field of vision.'

'Well, I'm sure you'll find some well-heeled cinephile who's willing to gamble on this . . .'

'Whereas you won't touch it – because that would mean investing in me.'

'Now that's a lousy thing to say,' I said, trying not to sound too angry or too hurt – and failing badly.

'But it's the truth. You have never trusted me, you have never believed I could succeed at anything.'

'How can you say that? I'm always telling you what a brilliant guy you are. I laugh at your jokes, I brag to my friends how talented and—'

249

'You don't have any friends.'

That comment landed like a right to the jaw.

'That's not true. I talk with Christy all the time . . .'

'She's three thousand miles away. Other than that, you see no one.'

'And how about you, Mr Solipsistic? You were living like Oblomov before I—'

'I have plenty of friends,' he said quietly. 'You simply never meet them because I know you'd look down on them. Just as you have already decided to look down on Adrienne and Stuart.'

'I am simply troubled by the idea—'

'That I might actually succeed at something and then leave you.'

'That is not what this is about,' I said, even though there was an uncomfortable truth to what he had just said. Our entire relationship was predicated, in part, on my fear that he would take the door marked Exit out of our lives – and I both hated and feared that knowledge.

'I would be thrilled if you succeeded with this film. And you know I would always support you in just about anything you'd want to do . . .'

'Then you have to invest in me.'

There was so much I wanted to say here: about how couples should never mix money and business; how, by investing in his project, I would be forced to confront my own doubts about Theo's sense of responsibility and that I would be giving him this rather substantial sum of money under duress. But I was in one of those tricky no-win situations. Refuse to plunk down the money and I would be telling him I had no faith in him. Invest the money and I would feel as if I had been strong-armed into this, with someone whose business sense was, at best, unevolved.

Trust your instincts. That is, perhaps, the best piece of advice you can ever heed, followed by: *Never put money into a movie.* So I decided to play for time and told him: 'I'll need to have some sort of partnership agreement. And I'll also need to meet your associate.'

Theo smiled the smile of someone who knew he was going to get what he wanted.

'No problem,' he said. 'No problem at all.'

Two days later, Adrienne came over to the apartment for dinner. Theo spent much of the day cooking an elaborate Indian meal. Though part of me was dazzled by the extent of his preparation (he'd sourced all the ingredients at a tiny Indian shop in Chelsea and even went so far as to hand-grind his spices) I couldn't help but think that he had only cooked me three meals in the two years we had now been together. He also insisted on buying champagne and several ridiculously expensive bottles of Bordeaux.

'It's an Indian meal,' I told him. 'The food is going to smother such rarefied wine.'

'This dinner will mark the beginning of our business partnership and I want it to be as special and important as this project.'

'You're talking about hawking a cheapie horror movie, not reprinting the Gutenberg Bible.'

'You really know how to piss all over everything.'

'That's not fair.'

'Nor is your insinuation that I am being extravagant for no other reason than to be extravagant.'

Five minutes later, Adrienne made her entrance.

'Entrance' was the apt word, though it was actually more of a performance. She showed up at our door wearing a floor-length coat that looked like a cross between a kaftan and an Afghan rug. She was very tall – somewhere over six foot – with densely curled hair, dyed virulently red. Everything about her instantly screamed 'extremity': the coat, the hair, the capped teeth, the huge bronze sunburst earrings, the vertical musky perfume that radiated from every pore. Then there was the matter of her voice. It was loud. Wake-up-the-neighbors loud. What made it even more grating was the way it oozed specious bonhomie.

'Oh, my God, you are as beautiful as Theo said you were.'

Those were the first words out of her mouth. Followed by: 'And – oh, I don't believe it – what an awesome apartment!'

This comment came when she was still in the doorway and hadn't yet taken in the 'awesomeness' of our place. But after throwing her arms around me like a long-lost friend she rushed inside and started talking in exclamation points about everything – from the color of our sofa to the 'fabulous' parquet floor to the 'gorgeous' new kitchen. And when it came to Emily . . .

'Oh, you are the most absolutely beautiful little girl . . .'

As Adrienne approached her with outstretched arms, my daughter instinctively curled herself up into a ball and turned away from this towering shrike. Emily, from the outset, always figured out who to trust and who to shun.

Now I do realize that I am engaging in excessive character assassination when it comes to Adrienne Clegg. But she was one of those people who didn't exactly provoke a neutral response. Within five minutes of her arrival, I was desperate for her to leave.

But there was no way I could say that. Instead I offered Adrienne a drink.

'A little Martini-wini would go down a treat,' she said.

'And do you want your Martini with gin or vodka?' I asked.

'You wouldn't happen to have Grey Goose by any chance?'

'No – good old boring Smirnoff.'

'I guess that will have to do . . .'

I headed to the kitchen and made the drinks. Then I returned to the living room where Adrienne was down on the floor, trying to bond with my daughter. She kept holding up building blocks and mouthing things like: 'Can Emily say the letter A?' 'Can Emily say the letter Z?' Being thirteen months old and unable to form words as yet, this was just a bit beyond her and Adrienne's shrieky voice sent her into floods of tears.

'Has Auntie Adrienne upset you?' she asked, all high decibels. Emily's response was to escalate her crying, causing me to scoop her up and whisk her off to her room.

'Guess you can see now why Auntie Adrienne is never going to be Mommy Adrienne,' she said as we left.

It didn't take long for Emily to regain her composure. Once out of Adrienne's range she relaxed.

'Sorry if she frightened you,' I whispered to her. 'She frightens me too.'

When I returned to the living room Adrienne and Theo had both slurped down their drinks. Noting that the cocktail shaker was empty, Adrienne insisted on heading into the kitchen and making a fresh batch.

'There's no need,' I said.

'Of course there's a need,' she said brightly. 'Another couple of Martini-winis and we are going to be bosom buddies.'

As soon as she was out of the room Theo said: 'I knew you guys would hit it off.'

'Very funny,' I said.

'Hey, don't blame me if you have no sense of humor.'

'That woman is an irony-free zone,' I whispered.

'You just can't stand anyone who's flamboyant.'

'She's a floor show.'

'And you are, as always, rushing to critical judgment.'

'That's not fair. I only want the best for you, for us.'

Adrienne was back with the drinks.

'You lovebirds having a little spat?'

'No, I was just being cranky,' I said, downing the Martini and accepting a second one. Vodka Martinis are an excellent poison. After the first you're moderately anesthetized. After the second, numbed. After the third you're either willing to make a pass at a fire hydrant or put up with a two-hour stream-of-consciousness monologue from Adrienne Clegg.

Fortunately the Martinis were augmented by all that Indian food which Theo had so lovingly prepared, and by all that extravagant Bordeaux bought especially for the occasion. I just sat back and ate and drank, as Adrienne did all the talking. I learned about her 'ultra-dysfunctional' childhood in Vancouver, her first brief marriage to a Hollywood set dresser who turned out to be a raving homosexual (or did she lead him to conclude that sleeping with men was a smarter option?), and her stint in some Betty Ford rehab center in British Columbia to break her Percodan habit ('At least Perc is cheaper than coke,' she noted). I also heard about how she helped discover at least three major film directors (none of whom I'd heard of) and about her previous professional lives in Paris and Berlin ('I was the first film distributor to get things moving in the old East Germany after the wall came down'). And, of course, there were her 'fabulous' years in New York where she 'knew everybody'.

Listening to her wasn't a vast strain. My brain, deadened by the vodka and the wine, shifted into neutral. I simply let her ceaseless monologue waft over me. There was something nonetheless fascinating about her self-absorption: the sheer loud narcissism of it all, the way she dropped film-industry names ('Steven' . . . 'Hugh' . . . 'George' . . .) and expected you to fill in the blanks; the fact that she viewed her life as an ongoing melodrama and didn't stop to think for a moment if it might be the least bit interesting for her audience. What did Theo see in her? Actually that wasn't difficult to fathom, as he seemed to take perverse pleasure in her campy extremity, the way certain gay men so love over-the-top divas. Perhaps it was her wild, unbridled self-assurance that strangely impressed Theo. For someone who had a degree of intellectual arrogance – and a geeky love of pedantic detail – he often hinted that he was ill at ease in that world of pure American ambition and wondered if he would always be someone on the financial margins of life. So Adrienne – with her aura of fiscal knowingness, of being *a player* – was an immediate source of attraction for Theo. As the evening wore on she started to talk about how she would market *Delta Kappa Gangster* – and so began selling me on her ability to turn this little blood fest into a highly profitable piece of merchandise. Yes, she was extreme and narcissistic, but it was clear she could push an idea. The more she talked the more I became convinced that, yes, Adrienne could (as she and Theo promised) treble my investment in under a year. Like any canny salesman, Adrienne knew how to be persuasive and dangle the possibility of multiplying money in front of you.

'I promise you this: the fifty grand you put into the enterprise will be completely guaranteed by us. What your money will do is let us travel to the big film markets – like the American Film Market in Santa Monica – and nail down big deals. With a film like this, it's a certainty that we can sell both theatrical and DVD. I mean, this movie is a gift. A fucking great lucrative gift. I showed it to an Italian distributor friend of mine just last week and he's already prepared to offer a hundred and fifty thousand for Italian theatrical alone. Now I know what your next question is going to be: If we're already being offered that sort of money, why do we initially need yours? The key here is the word "initially". As the distribution sales company we get thirty percent of all gross sales – but the money is only paid ten percent down and the distributors must make good on their offer within ninety days. So what we're talking about now is a short-term bridging loan – and one which we can repay to you once we have received the first hundred grand in deals. The thing is: not only will your investment be paid off in four months, but given your twenty percent cut of our commission . . . well, do the math, hon.

'I tell you, the demand for this sort of product is endless. People want to get the shit scared out of them. People want the visceral kick of extreme violence. We're living in a time of vapid consumerism and anemic expectations. What's more, though everything is superficially humdrum in most people's lives, the amount of silent rage out there is enormous. Rage at being in a dead-end job. Rage at being trapped in a sterile marriage. Rage at the fact that, for every average working stiff and middle-class office type, the money they're now making just doesn't cut it anymore – and they also know that there is no such thing as job security.

'So with all this rage around, how do people vent it? They need some exhaust valve: online porn, shopaholism, watching extreme stuff. This is where *Delta Kappa Gangster* really rings all the bells: a revenge movie in which you get the visceral kick of watching all-American assholes being mutilated. I mean, *ring-a-ding-ding* . . . it's a sure-fire winner.

'Now Theo told me about your time in hedge funds. Look at the apartment you got out of that. What we're offering you here . . . yeah, it's a risk. But you're the ex hedge fund gal. You know all about risk, hon. And you also know that a guaranteed return on investment in four months – coupled with the chance to easily triple your money within the year . . . and hon, when I say "easily" I am being prudent here . . .'

Hon. I hated her using that term of endearment, just as I also hated so much about her excessive personality, and her need to ingratiate herself with me. After she finished her sales spiel I said little, except: 'Well, I must think all this over . . .'

'Of course you must, *of course*,' she said. 'No pressure, hon, none at all.'

Then she manically began to tell a story about someone she knew who didn't invest in *Saw* and lost out on a cool million. But . . . '*No pressure, hon, none at all.*'

We finally got rid of her around midnight. Theo was ultra-solicitous, insisting that I go to bed while he did the dishes. When he snuggled up against me an hour later I didn't push him away. Nor did I object when I woke the next morning at eleven – it was a Saturday – to discover the house had been even more tidied up and that (according to a note he left – in easy view this time – on the kitchen counter) he had headed out to the supermarket with Emily to do the shopping for the weekend.

I saw right through all of this. And in the somewhat clear (but rather hungover) light of day I remained more than dubious about Ms Clegg. When I Googled her, I did come across many references to her presence at assorted film markets over the years and one 2002 *Hollywood Reporter* item (from when she was living in New York), noting that she was 'one of the real players in independent film sales'. Just as I also received, a few days after the dinner, a very thorough and very professional business plan from Adrienne, accompanied by a long and well-argued letter, explaining again the parameters of the investment and how, at the very worst, I would come out with the $50,000 I put into the company. Theo asked that evening if I was still dubious about making the commitment, also letting it be known that they were under immense pressure to sign up Stuart, as there were other better-established film sales companies now chasing him.

257

'Look, it would mean so damn much to me if you would take this gamble on me . . . especially as, when we make all this money, it will provide so much in the way of security for you and me and Emily.'

It was the first time he had ever spoken of the future in plural terms. That part of me which feared being abandoned again responded immediately to this articulation of commitment.

'All right,' I told Theo that night. 'I'm in.'

Adrienne called me up the next day, brimming with excitement.

'I screamed and screamed and screamed when Theo told me the news,' she said. 'And I promise, promise, *promise* we will not let you down. Of that you can be one thousand percent certain.'

She also said that it would be kind of cool if I was made an officer of the company, Fantastic Filmworks, that she and Theo were forming to distribute the film. It would mean I could come to board meetings and be kept fully abreast (and, indeed, could even influence) all the decisions they would be making about the sales of the movie.

'Why not?' I said, also thinking that it would be no bad thing to keep a watchful eye over how my investment was being handled.

A letter of general partnership arrived a few days later. It was all very straightforward – outlining my investment, a detailed schedule of repayments and bonuses, and (this was crucial to me) a clear statement indicating that, as a member of this partnership, I would have complete access to all books and corporate decisions about the sales and marketing of the film. That evening – when, as prearranged, Adrienne came by the house for a final discussion – I made it very clear that I wanted to be kept abreast of every major expenditure made in

258

the selling of the film and had to see full accounts whenever demanded.

'No problem, hon. There will be complete transparency here.'

Then, with several scribbles of a pen, I committed myself to a $50,000 investment in Fantastic Filmworks. As soon as the document was signed Adrienne brought out a bottle of champagne to celebrate the deal. Only this was not just any old bottle of champagne. This was a Laurent-Perrier 1977.

'There was no need for such an expensive bottle,' I told Theo later as we were getting ready for bed.

'There are moments when extravagance has its place.'

During the coming months – when Adrienne and Theo veered from extravagance to extravagance – I found myself in an increasingly enraged war of words with Theo about his profligacy.

Until, as the arbitrary nature of things would have it, the extravagant expenditure turned into extravagant profitability. Adrienne and Theo were right on the money about their little film. It was a monster hit.

Success can bring stability on all fronts. Success can also precipitate chaos. As I came to learn: never underestimate the need for self-sabotage when someone has finally gotten what they've always wanted.

Seven

EMILY. DURING ALL that went down over the next year and a half, the one and only great constant in my life was my daughter. Everything else around me turned very wrong – and I had no one to blame but myself. After all, by signing over all that money I'd handed them an opportunity to . . .

But I'm getting ahead of myself. First . . . Emily. By the age of eighteen months she was already forming basic but interesting sentences, and seemed as devoted to me as I was to her. Maybe I was super-conscious of my own complex family background – but from the outset, I vowed not to visit the same toxic guilt on my daughter, and to make Emily feel that her presence in my life was simply the best thing that ever happened to me.

Did she, as a baby, get this? Only a completely self-obsessive parent would think that. Honestly, I had no idea if *I* was getting it right. What I did know was that I so enjoyed every moment I had with my daughter. She never caused me trouble. Or maybe I simply decided that nothing she did was that troubling or distressing. If she knocked over the milk, if she ruined a night's sleep, if she was grumpy and unresponsive to my attempt to cheer her up, I seemed to ride with it. That's what surprised me the most about my response to her – the realization that nothing she asked of me was too difficult. It was revelatory, this feeling – for what it told me was the depth of my unconditional love for this little girl who also happened to be my daughter.

She coped with my absences, never putting up a fuss when she was dropped off at the crèche. Every evening when I arrived home she came tottering (and eventually running) towards me, announcing delightedly to Julia: 'Mommy home!'

Julia always went on about just what a charmer she was, and how easy it was to look after her.

'She is wonderful because you treat her wonderful,' Julia once told me in her still-shaky English.

'No,' I replied. 'Emily is wonderful because she is simply wonderful.'

By the age of three she was picking up books and saying things like: 'Mommy loves books – and I love Mommy.' Or she would climb into my lap when I was in my desk chair at home, grading papers, and would try to read the words I had written on the essays.

Every weekend, I made a point of bringing Emily somewhere cultural, but fun. The Science Museum, the Zoo, the Museum of Fine Art (she actually pointed to a Rothko hanging on one of the walls and went: 'Nice'), even the Wiedener Library at Harvard, where a friend named Diane who worked in the cataloging department brought us on a tour of the vast array of stacks. Emily found it all a bit claustrophobic and labyrinthine, and clung to me as Diane patiently explained to her how the books found their way onto shelves and how there were shelves for books about stories and shelves for books about things that happened in the past and shelves for . . .

'I write stories,' Emily suddenly announced.

'I'm sure you do,' Diane said, beaming.

Again I was told how poised and delightful my daughter was. On one snowy day I decided against taking the car and brought her to the crèche by the T. During the journey she happily colored away in her *Sesame Street* book, occasionally stopping to show me her handiwork, and an elderly woman sitting opposite me actually leaned over and said: 'I have grandchildren and they don't know how to behave in public and are always kicking up. But your daughter is just exceptional . . . and a great credit to you.'

Now I know I'm sounding just a little too fulsome here. But Emily made me feel fulsome. For the first time in my life, there was someone who was more important to me than anyone else in the world. A sweeping statement, but an accurate one. She was the great love of my life.

Meanwhile, her father was otherwise engaged. From the moment I transferred the $50,000 into the Fantastic Filmworks account, Theo was largely AWOL from our lives. With the money I gave them he rented an office with Adrienne off Harvard Square for $1,200 per month. It struck me as something of an extravagance.

'Harvard Square is the most expensive corner of Cambridge,' I told him.

'That's why we have to be there. Adrienne says that we'll have no street cred with the big-deal distributors if we're operating in some second-floor walk-up elsewhere. Everyone knows Harvard Square.'

'It's still fifteen thousand dollars a year in rent.'

'Don't sweat it. Adrienne says we should have an easy hundred Gs in our account within four months. Then you'll get your fifty back – and we'll have no more cash-flow problems.'

'You already have cash-flow problems?'

'I didn't say that.'

They flew off together to Milan for a big meeting there. Theo assured me – but only when I asked to be reassured – that they'd be sleeping in separate rooms.

'Don't sweat it. I'm not her type, she's not my type . . . and anyway she's got this guy she's seeing right now.'

'What's his name?'

'Todd something.'

'What's he do?'

'He's a journalist on the *Phoenix*, I think.'

I checked the masthead of the *Boston Phoenix*. There was no one with Todd as his first name listed there. I called their editorial office and asked them if they had someone named Todd who wrote for them. The woman on the other end of the line said they didn't divulge such information, but if I checked out all their back issues online, I might find what I was looking for. I did just that, using their search engine to check if there were any Todds with bylines. I went back two years. None whatsoever. If you were named Todd you were evidently barred from writing for the *Phoenix*.

I mentioned this to Theo. He got annoyed.

'What are you turning into – Edward G. Robinson in *Double Indemnity*?'

'I'm not trying to be a bloodhound,' I said, getting the reference.

'Yes, you are – otherwise you wouldn't be trying to find out if this Todd guy wrote for the *Phoenix*.'

'Well, he obviously doesn't.'

'So?'

'So she doesn't have a boyfriend named Todd.'

'No – she *definitely* has a boyfriend named Todd.'

'But he doesn't work for the *Phoenix*.'

'I obviously got that wrong.'

Theo did bring me back a fantastically expensive pair of black Ferragamo boots from Milan.

'They're magnificent,' I said, 'but far too indulgent.'

'Let me be the judge of that,' he said. 'Anyway, it looks like we have fifteen grand upfront for Italian theatrical.'

But the boots cost $1,500 (again the internet told all) and I was somewhat unnerved when I thought that he'd blown one-tenth of his first sale on me. Yet I decided not to challenge him on it as there were other more pressing concerns to be confronted.

'Hello there, thanks *sooo* much for calling Fantastic Filmworks.'

This voice – hippy dippy with those decidedly 'out there' inflections one associates with far too many hallucinogenics – greeted me when I called Theo at his office one afternoon.

'Who was that?' I asked when Theo came on the line.

'Our assistant, Tracey-Spacey.'

'You hired an assistant?'

'She's only part-time.'

'But she's still *an employee*. And what sort of name is Tracey-Spacey?'

'We need an assistant. Between my job at the archive and Adrienne being on the road all the time . . .'

That was another thing that was grating on me – Adrienne constantly being elsewhere, flitting between London and LA and Milan and Barcelona, and me occasionally receiving a phone call from the *grande dame*, all specious affability and reassurance.

'Jane, hon, you would not believe how damn expensive London is right now. I mean, eight bucks for a frappuccino in a Starbucks over here. Who pays that sort of money?'

'You evidently do.'

She began to laugh that hyena laugh of hers.

'You are such a card!' she said. 'But do I detect a teeny-weeny bit of worry-worry in your voice?'

'Yes, you do.'

'Look, the point of this call is . . . I've got goody-goody news! Ever heard of the Film Factory? One of the biggest distributors in the UK. They are ready to pony up two hundred and fifty thousand for theatrical rights in Britain.'

'And what about DVD rights?'

'They want to sell those on – but we'll have a forty percent share in that sale.'

'And they're thinking what sort of price?'

'Will you listen to you . . . Madame Business Head!'

'Thirty percent of two-fifty is seventy-five thousand. Not exactly riches beyond avarice, given that the UK is such a major English-language market.'

'It's a great price,' she said, a tone of annoyance coming through.

'They got seven-fifty for the UK theatrical sale of *Kill Me Now*,' I said, mentioning the name of a recent super-grisly horror film that had been a box-office phenomenon in thirty countries.

'How do you know that?'

'Because I know how to use a search engine. The search engine sent me to *Variety*, which had a story in their archive on the UK deal for *Kill Me Now*. Given that you've only been able to realize thirty-three percent of that price for UK theatrical distribution of our film—'

'You know,' she said, interrupting me, 'this wasn't *the deal* I agreed to when I accepted your investment.'

'You *accepted* my investment,' I said, sounding angry – which is exactly what I was. 'You came to me with my partner, begging me—'

'I have eighteen years' experience in the film business. I have been called the most important person in independent film distribution by the *Village Voice*. Anyway, two-fifty is a great price.'

'It's a mediocre price.'

'It pays back your investment.'

'There is that, I suppose.'

Theo came home that night, emanating passive-aggressive anger.

'I never knew you had such great experience in film sales,' he said, his voice mildness itself.

'I know how to compare a good deal maker and a bad deal maker.'

'And do you also know that Adrienne phoned me up from London in tears?'

'Am I supposed to be affected by that? I mean, I just pointed out that her deal wasn't up to snuff.'

'You're not to question her judgment in the future.'

'Is that an order, *sir*?'

'Let her do her job – which she's very good at.'

'Not if she got sixty-five percent less than—'

'No one knew at the time that the film-sales market would take a small dive. You've worked in finance, you know everything comes down to risk management, risk assessment. So why get all exercised about a good deal that isn't a great deal? You're getting your money back.'

But I didn't get my money back. Four months went by. Theo and Adrienne went to Los Angeles and the American Film Market, where they rented a convertible Mustang and took a suite in a hotel on the beach. How did I know such things? Because I saw the photographs that Theo took of himself and Adrienne posing by the electric-red Mustang, and a party they threw for assorted film types in their suite – which had (also in true Hollywood style) a very nice veranda facing the beach in Santa Monica. The reason I saw the photographs is because Theo had left his spiffy new Leica camera on the kitchen counter at home, with the image of himself and Adrienne (arms around each other's shoulders) in the digital display below the viewfinder.

Was I disconcerted by this? Just a little. As he'd left the camera out there for me to peruse I didn't think twice about picking it up and rolling through the other photographs that had been stored within. That's when I saw the pictures of the oceanfront suite, of the party they threw, of their carousing with assorted other partygoers on a king-sized hotel bed.

Why the hell had he left the camera out on the kitchen counter? The answer was an obvious one: he wanted me to find it. He wanted to share with me the fact that he was now sleeping with Adrienne. In that time-honored tradition of male guilt, he had to let me in on his grubby little secret – and, as such, transfer whatever guilt he was feeling onto me.

But when he arrived home that night and I confronted him about the photographs, his reaction was one of cool disdain.

'Why did you look at the pictures?' he asked.

'Because they were left out for me to see.'

'Bullshit,' he said, all calm. 'The camera was simply left out. You chose to pick it up.'

'And you chose to leave it out with a picture of you and Adrienne locked in an embrace.'

'We had our arms around each other's shoulders, that's all.'

'That's all? You were sprawled out on a bed in a hotel suite.'

'There were many people sprawled out on that bed.'

'But you had her head in your lap.'

'Big deal. We were all smashed.'

'You were in the same hotel suite.'

'That's right, *a suite*. As in a hotel apartment with many rooms. And there were two bedrooms. One for Adrienne, one for me.'

'You expect me to believe that?'

'I don't really care if you do or don't. It's simply the truth of the matter.'

'Even if – as you keep alleging – you haven't slept with the woman, it's also very clear to me that the two of you are engaging in absurd profligacy.'

'Oh God, this song and dance again.'

'Yes – this song and dance again. Because the seed money for the convertibles and the fancy hotel suite and all the extravagant travel came from me. And I've yet to see a penny of it back.'

'That's because we've yet to see any of the money from all the contracts signed.'

'How many territories are gone so far?'

'You'd have to talk to Adrienne. That's her division.'

'Her *division*? What are you, some multinational corporation with *divisions* in thirty countries? Surely you know exactly how many contracts you've signed to date.'

'Can't say that I do, really. A half-dozen, I think.'

'You *think*. And the States – the really big contract . . .?'

'Well, I was going to come to that. New Line might be offering us a cool million.'

This stopped me short.

'When did that happen?'

'A couple of days ago.'

'Why didn't you tell me?'

'Because it wasn't certain. And I didn't want you to be disappointed.'

'I'm an officer of this company. Surely I should have been told.'

'All right, it was an oversight. And I'm sorry. But aren't you pleased?'

'Of course I'm pleased. That's three hundred thousand to us. It's great news.'

'So you shouldn't be worrying about the money we've been spending to get the film sold. If we'd gone to the American Film Market and stayed in some Motel 6 and had been driving a rented Buick, everyone would have written us off as bit players. As Adrienne says, you throw some money around to make some money. That's the way the game works.'

'I still would like to see a full set of accounts for all the travel and all the signed contracts.'

'No problem,' he said, sounding evasive.

Evasive he remained. Every two weeks I would remind him that he still hadn't shown me the accounts or the contracts. He would promise them in a few days. When this went on three times too many, I blew up at him and said that he was to either show me the paperwork or face questions from my lawyer. And I would really like to know why the hell my fifty grand hadn't yet been refunded to me.

The next day I had a phone call at my office from Adrienne.

'Hon, hon, apologies, apologies. I have been very stupid-woopid . . .'

Stupid-woopid.

'. . . and I have been so fucking stressed with all the preparations for Cannes that I haven't gotten all the paperwork together that you not only need, but *deserve*. But I am happy to get everything couriered over to you tonight.'

'Why spend the money on a courier when Theo can bring it all home?'

'Didn't Theo tell you he was off to New York with Stuart to have a meeting with Focus and New Line and a couple of other mini-majors to talk about his next project?'

'No, he didn't tell me that.'

'Ooops! Me stupid again! He asked me not to tell you this. All this came up real sudden – 'cause thanks to us, Stuart is hot, hot, hot and everyone wants his new script. Of course we got in there first, giving him the money to develop it.'

'You what?'

'Oh, come on, don't sound so surprised. Surely Theo told you that we'd put up some seed money for the script?'

'What script?'

'*Dark Woods*. It's not as slasher funny as the last movie.

More Hitchcockian. A pair of homicidal adolescent twins are living in rural Maine with their trailer-trash mom and they decide to systematically take out all of her redneck lovers. Then they turn their attention to every wife-beater in their shitty little town. It's John Steinbeck meets *Death Wish*.'

'So you've paid Stuart to write this screenplay?'

'That is correct.'

'And how much exactly did you pay him?'

'One hundred thousand dollars,' she said.

'You're kidding me.'

'It's a great price, considering how hot he is now.'

'It's a great price, if you have the money.'

'We have the money.'

'Well, I know you have, on paper, a considerable amount of money in contracts. But I don't think Stuart agreed to write for you with nothing paid upfront, right?'

'Of course not. He's got studios circulating around him like vultures. He could command ten times that amount if he wanted.'

'So you wanted to get in there first?'

'Precisely, hon.'

'I'm not your "hon",' I said and hung up.

When Theo arrived back three days later his first words to me were: 'So you berated Adrienne about the script deal with Stuart.'

'I see your girlfriend has been keeping you up to date with our conversations.'

'She's not my girlfriend – but I know you can't stand her.'

'I never said that.'

'You don't have to. It's all over your face.'

'And that is because the woman is toxic. And like most toxic substances she's also dangerous.'

'You haven't a clue. She is held in such respect in the film business . . .'

'If she's held in that much respect, then what the hell is she doing in business with you?'

As soon as that comment was out of my mouth I instantly regretted it. But that's the problem with angry exchanges. Things get said and you can't easily take them back.

'Fuck you,' Theo said quietly.

'I'm sorry . . . I didn't mean . . .'

'Yes, you did. You meant every word. Just as you have always looked upon me as a loser whom you made the mistake of sleeping with a few times too often. So be it. But know this: if I had to choose between you and Adrienne, I'd choose Adrienne in a New York minute.'

He snapped his fingers in my face as he uttered the word 'minute'. Then, grabbing his coat and his Leica, he left the apartment.

I didn't see him again for another three weeks. Nor did I hear a word either. I tried ringing his cellphone. I sent countless emails. After forty-eight hours I called the Harvard Film Archive and was informed that Theo had taken a six-month leave of absence . . . and they didn't know where he was living right now. So I went to his apartment. It had been sublet to a Harvard graduate student from Mumbai. He too had no forwarding address for Theo – just a post-office box. Now I tried the apologetic approach, telling Theo in several emails that I let my emotions get the better of me, that I shouldn't have reacted so fiercely, that I truly regretted the way our conversation had turned so vile . . . and that, at the very least, we should sit down with each other and try to talk things through.

No response.

I rang Adrienne. Like him she neither answered my calls

nor returned my messages. I was absolutely certain that they both saw my number flash up on their LED screens and that they had agreed to freeze me out. Just as I was also certain that they were now living together – and conspiring against me.

'Of course he's fucking her,' Christy said when she passed through Cambridge a few weeks into his vanishing act. 'I mean, he's a guy. That's what they do with any woman who is available and willing. The thing is – how long are you going to put up with it and, for that matter, why are you putting up with it now?'

'There's a child involved.'

'But he's not that involved with Emily in the first place. So . . .'

'I know, I know . . .'

'If the man you're living with vanishes out of your life for a couple of weeks and doesn't even have the minimal courage required to tell you where he is, then you have to ask yourself why the hell you want him back.'

I hung my head and blinked and felt tears.

'There's other, bigger stuff going on right now,' I said.

That's when I told her about the phone call I had received last week from my mother. It was the first time we had spoken since that disastrous weekend with Theo. When Emily was born I did make the point of sending her photographs – and she replied with a polite, formal letter, telling me that, of course, Emily was a beautiful girl, and she hoped she would bring me much joy. That was it. I wrote back a proper letter (Mom refused to enter the world of email in her private life, even though she was forced to do so at work), saying that life was short and that if she wanted to visit us in Cambridge she would be most welcome. Two weeks went by and I was on the verge of calling her when I got a postcard from her:

Jane
  I honestly don't think a visit is on right now. Maybe
I'll change my mind in the future. If so I'll be in touch.
  All best
  Mother
  PS Please don't try to contact me to change my mind. I
know what I can – and cannot – handle.

I took her at her word, and didn't attempt to initiate any
further suggestions of visiting in person, though I was still
making a point of sending her new photographs of Emily
every six months, with a little card tucked in between them,
on which was scribbled something neutral like: '*Thought you'd
like to see how rapidly your granddaughter is growing up.*' Mom
always sent a brief postcard in reply, commenting on Emily's
poise, prettiness, etc. But she remained steadfast in her desire
to have nothing to do with me . . . until the week before
Christy showed up when, out of nowhere, she phoned.

'I'll be brief,' she said, sounding all businesslike. 'There's a
growth inside me that has gone funny and the doctor wants
me to go into the big hospital in Stamford for a bunch of tests.
I just thought you should know.'

'How serious did he say it was?' I asked.

'Now don't you start sounding all concerned, Jane . . .'

'That's not fair and you know it. I've always remained
concerned. It's you who've put up the brick wall between us.'

'That's a matter of interpretation.'

'Well, can I come down and see you while the tests are
happening?'

'I don't see the point.'

'If you don't see the point, then why tell me about all this?'

'Because I may be dying – and as my daughter you should
know that.'

She hung up. I called her back an hour later – my rage and guilt in competition with each other. She didn't answer the phone, so I left a message. Twenty-four hours went by. Still no word from her. I called her home again, left another message and then phoned the library and talked to one of Mom's colleagues. Mom had been checked into the Stamford Medical Center and her colleague hinted that things looked bad.

'How come we haven't seen you around here for a while?' she asked me.

'Long story,' I said.

I immediately phoned the Stamford Connecticut Medical Center and asked to be put through to her room. Mom answered on the second ring.

'I figured I'd be hearing from you, what with all the messages you left me. Feeling bad about having abandoned me all these years?'

'How are you doing?' I finally asked.

'My oncologist, Dr Younger, keeps running these damn tests. And they all end up telling him the same thing: The cancer is everywhere.'

'I'm coming down tomorrow.'

'Now why would you want to do that?'

'You're my mom . . .'

'It's so nice that you finally realize this fact after all these years.'

'That's not fair and you know it.'

'What I know is this: I don't really need your company right now, Jane.'

I toyed with the idea of dropping everything and rushing down to see her, but my class schedule – and being without night-time child cover – mitigated against it. Then on the morning that Christy showed up I received a call at my office from a Dr Sandy Younger.

'Your mother gave me this number,' he said, 'when she started chemotherapy a few weeks ago. She told me to only call you if things were beginning to look "final".'

That caught me short. Even though I knew – from what little information she had imparted – that she was terminal, hearing it directly from her doctor was like having a bony cold hand placed on the back of my neck.

'How long does she have exactly?' I asked.

'Maybe a month, no more. I would think about getting down here as soon as possible. At this stage of the cancer the situation can deteriorate very quickly. And excuse my intrusiveness, but as I gather that you are somewhat estranged from your mother—'

'Her choice, not mine,' I heard myself saying.

'There are always two sides to these stories. My one piece of advice is this: make your peace with her now. You'll find it far easier to cope later on if you've achieved some sort of . . .'

I knew which word was coming next: closure. A word which drove me apoplectic – because it posited the idea that you could actually get over certain things; that the sense of damage and hurt could suddenly be put on a shelf and filed away under: 'Been there, done that.' Closure was for closets, not people.

'. . . closure before she passes on.'

'All right, I'll get down there tomorrow,' I said.

When I related all this to Christy she immediately said: 'Don't worry about having someone covering for you at night. I'll stay with Emily until you get back.'

'I was thinking Mom might like to finally meet her granddaughter.'

'When my dad was in the last throes of his cancer he was so out of it he hardly recognized me. Anyway, if your mom hasn't shown the slightest interest in wanting a relationship with

Emily before now, why drag a little girl into the horrors of a terminal ward? That's an early childhood memory you can definitely spare her.'

I concurred with that, and set off the next day alone to Stamford. On the three-hour drive south I felt nothing but dread – not just at having to see my mother in the last stages of terminal cancer, but also at the immense waste of all our years on the same earth. We could never make each other happy, could never cross that threshold which separated disaffection from affection. It was always wrong between us. We both knew it – *always* knew it – and were never able to figure out a way of making it better.

And now . . .

Mom was in a three-bedded room in the oncology wing. I kept my head down as I passed by her roommates, all of whom were swamped by wires and cables and tubes and electronic monitors and all the other paraphernalia of life support. Mom, on the other hand, was relatively free of such high technology – just two lines running into each arm and one monitor *blip-blip-blipping* the metronomic rhythm of her still-beating heart.

Her appearance stunned me. Though I was prepared to see her in death's clutches, nothing really readied me for the appalling change she had been put through. Not only had she lost all her hair, but she had shrunken in size, her ashen skin drawn tight across her now-tiny skull. When she opened her mouth, I could see that only a handful of teeth remained within. The cancer had triumphed, denuding all her features. But when I sat down beside her and took her still-warm, emaciated hand, I was immediately informed that her vitriol towards me had not dimmed.

'So . . . you arrive for the final curtain,' she said.

'I arrived to see you, Mom.'

'And you didn't bring your daughter with you. My one and only chance to see her, and you deny me this . . .'

Don't get angry, don't get angry . . .

'You've never been denied access to her,' I said quietly. 'You've denied yourself access to her.'

She withdrew her hand from mine.

'That's a matter of interpretation,' she said.

'I simply didn't think this would be the right moment to bring Emily into—'

'Your father called me the other day,' she suddenly said.

'What?'

'You heard me. Your father called me. Told me that walking out on me was the worst decision he ever made in his life and that he was planning to come to Stamford in a couple of days and remarry me right here in this hospital.'

'I see,' I said, trying to sound neutral. 'And where did Dad call you from?'

'Manhattan. You know he's now the CEO of a very big metals company. All that bad stuff you revealed about him – well, it was all proven to be the lies I knew it to be. Not just lies, Jane – *slander*. But the truth will out and your father is now top dog again. He'll be here tomorrow to retake his vows with me.'

'How wonderful,' I said.

'Yes, it is. The ceremony is scheduled for noon.'

'And he's going to swear undying love to you?'

'Undying . . . because he now knows that leaving was the worst mistake he ever made. He told me that on the telephone, nearly breaking down, cursing himself for listening to you all those years ago and—'

That's when I got up and charged out of the ward and into the nearest restroom, locking myself in a stall and fighting back the need to scream and shout and pound the walls and get that woman's voice out of my head. But this desire was subsumed by the sobs that grabbed my throat and wouldn't let it go. *My mom is about to leave this life and all she can talk about is . . .*

Before the sobs could escalate into something more primal and extreme, a certain corner of my brain (the part that always argued in favor of self-preservation) said: 'Enough . . .' I let myself out of the stall and negotiated my way through the maze of corridors that was this wing of the hospital. Within five minutes I was back in my car and tearing north on Interstate 95, putting as much distance as I could between myself and Mom. I drove non-stop, arriving back in Cambridge just before midnight. Christy was awake, sitting in the living room with a glass of wine, but not surprised to see me.

'I've been trying to ring your cellphone for the past couple of hours. But I figured—'

'I had it turned off.'

'The hospital called.'

'Has she . . . ?' I asked.

'Around two hours ago. The doctors were wondering where you were.'

'I was . . . running away.'

Christy stood up and put her arms around me. But I didn't break down or convulse with sorrow or shake my fist at the heavens and demand to know why my mother had been such a sad angry woman who had to take it all out on the daughter who simply craved her love. No, I didn't have that purgatorial moment of grief which should accompany a parent's death.

All I felt was . . . exhaustion.

'Go to bed,' Christy said, seeing just how wrecked I was. 'Get nine, ten hours – and let me worry about bringing Emily to school tomorrow.'

'You're too nice.'

'Shut up,' she said with a smile.

I did as ordered – and actually slept ten straight hours without interruption. When I woke, there was a note from Christy:

> *By the time you read this, Emily will be happily ensconced at her crèche. I hope you are a little more rested – and as OK as you can be under the circumstances. And you might want to call your beloved Theo on his cellphone. He rang here while you were sleeping and wanted you to know that they have just done an American deal for the movie . . . for three million dollars.*
>
> *Congrats, I guess. You're rich.*

Eight

THE NEWS OF Theo's windfall was subsumed by a far more pressing concern: arranging my mother's funeral.

Upon waking up and finding the note from Christy that Theo was in the money, I immediately phoned the hospital and began to make arrangements. Within an hour not only had I organized the collection of the body by a funeral home, but I had also rung the local Episcopal priest in Old Greenwich and sorted out the service in two days' time. Then I called the library and informed her colleagues that she had died. I also asked one of them to contact any friends she might have in the community to pass on the news and tell them of the service Friday morning.

Once that was all completed, Christy was back in the apartment and making coffee. I accepted the mug that she placed in front of me, drew in a deep breath and phoned Theo. He answered on the first ring – and immediately sounded like a man who had just broken the bank at Monte Carlo.

'Well, hello there,' he said, all expansive and friendly. 'Listen, real sorry about your mom. That's tough . . .'

'Might you like to explain to me where you've been for the past three weeks?'

'London, Paris, Hamburg and Cannes – and do I have news for you . . .'

'Your news is less important to me than the fact that you have vanished from our lives for nearly a month.'

'I was off making us money. Big money. Like one million dollars to Fantastic Filmworks . . .'

'Congratulations, well done. The thing is, all that money is actually secondary to the fact that—'

'*Secondary?* You would think that. Because it's so you, so *Jane*. Piss on my parade and tell me how little value I have in your life.'

'You dare say that after telling me, if you had to choose between me and that psychotic freak you adore, you'd choose the freak in a New York minute.'

'Well, she doesn't belittle me.'

'I am not belittling you. I am angry – justifiably angry – because you abandoned us.'

'Jane, I'm sorry that your mother is dead, even though you understandably couldn't stand the bitch.'

'Thank you for that sensitive observation.'

'What do want from me? Lies?'

'You're sleeping with her, aren't you?'

'Do you have proof of that? *Documented* proof?'

That's when I threw the phone across the room.

There was a moment's shocked silence, during which Emily looked up from her coloring book and said: 'Mommy threw a phone.'

'Mommy probably had very good reason to throw the phone,' Christy commented.

'Mommy needs a drink,' I said.

But I didn't take the vodka that Christy proffered because I had to drive all the way back south to Stamford. Christy called the head of her English Department at the University of Oregon and spun some story about a family emergency and said she wouldn't be back for seventy-two hours.

'You don't have to do this,' I said after she hung up the phone.

'Yes, I do. And please don't tell me that you don't want to put me to any trouble. You've got more than enough on your mind right now. And if you want a piece of cheap advice, here it is: get your money back from Theo *now* . . . and with

281

interest. Once you've been refunded your investment, inform him that he no longer has a part to play in your lives. Not that he'll want to be a participant in Emily's upbringing. I hate to say it but the guy is a case of arrested development.'

'But you liked him when you first met him . . .'

'Sure I did. Because he's eclectic and original. And yeah, I encouraged you to keep the kid . . . not because Theo was destined to be named Father of the Year, but because I knew you would never live with yourself if you had—'

I put my finger to my lips.

'Oh, please . . .' Christy said. 'Anyway, look at Emily and tell me that my advice – which was simply a reflection of your own instincts – wasn't the right call.'

'You knew what I wanted, I guess.'

'No – *you* knew what *you* wanted – and you got it. And she is magnificent. Even if I still can never see myself crossing that frontier, I have to admit that whenever I lay eyes on Emily, I am very envious.'

As if on cue, my daughter looked up from her coloring book and said: 'Christy talks funny.'

A half-hour later they saw me off. I hugged Emily after loading my bag – packed with a black suit – into the truck of the car.

'Why Mommy goes?' she asked.

It was the one moment I almost broke down. Emily saw this.

'You're sad!' she said.

I shook my head and blinked back tears.

'Your mom is just very tired,' Christy said. 'Tired of other people making her sad.'

'I don't make Mommy sad,' Emily said.

Now I almost completely lost it. But I somehow managed to keep myself in check and held Emily close to me and whispered to her: 'You are the best thing that ever happened to me.'

Then, with great reluctance, I handed her back to Christy.

'You sure you'll be all right driving?' she asked.

'I'll be just fine,' I lied and promised to call as soon as I reached Stamford.

As it turned out I got through the drive without the requisite moments of guilt-sodden grief. Perhaps I was just too numb. Or perhaps the one-two punch of Mom and Theo had rendered me strangely defiant – as I told myself that there was no way I'd allow myself to fall apart at their expense. And yet . . . at extreme moments like this one, the regret nonetheless manages to swamp everything. Especially if it is rooted in the very simple realization that it didn't have to be this way. Even though you also know that when it's wrong, it remains wrong – and no amount of dialogue will ever make it right.

When I reached the hospital I was directed to the morgue. I had told the funeral director that I would be arriving around three p.m. – and sure enough he was waiting for me in the lobby of the hospital mortuary. I had expected some Dickensian stick figure in a cut-away frock coat and tall hat. But having been recommended by the hospital the firm of Sabatini Brothers, I should have realized that the funeral director awaiting me would be an Italian-American.

As it turned out, Anthony Sabatini was a short, bulky man in his early forties and dressed in the requisite black suit. He was so solicitous and decent, without being in any way oleaginous, that I took to him immediately. I sensed that, courtesy of his chosen profession, he was something of an expert when it came to sizing people up in extreme circumstances. Though I said nothing to him, he grasped right away that I was on my own here with no one to support me through the next few days.

'You can see your mom now if you like,' he said after introducing himself and insisting that I drink a cup of mediocre hospital coffee with him. 'But, to be honest, the last phase of cancer really robs the person of much of their original looks. It would be better if you let us do some restorative work first.'

'I saw her yesterday – I know how she was at the end. As it's going to be a closed coffin followed by a cremation—'

'If that's the way you want to go, Miss Howard, no problem. I'm not trying to shill for more business here. You tell me what you want, I'll make sure you have it. And I'll be here from now right until the end of the cremation to make certain that everything happens as smoothly as possible.'

Once we had agreed some basic things he approached the woman at the mortuary reception desk and informed her that we were ready for the viewing. She dialed a number. After a few minutes, she received a call back and then said: 'You can go in now.'

Anthony guided me through double doors, down a series of long, chilly corridors to a frosted-glass portal marked 'Viewing Room'. As he knocked on this door, he put a steadying hand on my shoulder.

'You ready, Miss Howard?'

I nodded. An attendant opened the door – and we followed him inside.

I had been preparing for this moment all the way down from Cambridge. As I had mentioned to Anthony, having seen her in the last throes of the cancer had indeed prepared me for the ravages that she had suffered. But once I was brought inside this plain unadorned room and looked down at the tiny shrunken figure on the hospital gurney – a blue sheet brought right up to her chin, her features so emaciated, her lips half-eaten away by the cancer, her eyes closed tight, never to open again – all I could think was: here is the woman who gave me life, who brought me up, who sacrificed so much for me . . . and who could never tell me that she actually loved me, if indeed she ever did. And I, in turn, could not tell her that I loved her . . . perhaps because . . .

Well . . . I always wanted her love. But when that love wasn't reciprocated, when it became clear to me that she saw me as the agent of her unhappiness . . .

Anthony Sabatini saw me lower my head and stifle a sob. It was the only moment that I came close to crying during the next few days. I didn't cry when, later that afternoon, I let myself into her house and sat on the narrow single bed in what had been my room and remembered how many times I had shut myself away here during my childhood and adolescence, thinking about a way to escape all this. I didn't cry when I saw her local lawyer and was informed that Mom had remortgaged the house twice over during the past few years as her hours in the library had been severely cut back. With no savings to act as a safety net, she had to keep borrowing against home equity in order to simply survive.

'*She knew I had money,*' I felt like telling the lawyer. '*And I had, against her will, helped her out in the past. Why couldn't she have asked me . . .?*'

But I knew the answer to that question.

I could have cried when the Episcopal priest who conducted her sparsely attended funeral (were there really only twelve people who cared about her?) referred to me as 'her much-loved daughter, Jane'. I could have cried when the tacky curtains opened in the tacky chapel of the crematorium and the coffin moved through ceremonial flames towards the furnace. I could have cried when a box was delivered the next day to her house and I drove out to Todd's Point Beach and scattered her ashes onto the angry waters of the Atlantic. I could have cried when I packed up two boxes of personal memorabilia – what little jewelry she possessed, some family photos, some of her prized Mel Tormé albums (she always went on about his voice being akin to a 'Velvet Fog') – and informed the lawyer that he should hire someone to pack everything else up and give it all to charity, then put the place on the market. I could have cried when the lawyer told me he doubted the house sale would actually cover all the mortgages, let alone the $23,000 in legal fees he had let ride with her over the past few years. And I could have cried when – on the way back to Cambridge – a public radio station played Mel Tormé singing 'What Is This Thing Called Love' . . .

Yes, there were ample opportunities to break down during the four days I ended up spending in Old Greenwich (Christy insisting that she could hold the fort until late Sunday morning). Though I could feel immense sadness for that which had been absent from our relationship, I found it very difficult to cry for someone who held on to a self-deception so skewed and sad that it corrupted everything to do with her one and only child. But if life teaches you anything it's this: you can never dispel another person's illusions. No matter how much empirical proof you have to the contrary, they will hang on to their false beliefs with a vehemence that might baffle and infuriate you, but which (you realize much later on) is their only defense against a truth that would undermine everything they hold dear. Once they have embraced the lie, nothing you can say, do or *prove* will shift them away from it. The lie becomes the truth – and it can never be challenged.

Halfway home on Interstate 95, my cellphone rang. It was a voice I didn't want to hear. Adrienne.

'Hi, partner,' she said loudly over the speakerphone,

286

pronouncing the last word with a faux-Texas twang, as if we were characters in a western.

'Hello, Adrienne,' I said, my tone suggesting the thinnest veneer of civility imaginable.

'Well, don't you sound bummed!' she said, following this comment with another of her hyena laughs.

'Maybe Lover Boy failed to tell you, but my mother was cremated two days ago.'

'Oh, stupid, *stupid* me,' she said. 'What a total goof I am. No wonder you hate me.'

'Is there any point to this call, Adrienne?'

'Look, for what it's worth, I'm sorry for your loss, OK?'

'Which loss are you talking about? The loss of my mother or of the man with whom I allegedly live?'

'Theo hasn't left you, has he?' she said, sounding all shocked.

'You know, Adrienne, I can take a modicum of hypocrisy, but not the sort of gold-plated bullshit you hand out.'

'Think what you like, Jane. But the point of this call is to reassure you that you will be receiving a transfer of one hundred and fifty thousand dollars from Fantastic Filmworks within the next four weeks.'

'Can I have that in writing, please?'

'You really don't trust me, do you?'

'You're sleeping with my guy . . . so, yeah, I really don't trust you at all.'

'I just wanted to bring you this good news. I hope you're pleased.'

'I will be pleased when I see the money – and I want an email from you confirming it will be paid within the month. As for Theo . . . I don't really care if I do – or do not – see him again. And you can pass that comment on to him. As far as I'm concerned we're through.'

'I don't know why you're blaming me exactly.'

'Because you're a ridiculous person, that's why.'

The line went dead. Our conversation was over.

I never did receive the email from Adrienne. For several weeks after this call, I didn't hear from Theo either, though I did run into one of his colleagues from the Film Archive on Brattle Street one afternoon. He seemed nervous in my presence and haltingly confirmed (when I pressed him) that he had recently heard from Theo by email, and that he was 'chilling out' for a couple of weeks on the Amalfi coast.

'You wouldn't happen to know where exactly on the Amalfi coast – and what hotel he might be staying at?'

'Uh . . . he didn't, like, share that with me.'

Liar. But I didn't feel the guy merited my anger, so I simply said that it was nice to run into him and quickly said my goodbyes. As soon as I got home, I Googled 'Amalfi Coast Five Star Hotels', figuring that Adrienne's need for extravagance would mean they wouldn't dream of staying anywhere but something palatial. There were nine such hotels in and around Amalfi. I hit pay dirt on the fourth call and was put straight through to 'Signor Morgan's suite'. And guess who answered . . .

'*Buon giorno, buon giorno,*' Adrienne said after picking up the phone, her voice at least three decibels too loud.

'The smoking gun,' I said in reply, my voice reasonably calm.

'Oh, hi there, Jane,' she said, trying to mask her surprise. 'I was just stopping by Theo's room to discuss some—'

'Sure you were. And it's a suite, not a room.'

'And it's all being charged back to the film.'

'Well, that's reassuring. What isn't reassuring – besides the fact that you are now evidently an item, and don't you dare try to suggest otherwise – is that, three weeks after our last call, I still haven't received the initial repayment of my fifty-thousand-dollar investment in your company.'

'You haven't? But I arranged for the transfer of that amount over ten days ago.'

'Sure you did.'

'I'm telling you the truth.'

'Sure you are.'

'I'll get on to my bank straight away and make sure you have that fifty grand in your account by the end of the week.'

'Can I have that in writing?'

'Of course, of course. I'll send you an email right away.'

'You promised me that email weeks ago.'

'Do you have any idea how busy we've been? I mean, the movie's sales have gone through the roof. And as I made very clear to you last time we spoke, not only will you be getting back your initial investment, but I can safely predict that another hundred and fifty thousand will be en route to you before—'

'Before *when*? The Twelfth of Never?'

A silence – during which I could actually hear her fuming.

'If you read through the letter of agreement that you signed with us, we are not bound to pay you any profits for another nine months. The very fact that I am willing to forward you the initial fifty thousand right now—'

'Please don't tell me how big-hearted and charitable you are. If that money isn't in my account this week, I'll be taking legal action against you.'

'I'm supposed to be scared by that? Oh, please . . .'

She concluded this sentence with a cackle. Again I had the urge to throw the phone across the room.

'You don't want legal trouble, Adrienne . . . especially if I decided to leak it all to the entertainment press. I'm sure all your investors wouldn't want to read about—'

'This is the film business, hon. In the film business everyone plays fast and loose. And if you think a stuck-up third-tier academic cunt is going to get away with threatening me . . .'

That's when I did throw the phone across the room. Again Emily's face registered shock as the cordless receiver ricocheted off a wall.

'Mommy's angry again,' she said.

I immediately had my arms around her, my fury quickly morphing into massive guilt.

'Not at you, my love,' I said. 'Never at you.'

An hour later, an email did arrive in my in-box from Fantastic Filmworks. But it wasn't the repayment guarantee that Adrienne had promised me. Rather it was a terse three lines from Theo.

> *Please pack up all my things at the apartment.*
> *Tracey will come by tomorrow to collect everything.*
> *I want nothing more to do with you.*

It was unsigned.
I shot back the following reply:

> *And I want nothing more to do with you.*

This too was sent unsigned.

I received this kiss-off on a Saturday morning. Had it come the day before I would have had to face my students and somehow maintain a veneer of stability at a moment when I felt that everything was coming apart. But instead of giving in to sorrow, I let my anger motor me through the next two hours, during which I raced around the house, dumping all of Theo's clothes into assorted suitcases, emptying his bookshelves, his desk, his DVD collection, and packing up his computer.

Emily watched all this with concern.

'Is Daddy going away?'

'Yes, Daddy's going away.'

'For ever?' she said, her face falling. Again I lifted her up in my arms.

Already my daughter was being damaged by her parents' inability to put her interests above their own. Do we ever get anything right?

'It's not your fault. It's just that Daddy's very busy right now and won't be around much. But you will be seeing lots of him.'

'Promise?' she asked quietly, as if she could see right through my weak assurances.

'Yes, I promise. And I promise not to get upset again.'

In the weeks after Theo and I ended it I actually stopped feeling permanently upset. Perhaps all my rage had been vented before the final break-up. Perhaps I was so prepared for it to be over that, when the final kiss-off came, there was no sense of shock or distress; just a resigned acceptance of that which was bound to happen. I could no longer dodge the knowledge that this had all been one huge mistake from the outset.

But whenever I looked at my daughter I also knew that the 'mistake' had given me the biggest gift imaginable. Perhaps the reason I could accept all the attendant *merde* in our so-called relationship was because Emily was so damn wonderful.

Weeks passed, then months. I didn't hear a word out of him. Part of me was astounded at his callousness. Surely he'd want to maintain some ongoing contact with his daughter . . . even the occasional email just to see what was going on in her life. But another part of me was actually pleased that he had so cut us off, so gone into hiding. It made it all the easier to write him off.

I taught the summer term at New England State. Emily and

I spent a week in a rented cottage on the shores of Lake Champlain. Though it took a little convincing I managed to coax my daughter into the water on a particularly warm day and helped her float on her back for the first time. She was understandably nervous at first. But I assured her I wouldn't let her go under.

'You'll keep me up?' she asked.

'I'll always keep you up.'

Because, truth be told, you'll always keep me up.

It was a very low-key, pleasant week – yet it was only a week, and I promised myself that, next year, I would take the full summer off and run away with my daughter to Paris for a couple of months . . . especially if I ever got the money back from Fantastic Filmworks.

Of course Adrienne's promise of reimbursing me the money came to nothing. I sent her a few stern emails. No reply. So I paid a visit to Mr Alkan at his one-room office down the street from me in Somerville. He listened to my story and looked over the letter of agreement I had signed with Fantastic Filmworks.

'I wish you'd brought this to me before you'd signed it,' he said.

'I wish I had too. Is there anything you can do to get them to honor the return on the investment they promised me?'

'I could send them a letter saying that – as their success in selling the film has been widely publicized in the entertainment press – they should now reimburse you. But contractually speaking they do have until December 1st to settle up. Still, if you'd like me to send them a wake-up call . . .'

'Yes, I'd like that very much.'

The letter that Mr Alkan sent was stern and legalistic. Not only did he demand prompt payment – especially as 'Ms Clegg had verbally promised my client the full reimbursement of her investment over three months ago' – but he also stated that, as an officer of their company, I was entitled to see their books and to monitor their expenditure to date.

Adrienne's reply was short and not very sweet.

Dear Mr Alkan

I do not remember promising your client any reimbursement of her investment before December 1st of this year when it is legally due. On that day I will also supply her with full company accounts. Any further attempts to demand money from Fantastic Filmworks before then will be ignored as your client has no legal right to demand anything more from the Company until the first of December.

Alkan told me he could try to tie her up in assorted writs ('There's always a way of putting the squeeze on people'), but asked whether I really wanted to run up thousands in legal fees when the prospect was that I still wouldn't see any money until the contractual date.

'I sort of knew it would end up like this when I handed over the money,' I said.

'I guess it's hard not to invest in your other half.'

'He was never my other half,' I said, the anger suddenly showing.

Alkan took this in.

'If it's any consolation,' he said, 'I won't be charging you for all this. And I'd like to keep the pressure on them to get the money to you as soon as possible.'

'Be my guest . . . and thank you.'

Good God, a moral lawyer. I wasn't prepared for such decency – any more than I held out any hope that Alkan could strong-arm the money out of Adrienne before its official due date.

But I decided to let him play the bad cop and hope that, just maybe, he'd surprise me with good news.

Two weeks later I received a call from him at my office. He had news . . . but it was anything but good.

'Fantastic Filmworks went bust three days ago,' he said.

Nine

'I DON'T UNDERSTAND,' I said.

This was an understatement. I was baffled.

'The company is broke, bankrupt, dead in the water.'

'But . . . how?'

'The way all companies or individuals go broke. They run up a mountain of debt which they cannot pay.'

'But the only way they run up all that debt is if they run out of funds.'

'That's the way it happens – and that's the way it has happened here. Since you've gotten me involved in this, I've been using a search engine to keep an eye on Fantastic Filmworks . . . and, you know, only a couple of years ago I'd never heard of a search engine. But I digress. According to a story in *Daily Variety* yesterday, Fantastic Filmworks have run out of money and are now facing debts of over half a million dollars.'

'Hang on . . . Theo told me they had signed contracts for more than a million dollars in film sales.'

'The *Daily Variety* story said the figure was closer to a million and a half. The problem was, the film they had . . . what was it called?'

'*Delta Kappa Gangster*.'

'Yeah, that's it. Not sure how I could forget a name like that. As it turns out, Fantastic Filmworks didn't have the rights to sell the film.'

'That's crazy.'

'It's the truth. They had letters of agreement from the director and his producer. But a letter of agreement is just that. An *agreement*, not a binding contract. The director and producer got approached by a big-deal French distribution company, Continental Divide, who told them they could take over the entire film-sales end. Plus they could give them, up front, three-quarters of a million dollars in cash. The director . . . what was his name again?'

'Stuart Tompkins.'

'That's it. Well, Tompkins was quoted in the article as saying that, given all the buzz surrounding the film a few months ago in Cannes, he and his producer were rather disappointed by the level of sales figures generated by Fantastic Filmworks and felt that Continental Divide could simply do better. Then there was the matter of Fantastic Filmworks's expenditures . . .'

While Alkan was talking I'd managed to go online and Google the article in *Daily Variety*. It was all there – exactly as he'd described it, with the additional following statement from Stuart Tompkins:

> '*I was genuinely troubled not just by Fantastic Filmworks's lack of transparency when it came to giving us a full financial accounting of all the sales to date, but also their refusal to disclose expenditure. It was apparent to me that Fantastic Filmworks had been spending an exorbitant amount of money selling the film – to the point where my advisers and I felt they could be accused of profligacy.*'

The journalist then cited several examples of Theo and Adrienne's extravagance – throwing a party for three hundred people at Cannes, at a cost of over $100,000; renting a suite at the Petit Majestic Hotel during the festival at a cost of $27,000; Adrienne having her very own car and driver during Cannes at an estimated cost of $5,000 . . .

The *Daily Variety* guy had done his homework. There were at least six other examples of Fantastic Filmworks's excessive expenditure, from 'chartering a helicopter to bring a dozen prospective buyers to lunch at the Colombe D'Or in St Paul de Vence', to 'co-managing director Adrienne Clegg ordering $800 of fresh flowers every day for their sales suite in Cannes'.

The journalist also managed to interview Clegg – and she was deeply unrepentant.

> *'I find it unbelievable that Stuart Tompkins accuses Fantastic Filmworks of profligacy when it is thanks to our phenomenal salesmanship that his little splatter movie stands to become an international sensation.*
>
> *'Why does he have these people fighting over him? Because Fantastic Filmworks took this little nothing and turned him into the directorial hot property that he is now. How does he repay our hard work on his behalf? He now tries to renege on a binding Letter of Agreement that clearly states that Fantastic Filmworks holds exclusive sales rights to his film.'*

But Tompkins's lawyer, a certain Bob Block of the Hollywood law firm of Block, Bascombe and Abeloff, begged to differ.

> *'A Letter of Agreement is not a binding contract and an allegedly experienced film-sales agent like Adrienne Clegg should know this. But she evidently does not – which is not at all surprising, considering how she has treated the film sales of* Delta Kappa Gangster *as her own personal expense account, allowing her to live the high life and indulge in overpriced whims.'*

There were several more paragraphs about how Continental Divide was one of France's best-known international film-production houses – and how the $750,000 advance to Stuart Tompkins was also being matched by an additional $150,000 for first option on his soon-to-be-completed new screenplay – which, though initially contracted by Fantastic Filmworks, had now been taken over by the French. There was another angry quote from Adrienne saying how her company had a signed agreement with Stuart for first refusal on the screenplay – and that she was planning to tie the entire film up in '*the biggest damn lawsuit Stuart Tompkins has ever seen*'. The *Daily Variety* reporter seemed to see right through such bluff, stating that he couldn't imagine a small-beer operation like Fantastic Filmworks taking on 'a major European player' like Continental Divide, '*because their pockets simply aren't deep enough . . . and they are now very empty after having their one and only "banker" taken away from them*'.

'Good God,' I said after quickly scanning the piece. Alkan was still on the other end of the phone.

'It is something of a mess,' he said. 'And I took the liberty of calling Bob Block and explaining that I was representing you as a duped investor in Fantastic Filmworks. He told me that Fantastic Filmworks were under siege on all fronts, as all that profligacy has resulted in such substantial debts. That's what's worrying me here, vis-à-vis you. The company was never incorporated or made limited liability. You are an officer of a partnership. From what I can gather, you are also the only member of said partnership who has anything in the way of assets or equity . . . unless I'm mistaken . . .'

'Theo's only asset is a vast collection of DVDs.'

'Are there any valuable collectors' items among them?'

'I doubt they're worth half a million.'

'And Ms Clegg . . . ?'

'Maybe she has Cayman Island accounts . . . but I tend to doubt it.' I could have added that the woman always struck me as something of a vagabond, always fleeing the last place in which she screwed up and setting up shop in the next city that would be taken in by her lies . . . for a while.

'I did check into Ms Clegg's background . . . and the reason why, perhaps, she was so reluctant to incorporate the company was because she already has three previous bankruptcies behind her. Had she asked for incorporation, checks would have been made—'

'And I wouldn't be in the situation I'm in right now.'

'It's sometimes very difficult,' he said quietly, 'to think in a cold pragmatic way about an investment when you are also investing in the person with whom you are sharing your life.'

'You don't need to make excuses for me. I knew what I was doing and I let neediness get in the way of clear thinking. The thing now, Mr Alkan, is to limit my liability as much as possible. So tell me this – what's the worst-case scenario?'

'The absolutely worst case?'

'That's what I said.'

'The creditors of Fantastic Filmworks commence legal proceedings to seize all your assets up to the amount of debt owing.'

'Jesus,' I said – even though I'd known this was coming.

'Now let me reassure you – that is absolutely the worst-case scenario and one that I will fight like hell to avoid . . . if, that is, you want to engage me to fight this.'

'Oh, you've got the job, Mr Alkan.'

'You don't have to decide this today, Ms Howard.'

'Yes, I do. We need to fight this immediately.'

'That's fine by me. And I do understand you are a college professor without bottomless pockets . . .'

'How much do you think this could cost?'

'At this point, without really knowing the extent to which the creditors might be pursuing you, that's difficult to say. I would probably need a retainer of, say, five thousand dollars.'

'Jesus,' I heard myself say again.

'Might that prove difficult for you to raise?' he asked.

'No, I have it,' I said. That was a half-truth. I had $9,352 (I dug the statement out of my desk as I was talking to Alkan) in a Money Market account at Fleet Bank, the result of saving a steady $300 month for the past . . . Well, I wasn't going to do the math right now, though I did know that this account was the start of a college savings fund for Emily – and that what little money I had left over from the Freedom Mutual days (around $16,000) was my emergency stash, to be touched only if I was absolutely destitute.

'I'll send you a check tomorrow,' I said. 'But if the legal costs run higher . . .'

'Let's not worry about that for the moment,' he said, the translation of which could be: *Actually the fees could run to five times that amount because, contractually speaking, you could lose everything you own.*

'My one and only major asset in the world is my apartment in Somerville. Were I to lose all that . . .'

'I'm going to make certain you don't.'

Even though it may cost me $50,000 to hold on to it.

'There are many loopholes we can use, like the fact that Clegg refused to provide you with up-to-date accounts as a way of shielding you.'

'But the worst-case scenario still is . . .'

'I wouldn't be honest with you if I didn't say that, yes, there are great concerns here. And I'm not trying to slap you on the wrist, but you should never sign a business agreement without having a lawyer read through it first.'

'I was dumb.'

'No – your intentions were good ones . . .'

'But naive. And now I'm going to be asset-stripped for my naivety.'

'I believe I can save you from that.'

'But you can't be definitive about that.'

'Ms Howard, my position here is akin to that of an oncologist. If an oncologist feels the situation is hopeless, then it is truly hopeless. If a lawyer believes the case is discouraging he also says so. I'm not saying that here. But like any cancer specialist I cannot give you a definitive answer to the question anyone in your situation wants to know: Will I unequivocally defeat the bastards? More than likely, yes . . . but I can't say more than that. Because life is never definitive, is it?'

After I concluded this call I sat in my office very quietly for around twenty minutes, trying to absorb all that I had just heard. Part of me was furious with myself for not having taken the necessary protective steps in the first place. Part of me simultaneously wondered whether I had subconsciously set myself up – as we all do so often despite our protests to the contrary. After all, I hated Adrienne Clegg on sight. And yet, I still – *still!* – signed over all that money and also allowed myself to be named an officer of the company. What was I thinking?

I was thinking: *I deserve all the bad stuff that is going to come down from this. Because . . .*

Because there is a part of me that always believes I deserve disaster.

And if the next few weeks proved anything it was the discovery that, when people want to get even, they always get vindictive.

I was in daily contact with Mr Alkan – as he was almost in daily contact with the long list of people and companies to whom Fantastic Filmworks owed money. Their landlord in Cambridge was still chasing for his $19,000 in back rent. The helicopter charter people in Nice were not responding well to two unpaid bills for over $17,000. A caterer in LA was still trying to chase them down for $9,400 that they dropped on a big bash when they were swanning around the American Film Market. And then there was—

No, you don't need to hear every last extravagance and frill and ridiculously irresponsible outlay Adrienne and Theo made in pursuit of . . .

That was a point which often vexed me – her need to spend in such a lavish and excessive way and Theo's ready compliance when it came to buying into her prodigality. What compulsive need was she fulfilling? What terrible damage was she trying to set right? Or was she simply one of those malignant people who couldn't help but wreak havoc wherever she landed? I had my theories (and like all such speculations they changed hourly) but what I did understand now was that – whether it was intentional or not – there was some trigger in the woman that made her want to fail. How else could you explain turning a $1.5 million windfall into financial catastrophe? And with Theo – *my Theo* – she found a willing accomplice.

For the biggest betrayal here was the one that Theo perpetrated on himself. By allying himself with such a psychotic loser he made me realize: *he wants the failure too*. It was something akin to an amateur poker player who – with beginner's luck – wins a vast pot. Then, terrified of this financial godsend, let alone the success, he doesn't bank a large portion of his money. Instead he decides to remain at the table and gamble recklessly with his good fortune until, of course, it's all been blown. He finds himself not only broke, but in serious debt to boot.

And then, like my father, he had to vanish into that geographic place called nowhere, leaving others to deal with the mess he'd left behind.

Vanished was the operative word here. A few days after I

read that *Variety* story online and sent a flurry of emails to Theo and Adrienne, demanding they speak to me (there was, of course, no response – nor any to the dozen messages I left on their respective cellphones) there was a new article in *Daily Variety*.

Mr Alkan saw it before me and phoned me at the university to tell me its content.

'According to the journalist who's been investigating all this, Ms Clegg and Mr Morgan have gone to ground. As in disappeared without a trace.'

I was online and on to the *Daily Variety* website within moments. There it was – replete with the headline:

Fantastic Filmworks Duo Disappear Owing Half a Million

The story went on to explain that only days after threatening lawsuits against their defecting star director, Stuart Tompkins, '*Fantastic Filmworks duo, Adrienne Clegg and Theo Morgan, have literally gone AWOL, with a bevy of creditors and lawyers trying to trace their whereabouts.*'

The journalist stated that the '*duo*' – last seen in London, staying at the '*minimalist chic Metropolitan Hotel*' – were due to board a flight from London Heathrow to Los Angeles, where they were planning to meet their own legal team – as well as have a thrash-out session with Stuart Tompkins's lawyers. But at the very last minute, they no-showed the flight.

Evidently smelling a great story, the journalist also explained how he spoke to the concierge of the Metropolitan in London, who confirmed that the couple did leave on the day in question and asked him to make reservations for them on a mid-morning Eurostar train to Paris. The couple spent one night in a Paris hotel – the George V (and he pointed out the $780 price tag they paid) – but then checked out with no forwarding address. They hadn't been heard of since.

'As you can imagine,' Mr Alkan told me in the first of many phone calls that day, 'all the creditors are swarming around us as you are the only accessible "partner" in the company. Now – a couple of ground rules here. I note that you don't have an unlisted phone number. What I want you to do is *not* answer your landline – or, at least, buy one of those old-fashioned answering machines where you can hear the message being left for you, so you can screen all calls. And if an unknown number pops up on your cellphone, don't answer it.'

'What happens if people start calling me at the university?'

'Again, I'd get one of those answerphones.'

'Everything comes through a central switchboard.'

'Then tell anyone who needs to contact you to use your cell – and simply don't pick up the phone. Sorry to sound dramatic but there are a lot of angry creditors desperate to find someone to cover the money they're owed. Never underestimate the awfulness of people when money is involved and the individuals in question take offense at being cheated. The fact that you are the innocent party here is, I'm afraid, secondary to it all. You are the only alleged representative of the company so you will be the focus of their anger. But it will pass – especially as I plan to contact every creditor and inform them that my client was simply an investor in the company and cannot be held legally responsible for their debts.'

I started calculating just how much this exercise would cost me. There were over thirty creditors. Say Mr Alkan spent ten minutes emailing and/or phoning each of them. That would be three hundred minutes. Or five hours . . . at two hundred dollars per hour. And then there were all the phone calls with me, and all the discussions with Bob Block at Block, Bascombe and Abeloff, and all the other attendant business to do with keeping me from being swamped by this mess.

'How much have you billed me for to date?' I asked.

'Let's worry about that later.'

'I need to know.'

'Around four thousand dollars. But look – all going well, this round of emails and phone calls to all the creditors will hopefully get them off your back and then we can get a court judgment stating that you are not responsible for Fantastic Filmworks's accrued debts, and that will be the end of it.'

'In other words, around another five thousand dollars on top of the five I've already paid over.'

A pause.

'I wish this could be cheaper for you,' he finally said. 'But all I can promise you is that I will try to end this all as quickly as possible. I'm very conscious of the fact that your resources are limited.'

'Is there any sign of the two outlaws?'

'None at all. Interpol are now involved, given that there are now allegations of fraud. I could, of course, engage a private investigator on our behalf, but the cost would be—'

'Forget it. Just keep the vultures away from me and I'll tough things out until everything dies down.'

Toughing things out turned out to be exactly right. For the next two weeks I was the subject of a frequently intense and vituperative campaign of intimidation by several of Fantastic Filmworks's creditors. According to Alkan, seventy-five percent of the creditors accepted his explanation that, as the sole investor in the company, I couldn't be held responsible for their financial mismanagement – but these were the big organizations (the hotels, car and helicopter hire companies and financial services groups) who could absorb a bad debt, and probably decided that it wasn't worth harassing a low-paid academic who was stupid enough to invest in a splatter movie. But then there were a handful of creditors who

305

wouldn't buy this explanation – and made it their business to frighten me into settling up with them.

The caterer in California – Vicky Smatherson – was one of the more aggressive ones. From the sound of her voice she was in her early forties – and she was very 'take no shit' in her tone. I was at home, playing on the floor with Emily, when she first rang. As soon as I heard the phone begin to chime I stiffened. As it continued to ring, Emily asked me: 'Why you don't answer the phone, Mommy?'

'Because I'm playing with you,' I said with a tight smile. Then the message kicked in, followed by: 'This is Vicky Smatherson – and your associates owe me over ninety-four hundred dollars for a big party they threw out here. Now maybe ninety-four hundred dollars isn't much to a bunch of big shots like you, but it's a goddamn fortune to me and I'm damned if I am going to let you get away with *not* paying me. If you think I'm being a little extreme here, tough shit. You will find out just how fucking difficult and relentless I can be if—'

I made a dive for the answering machine and turned the volume way down. Emily looked both bemused and unnerved by the call.

'That woman is angry at you,' she said.

'She's just upset.'

Then the cellphone sounded. I checked the screen. I didn't answer it. A moment later, the landline blared back into life. I double-checked that the answerphone volume was well and truly off. As it rang and rang, the cell also rang and rang. Emily smiled in the midst of all this cacophony and said: 'Lots of people want Mommy.'

I was so popular that the two phones kept ringing off and on for the next ten minutes until I had the good sense to unplug the landline and turn off the cell. After that I got Emily to bed, poured myself a double vodka and phoned Christy in Oregon – where I managed to catch her in her office.

'As always,' I said, 'I have something of a story to tell you.'

As always, the story came rushing out in one long rant.

'Jesus Christ,' she said when I reached the part about Theo and Adrienne vanishing to the ends of the earth or wherever the hell they were right now.

'My guess would be Morocco,' Christy said. 'A good place to go to ground – and handy for the South of France, should they want to sneak back across the Mediterranean for a decent meal.'

'I think you can eat pretty well in Morocco,' I said. 'Especially with other people's money.'

'You mean, especially with *your* money.'

'I'm absolutely certain that the funds are well and truly spent. Now their creditors are going to take my apartment away from me.'

'No, they won't.'

'How can you be so sure?'

'Because I won't let them. Anyway, I'm certain you'll get the favorable court judgment that your lawyer is promising you, and then everyone will be off your back.'

'And if that *doesn't* happen? If it goes the other way . . .?'

'Then you'll survive somehow – which is what we all do. If you lose the apartment you'll get another apartment. If you have to declare bankruptcy to meet all the debts, then you'll eventually recover from that. It's all very unfair, I know. But life is so often like that. Unfair, unjust, and more than a little cruel.'

Cruelty was something of a specialty of one Morton Bubriski. He was Fantastic Filmworks's landlord in Cambridge and he was very determined to collect the $19,000 in back rent that they owed him. Having found my phone number in the local directory he began a campaign of harassment that made Vicky Smatherson's angry phone calls seem like the height of politesse. He first phoned me around eleven one night at home – and thinking that Christy was about to ring me back (I'd left a message at her home earlier that evening), I grabbed the phone without thinking.

'This is Morton Bubriski and you owe me nineteen thousand, seven hundred and fifty-six dollars. I know you've got it because I know you're a professor at New England State. Just as I know where you live in Somerville and the fact that you own your apartment. I even know what crèche you drop your daughter into every morning—'

That's when I hung up. Thirty seconds later the phone rang again. When the answerphone kicked in he went vicious.

'Now you listen to me, you little bitch, you hang up on me again and I will not only fuck with your career, but I'll also destroy the rest of your life. Your associates completely screwed me around. And now I'm going to collect. And if you don't pay me—'

I grabbed the phone and shouted: 'Threaten me like that again and you'll have the police on the doorstep.'

Then I slammed down the receiver and pulled the cord from the wall.

'More yelling!' Emily said.

'That's the last of it.'

I kept both phones off for the rest of the night – but I couldn't sleep. My exhausted yet hyperactive brain began to picture all the legal proceedings I would be facing, and the very public disgrace of being evicted from my home and having it sold from under me. No doubt the university would soon learn about my financial disgrace and that, in turn, would be another black mark against me, further proof (as if that was needed) that I was trouble.

As it turned out I didn't have to wait that long for the university to discover that I was the target of a very angry group of creditors – the charming Morton Bubriski phoned the English Department the next morning and spent ten minutes haranguing Professor Sanders's secretary. He got so vehement and scatological that she too put down the phone – but only after having taped the entire conversation. ('It's a new university regulation,' she explained later. 'If someone starts going postal I hit the record button and we have his nastiness on tape.')

In turn, the record of Morton Bubriski's nastiness was played for everyone from the chairman of my department to the Dean of the Faculty to the university President himself. When the Dean of the Faculty demanded that I present myself in his office at three o'clock that afternoon I made an emergency call to Mr Alkan and begged him to drop whatever he was doing and accompany me to the Dean's office. To his credit he said immediately: 'No problem,' and was there just before three p.m.

The Dean was disconcerted when I walked into his office accompanied by 'my lawyer'.

'This is not a trial, Professor,' he said.

'I just thought it best to have counsel present,' I said.

'And it was me who *insisted* that she have counsel present,' Alkan lied, 'because she is a completely innocent party here.'

The Dean played us the call from Morton Bubriski. It wasn't pleasant listening – and when I was about to say something in my defense, Alkan put two restraining fingers on my arm right before I was able to open my mouth. (Did they teach him that move in law school?) Once the tape was finished Alkan informed the Dean that he was planning to have a restraining order issued against Bubriski by the close of business today – and 'the man will find himself in jail if he contacts you or my client in the future'.

Before the Dean could get another word out, Alkan kicked in with a detailed explanation about why I was being chased by assorted creditors, how I wasn't responsible for these bad debts, and how the two principal officers of the company had 'gone to ground'.

'Isn't Mr Morgan the father of your child?' the Dean asked me.

'I'm afraid so.'

'The problem for us – and I have actually spoken to the university President himself about this – is the perception that Professor Howard may have engaged in some sort of bad financial speculation. Were this to be made public – to end up in the press, for example – and were someone to start digging around in her background, they'd discover that her father also went on the run after being exposed for financial chicanery . . .'

'I'm not going on the run,' I said, sounding angry. 'And I resent the sins of the father being visited upon—'

Again Alkan put two restraining fingers on my arm.

'There will be no publicity surrounding this case,' Alkan said, 'because there is no case for Professor Howard to answer. As to your assertion that she is in any way following in the footsteps of her father when it comes to financial dishonesty—'

'If you both would allow me to complete the sentence I was attempting to finish . . . of course we knew when we hired Professor Howard that her father was a fugitive from justice. Of course we accept your assurances that she is not to blame for her partner's bad business management. And yes, as long as we do not have further threatening phone calls or any publicity about the case we foresee no problems . . .'

I asked: 'But if something is made public – or some angry lunatic phones you here . . . ?'

'Then we will have to reassess our position.'

'No, you won't,' Alkan said. 'Because I know all about the statutory clause in every university contract. Maybe you remember the Gibson vs Boston College case last year . . .'

I could see the Dean turn a little pale. Gibson vs Boston College involved a professor who had written a rather scandalous book about her extra-curricular sex life. Even though she published the book under a pseudonym (but was outed by that right-wing blogger Matt Drudge) the university tried to fire her on the grounds that her account of having had over four hundred lovers in the past three decades (not to mention picking up a recently ordained Jesuit outside the men's room at Boston's South Station) brought the university into disrepute. Not only did Boston College end up having to reinstate her and issue her with an apology, they were also forced to pay all her legal fees and offer her a year's paid sabbatical to make up for the unfair dismissal.

'Now, we're hardly dealing with a case like that here,' the Dean said.

'I'm glad to hear you say that,' replied Alkan. 'Because if you do try to dismiss my completely innocent client over bringing New England State into disrepute—'

'I can assure you we won't be taking such action.'

'Excellent,' Alkan said. 'Then I think we're done here.'

Outside the Dean's office I said: 'You were brilliant.'

Alkan just shrugged.

'Well, that's the university dealt with – for the moment anyway. And don't worry about Bubriski. I'll have him muzzled by nightfall.'

Even though Alkan later emailed me, enclosing the details of the restraining order that had been placed on Bubriski, the man filed a countersuit against me the next morning, demanding the $19,000 in back rent plus another $20,000 in assorted nonsensical damages, 'psychological stress' and the like.

'It's easily defendable,' Alkan said. 'Don't sweat it.'

But I did sweat it – and suffered another sleepless night.

Two days later Vicky Smatherson also filed a similar suit against me – as did six other Fantastic Filmworks creditors.

'The good news,' Alkan said, 'is that the sum total of all the demands is just under eighty thousand dollars, which means, at the very worst, that's all you'll be liable for. But that's the absolutely worst-case scenario. The truth is, once we go into court next week it will all be cleared up.'

'Until then . . .'

'I will send the requisite letters keeping all the vultures at bay. And I'm sorry to say this, but I will need another five thousand from you as a further retainer. All going well this will be the last payment.'

'And if things don't go well?'

'Try not to think that.'

But I did think that.

Again I didn't sleep that night – my third in a row. The next day I found myself increasingly unable to concentrate, to focus, to make it through a lecture without having a 'dead zone' moment when, out of nowhere, I would zonk out for a few seconds – much to the amusement of my students, one of whom trenchantly noted out loud: 'I think the Professor was wasted last night.'

When I snapped back into consciousness and scanned the classroom to see who out of the fifty students had made that comment, everything in front of me was a blur.

'I'm sorry,' I muttered. 'I haven't been sleeping . . .'

This comment got back to Professor Sanders who made a point of stopping by my office and catching me with the door open and in the midst of a doze at my desk.

'I hope I'm not interrupting you?' he asked, stepping inside.

'Sorry, sorry. It's just—'

'You haven't been sleeping. And you fell asleep in your class this morning.'

'I am just coping with a great deal right now.'

'Of course you are,' he said, all coolness. 'I really do advise you to get some sleep, Professor. The university might not be able to take action against you because of your association with deadbeats. But dereliction of duty while on the job, hinting at a larger psychological instability . . . that's another matter entirely.'

That evening – when I changed at Park Street for the Red Line train back to Somerville, I felt myself getting so shaky that I actually had to grip the platform bench when the train rattled into the station. Did I feel like throwing myself under the Red Line? I couldn't make sense of anything right now.

But I did manage to negotiate myself onto the train. I got off at Davis Square and went into a local pharmacy where I bought some over-the-counter sleeping aid that the druggist assured me would send me out for eight hours that night.

Emily was always able to read my moods – and when I came home that night she turned to her nanny and said: 'My mommy needs to go to bed!'

'How right you are,' I said, picking her up. But she stiffened as I held her.

'You're upset with me,' she said.

'No, I'm not.'

'You are.' Then to Julia: 'Mommy's cranky.'

'I've just got some stuff I've been dealing with.'

'Mommy's getting angry calls from people . . .'

'Emily, that is enough.'

My tone was far too sharp, far too 'end of my rope'. My daughter's face fell, she burst into tears and she ran off into her room. I turned to Julia and said: 'Sorry . . . there's a lot going on right now.'

'It's no worry, it's no worry. I go to Emily . . .'

'No, no, you go home. I'll calm her down.'

'You OK, Mrs Howard?'

'I just need one night's sleep.'

When I went into Emily's room I found my daughter curled up on the top of her bunk bed, her thumb in her mouth. As soon as I came in, she pulled her thumb out and guiltily shoved her hand under her pillow (I'd started trying to break her of the thumb-sucking habit). I sat down next to her and stroked her hair and said: 'I am so sorry for getting angry at you.'

'What did I do?'

'Nothing. I just overreacted.'

'What's that?'

'Getting angry unnecessarily.'

'Why are you angry?'

'Because I'm over-tired. I haven't been sleeping.'

'Because Daddy isn't here?'

'That's part of it.'

'You won't run away too?'

'And leave you? Never. Never in a million years.'

'You promise?'

'Of course I do. And I promise not to get angry again.'

'That's a big promise,' she said with a small laugh. At that moment I couldn't help but think: *This daughter of mine gets it all so damn fast.*

I took two sleeping pills that night, chased with a mug of chamomile tea. They knocked me out for around two hours, but then I was up again, staring at the ceiling, feeling as if my brain had been cleaved. I swallowed another two pills. I got up. I read through some papers. I waited for the pills to kick in. Nothing happened. I looked at the clock. It was now just one-thirty in the morning. I picked up the phone and called Christy. She too was up late, grading papers.

'You have me worried,' she said.

'I have me worried too.'

'It's not just insomnia you're suffering, it's depression.'

'I'm functioning just fine. A good night's sleep—'

'Bullshit. You're in a dark wood. My advice to you is to get to a doctor tomorrow and get some help. Otherwise . . .'

'OK, OK.'

'Stop dodging the obvious. Depression is a serious business. If you don't deal with it now—'

'I'll deal with it, OK?'

But the next morning I dropped Emily at nursery school and dozed off on the T. Later I caught sight of myself in the mirror in my office and saw just how strained and nether-worldly I looked. I drank three large mugs of coffee and got through my lectures, constantly sensing that I was a bad actor inhabiting the body of this alleged professor of English, trying to sound erudite and engaged with her subject matter while simultaneously knowing that I was nothing less than a sham . . . and that life as I knew it was nothing but a series of mis-adventures and setbacks, in which people disappointed you hugely and – worst of all – you kept disappointing yourself. And had it not been for Emily I might just now—

No, no, don't go there. But do go to a doctor. Now.

However, another voice in my head – the voice that didn't want to begin to face up to what I needed to accept, that, yes, I was in something akin to free fall – told me: *You'll sleep tonight and all will seem better tomorrow. Why add another goddamn wrinkle to your life by deciding you're depressed? Get home, go to bed. Show the bastards this won't bring you down.*

So even though the faculty doctor was on duty that

afternoon and I could easily have seen him and begged for some pharmaceutical way out of this sleepless hell, something in me forced me back across Boston on the T, and to Cambridge to pick up Emily. (Julia herself had a doctor's appointment that afternoon.)

'Mommy, Mommy!' Emily said as she saw me in the doorway of the nursery. 'Can we go get a treat?'

'No problem, my love.'

'You tired, Mommy?'

'Don't worry about it.'

And I helped her on with her coat and led her by the hand out the door.

'I think there's a coffee shop near here that does great sundaes,' I said. 'But first you'll have to eat something nutritious . . . like a hamburger.'

'Are hamburgers good for you?'

'They're better than ice-cream sundaes.'

Suddenly, in front of us, there was a commotion. An elderly woman had been walking her terrier. The lead had broken and the terrier was running free, heading towards us. The woman was yelling its name. Emily, all wide-eyed, broke free of my grip and chased right after it. I lunged for my daughter, screaming at her to stop. But she was already off the curb . . .

And at that precise moment, out of nowhere, a taxi came barreling around the corner.

Again I screamed my daughter's name. Again I lunged for her.

But I was too late.

Part Four

One

THEY FOUND ME in a snowdrift. It was around two in the morning – so they told me later. Had they arrived an hour later I would have been dead.

But that was the idea of driving into that snowdrift – and turning the engine off and taking the two dozen Zopiclones that I had in my pocket, and waiting for the moment when I could finally summon up the necessary . . .

Courage? No, that wasn't the right word, because there was nothing courageous about what I was going to do. Rather, the actual word here was '*finality*'. After all those weeks of an agony that was so unendurable, I was finally going to yield to the only bearable solution. And so, when I turned the corner of that backwoods road and saw the snow banked up on the edge of a dark wood, I suddenly braked. Digging the pills out of my pocket and flipping open the top of the bottle, I emptied all the Zopiclones into my mouth. I nearly choked as I chased them with water, the clustered tablets scraping my esophagus as they went down. Then I turned off the car's heater, unbuckled my seat-belt, disengaged the airbag and hit the accelerator.

All this was accomplished in under thirty seconds. It was a fast, instinctual decision, done without pause for thought. Maybe that's how many suicides work. Weeks, months, years of consideration and hesitation. Then, one morning, you're on a subway platform, you hear the approach of an express train rattling through the station and . . .

Heater off. Seat-belt off. Twenty-four heavy-duty sleeping tablets still burning my throat. Without further thought I slammed my foot down on the accelerator. The car shot forward, plunging deep into the snow before crashing into something solid. I was thrown forward. The world went dark. And . . .

That should have been it. The end – with either the crash, the pills, the cold (or a combination of all three) killing me.

But that wasn't the end. Because . . .

I woke up. And found myself on a narrow gurney-like bed. As the room came into focus I could see that the walls were painted some institutional color and the ceiling tiles were chipped and crusted with mold. I tried to raise my arms but couldn't. They were being held in place by straps. I blinked and realized that one eye was covered by a bandage. I touched my lips with my tongue. A mistake. There was a railroad track of stitches on both lips. My mouth was parched. When I squinted to my left I could see tubes attached to my immobile arms and assorted monitoring devices next to the gurney. I could also feel something sharp and unpleasant coming out of me. Even in this fogged-in, back-from-the-dead state I knew immediately that a catheter has been inserted into my bladder.

Oh God, I'm alive.

'Well, hello there. You're back.'

The voice was flat. Prairie flat. Plain, unadorned, dry. I tried to sit up. I failed. I blinked with my one good eye – and could make out the outline of a woman standing in front of me. Another blink and she came into better focus. She was rail thin with a lined face and sharply delineated features. But it was her eyes that unnerved me. They were eyes that tolerated no artifice, no self-pity. They were eyes that looked out on the world with a ruthless clarity. They were eyes that – even in my semi-conscious state – told me immediately: *She knows everything.*

'Guess you weren't expecting this, now were you?'

'Where am I?' I asked.

'Mountain Falls Regional Hospital.'

'Mountain Falls?'

'That's right. Mountain Falls, Montana. You had your "accident" just outside Mountain Falls, on Route 202, around two days ago. Do you remember that?'

'Uh . . . sort of. I lost control . . .'

I let the sentence die.

'You lost control of your car after ingesting a near-fatal amount of sleeping pills and driving right into a snowbank without a seat-belt. And I suppose the fact that the airbag was disengaged and you didn't have any heat on in the car was also an "accident", even though it was minus five the other night.'

'I lost control . . .'

'I know that,' she said, the tough tone slightly softening. 'We all know that. And we also know why . . .'

'How can you . . . ?'

Again I couldn't finish the sentence.

'Know *why*? You had a wallet on you. The wallet told the cops who found you who you were. They did a little investigating, being cops and all that. They found out what they needed to find out – and let us know about your situation. That's why you're strapped down right now. A precaution – in case you feel like doing yourself some serious harm again.'

I shut my eye, taking this all in. *They know. They know everything.*

'Name's Nurse Rainier, by the way. Rainier like the mountain in Washington State. Janet Rainier. I'm the matron on the ward here. Do you know what ward this is?'

'The psych ward . . .'

'Got it in one. You are in the psych ward – on suicide watch. My guess is that you kind of made a last-minute decision to end it all. Like you could have checked into a motel

321

with all those Zopiclone pills and a bottle of whiskey and done it in a bit of comfort. But you chose something kind of instantaneous, didn't you?'

I closed my eye and turned away.

'I'm being just a little gruff, right? That's kind of how I run things around here. Now I can completely understand why you might think I've got all the sensitivity of a car crash – and yeah, I know that is probably *not* the most opportune thing to say right now – but there you go. As long as you're on my ward you're gonna have to get used to my no-crap approach to things. 'Cause the goal is to send you out of here not wanting to drive into another snowbank again. You hear me?'

I stayed turned away.

'You hear me?'

She hadn't raised her voice a decibel, but she still unnerved me.

I nodded.

'Good. Now let me ask you another question: If I remove the restraining straps from your arms, are you going to play ball with me and *not* do anything rash, stupid and/or self-harming?'

I nodded again.

'I'd love to hear you express that thought.'

It took me a moment to summon up the ability to talk again. When I did speak, the mere movement of my lips was agony.

'I promise.'

'We are on the same page – and I am very pleased, Professor, to hear your voice.'

Professor.

'Now, the next question I have for you is: Would you like to try to drink something with a straw? That tube sticking out of your right arm is keeping you alive but IV feeding is no substitute for the real thing, now, is it? You've got the entire ward to yourself – things are surprisingly slow, considering how everyone in Montana loses a screw or two every winter – so I could easily whip you up something nice and bland like a vanilla milkshake. That sound good?'

I nodded.

'Words, please.'

'Yes, thank you,' I said.

'Three more words. I am impressed.'

'Can you take out the catheter?' I asked.

'Six more words. You are earning Brownie points by the minute. And yes, I can get that catheter removed – but only when we're certain you can walk again.'

'What?' I said, suddenly terrified.

'You fractured the tibia in your left leg. That's why it's in plaster. The resident orthopedist thinks you should be out of the cast in about four weeks tops. But we can't have you trying to make it to the ladies until we're sure you can stay upright. 'Course, we could put a bedpan under you . . .'

I became aware again of my left leg. The heaviness I had first felt in it turned out to be the cast.

'I can cope with a bedpan.'

'Then we can relieve you of the catheter.'

She came over to the bed and unbuckled each of the restraints. Though I had been out of it for two days I must have been struggling against the straps while unconscious, as there were deep red welts on both arms. Nurse Rainier caught me staring at these markings.

'They'll disappear in a day or two . . . unless you go postal on me and force me to chain you back down. But you're not going to do that, are you?'

'No.'

'That's my girl. Now I want you to very gently roll over on your right side – and, for obvious reasons, take it very slow.'

I did as ordered, but was unable to put my plastered leg on top of my good one.

'Now all you've got to do is take a deep breath and hold it until I tell you to let go.'

I could feel her lifting up the back of the green hospital gown into which I had been placed.

'Ready now?' she asked. 'One, two, three, deep breath – and don't you dare move.'

Again I did as ordered. I felt immense relief as the catheter was pulled free of me – followed by a cascade of urine.

'Shit,' I muttered through stitched lips.

'Don't sweat it. It's what always happens when the catheter is finally retracted. Anyway, it's about time we got you off that gurney before bedsores set in. Hey, nurse . . .'

A large shaven-headed man – with tree trunks for biceps, all adorned with tattoos – came through the swing doors.

'This here is Ray,' Nurse Rainier said. 'And he tends to be real pleasant unless one of our guests tries to engage in self-harm or leaves before they're given their walking papers. But you're not going to do that, are you, Professor?'

'No,' I whispered.

'I think we've got a real nice customer here, Ray. What do you think?'

Ray looked at his sneakers.

'We'll see,' he finally said.

'Well, how about getting the Professor out of bed and wheeling her down to the bathroom. I'll get Nurse Pepper to give her a bit of a sponge bath and get that disgusting nightdress off her. You up for that, Professor?'

I nodded.

'Language, language. I have got to hear you speak.'

'Yes, I would like to be cleaned up.'

'An entire sentence! This is progress! OK, Ray, she's

all yours. I'll see you later.'

'My eye . . .' I said.

'What about it?' Nurse Rainier asked.

'How bad . . . ?'

'You mean, will you lose it?'

I nodded, but just as Nurse Rainier was about to reprimand me for that, I managed to ask: 'Yes, will I lose it?'

'Not according to our ace ophthalmological surgeon who spent around five hours pulling shards of windshield out of your cornea and everywhere else. But you won't be able to use it for a while.'

'What else did I do to myself?'

'What did *you* do to *yourself*? Nurse Rainier said. 'I like it, I like it. The woman takes responsibility for her actions. You like that, Ray?'

'Can I move her now?' he asked.

'Sure thing. But be real careful of all those tubes and cables and everything else. We've got to keep her monitored.'

Ray may have looked like the sort of biker who had once possibly eaten a raw steer but he was a deft hand at disconnecting me from all my monitors, and hooking up my feed bag to a stand on wheels. Then – without asking if I was ready – he shoved his tree-trunk arms under me and hoisted me down into the wheelchair with surprising finesse and gentleness. As he was engaged in all this, Nurse Rainier kept talking.

'So besides fracturing your tibia, and doing a real number on your eye, you were severely concussed, and you've also got one big welt across your forehead. Then there was all the glass in your lips – but I've seen you running your tongue across the stitches, so I'm sure you're aware of that by now. What else? The concussion caused your brain to swell for around twenty-four hours – but the neurologist stabilized that one. You also had severe bruising around the chest and pelvis. Neat trick,

325

unstrapping the seat-beat and disengaging the airbag. Oh, you hit a tree, by the way. And when this Native American – name of Mr Big John Lightfoot – came down the road and saw your tail lights sticking out of the snowbank, not only did he stop to see what was going on, but he called the cops on his cellphone and even used a rope to attach his back bumper up to his rig and pulled you right out.

'I tell you, you've really got to thank Mr Big John Lightfoot for saving your life. The guy was right on the ball. As soon as he'd yanked you out of the woods, he opened the one car door that wasn't crushed and saw that you were suffering from hypothermia – the cops figured you'd been there around ninety minutes before Big John found you – and the guy sees that the car heater's off so he cranks it right up and starts warming you up. Then he finds the empty bottle of pills on the car floor, puts two and two together and – now this qualifies as heroic in my book – sticks his fingers right down your throat and makes you upchuck everything. Mind you, we had to pump your stomach all out when we got you here. You took that many Zopiclone, you're lucky you didn't wake up with major brain damage. But Big John's quick thinking probably saved you from that fate.

'So if I was you I'd write Mr Big John Lightfoot one major thank-you letter . . . if, that is, you feel like thanking him for your life.

'Anyway, that's all the news that's fit to print on the physical stuff you did to yourself. You're going to be in here for a spell – because though physically you could probably hobble out of here on crutches in around a week, well, it's the head stuff that's gonna want us to keep you hanging around. You'll hear more about that from our resident shrink, Dr Ireland, but only when she gets here in two days' time. We are the only psych ward in this corner of Montana, but with such slow business we don't merit a full-time shrink. Still, you'll like Dr Ireland. Woman about your age, from somewhere back East. Came out here to change her life and all that. Never met a patient who didn't rate her – except those whose cognitive faculties couldn't stretch to rating a candy bar. But I guess you're tired of listening to me. So let's get Nurse Pepper to clean you up . . . and we'll talk later.'

Nurse Ray wheeled me out of the empty ward and down a short corridor. I tried to take in my surroundings, but found that all visual perspective proved difficult. I could see everything and everyone who came close to me. Beyond that, nothing. Though Nurse Rainier had forced me to speak, I still found it difficult to articulate anything but the responses she demanded. I put my hands to my face. *I want to be dead. Because being dead means the absence of thought. And the absence of thought means . . .*

I was wheeled into a bathroom that had been specially equipped to handle the infirm. A young, stout woman in her mid-twenties was awaiting me. She introduced herself as Nurse Pepper. From her accent she sounded like she was from somewhere below the Mason-Dixon line. She immediately thanked Ray for 'delivering' me, then offered me a large, soft smile.

'I am so glad that you are back with us,' she said, all enthusiasm.

'And I hope you don't mind me telling you this, but I really was praying so hard that you'd make it. You're not offended by that now, I hope?'

I shook my head.

'Well, I am a great believer in the power of modern medicine – but I also know that Jesus can heal as well. But I bet you don't want to hear about that now.'

I started to sob. Within moments the crying was out of

control – the same sense of drowning that overcame me in the hours, days, weeks after the . . .

It was just a desperate accident, they all kept telling me. *Terrible, random – like all accidents. And there was nothing you could have done about it.*

I wouldn't accept a syllable of their consoling words. It was my fault . . . all my fault . . .

But the sobs now so intensified that I found myself no longer able to think one simple irrational thought. The grief had, as before, submerged me. Nurse Pepper kept trying to comfort me, putting her arms around me and saying she 'understood'. But when I veered into out-of-control territory, she suddenly let go of me and charged off. Moments later she was back with Nurse Rainier.

'What the hell did you say to her?' Nurse Rainier hissed. 'You pull that Jesus shit with her?'

Nurse Pepper started to whimper.

'Look at you, all pious and helpless,' Nurse Rainier said. 'You run right now and get me a syringe with five mgs of Sodium Pentothal. You get back here in less than one minute – or I will have your Christian ass suspended indefinitely. Now move.'

As Nurse Pepper raced off, Rainier crouched down beside me and locked her hands around both my arms.

'Professor . . . Jane . . . this is not the way to go. You hear me? I know how bad it is, how desperate and unlivable it all seems. But this is *not* going to do you any good. I'll say it again – you have got to cut this out now. Because you are going to—'

That's when I lashed out and caught her on the side of the head with my open hand. As soon as the blow was struck, she came right back at me, slapping me across the face. The smack was very precise – missing my damaged lips and landing on the cheek opposite my bandaged eye. But it still hurt like hell – and shook me out of my crying jag.

There was a moment of shocked silence between us. Then she stood up and smoothed out her uniform and stared down at me.

'You could have my job for that,' she said. 'But I don't think you want to go there, do you?'

I shook my head. Nurse Rainier was about to automatically say: 'Language!' but checked herself.

'Your face OK?'

I nodded, then managed to mutter: 'Your head?'

'I'll live,' she said. Nurse Pepper came running back with the syringe and a glass vial, handing them both to her senior colleague.

'She OK?' Nurse Pepper asked.

'I got her calmed down.'

Nurse Rainier held up the syringe in front of me.

'You think you need this, Jane?'

I nodded.

'You sure? I mean, it's guaranteed to knock you out for the next twelve hours.'

I nodded again.

'Have it your way.'

The needle pricked my arm – and I went under.

When I came to I was back in the gurney-bed, my arms again tied down, though somewhat looser than before. Everything still hurt – and my re-entry into consciousness was accompanied by the thick chemical fog that strong sedatives leave behind. I immediately felt the tubes and catheter back in place. Nurse Rainier was standing at my bedside, peering at me over her reading glasses.

'With us again,' she said.

I nodded.

'Language, Professor.'

'Yes, I'm here,' I muttered, my lips still in agony.

'Good. Very good. Shall we agree to deep-six everything that happened yesterday and start again?'

'Fine.'

'Then I'll get that catheter out of you and arrange for Ray to bring you back for that long-overdue bath. Trust me, Nurse Pepper won't try to "save" you this time. She'll just make certain you're nice and clean.'

It was exactly the same drill as yesterday. I rolled over on my side. I was told to hold my breath. The catheter was slipped out of me. Ray arrived, as silent and sullen as the last time – and as deft and gentle as before when it came to getting me into the wheelchair. Nurse Pepper was awaiting me in the bathroom, looking very nervous when I arrived.

'So good to see you better,' she whispered after Ray had deposited me with her. 'And I'm so sorry if I upset you yesterday . . .'

'It's OK.'

'Well, let's get you into a nice hot bath.'

It was quite an operation getting me into said bath. Nurse Pepper had to first wrap my cast in a waterproof casing – even though, as she explained, she would be keeping the leg suspended above the bath. Then she had to gently remove the bandages encasing my damaged eye so she could wash my hair.

'Don't worry about the eye being exposed to the light,' she said while cutting the bandages and trying her best not to take too much hair off with them. 'There's a separate internal bandage covering the eye. But I won't be able to wash your hair if I don't get the big bandage off. And your hair really needs a good washing.'

She ran the water in the bathtub, mentioning that she was putting in some salts to allow me a very good long soak. The bath was kitted out with a special clear-plastic seat that allowed the aged and the infirm to be electronically lowered into the water. Getting me into it took some work. So did taking off the sweat-and-urine-stained hospital gown, as the very act of raising my left arm upwards caused me immense pain in my midsection. Once she had me positioned in the seat she swung it around so I was directly over the bathtub. She wheeled a metal trolley over to the side of the bath. On it was a plastic sling, long enough to handle a leg. She winched the sling down so it was level with the bath. Then she gently lifted up my plastered leg and negotiated it into the sling.

'OK now, the seat's about to be lowered – so be prepared. And if the water's too hot, do tell me.'

But my attention was elsewhere. As I lay back in the bath seat – preparing for immersion like a Baptist convert – I caught sight of myself in a mirror on the right-hand wall of the room. For the first time I had full visual evidence of the damage done. The left eye wasn't just bandaged, but was also grotesquely puffed up. My forehead remained so deeply bruised that it appeared to have been smudged with black ink. The same sort of bruising covered my midsection below my breasts, while my stitched-up lips looked as if they had been encased in bloodstained barbed wire.

Nurse Pepper saw what I was seeing. She raced over and pulled a set of rolling hospital screens in front of the mirror.

'You don't need to be looking at that,' she said. 'And honestly, Jane, I know it all appears terrible now. But I've read your chart and I know that everything will heal just fine.'

'No,' I said. 'Everything won't heal.'

'You've just got to take every day—'

'Stop,' I said.

'I'm sorry.'

'Don't be. I just can't . . .'

Words vanished before I could get them out. I felt my eyes welling up again. Nurse Pepper put a steadying hand on my shoulder and said: 'Truth be told I would have done what you did – even though my church calls it a sin. But what happened to you . . . it's unspeakable.'

With that she pushed a button and I descended into the warm, lavender-scented water. I shuddered again as my skin was submerged. But the water was balming – and I felt so grubby, so toxic, that I gave in to its aromatic pleasures. After ascertaining I was comfortable – or as comfortable as I could be with a leg suspended above me and a battered body – she let me soak for almost a half-hour, sitting away from me in a corner of the room, leaving me alone with my thoughts – all of which were blacker than black.

Let them get me better. Let them help mend all the reminders of my botched suicide. Let them tell me I have to cope, that I have to be strong, that I must not let this destroy me – all the same platitudinous shit I heard in the weeks afterwards. *Let them get me back on my feet – and let them check me out of here. As soon as I am out of their grasp I will check into the nearest hotel and do the job cleanly this time.*

'Would you mind if I soaped you up now?' Nurse Pepper asked.

'I'd like that.'

Still wearing the surgical gloves she had on while lowering me into the bath, she took a bar of soap and gently worked her way across my skin, handing me the bar at one point and asking if I wouldn't mind soaping up 'down there'. Once my genitals and bottom were clean she used a shower hose to wet my hair and then lathered it up using Johnson's Baby Shampoo. The very sight of the curved bottle with its traditional yellow label provoked another long-suppressed sob. It was the shampoo I used to wash Emily's hair. Nurse

Pepper gauged my reaction and again put a forceful hand on my left shoulder while continuing to massage my scalp with her free fingers.

She rinsed off all the soap and used the electronic machinery to raise me up out of the now-scummy water. Then she disengaged my leg from the sling and sat me up and dried me off. After fitting me into a fresh hospital gown she spent a good ten minutes brushing out my hair.

'Thank you,' I said when she had finally finished.

'No,' she said. 'Thank you. I really do hope I haven't in any way upset you.'

'You've been very kind,' I said.

'And you will get better. Trust me.'

I was wheeled back to the ward. Nurse Rainier was there to greet me.

'Well, look at you,' she said. 'Almost human.'

As soon as I was settled back into bed again, Nurse Rainier said: 'Now we can chain you down again and hook you up to a feed bag. Or we can agree that you are going to play ball with us, and we can avoid the restraints and actually offer you something solid to eat. What's it going to be?'

'The latter, please.'

'You got it – but before we feed you, I'm afraid you've got to spend a couple minutes with one of our administrators. He's got a bunch of paperwork he needs to fill out.'

The administrator was a short, flinty little man with a name tag on his gray suit jacket that let it be known his last name was Spender.

'Miss Howard,' he said, greeting me with a curt nod, then introduced himself as the accounts officer for the hospital.

'This will only take a few minutes,' he said. 'I just have some basic questions, if it's all right to talk now.'

'Fine,' I said.

333

'When you were admitted we didn't have a chance to get some pertinent information on you, due to your . . . uhm . . . medical state. So, to begin with, we need your home address. Is it the same as found on your Massachusetts driver's license?'

'I don't live there anymore,' I said.

'So what is your new home address?'

'I'm in the process of finding one.'

'We need a definitive mailing address, Miss Howard.'

'Use the one on the license then.'

'Fine. Now . . . marital status?'

'Single.'

'Dependents?'

I shut my one good eye. I felt myself seizing up again.

'None,' I finally said.

'Profession?'

'I was a professor.'

'*Was.*'

'I left my job.'

'But New England State University informed me—'

'If you've been talking to my employers, why do you have to ask me what I do . . . *did*?'

'It's just the way the procedure works.'

'Procedure? This is a *procedure*?'

Spender was visibly uncomfortable.

'I'm certain this is not an easy time for you, Miss Howard. But I would appreciate it if—'

'Yes, I'm a professor at New England State University.'

'Thank you. And do you have any next of kin who need to be contacted now?'

'None.'

'Really?'

'That's what I said.'

A pause. Then: 'Now we did find the Blue Cross/Blue

334

Shield card in your wallet – and we did discover that you are part of the New England State University health plan. However, under the terms of the HMO, your hospitalization for a psychologically related accident is limited to twenty-eight days maximum, and does require the patient to pay for the first two thousand dollars in costs. As I'm certain you can appreciate, the nature of your injuries required extensive medical treatment – including ophthalmological surgery. So the two thousand deductible has long been surpassed. Now I noticed you have a Fleet Boston MasterCard and an American Express card in your wallet. Which card should I debit for the deductible?'

Welcome back to the United States of There Is No Free Lunch. But what does it matter, considering that I will be dead in less than a month?

'Either will work,' I said.

'I now need you to sign a few consent forms. I also know that a Professor Sanders from New England State was trying to get in touch with you, as well as a Mr Alkan who informed me he was your lawyer.'

'I'm not obliged to talk to them, am I?'

'Of course not.'

'Can I ask that no outside calls are put through to me?'

Again Mr Spender wasn't happy about this – and his disapproving look made it known that he had sized me up as a liability.

'Wouldn't you want the people who care about you to know that you are OK?'

'No,' I said, cutting him off. 'I wouldn't.'

Another awkward silence.

'Anything else?' I asked.

'Just your signature on all the lines I've marked.'

I didn't even bother looking at the documents even though

335

– the thought struck me – I could be inadvertently signing a document committing myself to the local loony bin. But that would cost the state of Montana money – and as they had probably assessed I was only a liability to myself . . .

Keep her for another twenty-six days, then: hasta la vista, *baby* . . .

After signing the documents I handed them all back to Spender.

'Thank you,' he said. 'And I honestly do hope you get better soon.'

After he had gone, Nurse Rainier returned with a breakfast tray – a watery omelette, toast, tea.

'So Moneybags Spender tells me you're playing Greta Garbo – saying you want to be all by yourself and won't talk to anybody.'

I looked away, the way Emily would look away if I reproached her for anything. That thought made me shudder again. Nurse Rainier took that in.

'It always hits you,' she said quietly.

'What?'

'*It*. The *event* which cannot be discussed – because if you start to talk about it, you will fall apart. Believe me, I know.'

'How do you know?'

'My son, Jack, wrapped his motorcycle around a tree when he was eighteen. That was twenty-four years ago. My only child.'

Her voice was steady, firm – a reporting of the facts, devoid of evident emotion. I took this in.

'How do you get over it?' I asked.

She stared at me straight on – a gaze I had no choice but to meet. Finally she said: 'You don't.'

Two

THEY KEPT ME in the hospital for exactly twenty-six more days. During that time I remained the only resident of the psych ward. Business – as Nurse Rainier kept noting – was indeed slow. I had daily physiotherapy. After the orthopedic resident discovered, during one of my weekly MRIs, that the fractured tibia had quickly healed, it was time for me to try to start walking on it again.

This was around fourteen days into my stay, by which time I had gotten to know the full range of Mountain Falls Regional's residents. The orthopedist was named Dr Hill. The ophthalmological surgeon, Dr Menzel. And the resident shrink, Dr Ireland.

Dr Menzel was a man in his late fifties. He told me he had emigrated from Czechoslovakia to Canada in the mid-seventies, and still had a considerable Eastern European accent. But he had gone native by wearing a string tie and cowboy boots. He was reasonably chatty, saying that he'd worked in Calgary for a decade, but drove down to Montana for a vacation in 1989 and was immediately smitten with the space, the light, the emptiness, the sheer epic grandeur of the place.

'Will I be able to eventually see Montana with my left eye?' I asked him.

'It will take at least four to six months to fully heal. We did have to do intensive micro-surgery after you were admitted, but we managed to remove absolutely all shards. Now it is simply a matter of time. The eye is a most regenerative organ. I am reasonably confident that you will regain eighty percent of its use, if not one hundred percent. Doctors have to be cautious. We can never promise miracles. But in your case, eighty percent retention of vision *is* a miracle.'

Dr Menzel arranged to see me twice a week. I was wheeled down to his office, the bandage was removed, and I put my head into a vise-like structure as he peered into the depths of my left eye to survey the impairments I had wrought on it. He was always chatty and didn't seem to mind that I didn't do much to maintain the conversation. So I heard all about the small ranch he had near Mountain Falls. And how he was breeding stallions as a pastime. And how his second wife used to be one of his nurses at the hospital, but now had a flourishing massage therapy business. And how their daughter was a freshman at Stanford, and was considered such a math genius that she had been given a full scholarship. And how he himself was a part-time painter – 'mainly abstracts, very derivative of Rothko, but I sense you might like Rothko . . .'

Why? Because he too tried to kill himself . . . but actually managed to succeed?

'Once you feel up to it, perhaps you might like to come out to our ranch one evening for dinner. I must tell you, Professor, that we get few Harvard Ph.D.s in these parts, let alone published authors.'

'It was an academic book that nobody read.'

'You do yourself a disservice. It was *a book*. It appeared between hard covers. It was reviewed in serious academic journals. This is nothing to be modest about. It is a fantastic achievement. You should be proud of it.'

Again I said nothing. Dr Menzel looked deeper into my eye. And asked: 'Who, Professor, is the greatest Czech writer?'

'Living or dead?'

'Let's say dead . . . as Kundera would win the "living" award.'

'Kafka, I suppose.'

338

'Kafka! Exactly! But try not to blink when you talk.'

'Maybe I shouldn't talk.'

'Oh, you can talk . . . but you cannot move your mouth as that simultaneously contorts the eye. Language, you see, is inextricably linked to sight. That which is seen is expressed. That which is expressed is also seen.'

'Unless the person is blind.'

'But the blind also see with . . . how did Shakespeare put it . . . ?'

'The mind's eye?'

'Exactly. The mind's eye sees everything, even if it cannot *see* everything. What is actually perceived through the act of *seeing* – and what is *seen* through the act of perception – well, therein lies a great human conundrum, would you not agree?'

'Everything is perception.'

'True – but who can actually ever see the internal workings of another human being? I look deep into your damaged cornea and what do I see?'

'Damage?'

'Scarring. Bad scarring . . . and the gradual development of scar tissue. The eye will adjust to this residue of harm. However, the fact remains that the lens itself has been inexorably changed by the damage done to it. It can never *perceive* the world in the same way again. Because the source of perception – the source of vision itself – has been completely altered by what has been inflicted on it.'

'And how does this relate to Kafka?'

'Well, what's the most quoted sentence of Kafka?'

' "One morning Gregor Samsor woke up to find himself transformed into a giant roach"?'

Dr Menzel laughed.

'How about the second-most quoted line of Kafka?'

'You tell me.'

' "When we look at each other, do we even begin to see the pain we both carry?" '

Ouch. I bit down on my lip.

'So . . . when you look into this damaged eye,' I asked, 'is the pain visible?'

'Absolutely. The "accident" came about because of pain. Desperate, terrible pain. That sort of damage . . . it will always be there. The scar tissue may mask it, may make it eventually tolerable. But still, trauma like that . . . well, how can you expect it to ever fully heal? All is changed afterward. The sense of perception is irrevocably altered. The world is a new and desperate place: implacable, random, pitiless. And we can never trust it again.'

It was the one and only time that Dr Menzel spoke to me this way. Afterwards, sensing my reticence on this subject, he restricted our conversations to my general ocular health and his increasing optimism that the bandages would come off soon. He understood that I no longer wanted to talk about what had happened – let alone explore its attendant metaphors. So he became strictly business, for which I was grateful.

Dr Ireland was also strictly business. She was a diminutive woman in her mid-forties, with a lean athletic frame and long red hair that was carefully braided. She always dressed smartly in black suits and never wore the white coat favored by the other residents. Only once did she mention that we shared the same alma mater, as she had done her undergraduate work at Harvard before going on to Dartmouth Medical School. Unlike Dr Menzel, she never spoke of her life outside of her 'drop-ins' twice a week at Mountain Falls Regional. But she was very tenacious when it came to getting me to talk about my current state of play . . . even though I fought her hard every step of the way.

During our first session she informed me that she was very

well briefed on my 'case'; that she had been in contact with New England State, with my lawyer, even with Christy (Professor Sanders told her where I was).

'I do hope you understand that what happened to your daughter was in no way your fault.'

'Think that if you wish,' I said.

'It's the truth. I requisitioned the police report, the autopsy report, the eyewitness accounts. Nothing, *nothing*, you did caused this.'

'And nothing I did stopped this.'

'Accidents happen, Jane. The circumstances that cause them are inherently irregular and unselective. Try as we might we cannot control their trajectory. They just *are* . . . and we have to live with the consequences, as terrible as that might be. But it doesn't mean that we should crucify ourselves for that over which we have little control.'

'Think that if you wish.'

'That's the second time you've used that phrase.'

'I often repeat myself.'

'Even if it causes you agony to hold on to such guilty feelings?'

'My guilt is my own business.'

'I couldn't agree with you more. The problem is, "your own business" turned so toxic and lethal that you saw no way out but to try to kill yourself. Now does that strike you as a sensible way out of hell?'

'Actually, yes, it does.'

'Do you still think that ending it all is the only solution to the grief you feel?'

Careful here.

'No . . . I feel somewhat . . . OK. Not totally OK, given all the injuries I suffered . . . but certainly OK about having made it through.'

'So . . . you want to live.'

'Yes. I want to live.'

'You are one terrible liar.'

'Think that if you wish.'

'That's the third time you've used that phrase.'

'Then I really am even more repetitive than I thought.'

'You haven't known much in the way of happiness in your life, have you?'

This stopped me short.

'There have been moments . . .' I eventually said.

'With Emily. That was her name, wasn't it? Emily?'

'I don't want to—'

'I'm sure you don't. But this is exactly what we do need to talk about. Emily. The one person in your life who—'

'You know shit.'

'Do I? All right then. Tell me who ever brought you happiness in your life? The father who was always absent and abandoned you, and then cost you your career in financial services? Or the mother who was hyper-critical and could not help but undermine you at every step along the way? Or maybe it was the first great love of your life, a married man who happened to be your thesis advisor and—'

'Who told you all this?' I shouted.

'Is that important?'

'I don't like being betrayed.'

'Quite. Knowing what I have found out about your background, I don't blame you. Your life has been one long sequence of betrayals, culminating in your partner Theo running off with—'

'That's it,' I said, grabbing the spokes of my wheelchair and steering myself around in a 180-degree turn towards the door. 'This conversation is finished.'

'Not until you tell me about your drive out here.'

'Trying to change the subject, are we?'

'You were found in a snowbank on Route 202 just over five days ago. Before that . . . what?'

'I don't have to tell you anything.'

'Yes, you do.'

'Why?'

'Because I could easily have you committed as someone who is a danger to the community.'

'I've harmed nobody.'

'Not this time. But say we let you go and you suddenly get the same suicidal urge again – only this time you decide to cross the central median on a highway and plow into a family of four . . .'

'I'd never do that.'

'So you say. But what proof do I have of that? None actually. Which makes you a suitable case for incarceration unless you are willing to—'

'I ended up in Montana because I ended up in Montana.'

'I need to know more than that.'

'I walked out on my job, my apartment, my life – and I started to drive.'

'This was how long after the . . . accident?'

'Three, four weeks.'

'And at the time had you been prescribed any medication to help you deal with—'

'Zopiclone . . . to help me sleep. Because I wasn't sleeping. Because I couldn't sleep.'

'The same Zopiclone found in your car?'

'That's right.'

'Prescribed by a Dr Dean Staunton – who also happens to be the staff doctor at New England State University?'

'No doubt you've already spoken to him.'

'He said that when you came to see him – in the wake of the

accident – you were in a very bad place, but trying desperately hard not to show it. You insisted on returning to work just five days after the funeral and would not listen to his recommendation that you take compassionate leave. What disturbed him the most was how controlled you were. Your colleagues were also astounded by this – and by the steely insistence you had about carrying on as normal.

'Until, that is, you attacked a certain Adrienne Clegg. Would you mind explaining to me what happened?'

'You know what happened – because no doubt somebody at New England State told you what happened.'

'I need to hear it from you.'

'I don't feel like talking about it.'

'Because . . . ?'

'Because I don't feel like talking about it.'

'You don't have to worry. Your lawyer, Mr Alkan, informed us that Ms Clegg decided not to press charges against you.'

'Lucky me.'

'Was there good cause why you attacked Adrienne Clegg?'

'I think so. The woman was my partner's business associate. Then she became his lover. Then they ran through a large financial windfall – and landed me with all the debt, then conveniently vanished from view. I was hyper-stressed because of this. I wasn't sleeping. I wasn't thinking too clearly. The insomnia was making me vertiginous. I couldn't concentrate. I couldn't negotiate even the simplest things. Which is why . . .'

The sentence fell away. Dr Ireland completed it.

'Which is why you blame yourself for what happened?'

'Yes,' I said.

'Do you also blame Adrienne Clegg?'

'Cause and effect.'

'And that's why – when she did come back to Boston – you attacked her?'

'Cause and effect.'

'You said that already.'

'I'm saying it again. And now I'm not saying anything more.'

There was a pause – and I could see the doctor sizing me up, wondering just how hard she could push me.

'We'll continue this again in three days' time. Meanwhile, don't you think it's important to contact your department chairman, your lawyer, your friends . . .'

'No.'

'We could contact them for you.'

'No.'

'Is that definitive?'

'Yes.'

'Depression is a normal response after—'

'Being clumsy enough *not* to kill yourself?'

Dr Ireland tapped her pencil against her clipboard.

'I'd like to put you on an antidepressant called Mirtazapine. It's largely to ensure that you sleep.'

'Will it stop me looking in the mirror and seeing the catastrophe that is my face?'

'All that will heal.'

'And then . . . What? . . . I'll eventually learn to come to terms with my "loss", and will find a way out of the "grieving process"? Is that the crap you're going to hit me with?'

Dr Ireland stood up and began to gather her things.

'I can be consoling when asked to be consoling,' she said. 'And I can be brutal when I need to be brutal.'

'I don't need consoling, Doctor.'

'Then here's the brutal truth of the matter: you are going to have to live with this every day for the rest of your life. Which is why you're planning to kill yourself as soon as you are out of our clutches.'

'You don't know that.'

'We'll continue this at the same time on Thursday.'

I was started on the Mirtazapine that night. Nurse Rainier told me that she was giving me 15 milligrams of the stuff ('Doctor's orders') because they wanted to ensure that I went under.

'Dr Ireland told me you attacked a woman with a sharp object. Then she told me the circumstances why. Can't say I blame you. Can't say I wouldn't have done the same.'

Oh, stop trying to humor me . . . to make me feel that everything that transpired wasn't my fault. I won't give in to the great new American tradition of refusing to accept the blame. I am guilty. Guilty of so much.

The Mirtazapine did help me sleep and I informed Nurse Rainier that I did feel the pills were smoothing out some edges.

'By which you mean you're actually feeling better?' she asked around a week after I had been started on the pills.

I knew this was a trick question. Antidepressants take weeks to gain purchase within the brain and the metabolism. Though they did knock me out I realized that they wouldn't begin to have any serious effect for some time to come. Best therefore not to raise their suspicions by saying I was feeling 'at one with myself' or some such pharmaceutical Pollyanna crap. Best just to say: 'They knock me out. They don't deaden anything.'

Nurse Rainier bought that one. Just as she also approved of the way I was starting to use a wheeled Zimmer frame to negotiate my way around the ward, and to my various appointments. I remained the only patient in the psych wing and though I was offered a television to keep me company I rejected it in favor of a radio on which I could listen to the local NPR station. I also discovered the limited resources of

346

the Mountain Falls Hospital library. Still, the hundred or so books on their shelves did turn up some surprises – like a dog-eared copy of Graham Greene's *The End of the Affair*, a novel that had greatly impressed me on my first reading around eight years ago, but whose themes of personal loss and the ongoing sentient echoes of the dead I now found hard to negotiate. Still I pressed on with re-reading it, trying to concentrate more on the precision of Greene's language, his immense readability, his understanding that we are all doomed by our impulses and the human need for emotional possession at all costs. It reassured me in the way that all good literature reassures – by showing me that everything is flawed, damaged, transient, and that we are all prisoners of our need to impose order on the chaotic business of life.

'Could we return to the accident in Cambridge?' Dr Ireland asked at the start of our next session.

'I'd rather not.'

'I'm certain you wouldn't. But it would be useful – for our work together – if I could hear from you exactly what happened.'

I hesitated.

'It's too early,' I finally said.

'Will there ever be the right moment? I don't need a big long story. Just a very simple recounting of what happened on that January afternoon five weeks ago.'

I stared at the floor. This was not me pausing for effect. I could hardly bring myself to replay all the events in my head, even though my brain did that for me ceaselessly. But to speak about them? To verbalize them, to give them narrative shape? That was too much.

'Please . . .' I whispered.

'Make it as fast as you want. Just tell me.'

So I sucked in a deep lungful of air and exhaled and spoke.

I must have spoken for only around two or three minutes. But I got through it all, right up to the moment in the hospital when they told me . . .

'And then . . . ?' Dr Ireland asked.

'Then I came apart.'

'Even though everyone spoke about how controlled and brave you were in the weeks that followed.'

'I was operating on autopilot. I was trying to pretend . . .'

'What?'

'Pretend that I could cope.'

'When did you realize you couldn't?'

'I knew it all along. But I kept telling myself: you somehow stick to your normal routine. You go to work. You give your classes. You grade your papers. You maintain your office hours for your students. And eventually – *eventually* . . .'

'Eventually . . . what?'

'Eventually . . . you'll be able to somehow manage.'

'Why this need to "manage"?'

'Why the hell do you think? I felt if I could manage I could somehow stay afloat.'

'Even though you knew you were coming apart?'

'Even though . . . all the while I felt as if my head was splitting open and the thought gradually began to overtake me that I couldn't endure the agony anymore.'

'But you weren't thinking of killing yourself at that time?'

'Yes, I was starting to think about that.'

'What stopped you?'

'Cowardice.'

'But when this Adrienne Clegg suddenly showed up again with your ex . . .'

'That incident . . . it was all rage.'

'I'm sure. Would you mind taking me through it, please?'

'Yes, I would mind.'

'I know it's probably not something you want to revisit. Nonetheless, it would be useful if—'

I raised my hand, like a traffic cop stopping traffic. Then I started to talk. Again I kept to the facts, determined to get through all this as quickly as possible. She only stopped me when I spoke about running off into the night after the attack.

'Did you have any idea what you were going to do next?' she asked.

'No. Like the attack itself, it was completely spontaneous. Afterwards I raced into the street. The next thing I knew I was in a cab. We made my apartment in Somerville in ten minutes. I raced around the apartment, throwing stuff into a suitcase . . .'

'Including all those Zopiclone . . .'

'Including my passport, my laptop, as many changes of clothes as I could squeeze into a bag . . . and yes, my pills. I tossed everything into my car. I cranked up the engine. I roared away. Actually, "roared" is an inappropriate verb. I stuck to the speed limits. I drove in a very steady, inconspicuous manner . . .'

'Because you thought . . .'

'I thought there'd be an all-points bulletin out for me. I thought that if I stopped anywhere to spend the night, I'd be traced there. So . . . I just drove.'

'Tell me exactly where you drove.'

'I drove everywhere.'

'What was the first road?'

'The 90.'

'Interstate 90?'

'That's right. I would only drive Interstates. I would only stay in Mom and Pop hotels – paying with cash, registering under an assumed name, not sleeping much.'

'By not much you mean . . . ?'

'One, two hours a night.'

'The rest of the time?'

'I would sit in a grubby bathtub, soaking in scalding water. I'd watch crap all-night TV. I'd think about hanging myself from the shower rail . . .'

'What stopped you?'

'I was just so exhausted, so deranged, so not here . . . and so terrified of the prospect, even though I was determined to leave the world. And when you are dead set on doing this you don't want to make contact with anyone who might convince you to do otherwise . . .'

'"*Leaving the world*",' she repeated, trying out the expression. 'I like it. It's almost romantic.'

'Suicide is often romantic.'

'Except for the individual who actually commits it.'

'Literature is riddled with romantic suicides.'

'Was your attempt romantic?'

'Look at my face and tell me if this is your idea of romance.'

'I was being ironic.'

'I know you were. But the road is romantic . . . especially for an American.'

'And all roads eventually come to an end. Yours did in Montana. Why here?'

'It's all random, isn't it? I must have clocked twenty-five hundred miles in all those days on the road and the one snowbank I chose is – *was* – here. Just think about that. Had I not decided, out of nowhere, to end my life at that one curve in Route 202 between Columbia Falls and Evergreen, Montana, you would never have known of my existence.'

'There's an old theory about people who get into their cars and head west. On one level they're fleeing their past lives. On another level they're heading towards a geographic extreme. The problem is, once they get to LA or San Francisco or

Seattle, the only thing left for them to do is drive right off the edge.'

'It's a nice metaphor, hitting the Pacific Rim and having no other recourse but to fall off the precipice of the continent. Too bad Margaret Atwood already used it in one of her novels.'

'Am I being accused of plagiarism?' Dr Ireland asked mildly.

'No – I'm just something of a fussy academic when it comes to sources.'

'Remind me never to take one of your classes, Professor.'

'There's no chance of that. I'm never teaching another class again.'

'That's a rather definitive statement.'

'Because I'm *rather* definitive about it. My academic career is over.'

'You don't know that.'

'Yes, I do – and that probably disappoints you. No doubt, you want me to find a way back to my old life . . . as that would mean accepting loss and all that.'

'Is it an "old life"? I mean, you were teaching classes up until two weeks ago.'

'Everything to do with that part of my existence is now "old". I won't be visiting it again.'

'Even though the chairman of your department informed me just a few days ago that he would like you back?'

'I don't want to say: "How dare you." But . . . how dare you?'

'How dare I what?'

'How dare you contact my employer and—'

'He actually contacted me.'

'I don't believe that.'

'The police had to call the university when they discovered

your New England State ID in your wallet. They spoke with Professor Sanders. He, in turn, actually went to the trouble to contact us here to see how you were faring.'

'The man always considered me a liability.'

'That's not what he said. Even the President of the university called the hospital administrator to find out your condition.'

'He's the type who wouldn't even dream of speaking to anyone below the CEO level.'

'And you are understandably bitter because . . .'

'I now hate the world.'

There was a long pause as Dr Ireland took that in.

'As I said to you the other day, you will not put this behind you. You will, in time, reach some sort of accommodation with it. But I will not attempt to sweeten that which is totally appalling. Your daughter is—'

'Shut up,' I hissed.

'The thing is, you tried to silence that thought forever. You failed. You are back here among the living. You again have to deal with that terrible reality. Or you can repeat history and kill yourself the moment your insurance runs out and the hospital administrators decide that, as you are able enough to walk out of here, off you go . . . even though I will do everything possible to keep you here. Because I would prefer to save your life. But I can't do that if you are so determined to end it. And you can reassure me all you want, or act receptive to what I say, or even pretend that you're getting better. But I won't believe a word of it.'

I hung my head. I tried to think of a response, but the words wouldn't come. I felt that drowning sensation overtaking me again.

'I remember when I was a resident in Chicago, the leading psychiatrist emeritus at the hospital was this elderly Germanic woman. I'm pretty sure she was Viennese, but that goes with the territory, right? Anyway, she was also a survivor of Dachau – and I learned that her husband and two sons had died in the camp. Not only that, but she had been subjected to medical experiments while incarcerated. But the woman I met was this formidable, steely clinician who'd emigrated to the States after the war and had made a new life for herself, marrying a very big noise in the U. Chicago philosophy department. Once I heard her give a lecture on guilt – specifically, survivor guilt. Someone asked her: Given all that she had endured – the absolute sheer horror of it all – how had she been able to not go under? Her reply was extraordinary. She quoted Samuel Beckett: "*I can't go on, I'll go on.*"'

'It's from *The Unnamable,*' I said.

'That's right. *The Unnamable.*'

We fell silent. Then I said: 'I can't go on, Doctor.'

'I know. But that's *now*. Perhaps in time . . .'

'I can't go on. I won't go on.'

Three

I SHOULDN'T HAVE made that comment. I shouldn't have spoken without thinking. But I *was* thinking. I knew what I was saying. I knew I was articulating the truth. By doing so I had confirmed Dr Ireland's worst suspicions. I was a hopeless case.

To her credit Dr Ireland didn't bring up this comment again. She simply increased my dose of Mirtazapine by 15 milligrams. They did knock me out, but they did nothing to alleviate the unalloyed grief that seemed to permeate every waking hour. Courtesy of the pharmaceuticals, I was managing to sleep nine hours a night. When I woke there was always a minute or so of pleasant befuddlement, during which I would wonder where I was. Then my tongue would touch my stitched lips and everything would instantly rush back. How I wish I could have preserved that moment between sleep and consciousness when my brain seemed to be devoid of a memory; when I was just living in a woolly moment. Because once the mental trigger was pulled – and all retained thought was returned to me – I simply wanted to die.

Nurse Rainier was always on duty first thing in the morning and she seemed well aware of the processes by which the post-wake-up gloom would descend upon me. Within five minutes of me opening my eyes she'd be handing me a glass of orange juice and ordering me to get it into my system as soon as possible.

'It'll push your blood sugar up,' she'd say.

Nurse Rainier never spoke again about the child she lost, nor did she ever mention my failed suicide or the sorrow that haunted every waking hour. *Sorrow.* It was too controlled a word for what I was feeling right now. There were moments when I felt seriously unhinged; when I was convinced that I would never, *ever*, recover from what had happened, when it was absolutely clear to me that life from this point on would be constant agony . . .

Though I tried my best to hide this incessant despair, Nurse Rainier let it be known she was on to me. If she found me curled up in a ball in my bed, she'd tap me hard on the shoulder and say: 'I'm sending you to the physio now.' If she sensed that I was lost in gloom, she insisted on turning on the radio by my bed and getting me listening to NPR. If I was uncommunicative she would force me to talk with her.

Every morning she managed to drop a *New York Times* on my bed, telling me she'd found the one shop in Mountain Falls that sold it and commanding me to 'read about the world'. Even though the leg was still encased in a cast, she made me walk around the hospital for at least a half-hour twice a day, initially with a walker, but after a week or so with a cane. And when the bandage came off my eye, she brought a television to my bedside and forced me to watch an hour of news every day.

I knew why she was getting me to read a proper newspaper and listen to NPR and see what was happening in the world at large. It wasn't merely to distract me and fill up time, but also to somehow make me engage with something beyond my anguish.

Dr Ireland was also trying to push me towards some sort of acknowledgement that there was life beyond this hospital and all that it represented. She didn't return to my statement that I couldn't live with the grief. But she did insist that I talk about my daughter, recalling as much as I could bear to talk about – which wasn't much because every time her name crossed my lips, it was as if I had been seized by an impossible sadness. But she kept pressing me – just as she also wanted to know everything about my relationship with Theo and how my heightened anxiety in the final weeks had made me distracted for that crucial moment when the dog broke free in front of us and . . .

'Do you blame Theo for what happened?'

'He wasn't there. I blame myself.'

'But his business failure – the debt he ran up with that woman, the angry creditors, the very real fear you had that your home might be taken away from you . . . surely you must somehow feel that if these pressures hadn't been piled up upon you . . .'

'I take responsibility for what happened.'

'But don't you hate him for it?'

' "Hate" is a terrible word.'

'You've been through a terrible experience – and his irresponsibility, his complete disregard for your feelings, your welfare . . .'

'Stop attempting to make me feel better about what happened. I know the game: *when bad things happen to good people* and all that self-denial crap. I won't buy into that.'

'Or maybe you'd simply see that the accident was just that – an accident. And that you yourself were, at the time, coping with terrible pressures, terrible—'

'I despise Theo Morgan, OK?'

'And I'm here to tell you that everything you feel is valid and—'

'Oh, *please*. Everything I feel is awful. Maybe when I'm watching the nightly news that Nurse Rainier insists I watch I have a half-hour when I am distracted from it all. And thanks to your high-powered pharmaceuticals I do manage to sleep. But that's it. Otherwise it's there, day in, day out. Omnipresent. Hanging over every thought, every action.'

'Your lawyer called yesterday,' she said, changing the subject. 'The switchboard, acting on your instructions, didn't put the call through. But he did speak to me.'

'You mean, you asked to speak to him.'

'No, I mean he called me at my private practice in Mountain Falls. We had spoken twice before. I don't sense it's anything that dire. But he does need to talk through some things with you.'

'You evidently feel that, clinically speaking, this would be a good thing for me to do,' I said.

'I feel . . . he's your lawyer and you simply should speak with him.'

So I accepted a call from Alkan the next day.

'I'm glad to hear you survived your accident. After everything you've been through . . .'

'It wasn't an accident, Mr Alkan. It was an attempt to kill myself. Botched like everything else I do.'

'I'm certain that's an overly harsh statement.'

'To what do I owe this call, Mr Alkan?'

'You may have heard from Dr Ireland that Adrienne Clegg decided to drop all charges against you . . .'

'Yeah, I heard that. And what caused this Pauline conversion?'

'I had a talk with her lawyer – and made it very clear that I would eviscerate her if she dared take action against you.'

'So she completely backed off?'

'Better than that . . . she signed a document drafted by me, saying that she would never take any legal action against you and that all debts accrued by Fantastic Filmworks were not your responsibility.'

'Well . . . thank you.'

'You are most welcome. But there are a couple of other

things to discuss. The cab company . . . their insurers phoned me with an offer.'

'An offer?'

'A compensation offer.'

'I don't want their money.'

'Be that as it may, they still offered—'

'I don't care what they offered.'

'In situations like this one – and given the age of your daughter – the amount is never—'

'Did you hear what I said, Mr Alkan? I don't want their money.'

'It's one hundred and fifty thousand dollars.'

'Give it back to them.'

'Surely you're being a little rash here . . .'

'Don't tell me what I am – or am not – being. I don't want their damn money. Period.'

'I'll give you a few days to consider that.'

'Tell you what – accept their offer, but give the money away.'

'Miss Howard . . .'

'You heard what I said: give it all away.'

'To whom?'

'Is there a charity for parents who lost a child?'

'I'm sure there is. I'd have to do a little digging around . . .'

'Well, that's who it goes to.'

'I really wish you'd consider this for a few days.'

'Why? I might change my mind.'

'All right then.'

'By the way, what do I owe you for your services for all this?'

'Nothing. As you're making a charitable donation here I'm waiving my fee.'

'You're just doing that because you feel sorry for me.'

'That's right – I do feel sorry for you. As anyone would.'

'Anything else we need to discuss here?'

'Your life in Boston. When are you planning to come back here?'

'I'm not.'

'Isn't that a slightly premature decision? I mean, New England State has been in touch with me. They do want you to return as soon as possible. They consider you a most valued member of the department. Of course, I can't force you to do one thing or another. But I do know, from my discussions with your department chairman, that the university is willing to put you on fully paid compassionate leave for the rest of the year.'

'I don't want their money either.'

'It's being paid to you as we speak. Not only are they being very understanding, they're also showing real concern for you.'

'My mind is made up. And there's something else I want you to do for me. I want you to find a realtor and sell my apartment. Get rid of everything. Give away all the furniture, the electronics stuff, the books, the CDs. The lot. And then sell the place.'

'Where do you want the money to go?'

'Your call. Just give it away.'

'Jane . . .'

'Don't try to reason with me, Mr Alkan. Don't try to tell me I need more time to figure out my next move and all that blah, blah, blah. Sell the apartment and do whatever you want with the money.'

'I simply can't do that.'

'Get me the necessary paperwork and you can.'

A silence. Then: 'All right, Jane. As you are the client I have no choice but to follow your instructions. I'll send all the relevant papers to the hospital.'

'Thank you.'

'One last thing. Your friend, Christy, has been in touch with me regularly, trying to find your whereabouts. She seems genuinely concerned about your welfare. Will you speak to her?'

'No.'

'She did tell me she was your closest friend.'

'That's right. She is my closest friend. But I won't speak with her.'

'Mightn't it be worth your while to——?'

'My decision is final, sir.'

'Very good then. I'll FedEx everything in the next few days.'

'Please get them to me as soon as possible. They'll be kicking me out of here in fourteen days.'

'And then?'

'We'll see.'

The documents arrived forty-eight hours later. An extended form from Standard Life Insurance, in which I agreed to accept $150,000 from the company in exchange for never making another claim against them 'in this matter' again. There was also a document agreeing to the transfer of said $150,000 to the Samaritans. ('After some research I decided that they were the best of the organizations dealing with the bereaved and anyone else thinking about taking their life.') And there was a power-of-attorney form, granting Mr Alkan the full legal right to do whatever the hell he wanted to do with all the proceeds from my apartment . . . and anything else to do with my financial life.

I signed both forms and gave Nurse Rainier $30 in cash and asked her to FedEx them all back to him.

Having signed my life away I felt a strange sort of calm. I knew what all my next steps would be. Just as I knew that, with only twelve days to go before the insurance ran out, Dr

Ireland would be doing her best to make certain I was on the straight and narrow in time for my release.

'I must come clean about this and tell you that I telephoned your lawyer in Boston,' she said. 'He did inform me about the contribution you made to the Samaritans. That's most admirable.'

'Glad you think so.'

'He also told me you asked him to sell your apartment and give everything away.'

'Bet you find that less "admirable".'

'Just troubling, to tell the truth. I mean, say you decide to return to the Boston area and recommence your job at the university?'

'I'm not certain what my next step will be. But fear not, I won't be buying another car just to ram it into another snowbank.'

'Glad to hear that. Your friend, Christy, called me. She's incredibly concerned about you and actually wanted to come out here to see you.'

'But you talked her out of it?'

'I said that, given your somewhat fragile state – and your refusal to have any contact with the outside world – it mightn't be advisable.'

'Thank you for that.'

'She told me she lives in Oregon – which is less than a day's drive from here.'

'I'm not ready to see her.'

'But she told me she was with you in the weeks after Emily—'

'Correct,' I said, cutting her off. 'But that was then. And now . . .'

'Are you afraid of seeing her because of your failed suicide?'

'Yes, absolutely. But also because . . .'

'Yes?'

'Because I don't want . . . need . . . the kindness of others.'

'You mean, you think you don't *deserve* the kindness of others because you still wrongfully blame yourself for—'

'You're not going to convince me otherwise. I know what happened . . . and I have no alibi against that.'

She reached under her chair and pulled out a pad of paper and a pen. She uncapped the pen and starting drawing on it. Then she showed me her handiwork – a small blackened dot surrounded by a large circle.

'Know what this is?' she asked.

'Haven't a clue,' I said.

'The black dot . . . that's the world. And the circle . . . that's the grief you are suffering. In other words, your grief makes the rest of the world appear minute.'

She flipped a page and started drawing again, then showed me this new diagram: the same-sized circle, but a black dot that had trebled in size.

'Now, in time – and, as I have said during so many of these sessions, it will take a considerable amount of time – your grief will remain the same, but the world will get bigger. And when that happens—'

'I'll be a happy camper again?'

'You'll never be that. What will happen is that life will reimpose itself and force you to re-engage with it. The world will seem larger.'

Bullshit.

But I said nothing. I just shrugged.

'In the meantime,' Dr Ireland said, 'you would benefit from as much support as you are willing to accept.'

'You mean, once the insurance company kicks me out of here.'

'Your physical condition is very much on the mend. Dr Menzel tells me your eye is going to be near-fully functional in a few weeks – and the orthopedist is also very pleased with your progress. But I do worry that, if you are left on your own, you could psychologically regress . . .'

'As you said, it's not a simple "fix".'

'But say your friend Christy took you in for a while . . . ?'

'No sale,' I said.

'Hear me out, please. Christy told me she has plenty of room at her house in Eugene, Oregon. She is more than willing to drive out here, pick you up, and put you up at her place for as long as—'

'I don't want to be beholden to anyone.'

'This is not a matter of being "beholden" to anyone. This is – put baldly – trying to save you from yourself.'

'Good luck,' I said.

I dug my heels in on this one. Though Christy tried ringing me every day I refused to take her calls. I also informed Nurse Rainier that if she was to show up at the hospital I wouldn't "receive" her.

'Because Your Majesty is otherwise engaged,' Nurse Rainier said. 'Feeling sorry for herself.'

'Think what you like.'

'Believe me, I will. Especially as I know exactly what you're going through – and how easy it is to think that isolation is the only solution. But, as I learned, if you find yourself in hell, the only thing you can do is keep going.'

'I'll always be in hell.'

Nurse Rainier just shrugged.

'You can think that – and if you want easy answers, I can get five different men of God in here within the next half-hour and they'll sell you a bill of goods about the paradise to which you're bound if you accept that telephone call from Jesus.

363

They'll probably tell you that once you get to the other side, you'll meet up with—'

'Why are you doing this?'

'Been there, done that – that's why. I can't give you bromides, Professor. I can't give you much in the way of hope. Except what I told you before: if you're going through hell, just keep going. Though if I were you, I'd also think about staying with my friend in Oregon for a while.'

Christy continued to ring the hospital on a daily basis – I continued to refuse her calls. Just as I also wouldn't speak again with Mr Alkan – though he too phoned regularly.

If you're going through hell, just keep going . . .

Until you decide simply to reject the act of self-persuasion – of telling yourself the agony will, in time, be manageable – and bow to the inevitable.

So I counted off the days. I took my pharmaceuticals and had my sessions with Dr Ireland and did even more intensive physio once the cast came off, and readjusted my damaged eye to life without a bandage. All the while I prepared myself for the denouement that could not be sidestepped.

And so it came to pass – exactly twenty-eight days after my 'accident' – that I was turned loose from my convalescence. On the morning of my departure I had one last talk-fest with Dr Ireland. It was clear that she feared for me.

'I regret having to discharge you, Jane. Should you feel at any time, day or night, that you cannot cope, you must call me and talk things through.'

'Sure,' I said.

'I wish I could believe you . . .'

'Believe what?'

'Believe that you won't give in to despair. We all have to travel hopefully . . . even when events dictate otherwise.'

'I'll keep that in mind.'

I organized a taxi to pick me up at the hospital. Nurse Pepper insisted on giving me one last bath – and telling me that she hoped I would find 'the benevolent hand of a higher power' guiding me wherever I went. Nurse Rainier insisted on escorting me out to the waiting taxi. As the driver loaded up my suitcase and helped me into the back seat, she thrust a plain wooden cane on me.

'Brought this along as a little goodbye gift. Something to lean on.'

'Thank you . . . for everything,' I said.

'I don't want your thanks. I just want you to survive.'

I asked the cab driver to take me to a Holiday Inn on the edge of Mountain Falls. En route to the motel, I asked the driver to stop at a pharmacy. There I bought a bottle of one hundred and twenty Tylenol PM tablets. Then we continued on to a liquor store, where I scored a fifth of vodka.

The guy insisted on helping me in with my bag, even holding my arm as I leaned on the cane and I hobbled towards the hotel reception.

'How many nights are you planning to stay?' the woman behind the desk asked me.

'Just the one,' I said.

'You don't have a vehicle?'

'No.'

The Holiday Inn was a motel arrangement – you drove right up to the door of your rented room. The cabbie – a guy in his forties with thinning hair, wearing a check hunting shirt – again insisted on bringing me to its portals and helping me inside. It was a classic Holiday Inn with shit wallpaper, shit carpet, shit bedspread. I peeled off two twenties from my small wad of cash and handed it to him.

'The fare's only twenty,' he said.

'Well, you deserve forty.'

He looked unsettled as he said goodbye to me – as if he had a premonition of what I intended to do and was fearful on my behalf. As soon as he was gone I called the front desk and asked them if they might have a roll of duct tape behind the counter, as I needed something to repair a torn handle on my suitcase.

'You're in luck,' the woman said. 'We had an electrician doing a job for us here a couple of days ago and he left a roll behind.'

Using my cane I limped back to reception and picked it up.

'Can you get it back to me before you check out tomorrow?' she asked. 'Just in case the guy comes back looking for it.'

'No problem,' I said.

I returned to the room. I put the pills and the tape in a bedside drawer. I found a plastic laundry bag in a shelf in the closet. I pulled out the pills and the plastic bag and the tape.

Do it fast before you can think about it. Pour yourself three fingers of vodka to steady your nerves, then take the pills – ten at a time, all chased with more vodka. Once they're all ingested, place the plastic bag over your head. Seal it tightly around your neck with duct tape – by which time the Tylenol/vodka cocktail will have done its chemical work and you will begin to drift off into . . .

I found a plastic cup in the bathroom. I returned to the bed. I spread all the pills out on the bedside table. I half-filled the cup with vodka. I took a long sip. The alcohol burned as it slipped down. I raised the cup again and downed its contents. The vodka went straight to my head. I grabbed a notepad by the bed and scraped half the pills into my left hand. But just as I was raising them to my mouth, I heard a woman's voice. A shrill woman's voice, raised in anger.

'You little bitch . . . you ever fucking sass me again . . .'

Then I heard the distinctive sound of a slap, followed by a howl from a little girl.

366

'No, Mamma, no . . .'

Another slap, another howl. Then: 'You get that look off your face, you little . . .'

Suddenly I was on my feet, throwing the pills to the ground and hobbling to the door. As I yanked it open I saw the shrill woman – large, overweight, a shock of black hair – slapping a little girl across the side of the head. The girl couldn't have been more than five – and, like her mother, she was already oversized. Without thinking what I was doing I grabbed the woman's hand just as it was about to land again on her daughter's head.

'You stop that,' I heard myself yell.

'Who the hell are you?' the woman screamed back at me, struggling against my grip.

'You stop that right now.'

With her free hand she punched me right in the abdomen. It landed with full force, doubling me over, making me retch up vodka.

'You've got some nerve, lady,' she said, pulling the little girl into a car. I tried to get up. I couldn't.

'You can't do that to a child.'

The woman doubled back on me.

'You tellin' me how to treat my daughter?' she screamed. 'You givin' me parent lessons, Miss Fancy Pants?'

With that she kicked me right in the ribcage. I fell to the pavement and was sick again. There was the sound of an engine starting up. Over this: 'See what you caused, you little bitch?'

The girl begged her mother to forgive her. Then, with a shriek of rubber, the car pulled away and they were gone.

The entire incident couldn't have lasted more than a minute and it was witnessed by no one. I spat out the toxic bile that was now swimming around my mouth. Picking myself up

367

I staggered back into the room. As I walked inside, my shoe landed on top of all the pills I had scattered on the floor. All at once I was crying and sweeping the remaining pills off the bedside table and crushing them with the heels of my shoes, and grabbing the bottle of vodka and racing into the bathroom and smashing it in the tub, and finally collapsing on the bed, sobbing wildly, feeling beyond lost.

When the sobbing eventually subsided I lifted myself up off the bed and went into the bathroom and picked up every shard of glass in the bathtub. Then I found a dustpan and brush in the closet and swept up all that now-powdered Tylenol, thinking: *Even when you've been assaulted and have botched another attempt at suicide, you have to tidy up. Because you're a bad girl. And bad girls who want to be good girls always try to clean up the mess they've made, even though they know that they still won't feel better about themselves. Because . . .*

How could that woman do that to a child? *Her child.*

I felt another sob lodging in my throat. But I caught it and wouldn't let it escape. No more of that. Nurse Rainier was right: crying in the face of hell was just crying in the face of hell. And another failed suicide was just . . . pathetic.

I stood up. I went into the bathroom. My ribcage hurt and my mouth was noxious. Before splashing water on my face, I stared at my red eyes, the small lingering abrasion across my forehead, the lips now free of stitches but still marked by scars. As I turned away in disgust, a question formed in my addled brain.

When you can't self-destruct, what is the only other option open to you?

The answer arrived without much in the way of rumination . . . because it was so damn obvious.

You leave the world.

Four

IT TOOK AROUND twelve hours to divest myself of myself. It was fast work. After telling the woman at the front desk of the Holiday Inn that I would be staying there for the next two nights I used my cane to limp across the road to a grim little strip mall. There I bought a $20 telephone card, some cold cuts and bread, a pair of scissors and a few bottles of water.

Back in the room I started to work the phone. I called American Express, Visa, Discovery and MasterCard and cancelled all my accounts. All four of the 'customer services agents' I spoke with professed horror at my decision to end business with their companies, the Amex woman actually asking me: 'Have we done anything to upset you?'

'No,' I said. 'I've just decided I don't need your card anymore.'

'But we'd hate to lose you.'

'I'm sure you'll get over it.'

I phoned the telephone service of my bank in Boston to transfer the necessary funds to clear what remained on these accounts, then cut the cards in half. I did keep one piece of plastic: the debit card for my checking account, which, at close of business today, had a balance of $23,863.84. Enough to keep me going for a while – especially as my salary from New England State was still being paid into it monthly.

New England State. That was, so to speak, my next port of call. Opening my laptop, I found the wireless connection for the hotel and went online. I hadn't opened my mailbox since running away from Boston over five weeks ago. There were 338 messages. I deleted them all without reading a single one, even though I noticed many from Christy and from colleagues and even from old classmates, someone evidently having supplied my email address to everyone in the wake of . . .

But I couldn't bear reading words of condolence now, any more than I could deal with my best friend and her tough-love stance about getting me installed at her house. I counted eighteen emails from her. *Click, click, click* . . . and they were consigned to oblivion.

After also emptying the Recently Deleted folder of my server, I wrote Professor Sanders an email. It was short and to the point: in the wake of recent events in my life, I felt I had no choice but to resign my position at the university, effective immediately. And I thanked him for the support he showed me after . . .

Fifteen minutes after sending this, a reply came bouncing back to me.

Dear Jane

I'm online right now – hence the immediate response to your email. Everyone here has been naturally worried about you and were very relieved to hear that your automobile accident, though horrendous, didn't prove life threatening or crippling. As to your letter of resignation, the university is very much committed to keeping you on staff. Your post is currently being covered by a graduate student, Tim Burroughs, who is talented, but is not you. The President himself wants you to know that you are a valued member of our department – and has assured me you will remain on full pay until, hopefully, you return for the fall semester. That 'hope' is shared by all your colleagues in the department – especially by me.

Given what you've been through I can fully understand why you might want to sever ties with everything to do

370

with the recent past. But do know this: for all the complexities of your time at New England State – and I do appreciate that it often hasn't been easy for you – you are much respected here and enormously liked by your students. In short, we don't want to lose you.

I don't know if you read the letter I wrote to you after the accident. When my sister lost her nine-year-old son to cancer some years ago she couldn't bear to read a single letter of condolence. But I want to re-emphasize what I said in that note: a tragedy like the one you have suffered is so awful that you must give yourself the necessary time to somehow find a way forward. So – for the time being – I will not accept your letter of resignation. We have three or four months in hand before having to act on filling your position, should you not change your mind. But I sincerely hope that you will return to us in the autumn.

In the meantime, if you would like to discuss any of this – or simply feel like talking – please call me at any time.

Sincerely

Without pausing to reconsider I clicked the Reply button at the end of this email and wrote:

Dear Professor Sanders

I greatly appreciate your kind words and your support. However, my decision is final. I will not be returning to New England State in the autumn as I am resigning my post with immediate effect. There is no need to continue to pay me for this term.

Sincerely yours

Around a minute after sending this, there was an instant

reply from Sanders. I deleted it before it could be opened. Then I sent an email to Mr Alkan.

I presume the insurance payment has been handed over to the nominated charity. I presume the contents of the apartment have been given away and that the apartment itself is on the market. There will possibly be an insurance payout for my totaled car. Please also give this sum away. I don't want it.

In closing, this will be my last email to you. I am now vanishing from view. As you have power of attorney over my assets I leave you to administer their disbursement and deduct any fees that you incur in doing so.

I thank you for all the good counsel and kindness you have afforded me.

Over the next few hours I also cancelled all health insurance premiums, all pension plans, all monthly saving schemes. Then I spent over two hours stripping the hard drive of my laptop computer of every file, email and software program. Before doing so I also canceled my email account with AOL. I wouldn't be using email again for a very long time.

By the time I had completed all these tasks it was midnight. I took a long bath. I climbed into the stiff, rough Holiday Inn sheets. I popped a Mirtazapine and turned on the television and watched crap until the pill did its work and I faded into nocturnal limbo.

I slept straight through until nine the next morning and woke with a curious sense of disengagement. The dreaded instant still arrived when sleep gave way to consciousness and the world rushed in. But today, accompanying that 'each dawn I die' moment, was a grim resolution to get through the day . . . and to do so with the knowledge that my former life was just that: a part of a now-eradicated past. The laptop had been stripped clean. I had no instruments of credit, no debt, no material possession, a modest sum of money in the bank, $2,000 in cash, $1,800 in traveler's checks, no job, no family, no dependents, no obligations. Had I been of a philosophical bent I could have described my current condition as one approaching existential purity – a state of complete individual freedom, devoid of responsibility to anyone bar myself. But I knew better. I was engaged in the act of wiping the material hard disk of my life – with the bleak cognizance of the fact that I would never erase its emotional content.

Still . . . *keep busy, keep busy*. So I rang the front desk and asked them if they knew the number for the bus depot in town. They did. I called them up and found that there was a bus which left Mountain Falls tomorrow morning at nine a.m., crossing the frontier into Canada at one p.m. and then continuing non-stop to Calgary, arriving there around four p.m. One-way $47 – payable at the depot in town.

Why Calgary? It was the nearest city that was not in the United States. And if I was in the process of deleting the past, then the act of geographically detaching myself from my country had a certain logic to it. Had I been in Texas, I would have headed south to Mexico. As I had crash-landed myself in the higher reaches of Montana, there was only one place to go from here: up. Calgary was the first big city due north of where I now found myself. There was the extra bonus of having a Canadian passport (courtesy of dear old Dad). So Calgary was the obvious destination. I didn't care what it turned out to be. It was *there* – and *there* was where I was heading.

But before I caught that bus over the border there were a few final pieces of business to which I needed to attend. So I showered and changed into clean clothes and found a housekeeper doing the room next to mine and asked her for a large plastic bag. Then I went back to my room and opened my suitcase and dumped every item of clothing I owned into the bag. I also added the three pairs of shoes I'd thrown in and the extra coat that I'd grabbed as I fled my Somerville apartment.

If you're going to purge the past, everything connected with it must go.

Then I called a cab. When it arrived I told the driver to take me downtown. He looked warily at the large plastic bag I was toting with me.

'Know of a charity shop in town?' I asked. 'I want to make a donation.'

He dropped me in front of an American Cancer Society storefront. I paid him off and went inside and handed the bag to the large cheery woman behind the counter.

'Well, gosh . . . this is most generous of you,' she said.

Being a university town Mountain Falls had plenty of clothing shops. Within two hours I had bought two corduroy skirts, three pairs of jeans, three sweaters, half a dozen T-shirts, a pair of winter boots, a parka, a week's worth of underwear and socks, a duffel bag with wheels, and a new leather jacket which was on sale for ninety-five dollars. In all I dropped around seven hundred bucks – but I was now outfitted for the rest of the winter.

The saleswoman who helped buy the jacket told me that there was a 'real fine hairdresser named January' at a salon called Fine Cuts just two streets away. The woman even insisted on phoning January for me and telling her that I was en route to her: 'You look after my new friend and be real nice to her.'

Though I was touched by her neighborliness, all the questions she bombarded me with – *'New in Mountain Falls?'*, *'What do you do for a living?'*, *'Got a fella?'* – re-emphasized all the reasons why I couldn't inflict a small town on myself.

Before I had unpacked my small suitcase, they'd be on to me. Google tells all – and they would know all. Granted, they might be on to me in a big city as well, but at least there I could choose anonymity.

January turned out to be twenty-two or thereabouts. She was short and hyper-thin. She snapped gum and had a stud in the left side of her nose and purple painted nails. As I sat down in her chair and she mussed my straight brown hair that fell somewhere south of my shoulders and asked: 'So what are we going to do with this?', my reply caused her to smile.

'Cut it all off.'

'You want me to, like, shave your head?'

'Nothing so radical. But I would like it short.'

'Like short and spiky?'

'Like Joan of Arc short.'

'Who?'

'It doesn't matter. Have you ever seen an Audrey Hepburn movie?'

'Who?'

'Pageboy style?'

Working at the next chair was a hairdresser in her mid-fifties. This was Estelle – who owned the place. She heard our little exchange and nudged January.

'Winona Ryder.'

The penny dropped and January said: 'Oh, right, yeah, cool.'

An hour or so later I was most definitely the owner of a new look. January hadn't gone so extreme as to give me short back and sides, but my hair was now tightly cut around my head, though not to the point of rendering me androgynous.

'Didn't want to make it too mannish,' January said as she gave me the final blowdry. 'But didn't want it to be too girlie either. You cool with it?'

I looked at myself in the mirror. The lips were still marked. Ditto the forehead. But January's handiwork had, indeed, altered my appearance. I had lost the severe New England professor look. I now seemed . . . well, different.

'You've just lost five years – not that you looked that old to begin with.'

My eyes – hooded, ringed with dark circles – said otherwise.

'Mind me asking, but were you in some kind of accident?' January asked, as she brushed out my hair, her left hand touching the still-bruised forehead.

'Yes. I had an accident.'

'At least you walked away from it.'

'Sort of.'

'And at least it wasn't some guy who did that to you.'

After handing over $50 – and giving January another $10 for herself (she was genuinely chuffed by such a large tip) – I thanked her and left. There was a bookshop a few doors down from the salon. It had a café, a good selection of magazines and a very well-stocked literature section. I picked up several long books: Stendhal's *The Red and the Black*, Thomas Pynchon's *V* (which I had always meant to read), the collected stories of John Cheever and assorted magazines. Then I found a small diner that did stylish food. I had a plate of pasta and a glass of wine. I was back at the Holiday Inn by three. I read my magazines. Afternoon passed into evening. I listened to a Chicago Symphony concert on the local NPR station. I read one of the Cheever stories, marveling at his ability to find the elegiac amidst all that suburban sadness and frustration. The Mirtazapine did its chemical magic. The radio alarm woke me at seven. I showered and changed into a new pair of jeans, a T-shirt and a black turtleneck sweater.

Forward momentum, forward momentum. It was the only solution.

So I balled up the last of my old clothes and put them in the trash can by the desk. I picked up my laptop and went outside. The maid — a Hispanic woman in her mid-thirties — was pushing her housekeeping cart between units.

'Hi there,' I said.

The maid looked up at me with a questioning look on her face.

'You want something?' she asked.

'I was just wondering . . . might you need a computer?'

The questioning look now turned to downright puzzlement as I explained that I wanted to get rid of this laptop and was wondering if she'd like to take it off my hands.

'You want to sell it to me?'

'No, it's a gift.'

'Something wrong with it?'

'Not at all — and I've even stripped the hard disk of all old files, so it will be like a new computer for you.'

'Something bad inside it?'

'Like I said, I just don't need it anymore.'

'Everyone needs a computer.'

'I agree. However . . .'

I realized some fast thinking was necessary to convince her I wasn't a crank or dangerous or a combination thereof.

'I'm starting a new job next week and they're giving me a new computer so I won't have a use for this one. If you'd like it . . .'

'You trying to stick me with something?'

'Tell you what. Take it off me now. Bring it home. Open it up. Check it out. You'll see there's nothing dark or dangerous contained within. But if you still don't want it, take it to a pawn shop and get some money for it.'

Again she sized me up with suspicious eyes.

'You crazy, lady?'

'I'm just offering you something for nothing.'

'That makes you totally crazy.'

I held out the computer. The maid hesitated, but then reached out and accepted the laptop.

'You do this often?' she asked.

'It's a first for me. I hope you get some use out of it.'

That was the last vestige of my past. I returned to my room, zipped up my new duffel on wheels, rolled it over to the reception area and settled my bill for three nights. The receptionist looked at me quizzically.

'You get a haircut or something?'

She called me a cab. Ten minutes later I was at the bus depot. Half an hour after that, I was on a Trailways bus heading towards the border. I read another couple of Cheever stories on the way north, trying not to look out the window. The sight of such wild beauty was too much to bear. It spoke of natural splendor, of the pantheistic belief that God is the universe. But I knew better than to buy into that absurd notion of God being everywhere . . . and, as such, very busy. If the past few weeks had taught me anything, it was that we were all alone in a hostile universe – and that destiny had no logic, no plan, no grand intelligent design.

So I kept my head down and in my book as we traversed the edge of Glacier National Park and then headed into bleak open prairies. I was one of the few non-Native Americans on the bus. I looked up once to see that we had crossed into a First People's Reservation. Everything here was frozen and empty, the roads narrow and switchbacked, the terrain what I imagined the steppes of Central Asia to be: a bleak, ever-wintery void.

Most of the passengers got off at the town of Jefferson, a dispiriting collection of fast-food joints and a huge jerry-built casino that was undoubtedly owned and operated by the First People's Tribe, but was still a testament to all-American bad taste. There were only four of us left for the drive into Canada. The road to the customs post was even more treacherous than the one we had already negotiated, as the winds suddenly began to gust and the bus was enveloped in thick blowing snow. The driver was doing his best to manage the hairpin turns, the torturous steep descents, the complete lack of visibility. I put my book down as it began to dawn on me that I might be heading for another accident. But then I raised it again with the thought: *So what?*

The driver was a total pro and somehow managed to get us out of this slalom course and land us in Canada. The last few hundred yards were a lesson in modern *Realpolitik* – signs informing all comers that they were about to leave the United States (as if this was akin to falling off the edge of the world), then concrete bollards narrowing the road as you passed by the American customs post and continued right on into Canadian terrain.

The bus pulled up in front of a squat institutional building with a large maple-leaf flag blowing in the wind.

'All off, please,' the driver said.

It was minus something outside, and we had to wait as the lone immigration inspector in the glass booth interviewed each of the four passengers. I was last off the bus and last to be questioned. I handed over my Canadian passport.

'How long have you been out of Canada?' the officer asked me.

Here we go again, I thought.

'I've never lived here, but I did visit Nova Scotia a couple of years ago.'

That was the truthful answer, but not the smart one as it led to him bombarding me with questions about how I claimed my Canadian citizenship, why I hadn't resided in the country before now, why I was returning, blah, blah, blah. Rule number one with officialdom: give them simple answers. Had I said I'd been out of the country for a week he would have waved me through. As it turned out he still waved me through – but only after a pointless third degree that (I sensed) had more to do with his general sense of boredom than his worries that I might be a subversive traveling on false papers.

Once approved for entry I reboarded the bus, fell back into my seat, tried to read, surrendered to sleep, and only woke when we jolted to a halt and the driver announced that we had, indeed, arrived in Calgary.

I opened my eyes – and within half an hour wished that I hadn't.

Maybe it was the paucity of the light, the gray tire-treaded snow everywhere, or the reinforced concrete that seemed to characterize every corner of the cityscape. But from the moment I first laid eyes on Calgary I loathed it. Loathed it on sight.

In that initial first half-hour when I left the bus depot and got into a taxi and asked the driver to take me to the nearest hotel, I kept telling myself: *It will have to get better.* This corner of the city – with its faceless tower blocks, its wide nondescript streets, its strip malls, its brutalist style of architecture that seemed to be lifted right out of some Polish Communist-era film – all conspired to make me wonder what had possessed me to decide on Calgary as a destination . . . and to simultaneously consider it apt for my current state of affairs. *Just when you thought you couldn't travel further down into the abyss, you landed yourself here.*

The driver – a Sikh, wrapped up against the chill – asked me what sort of hotel I was after.

'Something cheap.'

Another bad mistake. He brought me to a place on what seemed to be the edge of the city – an in-town motel of the sort used by working girls and pensioners very much down on their luck. A room was just forty five Canadian dollars a night – and it lived up to its price. A dump. Painted breezeblock walls, yellowing linoleum floors, a double bed with a stained bed-spread and a mattress that sagged everywhere, a kitchenette with rust stains, a toilet which hadn't been properly cleaned in . . .

I wanted to leave immediately. But a snowstorm inconveniently began to kick up right after I checked in. I was tired and disorientated and veering into that shaky realm which always hinted that I was heading into the 'It's all unmanageable' zone. So I did what I had taken to doing whenever I felt myself tipping over the edge. I went to bed – this time taking double the dose of Mirtazapine to make certain that consciousness did not arrive for at least twelve hours.

As it turned out I managed eleven, and woke at six in the morning, stuporous and confused. The world rushed in. The grief hit – and, just to augment things, I was in the most joyless of surroundings.

I had checked out by six forty-five, stepping out into the snow-bound streets, a boreal wind howling down the empty boulevard. According to a street sign I was on 16th Avenue NW – and in a place called Motel Village. There were ugly motels to the north, south, east and west of me, a 7-Eleven, a Red Lobster, a McDonald's and a Tim Horton's doughnut joint. The sky was the color of cold porridge. The cold was so pronounced and severe that the skin on my face felt grated within a minute of leaving the motel. I passed by a newspaper box. Taking off my gloves to dig out a couple of quarters risked frostbite – but I still managed to buy a copy of the *Calgary Herald* before dashing into the safety of the Tim Horton's.

Inside, the atmosphere was fast-food depressing. Truckers and sanitation workers (judging by the vehicles parked outside) and the urban poor all eating thick clumps of frosted dough, washed down with indifferent coffee. *You Ivy League snob. You're no longer in Cambridge. You're in a High North shithole.*

I ordered two maple-glazed doughnuts and a cappuccino. Maybe it was the fact that I hadn't eaten in over sixteen hours, but they all tasted pretty damn good. I opened the newspaper, turned to the property pages and scanned the Apartments for Rent ads. One of the fundamental problems of coming into a city about which you know absolutely nothing is that street coordinates and neighborhood references make absolutely no sense: *Eau Claire: superb 1-bed exec with magnificent Bow River views.* Or: *Best of 17th SW – stylishly furn 2-bed unit, walk to CBD, $1750. References.* Or: *Magnolia Heights – sparkling clean home in the friendly neighborhood of Saddle Ridge!*

Even though I knew nothing at this point about Calgary I still sensed that any area named Saddle Ridge was probably stuck out in the 'burbs.

I checked my watch. It was seven-thirty. There were a couple of beefy guys at an adjoining table.

'Morning,' I said. 'I just arrived in town last night . . .'

'And you ended up here?' one of them said, causing the other two to laugh. 'Lady, you've got a nose for the wrong side of the tracks.'

'It's a mistake I won't make again. But listen, what's a decent hotel in Calgary?'

'A decent hotel in Calgary?' the same guy said again, repeating my question with a certain mordancy. 'You really think we know stuff like that?'

'Sorry to have troubled you.'

'Hey,' one of his colleagues said to the guy, 'show the lady some respect.'

'I wasn't being disrespectful.'

'The Palliser,' the third man said. 'Was in there once when there was a fire in the kitchen.'

'Was that back in 1934?' the first guy asked.

'You got to excuse our friend here,' the third man said. 'He thinks he's a comedian, but no one at the station house ever laughs at his jokes. You want a good hotel, you go to the Palliser. But it'll cost ya.'

I did a very fast calculation of the money in my jacket pocket – between my cash and my traveler's checks I had not far off $4,000 Canadian. I could afford a few nights in a decent hotel. Check that: I needed to be in reasonable surroundings while I got my bearings.

'Do you know if there's a phone around here?' I asked him.

'Who you wanna call?'

'A taxi.'

He pulled out a cellphone.

'Consider it done.'

The cab arrived in minutes. It took nearly half an hour to reach the Palliser.

'I didn't realize I was so far from downtown,' I said to the driver.

'Calgary's a sprawl.'

Calgary was also a non-stop construction site: condos, bedroom communities, new developments, new strip malls. There were few extant historic buildings . . . bar the Palliser. It was located on 8th Avenue in what appeared to be the downtown. From all my years teaching the literature of America's Gilded Age, I immediately responded to the Palliser. Its facade was Robber Baron. Its interior was updated

383

faded glitz – an accurate oxymoron (which, in itself, *is* an oxymoron). It was an old railroad hotel which a century ago catered to the leisured class who had somehow managed to find themselves in this isolated outpost – arriving by the Canadian Pacific from the East, laden down with steamer trunks that were carried by a manservant who probably slept in cramped downstairs quarters while his oil-magnate master and his overfed wife retired to a vast suite on a higher floor.

All right, all right – I was mentally riffing. But it was rare to come across such a relic from the era in which (academically speaking) I had lived for so long. This was a hotel out of a novel by Dreiser or Frank Norris. It was also exactly the sort of place about which my father spoke so often back in the days when he spoke about such things – waxing lyrical about his long-vanished Canadian childhood when his father once brought his then ten-year-old son on a trans-Canadian trip, during which Granddad was drunk from eleven in the morning onwards. I'm certain he once mentioned staying in 'some big old pile' in Calgary, how it was right after Christmas and he'd never been colder in his life . . . until, a couple of days later, they ended up in Edmonton.

'You should've seen winter back then,' he told me.

You should see winter now, Dad. And you should see where life's random cruelties have landed me.

'Can I help you?'

It was the woman at the front desk. In her twenties, black-haired with a decided Eastern European accent. How had she landed herself in Calgary?

'I was looking for a room for a couple of nights.'

She explained that they had rooms from $275 to $800 per night. I blanched – and she noticed that.

'It's a bit beyond my budget,' I said.

'How many nights would you be with us?'

'Maybe four or five. I'm new in town and will be hunting for a place to live.'

'When did you arrive?'

'Just last night.'

'You have a job here?'

I shook my head.

'Family? Friends?'

Again I shook my head.

'Why Calgary?' she asked.

'Random selection.'

'Like evolution,' she said with a smile, then added: 'I studied biology back in Poland.'

'And here?'

'I still study biology at the university – and do this to pay my bills.'

'But why Calgary?'

'Random selection.'

She tapped away at her computer terminal for several minutes, then picked up the phone and spoke in a low voice to someone. When she ended the call she was all smiles.

'Things are a bit slow at the hotel this week – so if you are willing to commit to five nights here I can offer you a special employee's rate of a hundred and fifty per night. It won't be one of our larger rooms, but it's still pretty nice.'

'Thank you,' I said, handing over my debit card.

'Jane Howard,' she said, reading my embossed name. 'Any thoughts on what you'll be doing in Calgary?'

'None,' I said.

'That's a start.'

As described, the room wasn't big – maybe 200 square feet. But after the nightmare motel, it was more than adequate. There was a queen-sized bed, a good armchair, a desk, a very clean functioning bathroom. I unpacked my bag, turned on my radio, found the classical music station of the CBC, ran a hot bath, undressed and sat in it for the better part of an hour, contemplating my next move, trying to grapple with the daily gloom. But 'to grapple' is to attempt to come to terms with a set of circumstances. There was no antidote to all this. There was just the matter of trying to get through the day.

So, after my bath, I picked up the phone and called the concierge – and explained that I was moving to Calgary and wanted to rent an apartment, but knew nothing of the city. The concierge was named Gary – a very friendly type, eager to help.

'You in the oil business?' he asked.

'Uh, no . . .' I said, just a little bemused.

'Calgary's a big oil town – the Dallas of the North – so most of the relocating executives we get staying in the hotel are in petroleum.'

'I'm a teacher.'

'Then I guess you're not going to be after some big executive pad.'

'My budget's pretty modest.'

'Any idea where you want to live in town?'

'None.'

'Do you have a car?'

'No.'

'Will you have a car?'

'I don't think so.'

'And you teach what?'

'Literature.'

'In high school?'

'I was a professor.'

'Right – then you'll probably want to be near some bookshops and decent cafés and not far from the art cinemas in town.'

'There are art-house cinemas in Calgary?'

'Don't sound that surprised. There are three – and even a couple of very good theaters and not a bad symphony orchestra.'

Well, this was news.

'Anyway,' he continued, 'my advice to you would be to look either in an area called Kensington or somewhere around 17th Avenue SW – and I do know a realtor who might be able to help you. How fast are you wanting to move?'

'I need a place in a couple of days.'

'OK – I'm on the job . . .'

Within fifteen minutes he called back to say that a realtor named Helen Ross would be calling momentarily. This she did.

'Understand you're looking for a rental unit in either Kensington or Mount Royal. What's your budget?'

'I really couldn't spend more than seven hundred a month.'

'Furnished or unfurnished?'

'Furnished would be preferable.'

'Then we're probably talking a studio, if that's OK with you.'

'That's fine.'

'Mind me asking what you do?'

I knew this was coming – and had a straightforward answer prepared. I had taught university. The contract had ended. I was now looking for work.

'So no gainful employment right now?'

'Is that a problem?'

'Not if you can show you have adequate funds to cover the year's lease.'

Damn. That would mean contacting my bank in Boston – as she would probably need a reference as well. By getting in touch with the bank I'd be informing someone of my whereabouts . . . unless my guy there could be trusted to stay shtum about this. Are bankers like priests?

'I can provide you with anything you need,' I said.

'Very good then. I have a viewing this morning, but say I came by the hotel at three this afternoon?'

I was waiting for her in the lobby when she drove up in a silver Lexus. Helen Ross was in her fifties. Well preserved. Well dressed. Two serious diamond rings on her left hand. A hint of Botox around the eyes. Direct, pleasant and evidently not wanting to spend too much time on such a small-beer letting, but still determined to be professional and courteous. I could see her looking me over, sizing me up, probably categorizing me as an eternal-student type . . . which wasn't too off the truth. In a very casual way she asked me about my background. I provided her with just enough to satisfy her curiosity, mentioning my Canadian father, my doctorate from Harvard (that made her glance at me with care – gauging whether I was being straight with her or was some fantasist) and how I was now 'between jobs' and had decided on 'a change of life, a change of scene'.

'Divorced?' she asked.

'We weren't officially married, but . . .'

She nodded grimly.

'My husband left me last year – after twenty-three years together. I got the big house and the Lexus and a lot of grief that doesn't seem to want to go away. You know about that too?'

'I know about grief.'

Helen Ross took that in – and correctly sensed from my tone that I didn't want to pursue this subject. Instead, she changed course, telling me that Calgary was now booming. House prices had doubled in the last eighteen months. Biggest growth of any Canadian city. Some of the best restaurants in the country. Cool arts scene, the city having finally gotten wise to the idea that fostering a 'creative community' was a boon to business. And, of course, with the Rockies just forty minutes away by car . . .

It was like being with a one-person Chamber of Commerce. But I liked Helen Ross – and her forthrightness with me about her post-divorce emotional injuries immediately made me realize that I was wrong to judge her simply on the material evidence of her well-upholstered life. She bled like the rest of us and she wanted me to know that as well . . . which, coming from a complete stranger, had an honest poignancy.

'Now I have only three places I can show you – and the first is the best.'

It was located in an area called Mount Royal, right off 17th Avenue SW.

'This is one of the trendiest parts of town.'

At one end of 17th Avenue SW were some ugly apartment blocks (they seemed to be a Calgary specialty) and a 7-Eleven. As the avenue progressed I did note some cafés, some boutiques, a collection of renovated brick buildings, a few bookshops and quite a number of restaurants. All right, it wasn't Harvard Square. But after my initial shell-shocked impressions of Calgary . . . well, this wasn't bad at all.

We turned into a side street and pulled up in front of one of the few old buildings in the area. By old I'm talking 1930s – and judging by its institutional girth, it had started life as an educational establishment.

'This was an old schoolhouse,' Helen Ross said, 'but is now a very nice apartment building.'

The 'unit' that Helen had earmarked for me was located on the second floor, right in the back of the building. ('But it still gets great morning sunlight.') As promised it was a studio – maybe 250 square feet at most – but nicely renovated. Plain off-white walls. Stained hardwood floors. A modern alcove kitchen with all the basic equipment. A modern neutral bathroom. A sofa in gray fabric. A matching armchair with an ottoman. A floor-to-ceiling set of doors that opened to reveal a queen-sized Murphy bed with a reasonably hard mattress. A Paris-style café table and two mahogany bentwood chairs.

'There's one very decent walk-in closet. There's a communal laundry in the basement. There's room for a desk on that wall over there by the window. It's wired for cable and broadband . . .'

'*I don't watch television and I don't have a computer anymore,*' I was going to tell her, but decided not to sound like a Luddite crank.

'And if you're willing to sign a two-year lease I can get the price down by a hundred a month to six twenty-five.'

'Sold,' I said.

But I still needed to provide references. So the following morning, I called Laurence Phillips, the manager at the local branch of Fleet Bank in Somerville, where I deposited my money. We'd had few dealings with each other – and though he took my call immediately, he seemed genuinely surprised to hear from me.

'I was aware of the fact that you had left the Boston area . . . just as I had also heard about your dreadful loss. I am so sorry. I don't know if you received our letter of condolence . . .'

'I couldn't read any of them.'

'Of course you couldn't. How can I help?'

'Are you good at keeping a secret, Mr Phillips?'

'As long as it doesn't entail anything illegal.'

'It's nothing illegal. It just has to do with my whereabouts.'

Then I explained about how I had landed in Calgary, leaving out the failed suicide attempt . . .

'I simply need you to fax the realtor my bank statement and

a letter from you stating that I'm a client in good standing etc . . .'

'I'm happy to do that.'

'I also need you to promise me that you will not mention my new location to anybody.'

'You have my word.'

Later that afternoon Helen Ross phoned me at the hotel to inform me she had received the necessary bona fides from Laurence Phillips and the lease would be ready to sign tomorrow. I would have to provide one month's rent in advance and an additional one month's deposit.

'No problem,' I said.

We met at the apartment the next day. I signed the lease. I handed over $1,250 in cash. I went shopping. At Helen's suggestion I also rented a car for a couple of days – she had a friend at the downtown branch of Alamo who gave me a sub-compact for three days for $100, all taxes and insurances included (I was conscious of every dollar I spent). She also pointed me in the direction of a mall called Chinook just fifteen minutes from my house where she told me I could buy everything I needed.

Before we parted she put a hand on my shoulder and said: 'We naturally had to run basic background checks on you. And I did use a search engine to find out about your academic career. That's when I also read about your tragedy.'

I suddenly stiffened . . . and wanted to be anywhere but here.

'I'm so sorry,' she continued. 'I don't know how—'

'Stop, please,' I said.

She withdrew her hand.

'Excuse me. I didn't mean to seem like I was prying.'

'You weren't prying. It's just . . .'

So this is how the world now worked. You met someone,

you discovered they might have a credential or two, you Googled them, and you found out . . .

But this knowledge simply made me resolve to limit all human contacts to an absolute minimum. I just couldn't bear any form of decency or kindness right now. People always asked questions about you. Even though they were usually well-meaning questions they were still *questions*. And questions led to answers. And answers led to . . .

So I would withdraw completely.

But before that, I needed to buy some essential items for my new 250-square-foot world.

The Chinook Mall was like all other malls – all those brand names and designer emporiums tempting you to purchase all sorts of things you didn't need. Still, I did find a household goods place where I bought two sets of dark gray sheets, two pillows, a duvet and two gray covers, bathroom towels, a coffee maker, basic pots and pans, a set of white plates, cutlery, glassware. All in, I dropped just under $1,000 – but for that money the apartment was completely set up, bar a small stereo which cost me an additional $200.

I returned home. I unpacked everything. I plugged in the stereo. I found CBC Radio 2 – the classical service. I sat down in the armchair. Out of nowhere, it all hit me again, and I found that I simply couldn't stop weeping until I was so wrung out there was no choice but to stagger into the bathroom and splash cold water on my face and grab my coat and car keys and . . .

Drive.

As I had the car for another two and a half days I decided to take advantage of it and . . . drive.

So I spent the time exploring as many parts of Calgary as possible. And what did I discover . . . ?

That cab driver I met on my first morning in Calgary was

right – the city was a sprawl. Like all sprawls – especially those set on prairies – it often had the feeling of being jerry-built, thrown up in a hurry, half thought out. There was no sense of a past, a heritage, a coherent urban identity. In a used bookshop on 17th Avenue SW I came across some 1920s photographs of Calgary, all of which showed a bustling North American cityscape of the type that mixed frontier architecture with certain turn-of-the-century Chicago flourishes. Bar the occasional remnant in the downtown core, it had all been detonated away, replaced by towers of glass and steel. There were some interesting neighborhoods. Kensington – which fronted the Bow River – had an excellent bookshop, an old-style picture house which showed art films, a couple of terrific coffee places and a general Cambridge-style atmosphere. There was also a nearby area called Mission with similar trendy shops and restaurants, and Inglewood, a warehouse district just beyond the 'downtown core' (as Calgarians seemed to always call it) with a burgeoning attempt at what design magazines call 'a loft scene'.

Then there were the millionaire-oilmen houses in Mount Royal, the expensive bachelor pads around Eau Claire, and the endless 'burbs – track after track of the same ranch-style house or bungalow, stretching into near-infinity on the prairie. All these subdivisions and estates had fanciful names: Killarney, Sweetwater, Sunridge, Westhills. All were grouped around shopping centers and strip malls. All had the sort of uniformity one associates with military housing. All represented so much of the prosaic and the stifling in modern life. As I toured their byways, the sight of a mother loading up her daughter into the family SUV would detonate a sorrow that still seemed limitless. This was accompanied by the knowledge that, no matter where I turned, I would always see children. They would be in shops, in malls, being pushed in strollers, getting off schoolbuses, being guided through museums, walking home with parents after school. It wasn't just the three-year-olds who cut me to the quick. From this time onwards, every child at every stage of life – right up through adolescence and beyond – would remind me of all those stages we would have gone through together . . . what could have been, what now never would be.

So I decided to steer clear of these suburban enclaves because they had a higher density of children than the area around my neighborhood. I did a little more shopping for the apartment – a desk lamp, a floor lamp, a rug for the floor – and then returned the car, vowing not to venture outside the central core of the city again.

Once I had the apartment set up, a routine developed. I would wake most days around noon. Then I would walk down to 17th and 9th – and my morning haunt, Caffé Beano. It was a 1950s retro coffee joint. They knew how to make excellent espresso. They served proper bagels and muffins. They sold that morning's edition of the *Globe and Mail* and the *Calgary Herald*. They left you alone . . . though, after I had showed up every morning for a while, the barista on duty asked me my name.

'Nice to meet you, Jane,' he said. 'I'm Stu.'

'Nice to meet you, Stu.'

End of conversation.

I would spend over an hour and a half in Caffé Beano, then I would haunt the two or three used bookshops on 17th. Here too the staff got to know me, especially at Prism Books, where I scored a complete hardcover edition of *Remembrance of Things Past* and a 1902 English edition of the complete Dickens. I could have kept buying more, except that my small apartment would only take so many books and I was very conscious about curbing my expenditure.

Jan was the girl behind the counter at the bookshop. She was somewhat punky – her hair had been dyed the color of cotton candy – and she told me she'd already had a couple of 'out there' stories published in small magazines. She also tried to engage me in dialog.

'You're in here every afternoon,' she said.

'I'm a person of routine.'

'And a good customer. You wouldn't happen to be a writer?'

'Just a reader.'

'You mind me asking you your name?'

We introduced ourselves.

'Well, if you're not a writer – and you're in here every day – what do you do?'

'I'm just taking a little time out from everything right now,' I said.

'And you chose Calgary to do that?'

'I kind of fell into the place.'

'Tell me about it. I was raised in Regina – a dump – and came here to the U. of C., and kind of never left. And, like, half of me thinks that the city is an ugly shithole – but one with these little pockets of cool which just about counterbalance the fact that the place looks like the set of one of those Kieslowski movies located in some Warsaw housing estate. You ever see *The Decalogue*?'

'Yes, I know all ten full-filled episodes.'

'Well, there are a bunch of us who get together every Thursday night in a room above here – and we show a couple of interesting movies and drink a bit too much and pretend we're in Paris or Prague or Berlin. If you were interested . . .'

'I'll think about it,' I said. My tone hinted that I wasn't in a sociable place right now.

Jan seemed to understand as she said: 'Anyway, if you're

ever up for hanging out with some like-minded souls, consider this an open invitation. We all think of ourselves as being in internal exile here.'

But I didn't take Jan up on her offer. Because that would have meant actually talking with other people. Which, in turn, would lead to questions. And the questions would lead to . . .

Still, Jan seemed to grasp that I needed to play the solipsistic card right now, as she never pushed me for any further details about myself. I would drop in, browse, occasionally make a big purchase, and otherwise would pick up a book or two a week – and our talk would be limited to literature, something in the news, a new movie that just opened at the Uptown or the Globe or the Plaza: the three decent cinemas in town.

I had this sort of genial but distant relationship with every shopkeeper I got to know in my area. The guy at International News (where I could buy the *New Yorker* and the *New York Review of Books*), the woman at Reid's stationers where I purchased ink and notebooks, the guy in the wine and cheese place on 11th Avenue where I dropped by twice a week to stock up on drink and comfort food . . . they all knew my name. They all exchanged pleasantries with me. They never tried to engage with me – because the signal I sent out to the world was: *Please don't come too close.* This may have been a small city, but it was still *a city.* As such, if you chose a certain form of anonymity, people would accept it. Because that was the urban code . . . even in Calgary.

Time. I suddenly had a great deal of it on my hands. With no employment, no ties, no responsibilities, no clear need to do anything other than get through the day, I found myself still looking for ways to keep busy. The café. The bookshop. Home to read for three hours. A longish walk, during which I'd also buy groceries. Home again to do ninety minutes' worth of French (I bought grammar books and some basic texts, determined to finally crack the language . . . but also knowing that it filled a gap during the day). Then I would force myself out most nights – to a movie, a concert, a talk at a bookshop, anything that could divert me.

Time. Time. Time. By the end of April the temperature was gradually heading north. I bought a second-hand bicycle with a decent set of panniers large enough to fit in several days' worth of groceries. It also brought me around town. With the exception of events at the University of Calgary, the bike would get me pretty much everywhere I wanted to go: to the cinemas, to a coffee place in Kensington which roasted its own beans, to the bi-weekly literary readings at the McNally bookshop on 8th, to the occasional classical concert at the Jack Singer Hall . . .

Had I wanted to, I could have rented a car and headed out of town in the direction of Banff and the Rockies. But I knew I still couldn't bear the idea of looking at anything scenic, dramatic, momentous. Best to stick to Calgary's concrete mundanity. Its habitable bleakness perfectly reflected the inside of my head.

Time. Time. Time. I broke down and bought a small television and a DVD player. Though I never signed up for the cable television service in the building, I did start to make use of a very good film library a few streets away from me. It proved useful on those nights when the pills didn't do their chemical magic and I jolted awake and had to read or watch something to keep the darkness at bay. I found that, in the middle of the night, I couldn't handle anything life-affirming or consoling. No Frank Capra movies, no re-viewings of *ET*. I worked my way through Dickens's *Bleak House,* fascinated by the way he could write a social novel that also grappled with melancholia. I watched Carl Theodore Dreyer's *Day of Wrath*

– about witch burning in seventeenth-century Denmark – and all of Bergman's island films. When I found myself in the film-rental place reaching for Klimov's *Come and See* (about the Nazi massacre of a Belarus village) I actually had a manic fit of the giggles and wondered: *Will there ever come a moment when I can get through a night again without a medicinal dose of desolation?*

The problem was compounded by the amount of booze I was putting away. I'd get home from a film or a concert. I'd down three glasses of wine and then take my pills. Sleep would hit. Four hours later I would be wide awake again. So I'd open Dickens or pop on Bergman's *The Passion of Anna* and down another three glasses of something red – and maybe surrender to sleep sometime just before seven, staying in bed until noon. But after around three months of broken nights I woke up yet again with another hangover and thought: *Maybe I do need to take this in hand.*

This meant going to a doctor. In turn this also meant finally dealing with officialdom. After four months in Calgary I was finally informing Canada that I was residing in their country. So I went to the payphone I used outside the Shopper's Drugstore, called Information and asked the woman on the line: 'How do I register for social security?'

'You mean social insurance?'

'Is that what they call it?'

'Yes, that's what they call it,' she said, polite but just a little tetchy. 'Here's the number . . .'

That afternoon I presented myself at a government building. I filled out the requisite forms. I proffered my passport. I was interviewed by a courteous if chilly woman who asked me a lot of questions about why I had only now, at the age of thirty-three, registered for a social insurance number.

'I've never lived in Canada.'

'And why was that?' she asked, her tone officious.

'Because I was brought up in the United States.'

'So how do you have a Canadian passport?'

'My father was a Canadian.'

'And what made you decide to suddenly move to Canada?'

'Is that relevant to me receiving a social insurance number?'

'I have to follow procedures here. I have to ensure that you are legitimately entitled to a SIN.'

'You have my passport. You can, no doubt, check with Ottawa to ensure that it is valid. What else do you need from me?'

'I have asked you a question. I now expect an answer. What made you leave the United States for Canada?'

Without a moment's hesitation I blurted out: 'My three-year-old daughter was knocked down and killed by a car. Happy now?'

My voice was so angry and loud that it silenced the room. All the other clerks, all the waiting citizens, seemed to freeze. In the shocked moment that followed, the clerk's eyes filled with fear – as if she instinctually knew what was coming next.

I remember something David once told me when a waitress in a restaurant was rude to us for no apparent reason.

'You never know what sort of day she was having before she got here – so don't think it was about you.'

Behind where the clerks sat at their windows was an office, its door open, a besuited man working behind a desk. He too must have heard what I said, as he was instantly on his feet, hurrying towards us. The woman clerk nervously glanced in his direction. That's when I realized this was not the first time she had seriously overstepped a boundary . . . though this observation was secondary to the anger I was still feeling after my outburst.

'Mr Russell,' the clerk said, 'if I could just explain—'

'That won't be necessary – as you can go home now for the rest of the day.'

'But I was only trying to carry out—'

'I heard exactly what you were doing – and you've been darn well warned about this before.'

'I just thought—'

'Go home, Mildred. You will hear from us tomorrow.'

Mildred didn't look like she wanted to move. But realizing she had no other option she quickly got up and left, running off and appearing to burst into tears at the same time. Mr Russell picked up my file off her desk and glanced at it.

'She should have had the good grace to apologize, Ms Howard. But as I'm her supervisor I'll do it for her – and for this department. I'm truly sorry about all that. I'm afraid it's her style – and she's been warned before to amend it. Now, if I have my way, she'll be amending it in Medicine Hat.'

He opened my file and said: 'I'll have your SIN in five minutes.'

Which indeed he did – again apologizing as he handed me my passport and my new social insurance card.

'I hope this experience won't make you think all civil servants here are so graceless,' he said before wishing me goodbye.

Graceless? Passive-aggressive was the true Canadian style – and it didn't just apply to the bureaucrats. Everyone up here was, by nature, polite. It was part of the social make-up – something that was expected of you. But the politeness was tinged with a testy petulance; civility through gritted teeth. Mildred was a case in point. She never raised her voice once when pressing me for an answer. But, in a fusty, school-marmish way, she played the passive-aggressive card firmly: *If you want what I can give you, you heed my command.* Until my very American outburst sabotaged her strategy.

In the aftermath of it all I was strangely grateful to Mildred. By angering me she had provoked me into doing something I had refused to do, even during all my sessions with Dr Ireland . . . actually spitting out the appalling but undeniable truth: my daughter is dead.

I articulated this verity a few days later when I showed up at the medical practice to which I had been assigned. My doctor was named Sally Goodchild; a woman in her forties, quiet, straightforward and, as I discovered, a quick diagnostician. As soon as I came into her consulting room I could see her sizing me up.

'So, Jane,' she said, reading through my health questionnaire, 'you're new to our practice. New to Calgary as well, I see. And you're having trouble sleeping – even though you're on 30 mgs of Mirtazapine per day. So, to cut to the chase, how bad is the depression?'

'I just can't sleep.'

'If you can't sleep while taking Mirtazapine, you are seriously depressed. And the doctor who first prescribed you the pills, she was in the States, yes?'

I nodded.

'And was there something *causal* – as we medical types like to call it – which brought about your depression?'

Again I said it.

'My daughter Emily . . .'

I got through the sentence, staring down at my hands. Dr Goodchild was evidently unsettled by this revelation – and, to her credit, did not try to hide it.

'That's terrible,' she said. 'I'm not surprised the dosage of Mirtazapine isn't proving effective anymore.'

'I need to sleep, Doctor.'

She asked if I would like to speak to a therapist.

'Been there, done that,' I said. 'And it did no damn good.'

'Are you working right now?'

I shook my head. She thought that over for a moment, then said: 'All right, I'm going to up your intake of Mirtazapine by a further 15 mg – and I'm going to also ask you to consider the idea of finding a job. It would give some focus and shape to your day.'

'I don't want *focus* and *shape*.'

'So what do you want, Jane? What would help you here?'

'What would help me here? My daughter. Alive.'

'But that can't be.'

'And as I can't kill myself . . . as much as I want to every hour of every day . . .'

'You think yourself a coward because of that?'

'Actually, I do.'

'Whereas I think choosing to live when you realize there is no solution . . . well, it's almost heroic.'

'No, it's not heroic at all.'

'Think what you like. You have chosen now to live. But with that choice comes a realization: there is no solution. There is only one antidote to this all – an antidote which won't drain any or all of the poison away, but which might prove temporarily palliative.'

'And what's the antidote?'

'Go back to work.'

402

THERE WERE PLENTY of jobs in Calgary. Every week there was a story in the *Herald* about the labor shortage – how Boomtown lacked enough workers to serve up fast food and mop offices and even teach their children.

I scanned the employment pages in the newspaper. I nosed around a few job agencies. It was true – there were job openings for teachers. With my qualifications I sensed it would be reasonably easy to land something. But then I'd have to get up in front of a group of kids and talk. That would mean having to be with children. Even if they were pre-college adolescents, they'd still be children. And that would be too much to bear.

Then, by accident, I discovered the city's Central Public Library. I was heading on my bicycle to an afternoon movie at a multiplex located in the Eau Claire marketplace and decided to stop en route in Chinatown for a fast plate of dim sum. This meant taking a different route, turning left down the McLeod Trail (many thoroughfares in Calgary were called trails) and passing an ugly cluster of municipal buildings. I'd cycled this way many times before – but never really took much notice of these administrative edifices, all of which were straight out of the Stalinist School of Architecture. Today I happened to look up and see a sign which said: Central Public Library. I braked and pulled over. The library was all reinforced concrete and prison-style slitted windows. What were the municipal authorities thinking when they approved this monstrosity? Still, I locked up my cycle and went inside. There – on the bulletin board in the lobby – was a notice:

CALGARY CENTRAL PUBLIC LIBRARY SEEKS ASSISTANT LIBRARIANS

They were offering a forty-hour week at $12 per hour. Though they would prefer candidates with 'some knowledge of library science', it was not essential. There were three posts open right now and candidates should submit their résumés to . . .

And they gave the name of a Mrs Geraldine Woods, Chief Librarian.

I walked into the library and asked if they had a computer room.

'Ground floor, turn left. But it costs $2 for an hour's internet access.'

I didn't want to go online. I just wanted to use a word processor and a printer. Over the course of the next hour I sat and wrote my résumé, along with a covering letter to Mrs Woods. When I finished and was about to hand it in, the thought struck me: How will she get back in touch with me if I don't have a telephone? As much as I didn't want this rather essential instrument of communication I knew that a résumé without a telephone number would raise suspicions – and probably make her wonder if I was living a life like the Unibomber. Best to bow to the inevitable and get a cellphone.

So I printed up the résumé and the letter, leaving a space blank for the phone number. Then I went outside and cycled over to Chinatown and found around eight different shops selling electronic goods. The one I chose was run by a nervy man in his thirties who was chain-smoking and simultaneously shouting down a cellphone that was so petite he had to hold it between his thumb and forefinger. He ignored me for around five minutes – not an easy trick in a shop that was nothing more than an eight-by-eight space. When I finally got fed up with waiting and turned to leave, he immediately ended his call.

'You stay, you stay . . .' he shouted. 'I get you nice phone, nice price.'

Half an hour later, having been relieved of $75, I left with a pay-as-you-go phone, topped up with $20 worth of calls. More importantly I had my very own number – which I hand-wrote at the bottom of the covering letter. Then I cycled back to the library and handed in my application at the front desk, thinking to myself: *She'll probably look at the résumé and think I'm a crank* . . .

The next day, I received a phone call around nine-thirty from Mrs Woods. She sounded pleasant and brisk.

'Any chance you could come by the library today for an interview?'

I showed up, as requested, at three p.m. I dressed soberly: a black corduroy skirt, black tights, sensible shoes, a V-neck sweater beneath which was a white T-shirt. Mrs Woods, on the other hand, wore a beige pantsuit with a floral blouse. She was large and, like just about every librarian I'd ever met, only semi-comfortable with other people. But as she was the head honcho here she obviously had more advanced social skills than her colleagues. (Something else I learned during all my years in academia – the chief librarian in any institution was usually chosen for that role not just because of their experience, but also because she could actually maintain eye contact with someone else.)

'Now, to be honest with you, Ms Howard, when I read through your résumé I did think to myself: Are we dealing with an imposter here? Because, quite honestly, I've never had anyone with your credentials apply for a job with us. Then I did do a little background check . . . and discovered that you do have a doctorate from Harvard, and you really did publish that book on American Naturalism. And you really were a professor at New England State. So, my question to you is an obvious one: Why take a low-paying job with us in Calgary?'

'How far did you research my background, Mrs Woods?'

'I Googled you, of course.'

'Then you must have read about my daughter.'

She met my gaze. 'Yes, I did see that.'

'Then you have your answer why I'm here.'

'I have to level with you – I also saw an article online about an assault you committed in the wake of the . . . accident.'

'Did you read the circumstances of the attack?'

'Indeed . . . and part of me sympathized. But another part of me . . .'

'Worried you might be hiring a sociopath?'

'Hardly. I emailed your Professor Sanders at New England State. He wrote back a glowing recommendation – and asked you to get in touch with him.'

This was the double-edged sword of applying for this job: knowing full damn well that I would have to supply references. And knowing this meant revealing to my former colleagues back East where I was right now. In turn this could mean Christy finding out my whereabouts . . . though I gambled that she wouldn't be in further touch with Sanders and I also had a plan of action to make certain he didn't give out my new address.

Mrs Woods continued: 'He also explained the events surrounding the incident. And he reassured me that it was a one-off, brought about due to the extraordinary circumstances you were coping with. I am so sorry. I can't begin to imagine how—'

'I am not in the habit of attacking people,' I said, cutting her off. 'But I do like books. And having spent so much of my life in libraries . . .'

406

Ten minutes later I had the job. $480 per week gross pay, with twenty-seven percent deducted for federal tax and an additional 10 percent to the provincial government of Alberta – which meant I'd be taking home $350 dollars per week. That was fine by me as my monthly outgoings were around $1,300. Though my salary from New England State continued to be paid into my Boston account (Professor Sanders evidently ignoring my directive to stop it), I decided not to touch what cash reserves I had. Instead, I lived on a tight budget – but one which never left me feeling constrained or impoverished. On the contrary it became something of an interesting challenge bringing expenditure down to the essentials; deciding that, in exchange for the hour or so I spent in a café every day, I would forgo eating out a couple of nights a week. More importantly, the job meant there would now be eight hours a day when I would be preoccupied with something other than the inside of my head. With a little bit of strategizing I was certain I could be a model colleague to everyone else in the library, while also politely slamming the door on any contact outside polite staffroom chat.

And if anyone at the library ever asked me about my past . . .

But nobody at the library did that. On the contrary all my new colleagues were pleasant, but also just a little distant from me. They wanted to make me feel welcome but I could see they were also handling me like a fragile china doll who might easily break. After getting the overall library tour from Mrs Woods, I was handed over to a sinewy, flinty woman named Babs Milford: the Chief Cataloger.

'Figured with your background you might want to be doing something a little more cerebral than stacking books, so you've been assigned to me. A lot of people find cataloging tedious. I'm not one of them – and I'm gambling on the fact you might find it interesting as well.'

Babs was from the Prairies. A small farm near Saskatoon. She had this dry, reedy voice, tobacco cured (at every break she always dashed outside for a smoke), with a somewhat sardonic edge that seemed to define her world-view. She was in her late fifties – widowed, with two grown girls who both lived in Toronto and (from what I could gather) weren't in close contact with their mother. Information from Babs only rarely seeped out, like the occasional drop of moisture on a concrete plinth. But she still indicated that her marriage had not been a particularly happy one, and her husband's sudden death from a heart attack six years ago came just when they had decided to separate.

Babs only revealed this fact to me after we'd been working together for four months. Even then it was mentioned in a side-of-the-mouth way, when I was re-cataloging all the John Updike novels we had in the library, and Babs asked me if he was 'the guy who always writes about unhappy marriages.' This style of 'plain speak' belied a real intelligence and knowledge of books . . . but she maintained what I came to see as a certain Canadian prairie style, in which overt displays of the highbrow had to be undercut with a certain backwoods naivety.

When I confirmed that, yes, Updike often wrote about domestic unhappiness, she smiled a rueful smile and said: 'Maybe I should read one of his, find out what went wrong in my own marriage.'

That's when she let drop the fact that she'd been on the verge of divorcing her husband – 'on the grounds of his endless grumpiness' – when he happened to keel over on a trail somewhere near Lake Louise while returning from a fishing trip with 'another of his taciturn friends'.

That was the only moment I got a glimpse of Babs Milford's interior life – except for a mention that she hadn't had a visit from either of her daughters in over two years. Other than that, we simply made small talk when we worked. Babs was quite the political junkie. She taught me massive amounts about Canadian politics. For someone who had lived so long in ultra-conservative Alberta – which always fancied itself as the *Texas du Nord* of Canada – she was surprisingly liberal on all social issues, from women's rights (especially when it came to abortion), to the legalization of gay marriage, even to the idea that most drugs should be available in state-run liquor stores.

'Of course, I don't articulate such things publicly,' she said in that mordant tone from which she never varied, 'especially because every second person you meet in Alberta is either a Bible-thumper or someone who really does espouse a Marie Antoinette doctrine when it comes to the less fortunate members of our society.'

Babs rarely asked me anything about myself – though she did make a point of ordering my one and only book for the library and showing it to everyone in the staffroom during a coffee break, and even taking it home to read.

'You've got one big brain,' she told me a few days later.

'Don't be so sure of that,' I said.

'You don't get into Harvard and write a book like that without serious smarts. You ever think you might go back into teaching?'

'Not at the moment.'

She acknowledged this comment with the briefest of nods. That's when I knew that *she knew* . . . even though, from the moment I started work at the Central Library, I realized that Mrs Woods had briefed everyone on 'my background' and they had all collectively and individually decided to steer clear of any subject to do with children whenever I was in the room.

There were over fifty employees in the Central Library but I only had ongoing contact with four of them. Besides Babs, there was Dee Montgomery, a woman in her mid-thirties who had pronounced buck teeth and was endlessly enthusiastic about everything and everyone.

Dee was the Reference Librarian – and when she found out the subject of my book she made a point of taking me to 'the crypt' (librarian slang for the room in which all the old bound periodicals and major source books were kept) and showing me a complete collection of *Munsey's Magazines* (a key muck-raking journal during the early twentieth century), a first edition of Veblen's *The Theory of the Leisure Class* and even several signed volumes of Mencken.

'This is your era, isn't it?' Dee asked me.

'That it is . . . and I didn't realize how much you had here.'

Actually, this was a lie. On one of my first days working at the library, I started rummaging around their computer files and discovered that they had very substantial research resources when it came to American Naturalism and the Progressive Era. But I stopped myself from getting too interested in their collection. That would mean revisiting the past. And revisiting the past would mean . . .

'If you're thinking about writing another book,' Dee said, 'I sure would like to help you. We can requisition so much from other libraries around Canada. And then there's an entire database of—'

'My book-writing days are over,' I said.

'Don't say that.'

'It's the truth.'

'You never know. In time, when things are—'

But she cut herself off, saying: 'Oh, Lord, listen to me. I just never know when to keep my big trap shut. I mean, I don't even know you and already I'm saying . . .'

410

'It's OK,' I said. 'No offense taken.'

'Well, I am truly sorry. I just wanted to help.'

'Don't sweat it.'

From that moment Dee assiduously steered away from *that* subject . . . but could never shake off the tendency to put herself down or always point up her inadequacies.

'Dee can't get through the day without beating herself up,' Ruth Fowler said. 'That's why her husband eventually ran off with her best friend. I think he got fed up with listening to his wife tell him what a screw-up she was. Eventually he decided she might be on to something – and sought refuge elsewhere. Poor Dee. She's ace at what she does and she's probably the nicest person working here. But talk about self-esteem issues . . .'

Ruth Fowler was the wittiest person working at the Central Public Library. She was tiny – around five feet tall – with round rimless glasses and a predilection for tweed suits. At times I thought she resembled something out of a 1920s English drawing-room comedy – the herringbone-clad favorite aunt of some bounder named Sebastian, and the woman who – throughout the play – dispersed genuine words of wisdom through a veil of sarcasm. She was Head of Reception, which meant she manned the front desk and – as such – was the public face of the library. She also dealt with all information queries regarding the resources of the library, organizing school visits, open days, public events. She was the ideal person for such a public job. Along with Geraldine Woods she was also the only member of staff I met who could be described as externally comfortable in her own skin.

In private she had a wicked sense of humor. And when it came to the 'thing' which everyone else on the staff danced around she let it be known that she was very much in my corner.

411

'You probably know that I function as the staff chaplain. You've got a personal problem or a peeve against another member of staff, you come to me and I'll try to sort it out. So I'll be straight with you. Mrs Woods briefed everyone on the death of your daughter. The fact is, no one really knows how to deal with it – because it's so damn awful, and because, people being people, they don't want to say the wrong thing and upset you. More to the point, we're all terrified of other people's tragedies, because they point up the fragility of everything.

'Anyway . . . I just want you to know that Dee came to me horrified about that little exchange she had with you about maybe writing another book.'

'I did tell her I wasn't upset.'

'Yes, she related that back to me. But Dee being Dee, your exchange gave her the excuse to indulge in a self-criticism that hasn't abated for seven goddamn days. That's her problem – and I just wanted you to be aware of a certain awkwardness people have with you. Just as I also want you to understand that if there is any moment in the future when you're having one of those days . . . or one of those weeks . . . when you are in a dark wood, when you just can't cope, whatever, all you have to do is call me and I will arrange compassionate leave for however long you need—'

'That won't be necessary,' I said, interrupting her.

'Fine, Jane . . .'

'I do appreciate the thought.'

'I'll say no more about it.'

'Thank you.'

She did say some more about Vernon Byrne – the Music Librarian and perhaps the most taciturn of any member of the staff.

'I think his problems began with his name,' Ruth said. 'I

mean, everyone calls him Vern. And who the hell could go through life with a name like Vern Byrne?'

Vern was in his late fifties. He was a thin, reedlike man who always dressed in identical clothes: a dark gray jacket, gray flannels, a tattersall shirt and dark blue knit tie, well-polished heavy cordovan brogues. The tattersall shirts showed occasional variety. One day the pattern would be blue, the next day green.

'I think he has three of everything: the same jacket, pants, shoes and so on,' Ruth said. 'It's very Vern. He doesn't care much for externals. But get him talking about music and everything changes.'

Vern sported a military-style haircut – short back and sides with a precisely groomed flat top.

'He must use a serious pomade and the stiffest brush on the market to keep it so perfectly planed,' Ruth said. 'I keep wondering if, at home, Vern has a small bird that sits atop his crewcut and keeps the man company. God knows, he could use some sort of companionship.'

That was the other known thing about Vern – the fact that he was an inveterate loner who had always lived by himself in the house he had inherited from his late mother in an inner suburb of the city. He had no known interests outside of classical music.

'He's so closed off, so closed down,' Ruth said, 'that he strikes everyone as seriously weird, seriously damaged; the sort of guy you wouldn't want to go near young children. But I've been working with him for sixteen years – and I must say I'm fond of the man. We all have our weirdnesses. His are just a little more on display than the rest of us.'

Vern's domain was the collection of compact discs and music texts – all grouped in a quarter-acre of the library's third floor. When I was first introduced to him in the staffroom he

413

proffered a dead right hand lacking in any reassuring grip. Then he stared down at the tips of his shiny shoes.

'Nice to meet you,' he mumbled.

A week later I was trying to track down a missing volume from the *Grove Dictionary of Music and Musicians* and had to venture over to his 'lair' (Ruth's term). As I approached him he was huddled over one of the CD players that allowed browsers to listen to a disc before taking it away for a few days. A large set of headphones covered his ears. He had his eyes closed and he was engaged in a moment of such intense musical concentration that, from a distance, he almost seemed to be experiencing some sort of religious rapture. But when he realized I was standing nearby, watching him enthralled by the music, he jumped up as if I'd caught him in an obscene act and wrestled the headphones off his ears. From the dislodged headset I could hear booming strings followed by a wall of brass – at an exceptionally loud volume.

'Sorry, sorry,' he muttered, 'I was just . . .'

'What's the piece?'

'Bruckner 9. The scherzo.'

'The one with the heavy use of the double bass and then the *länder* theme coming in as a counterpoint to all the forward momentum?'

'Uh . . . yes . . . absolutely,' he said, genuinely surprised by what I had just said. 'You know your music, do you?'

'A bit. Whose version were you listening to?'

'Günter Wand with the Berlin Philharmonic. It was released before Wand's death in 2002.'

'And?'

'And what?'

'Do you approve of it?'

'Oh, yes, absolutely. He understands the architecture of the symphony which . . . uh . . . is absolutely key to any reading

414

of Bruckner. But he also has this *kappelmeister* control when it comes to metronomic markings and a refusal to—'

He suddenly cut himself off.

'Is this of any interest to you?' he asked.

'Sure. But I'm hardly in your league when it comes to—'

'So who do you like when it comes to Bruckner?'

'Well . . . I always had the Karajan set. But I sense the interpretations were all a bit like thick-pile carpet – easy on the toes, but lacking a certain edge.'

Vern Byrne smiled a nervous smile.

'That was Karajan all right – everything plush and beautiful, but no sense of the . . . uh . . . metaphysical, I guess. Kind of a pretentious word, I'm sure.'

'Not at all,' I said. 'Anyway, with Bruckner, the metaphysical is all-encompassing.'

'A kind of Catholic metaphysic. He was a little too devout for his own good.'

Another shy smile from Vern Byrne.

'So if you were to recommend me a lean, non-upholstered version of Bruckner 9 . . . ?' I asked.

He raised a finger and went over to the top shelf of the 'Symphonic' shelves, pinpointed the Bruckner section instantly, ran his finger along the tightly stored CDs, stopped at precisely the disc he wanted, pulled it out and handed it to me.

'Harnoncourt – also with Berlin. Period-instrument technique but with a modern orchestral sound. As I'm sure you know, Harnoncourt was one of the early pioneers of the "authentic performance" school, and he did really innovative things with baroque and classical repertoire. His Beethoven symphonies were an absolute revelation – and better than John Eliot Gardiner, who has always struck me as a bit up himself. Anyway, give it a listen and let me know what you think.'

I brought the disc home, sat down in my easy chair and listened to the entire symphony without interruption. I had heard Bruckner 9 before – and even remember a live performance with the Boston Symphony under Ozawa which I attended with David, and which he wrote off as 'classic Ozawa: all flash, no depth in the backfield'. (Trust my David to wonderfully integrate a baseball-ism into a discussion of a Bruckner symphony.) But I had never truly *listened* to the 9th before now. And what did I discover in this unadorned but still very dynamic reading by one Nikolaus Harnoncourt? That Bruckner didn't simply write music, but cathedrals of sound that sucked you into their vortex and made you consider worlds beyond your own. There was an epic struggle going on in this symphony. Unlike Mahler, however, the fight wasn't between the individual and life's remorseless march towards mortality. Rather, Bruckner seemed to be aiming at something altogether more incorporeal: the search for the divine amidst the whirligig of the quotidian; the notion that there are large, ethereal forces at work in the universe.

Listening to the symphony, how I so wished I could be a believer at that moment. How I wanted to think that Emily was there in some soft-focus afterlife, forever three years old, forever playing with her dolls, humming the songs she so loved, not afraid of being on her own because heaven is a place where fear and loneliness never exist; where even those taken so early from this life are in the most celestial of crèches. And since time no longer matters, it's just a flick of an eye to them before sixty years has passed and the parent who never got over their loss has suddenly succumbed to some horrible cancer, and there is this reunion with their ever-adored, ever-mourned child, and they all live happily ever after under God's benign hand. But they're not really *living* because this is not life, this is heaven: a place where nothing really happens . . .

How can people buy into such pathetic nonsense? How can they try to convince you that such a fatuous construct exists, in the well-meaning but wretched hope that it will somehow ease the agony? You want to find a notion of the celestial – listen to Bruckner or a Bach cantata. Go take a hike on a high-altitude pass (if, that is, you can stand to look at all that beauty). Hop on a plane and walk around Chartres. But don't . . . *don't* . . . try to tell me that the next life is babysitting my beautiful daughter for me while I sit here in torment, knowing that I will never get over it.

I had to drink myself to sleep that night – the first time I had done so since the doctor had upped my dose of Mirtazapine. The next morning I felt fogged in and low. Staring at myself in the mirror was not a pleasant experience. I looked like I'd been on a bender. At work Ruth asked me: 'Rough night?' To which I simply nodded, ending all further discussion on the matter. When I returned the disc to Vern I could see he too was disconcerted by my appearance, but said nothing.

'Good recording,' I said, handing it back to him.

'Glad you liked it,' he muttered, staring down at his shoes.

'I'll come back soon for another recommendation,' I said, then left.

But I didn't return to his lair for a couple of weeks – because I was fearful about getting sideswiped by Vern's next musical offering; because Vern sensed a sympathetic ear for his musicological monologues; and because I didn't want to feel beholden to him to play nice and interested and . . .

God, how hateful I sounded. But the Bruckner had seriously thrown me, opening up a new rich seam of grief. It was like a cancer that constantly metastasized. Every time you thought you could zap it and keep it in one specific locale, *shazam*, it attacked another part of your psyche. And it was so tricky, so ruthless, that – even if you were distracted away from *it* for several hours – suddenly there it was again, reasserting itself, letting you know that this sort of torment was ceaseless, terminal.

I certainly couldn't blame Vern for all that, but, even so, from that moment on I maintained a polite distance from him.

'You know,' Ruth told me one afternoon, 'when I found out the truth about Vern Byrne . . . well, I vowed never to make presuppositions about other people – even though that resolution lasted about ten minutes. *Vern Byrne.* Here I was typecasting him as something out of a Southern Gothic. As it turned out I was so damn off-beam. The man was a music teacher back East. His wife ran off with some RCMP guy and hit him with a nasty divorce which wiped him clean. Meanwhile, their only daughter was diagnosed as severely schizophrenic in her early teens and has essentially been in institutions since the late eighties. That's around the time poor Vern started to drink heavily – and lost his job because of it. Had no choice but to move back in with his widowed mom in Calgary. But you got to give the man credit. When he got back here, he completely sobered up – joined AA and all that – and got himself this job at the library. According to what I hear, he was kind of a quiet man before all this happened to him. Since then he's become real quiet. And when he got hit with prostate cancer five years ago . . .'

'Good God.'

'You can say that again. But that's the thing about other people's lives. You scratch the surface, you discover all this dark stuff. We've all got it. Anyway, since the cancer surgery, which was successful, I gather he's started drinking again, but he seems to have it under control. And he is sitting on a nice piece of equity with his mom's house. It isn't much – one of

418

those bungalows they put up here in the early sixties. But "isn't much" in Calgary still means four to five hundred thousand these days. Anyway, that's the Vern Byrne story. And now you know why they call me "The Stasi" around here. Because I know everything about everybody. But that's the thing with a library – you've got to do something to make the hours go by. But hey, I may be a gossip, but I'm not a malignant one. I actually like most of my co-workers, even if I do talk about them all the time.'

'You mean, you even like Marlene Tucker?' I asked.

'Nobody likes Marlene Tucker,' she replied.

Marlene Tucker. She was the Head of Acquisitions – which gave her a certain amount of power in our small world, and which she didn't mind wielding to everybody's annoyance.

'The Decider', Ruth called her, because Marlene was always telling you that she would, 'in time', make 'an informed decision' on whether a book you felt had to be in the library's collection would, in fact, be approved by her.

She was a very average-looking woman in her mid-forties who favored the sort of floral dresses that went out of fashion after Laura Ashley took that fatal dive down the stairs. She was always super-polite and super-formal – a hint of *noblesse oblige* always leaking out whenever she played 'the Decider' card.

'It is a wonderful attribute for the library to have someone with your credentials on the staff,' she told me just after I joined. 'And perhaps you could advise me on our new literature additions.'

Some months later – when, on her directive, I ran up thirty hours of overtime compiling a lengthy list of gaps in the library's fiction collection – she immediately stiffened when she saw the more than four hundred books I felt must be added to our shelves.

419

'Four hundred books!' she said, the tone suggesting that I had way overstepped my assigned undertaking.

'Well, you did ask . . .' I said.

'Yes, but I certainly didn't expect you to come up with such an impossibly long list of titles.'

'Four hundred and eleven books is pretty modest.'

'Not if you are trying to work them into a tight annual acquisition budget.'

'Didn't the provincial government allocate another four hundred thousand dollars to this library for new acquisitions? Isn't that why you commissioned this list from me?'

'I did think that you would be the best-equipped member of staff to deal with it. But honestly . . . the purchase of a complete first edition of Stephen Leacock. That must cost . . .'

'There's a rare-book dealer in Victoria who could get us a complete set for around nine thousand.'

'Why would the Calgary Central Library want to spend nine thousand dollars on a first edition of Stephen Leacock?'

'Two reasons. The first is: he's the Canadian Mark Twain—'

'I know who Stephen Leacock is.'

'And the second reason is: your investment will probably double in five years.'

That caught her unawares.

'How do you know that?'

'I did some research on the internet. I also found out that there are only four complete Stephen Leacocks in the original 1903 first edition on sale in Canada. Three of them are with Toronto dealers, which means they're charging anywhere from seventeen to twenty-four for the same edition.'

'Why is the one in Victoria so much cheaper?'

'It's an independent dealer. He operates from a garage next to his house, so the overheads are considerably lower. More to the point, he bought this first edition in an estate sale – and wants to shift it quickly.'

'Have you checked out his bona fides as a dealer?'

'Absolutely,' I said, reaching into my desk and handing her a file. 'It's amazing what you can find on the net. I've also asked him for photocopies of the frontispieces of all the books and have even found a retired Leacock scholar who lives in Victoria and – for an agreed fee of two hundred and fifty dollars – is most happy to go over and vet our investment before we pay the nine thousand.'

'Is that his best price?'

'Considering that I got him down from thirteen, yes.'

That also made her tense up.

'How can you be sure that the edition will double in value in the next five years?'

'Read the documents I've printed up for you – including one from the Antiquarian Booksellers Association of Canada, which talks about the rarity of this set and how its value is going to exponentially grow in the next decade. You'll win Brownie points with the board for this purchase, believe me.'

One thing I was learning about Marlene Tucker was that she distrusted the intelligence of other people – unless it could be used to flatter her own image. So when she told me that: 'In time I'll make an informed decision about this' – and I countered that the dealer would only guarantee us this price for the next seven days – she smiled another tight smile and said: 'I might just give Mr Henderson a ring tonight.'

Stockton Henderson was the chairman of the library's board – a big-deal corporate lawyer in town with a very high opinion of himself. He treated the library as if it was his own personal fiefdom and marched around the place like Charles Foster Kane on an inspection tour. When the Leacocks arrived seven days after my conversation with Marlene Tucker, he

421

came by personally to inspect the merchandise. They were laid out on display in the boardroom – and I was summoned by Mrs Woods to personally meet the 'great man'.

Everyone had told me that Stockton Henderson was a latter-day Babbitt – bumptious, arrogant and lacking in social niceties. But nothing prepared me or Mrs Woods or Marlene Tucker for his first comment: 'So you're the Harvard woman with the dead child . . .'

The silence that followed was immense. Stockton Henderson registered it.

'Did I say the wrong thing?' he asked Marlene Tucker.

'Not at all,' I said, deciding to play along. 'You're right on both counts: I do have a doctorate from Harvard and my daughter was knocked down and killed by a car.'

Stockton Henderson didn't even flinch when I addressed this directly to him. That's when I realized the bastard hadn't made the comment in an offhand, unthinking manner; that it was completely calculating and designed to get a rise out of me. The very fact that I answered it coolly impressed him.

After acknowledging my answer with a quick nod of the head, he then said: 'I read through both your research into and your report on the purchase of the Leacock. Your Harvard pedigree comes shining through – but also the fact that you have a nose for a good deal; that you are actually looking in a forward direction when it comes to increasing the value of the library's collection. Wouldn't you agree with that, Mrs Woods?'

'No doubt about it. It was first-rate work on Jane's part.'

'And what would you say, Mrs Woods, if I were to negotiate with the legislator up in Edmonton about finding a fund of, say, half a million dollars to augment the library's collection?'

'You mean, in addition to the four hundred thousand that

the legislator has already allocated to us?' Marlene Tucker asked.

'I don't remember asking for your opinion on this, Mrs Tucker,' Henderson said.

Marlene Tucker stared at the floor, suddenly cowed and sensing what was coming next.

'Mrs Woods . . . ?' he prompted.

'I believe that the half a million, if properly invested in rare and highly collectable books, could be the beginning of a small but genuine endowment for the library.'

'That's exactly the answer I was hoping to hear,' he said. 'Now I understand you're a published author, Miss Howard.'

'I just wrote one book, sir.'

'It's still a book. And we certainly have no one on the staff of the library with your literary credentials, let alone your degrees. So say I was to offer you the job of Head of Acquisitions – with simultaneous responsibility for creating a rare-books department in the library?'

The pause that followed only lasted around three seconds. Any longer and Henderson would have written me off as weak. If my time in finance had taught me anything it was that men like Stockton Henderson took comfort in decisiveness. It allowed them to believe that people saw the world in the same Manichean, free-of-doubt way they chose to perceive things . . . doubt being a sign of spinelessness in their eyes.

'I'd say yes,' I answered.

'Excellent. Then that's how it will be. You have no objections to that, Mrs Woods?'

Geraldine Woods – who always considered Marlene Tucker to be a liability (and someone who was not-so-secretly gunning for her job) – fought hard to suppress a very large grin.

'None whatsoever, sir.'

'That's settled then.'

'But Mr Henderson . . .' Marlene Tucker said. 'It was agreed between us that I would remain Head of Acquisitions until—'

'That *agreement*, Mrs Tucker, was made on the basis that you would succeed at the job. But what have you achieved to date, except the maintenance of a certain bureaucratic status quo?'

'I don't think that's a fair assessment—' she said.

'I'm sure you don't,' Henderson countered. 'But the truth is often unpalatable. Any further questions, Miss Howard?'

'Would you like me to draw up a list of possible "investments" we could make in the rare-book field in advance of your discussion with the powers that be in the legislature? I could completely research how best to allocate the half a million dollars and what the return on this investment could be.'

'Now *this* is the sort of forward thinking I like. Yes, I would very much appreciate such a document. Might you have it to me within seven days?'

'No problem, sir.'

'Then we're all on the same page – pun intended!'

And we all laughed at this lame joke.

As soon as Henderson left the room, Marlene Tucker turned to Geraldine Woods and said: 'I will not be accepting this decision. I will be contesting it – and if that means having to take legal action or go to the board . . .'

'You are more than welcome to do that, Marlene,' Geraldine Woods said. 'But that will mean coming up against our chairman – a man who hates to be contradicted. But if you want to do that, be my guest. I can promise you he will insist you be demoted down to the sorting division, rather than the nice comfortable job in cataloging . . .'

'Cataloging! I started in cataloging twenty-three years ago.'

'Then there's something rather elegant about your returning to your professional roots.'

'You haven't heard the end of this,' Marlene said, then stormed out.

As soon as she had left the room, Geraldine Woods let out a long exhalation.

'Well, bless you for coming into our lives and ridding us of that woman.'

'That wasn't my intention.'

'Believe me, I know that. And Stockton Henderson knows that too. You were darn impressive when it came to fielding that snarky comment by our chairman. It's his style, I'm afraid.'

'You forget, I spent a little time in the business world.'

'Oh, I'm well aware that you are a woman of many parts, Jane. I also know that you will do this job wonderfully. You'll be on a salary of thirty-eight thousand thanks to this promotion. Once we get that half a million from the legislature, I will want to go public with the job you're doing, building up our collection.'

'Count me out of that,' I said.

'But it would be incredibly important for us to have you – a published author, a serious academic – be the public face of this new project.'

'Sorry, I can't . . . *won't* . . . do it.'

'Would you, at least, sleep on it for a couple of days?'

'I'm happy to do all the research, all the negotiations, all the buying . . . and to take on the duties of Head of Acquisitions. Just don't make me do anything in public. I'm certain you can find someone else to be the front man for all this.'

Stockton Henderson wasn't too pleased when Mrs Woods

informed him I wouldn't do any press in my role as the Head of Acquisitions, until she suggested that Henderson himself announce this 'new initiative' and simply say that the library was working with several rare-books experts who were personally advising him on the best investments to be made . . . but that the final decision was made by himself.

Being both pompous and massively self-important, Stockton Henderson relished this idea. Within two months he had convinced the provincial legislature to part with a further $500,000 to start this new collection.

'They're largely such a bunch of philistines,' Ruth Fowler noted after the money came through, 'that it takes a fellow oaf like Henderson to muscle the extra funding through.'

'I'm not complaining,' I said, knowing that between the two grants I now had close to $1 million to spend on books. And spend I did. On the general-collection side I took on board every recommendation made to me by all the heads of divisions when it came to where their collections were lacking. We had a part-time graduate student from the University of Calgary working in the fiction section – a smart guy named Ron, who seemed to be something of a whizz when it came to identifying our deficits. I commissioned him to see how he could bump up our literature holding – and gave him a budget of $50,000 to work with. He was like a kid in a candy store. Within two weeks he came back with all sorts of ideas – an entire section devoted to the Beats, to Québécois writers (in French and in translation), to forgotten Albertan novelists, to the French *nouveau roman*.

Mrs Woods had to defend many of these purchases to a board of directors who – fuelled by a nasty-letter campaign by Marlene Tucker (who simply refused to speak to me in the wake of her demotion) – were appalled that we were spending 'good taxpayers' money' on 'beatniks' and 'Francophones' and 'books that nobody will ever read' (exact quotes from the meeting). Shrewdly, Mrs Woods had contacted several sympathetic journalists in Calgary – on both the *Herald* and *FastFwd* – both of whom wrote glowing pieces about the vast improvement in the Central Public Library's collection and how (according to *FastFwd*) it was 'a tribute to the Library's Board of Directors' that they had 'approved such an impressive overhaul of the CPL's collections – and one which, with both its eclecticism and depth, makes it one of the best metropolitan libraries in Canada'.

The board loved this flattery – and Mrs Woods threatened Marlene Tucker with summary dismissal if she continued her poison-pen campaign. But the person who most adored all the good press was Stockton Henderson. When I scored a rare edition of Dickens's *Dombey and Son* in the original parts for a bargain $14,000 from a dealer in London and a numbered Shakespeare and Co. first edition of Joyce's *Ulysses* for $58,000, Henderson invited a few journalists over to the library to inspect the goods. He also informed everyone that he himself had tracked these finds down. He basked in the journalistic copy that followed: how this big-deal oilman lawyer was, in private, a rarefied bibliophile.

'Jesus, I nearly gagged when I read that,' Ruth said the next day. 'The guy thinks he's a Medici, when he's nothing more than a Borgia Pope – of the provincial Canadian variety. "Rarefied bibliophile." Yeah, and he's also Pierre Trudeau.'

I smiled a weak smile. Ruth noted it.

'How're you doing today?' she asked.

'I'm fine.'

'You sure?'

'Of course I'm sure. Why wouldn't I be sure?'

I could hear the defensiveness in my voice, just as I also realized: *She knows.*

'You didn't have to come to work today, Jane.'

'But I wanted to come to work. I *needed* to come to work.'

'Well, as long as you're OK.'

Of course I'm not OK. How can I be OK on the first anniversary of my child's death?

'You know, if you don't feel like being here,' Ruth continued, 'you should just go home. Everyone will understand.'

'That's where you're wrong, Ruth. No one will *ever* understand. Nor do I really expect them to. And now if you'll excuse me I'm going back to work.'

I shut myself in my office for the rest of the day. Ruth was right. I shouldn't have come in. I had been fretting about this day for weeks. Everyone says that the first anniversary of a bereavement is excruciating – not simply because you realize that a whole year has gone by since your world collapsed, but also because time heals nothing. So I kept the office door closed and I stared into my computer screen and tried to concentrate on tracking down a first edition of *The Scarlet Letter*. I found a dealer in Cape Town (of all places) who had one copy. But he was demanding an exorbitant $30,000. I tried to gauge whether this was a fair market price, and whether it was worth committing so much of my budget on one volume (I decided against it), while also knowing that all this first-edition detective work was nothing more than a series of diversionary tactics, allowing me to sidestep, for a few minutes at a time, the terrible reality that still, twelve months later, haunted every hour of every day.

Finally it was six p.m., and I could get on my down coat, my hat, my scarf, my gloves – all the layers one needs against a Canadian winter – and abandon ship for the night.

It was a cold night – the mercury in the minus teens, with snow beginning to cascade down. There were two films playing at the Uptown which I wanted to see. It was a twenty-minute walk down 8th Avenue from the library, and I figured I could time it to stop in a wine bar called Escoba a few doors down from the cinema and have a plate of pasta and several glasses of something red and hearty, then duck into the cinema and kill the evening staring at projected shadows in a darkened room. But as soon as I walked out of the library, I did something rather strange. I sat down on the pavement outside its main entrance and just remained there, oblivious to the cold, the snow, the passers-by who glanced at me as if I was mad . . . which, perhaps, I was.

A cop came by – a middle-aged man wearing a furry hat with ear flaps, the badge of the Calgary police pinned across its front.

'Are you all right, ma'am?'

I didn't look up at him, but turned and stared into the gutter.

He crouched down beside me.

'Ma'am, I asked you a question. Are you all right?'

'I'll never be all right,' I heard myself saying.

'Ma'am, have you had an accident? Are you hurt?'

'I did this last year.'

'Did what, ma'am?'

'The night after my daughter died, I sat down in the street.'

'I'm not following this . . .'

'I went back to where the accident happened and I sat down in the street, and I couldn't get up again until the police came and . . .'

'Ma'am, I need to know your name, please?'

I turned away. I felt his gloved hand on my shoulder.

'Ma'am, do you have any identification on you?'

I still refused to look at him.

'OK, ma'am. I'm calling for back-up and getting you somewhere safe for the night.'

429

But as I heard him reach for his walkie-talkie, a man came hurrying over.

'I know her,' he told the officer.

I glanced up and saw Vern Byrne. He crouched down by me.

'Did something happen, Jane?'

'A year ago . . .'

'I know, I know,' he said quietly.

'How do you know this woman?' the cop asked.

'We work together.'

'Is she always like this?'

Vern tapped him on the shoulder. They both stood up and spoke in low voices for a few moments. Then the cop crouched down again beside me and said: 'Your colleague has assured me he's going to get you home. He told me what you said about your daughter is true. And that's really hard – and I'm sorry for you. But this is my beat – and if I find you again in the street like this I am going to have to get you admitted to the psych wing at Foothills Hospital . . . and, believe me, that would give me no pleasure.'

'This won't happen again,' Vern said.

'All right,' the cop said, 'but you promise you will get her home?'

'You have my word.'

The cop left. Vern helped me to my feet, putting a protective and steadying arm around me.

'Let's get you home,' he said.

'I'm not going home.'

'You've got to go home. You heard what the officer said.'

'I am *not* going home.'

My body stiffened. I was suddenly determined to be immobile.

'Please, Jane,' he whispered. 'If the officer comes back and finds us still here . . .'

'A drink,' I said.

'What?'

'Buy me a drink.'

Six

VERN HUSTLED ME into the first bar he could find. It was located diagonally across the road from the Central Public Library. The wind was scalpel sharp and the blowing snow made visibility difficult. Vern grasped my left arm with the force of a lifeguard pulling a half-drowned swimmer out of deep water. We all but fell into the bar.

'Jeez,' Vern said under his breath as he looked around. 'Kind of fancy.'

The bar was actually a restaurant called Julliard. There were booths. Vern steered me into one. A waitress approached us, all smiles.

'You guys look like you need some anti-freeze! So what's it going to be?'

'What's your pleasure?' Vern asked me.

I just shrugged.

'You like rye?' he asked.

'Sure.'

'Two Crown Royals, straight up, water back,' he told the waitress.

When she was out of earshot he leaned over and asked: 'You OK now?'

'Thank you for getting me here.'

The drinks arrived. I picked up the glass and downed the rye in one go. It didn't burn the way so many whiskeys do when they hit the esophagus. It had a slight sweetness and a hint of honey that was immediately warming. I put the glass down and turned to the waitress who still hadn't removed our glasses of water from her tray.

'Could I have another, please?'

'No problem,' she said, then added: 'You sure as heck must have been cold.'

'Know what I can't stand about Canada?' I suddenly said to Vern. 'All the goddamn politeness – and the way everyone uses namby-pamby language. *Heck . . . jeez . . . sugar . . . freaking*. Can't you people swear in this country? Do you all have to be so inanely polite? Know what I think? You all sit on your hands so much you can't come out swinging. I mean, they broadcast all that politically correct Inuit Throat Singing shit on the CBC . . . and you don't fucking object. Not "freaking" object. *Fucking* object. That's right, *fuck*. I'm from South of the Border and I say *fuck . . .*'

This rant was delivered in a very loud voice. It silenced everyone around us. All eyes were upon me. Before I knew what was happening, Vern was throwing some money on the table and hustling me out the door. Again he steered me by the arm as we hit the cold. He said nothing, but the lifeguard grip had become that of a cop making an arrest. We turned left up 8th Avenue.

'There's always a taxi outside the Palliser,' he said.

'I'm sorry. I'm really . . .'

'Don't worry about it,' he said.

'I messed up in there. I . . .'

'Stop, *please*,' he said, the tone more worried than angry.

'All right, all right. Just get me home and . . .'

'I don't think you should be left alone.'

'I'll be fine.'

'That's not my reading of the situation.'

'I can handle things.'

Vern said nothing. He just gripped me tighter and pushed me forward. The wind was now cruel, grating any exposed skin. We made it to the Palliser in five minutes, by which point my fingers had so stiffened that it pained me to bend

433

them. There were three cabs outside the hotel. Vern bundled us into one of them and gave the driver an address on 29th Street NW.

'I live just off 17th Avenue SW,' I said.

'We're not going there.'

'You hijacking me?' I asked.

Vern said nothing, but leaned over and locked the door beside me.

'Trust me: I'm not going to jump out of a moving vehicle,' I said.

'I did once.'

'Seriously?'

'Seriously.'

'Why?'

He stared down at his hands and spoke slowly.

'My daughter had just been committed. More to the point, I had signed the papers committing her. After that I went on a seven-day bender. It ended with me jumping out of a moving car. I was hospitalized for three weeks. I broke my left leg. I cracked three ribs. I fractured my jaw. They also put me in a psych ward. I ended up losing my job. It was awful – and I'd rather not see you go through something like that.'

'I've done the psych ward already.'

He registered that with a quiet nod – and we said nothing until we reached 29th Street NW. The cab pulled up in front of a modest split-level bungalow. Vern paid off the driver and got me inside. As we crossed the threshold he hit a light. We were in a hallway – and one which looked like it was last decorated in 1965. There was faded brown floral wallpaper, an old antique coat rack, a side table covered with two lace doilies. (Does anyone still use doilies?) He took my coat and hung it up and told me to make myself at home in the front room.

434

'You want to stay with rye?' he asked.

'Rye works,' I said.

The front room was decorated with the same wallpaper and had heavy mahogany-toned furniture similar to the coat rack and the table in the hallway. Again lace covered the headrests on the oversized armchair and the sofa. There was a venerable baby grand piano covered with sheet music and a pair of Tiffany lamps on two end tables. But most conspicuous were the floor-to-ceiling bookshelves, all heaving with music texts and thousands of CDs. The CDs were all alphabetized, with little dividers noting major composers. There was also a serious stereo system covering two shelves and two large floor-standing speakers.

Vern came in carrying a tray, on which stood two crystal whiskey glasses, a bottle of Crown Royal, an ice bucket and a small water pitcher. He set the tray down on the coffee table.

'This room is amazing,' I said.

'Always strikes me as rather ordinary.'

'But the CD collection. There must be over a thousand discs here.'

'Around eleven hundred,' he said. 'The rest are in the basement.'

'You have more?'

'Yes. A few.'

'Can I see?'

Vern shrugged, then pointed his thumb towards a doorway off the living room. He opened it, flipped a switch and I followed him down a narrow set of stairs into . . .

What I saw completely threw me. Because there, in this completely finished basement, was shelf after shelf of CDs, again meticulously organized in library style, with a high-end stereo system connected to two massive speakers. One

435

oversized leather armchair faced these speakers. There was also a large trestle table and a high-back swivel chair, strewn across which were papers, books, a laptop computer – and behind which was a shelf on which rested the entire *Grove Dictionary of Music and Musicians*. The basement felt like both a serious musicological shrine and something of a command center. If Dr Strangelove had been a classical music fiend he would have felt most at home in this subterranean cavern.

'Good God,' I said. 'It's extraordinary.'

'Uhm . . . thanks,' Vern said.

'Did you buy all the CDs?'

'Uhm . . . around a quarter of them. The rest . . . well, ever heard of the British magazine *Gramophone*? Or *Stereo Review* in the States? I've been reviewing for both of them for around fifteen years.'

'And this is where you write your reviews?'

'Yes . . . and also work on . . .'

Again he broke off, not sure if he wanted to share another piece of information with me.

'Go on,' I said.

'I'm writing a textbook.'

'But that's fantastic. Is it commissioned?'

He nodded.

'Who's the publisher?'

'McGraw-Hill.'

'The biggest textbook publisher in the States. I presume it's a music textbook?'

'It's sort of like the *Oxford Dictionary of Music* – but aimed at high-school students. Potted histories of major composers from Hildegard of Bingen right up to Philip Glass.'

'How did you land such an amazing gig?'

'I wrote them a long letter, explaining my background, my teaching experience, my degrees, my writings for various magazines – and also included a pretty extensive outline. Never expected to hear anything from them but, out of the blue, I got this call from an editor there named Campbell Hart. Asked me if I would come to New York to meet him. Even offered me a plane ticket and a hotel room for one night if I'd make the trip. Hadn't been in New York since . . . Jeez, since I was a university student back in the late sixties.'

'Where did you go to university?'

'Toronto – and the Royal College of Music in London. But that was a long time ago.'

Now it was my turn to look at him carefully to see if he was being on the level with me.

'What were you studying at the Royal College?'

'Piano.'

'You were accepted there as a pianist?'

'It's ancient history.'

'But . . . the Royal College of Music *in London*. You must have been some pianist.'

'Let's go back upstairs,' he said.

He started turning off all the lights, then escorted me back into the living room.

'You ready for that rye?' he asked.

'Please.'

'You want water back or some ice?'

'No – I'll take it neat.'

As he poured out two fingers for me I noticed just the slightest tremble in his hands. He handed me the glass, then slowly measured out a small amount for himself, fussing over its size, making certain it didn't exceed a specific amount.

'I like your house,' I said.

'I haven't done much to it.'

'But it's very solid – and the furniture is so late nineteenth century . . .'

'My mom would have liked to have heard you say that. She picked it all out.'

'What did she do?'

'She was a music teacher in a high school here in Calgary.'

'Was she your piano teacher?' I asked.

He nodded slowly, then followed this with a small sip of his rye.

'She must have been so proud of you when you got into the Royal College of Music.'

He fell silent and downed the rest of the whiskey in one go. Then he stared down into his glass for a very long time.

'Have I said the wrong thing?' I asked.

He shook his head and started fingering his glass while furtively glancing at the bottle of Crown Royal. It was clear he so wanted another drink – but had to limit himself to just one.

Finally: 'I had a full music scholarship to the University of Toronto. While there I studied with Andrei Pietowski. Polish émigré. Brilliant and very demanding. He thought I had "it", that I was going to be the next Glenn Gould. He even had me play for this Austrian pianist named Brendel when he came through Toronto. Brendel was living in London. He had connections at the Royal College. I got a full scholarship there. That was 1972.'

'And then?'

'I arrived in London. I started at the Royal College. And . . .'

Another of his fall-silent moments.

'You want another rye?' he asked me.

'Sure,' I said, holding out my glass. He splashed a few more fingers of whiskey in it. Then, with two distinct globules of sweat rolling down his face, he poured out another finger of rye into his own glass. As soon as he'd done that he stood up and disappeared into the kitchen with the bottle.

When he returned he said to me: 'If you want another top-up it's by the sink. If I start going for it, tell me not to, OK?'

'Sure,' I said.

There was a slight quiver to his lips as he raised the glass. Once he had downed the shot in one go, he shut his eyes tightly, an anxious glow of relief filling his face. He put the glass down.

'In London I had a breakdown,' he said. 'It happened around a month after I got there. I'd been assigned by the Royal College to this big-cheese Viennese guy named Zimmermann. Tyrannical, exacting, never kind. I was his star pupil. He told me that two weeks into our "collaboration", as he called it. He thought I was so good he insisted we "immediately try to scale Everest". "So what if you fall, Canadian," he said in this thick Viennese accent. "I will be the one with the rope to pull you back up again. So come now, we scale Everest."'

'What did he mean by that?'

'The Hammerklavier Sonata by Beethoven. It's number 29 – the last sonata and the most taxing. You can't approach it lightly. It's fiendish – and perhaps the greatest exploration of the infinite musicalness of the piano that has ever been composed. I went to the library. I got the score. We started to work on it during our three one-hour sessions each week. Zimmermann was – as always – scathing. But that was part of his strategy as a teacher, and I always responded to it. I aimed to please.'

'And he was pleased?'

'By the end of the second week, he told me: "You will be playing the Hammerklavier on the concert platform within eighteen months. You *will* scale Everest."'

'The next day I was working alone on the scherzo in one of the soundproof rooms at the Royal College. Third movement, bars 3 to 8. Suddenly my fingers froze. They literally stopped dead over the keys. I couldn't move them, I couldn't move myself. I don't know what happened. It was like someone flipped a switch in my brain and rendered me immobile. Another student found me there an hour later, catatonic, unresponsive to anything he said. They called an ambulance. I was admitted to a hospital. I stayed in that unresponsive state for about four weeks. Finally, my mom – who flew over to be with me – agreed to let them try electric-shock treatments to bring me back. The shocks worked. I came back.'

He fingered the whiskey glass again, so wanting another drink.

'But I never played the piano again,' he finally said. 'No, that's a lie. I played the piano all the time. Because once Mom got me repatriated to Canada and I started to function again, I did start teaching piano . . . in Hamilton, Ontario.'

'Why Hamilton?'

'I spent around six months in a psychiatric hospital there when I got back. There was a shrink in residence who specialized in my sort of manic depression, and my consultant in London had once worked with the guy, so it was decided to send me to him. That's where I met my wife, Jessica. She was a nurse on my ward.'

I really didn't know what to say, so I said nothing. We fell silent for a few moments. Vern kept fingering his empty whiskey glass.

'I've talked too much,' he said.

'Not at all.'

'I don't have much in the way of company, so . . .'

'How did you and Jessica get together?'

'Not tonight. I've already bored you with the half-story of my life.'

'It's hardly boring. Anyway, you shouldn't be apologizing

to me when I'm the one who caused the scene on the street, in the bar, in the cab . . .'

'You had just cause to do that, given that it was a year ago today.'

Now it was my turn to stare down into my whiskey glass.

'You're well briefed,' I said.

'It's a small place, the Central Public Library.'

'You saved my ass tonight.'

'There was no choice in the matter.'

'Still . . . you did that. For me. And I'm very grateful.'

'I just know what that first anniversary is like. When I had to commit my daughter Lois . . . it was April 18th 1989. And since then . . .'

Silence.

'Her schizophrenia is of a type that never seems to be cured. Even if she wanted to be let out of the institution where she's lived since then, the state wouldn't let her. She's considered a danger to society. And that's that.'

Again his index finger began to rub incessantly against the whiskey glass.

'What sort of meds do they have you on?' he asked.

'Ever heard of Mirtazapine?'

'It's been my constant companion for the past five years.'

'That's a long time on one drug.'

'I sleep because of it. That's something I didn't do for years.'

'Oh, it does make you sleep.'

'How many milligrams are you on?'

'Forty-five.'

'I've got a spare room top of the stairs to the right. It's even got its own en suite bathroom.'

'I'd rather go home.'

'And I'd rather you not hurt yourself tonight.'

'I'm OK now.'

'I jumped out of that moving car an hour after I assured a friend I was OK. You wait here until I get the pills, then you go upstairs and sleep. There's a radio by the bed and some books. But the pills should do their stuff – and when you wake up tomorrow, that anniversary will be behind you.'

'I'll still feel terrible.'

'That's right, you will. But at least you won't be obsessing about the day in question.'

He returned a few moments later with the pills, a glass of water and some towels. Part of me told myself: *This is all too weird.* Another part of me wanted to simply bolt out the door and into the night. But there was a small rational voice still operative inside my jangled brain which counseled: *Take the drugs and go to sleep. You just don't know what might happen if left to your own pitch-dark thoughts.*

So I accepted all that he offered and went upstairs. The room had the same sepia floral wallpaper and a sleigh-style bed, decorated with dolls. There were several framed portraits of a young girl, taken when she was a baby, a young girl, a teenager. Was this Lois? Were these her dolls? Was I about to sleep in the room of his lost daughter, a room she herself had never slept in, as Vern had only moved here after she was committed . . . ?

Again I wanted to flee. Again I told myself: *It's just one night and – unless I've misjudged all this entirely – he's not the type who's going to strut in here naked at three a.m.* I downed the pills, thinking: *That's decided the matter.* I used the bathroom. I climbed into the elderly pink floral sheets. I switched off the light. My watch glowed in the dark. It was only eight p.m. The bedtime of a child. But tonight I was a child sent to bed early in the room of a child who never lay in this bed, and whose presence hovered above me as the pills did their magic and . . .

It was five-thirty a.m. That's what my watch told me. Nine and a half hours of sleep. I couldn't complain – even if it was disorienting to wake up in this strange bed in this strange house, wondering if the loud rasping sound I could discern nearby was Vern snoring.

I got up and used the bathroom, then dressed and remade the bed with great care. Once downstairs I found a phone in the kitchen and called a taxi company and asked them to send a cab to . . .

I actually remembered the address and told the dispatcher to inform the driver that he shouldn't ring the doorbell when he pulled up. The kitchen, like the rest of the house, was from another era. The fridge must have been thirty years old. There was a linoleum table with photographic placemats depicting 'Great Canadian Scenes of Natural Beauty'. There was no dishwasher, no microwave, no fancy espresso machine, and the front-loading toaster was one of those lost-in-time jobs that was made from tin. Vern spent thousands on the most up-to-date stereophonic equipment, but ignored all mod cons elsewhere. We all have our priorities, I suppose.

I scribbled a note on a pad that he had picked up from a local realtor's.

I slept so well I was up before the dawn. You were extraordinarily kind and decent to me at a moment in time when I didn't merit such decency. I hope you will now consider me your friend – as I do you.

See you later today at the House of Mirth.

My best

I got into the cab. It headed up 29th Street, passing the Cancer Center of the Foothills Hospital. Was this where Vern was treated?

The driver must have been reading my thoughts. As we

passed it, he said: 'Every time I drive by that place and see the words "Cancer Center", it gives me the willies. "There but for the grace" and all that stuff.'

'Know what you mean.'

Back in my little apartment I took a hot shower and changed my clothes, then went to Caffé Beano for breakfast. When I reached the library at my usual start time of ten Ruth greeted me with a look of concern.

'You had me worried yesterday. I was going to suggest taking you out last night, but you were gone by the time I came looking for you.'

'I just went home.'

'You shouldn't have been alone last night.'

I said nothing.

Later that day, Babs came up to me in the staffroom and also asked how I was doing.

'Just fine,' I said quietly.

'Well, if you ever feel in any way like you want a shoulder to cry on—'

'Thanks,' I said, then quickly changed the subject. People want to be kind. People don't know what to say. In turn, you don't know what to say to them. What can you say? What can be said? Just the usual bereavement banalities – and the acknowledgement that it's all still so awful. After that . . .

There was no solution. There was just work – and I threw myself into it. I chased down a Bodley Head edition of the complete Graham Greene for a bargain $2,300. I asked Marlene – now functioning as Head of Children's Books (and endlessly grumpy) – if she would like to spend $20,000 on updating her collection.

'Will I have carte blanche to do what I want with it?'

'Did you ever give anyone else carte blanche when you were in charge of acquisitions?'

'You're not answering my question.'

'And you're evading mine. But I'll cut to the chase. Yes, you can have virtual carte blanche – insofar as you can draw up your dream list of how you plan to spend the twenty thousand. Unless I seriously object to anything on the list, you can go ahead and order all that's there. Fair enough?'

'What exactly would you "object" to?'

I sighed a long sigh – and stopped myself from saying something genuinely angry, like: *Why do you have to be so goddamn contrary? Why is everything a problem in the making for you?* And I could have added to this the thought: *Why is every workplace a minefield of petty politics and smoldering resentments? It's as if people need to turn their own insecurities and boredom into something malignant and displacing. Internal politics are all bound up in the ennui of the quotidian – and the terrible realization that there is only a finite amount of interest to be found in what you do from nine to five every day; that, like it or not, it's meaningless. So why not turn the banal into the melodramatic by finding people to dislike, by sniping at your co-workers, or getting paranoid about what they might be saying about you . . .*

Vern had the right idea. He came to work and rendered himself invisible. He did his job. He did it well. He remained cordial, but distant from his fellow workers. He went home – and immersed himself in the music writing that, I sensed, gave his life the passion it otherwise lacked . . . or that he no longer wanted.

Vern. After that night at his house, he simply greeted me with a courteous nod in the hallway or a fast 'Hello, Jane' the few times I saw him in the staffroom. He seemed to be avoiding me, as if he had said too much about himself that evening, revealing more than he wanted to. Though it struck me that all that stuff about his secret writing life should be known and celebrated, I also understood why he kept it to himself. In a small world like our little library, everything can be taken down and used against you – especially if you show initiative above and beyond our own prosaic horizons.

'*And he really thinks himself a music critic? . . . Who in their right mind would commission a textbook from him?*'

No wonder Vern lived in a sort of internal exile. When life has so conspired against you – and you find a little something that re-establishes your sense of wonder – you have to guard it fiercely. Because malignancy is all around you, and kindness is not as commonplace as we so want to believe.

Vern. A week went by – and still nothing more than a monosyllabic greeting. Fair enough. A second week went by – and I had a request from him, via email, about purchasing the *Complete Mozart*, a one-hundred-and-fifty-disc set on Philips. He wrote:

> *If I had my way, I'd buy each work individually – but that would be bad waste of public funds. The set is on special offer for $400. It strikes me as great value – and an essential addition to our collection. They're all very credible readings of the Mozart oeuvre.*
>
> *I hope you will approve this.*
> *Vernon.*

I wrote back:

> *Approved. Aren't there also complete Bach and Beethoven and Schubert sets? At the price you mentioned it strikes me as a steal. Please investigate and get back to me.*
>
> *You well, by the way?*

He wrote back:

> *The Bach and Beethoven and Schubert are also $400 each and, as such, excellent value. The Beethoven and*

Schubert piano sonatas, for example, are performed by
Brendel, Kovacevich, Lupu and Uchida . . . the major
league of contemporary pianists, so to speak. So yes, these
would be ideal recordings for us.
PS I have two seats for the Angela Hewitt concert next
Thursday night. Might you be free?

My God, Vernon Byrne was inviting me out. I didn't know
how to take this, except to think that Angela Hewitt was the
greatest Canadian pianist since Glenn Gould. And she was
going to be here in Calgary and Vern had an extra seat, so . . .
why the hell not?

I wrote back.

The Bach and Beethoven and Schubert Collected Works
are approved for purchase. And yes, I'd be delighted to go
to the Hewitt concert with you. But let me buy dinner.

He wrote back:

No, I'm buying dinner. I've reserved Teatro at six p.m. on
the night. See you then.

I must have bumped into Vern half a dozen times between
his invitation and the dinner itself. Every time I saw him he
tensed and simply nodded hello. I felt like telling him: *It's just*
a dinner and a concert. Stop acting like we're having an affair
and I'm married to a trigger-happy, alcoholic, wildly jealous
Marine . . .

'You know, I believe that Vern is intimidated by you,' Ruth
said to me on the day before the concert.

'What makes you think that?' I asked.

'The way he averts his eyes every time you come into his
field of vision.'

'Maybe he has better things to be looking at.'

'Maybe he has a crush on you.'

'Maybe you should stop acting like we're all still in high school. He's a shy man, end of story.'

He was a very nervous man, fingering an already-poured shot of whiskey as I entered Teatro. It was one of Calgary's big-deal restaurants – located only a block from the library and opposite the Jack Singer Concert Hall where Ms Hewitt was to play tonight. I'd passed by it a few times and never looked inside or glanced at its menu – big-deal restaurants not being something that was ever part of my life, even in those brief Freedom Mutual days when I was making stupid money. But I had dressed nicely for the evening out – a longish black skirt and a black turtleneck and black boots. The fact that I had come to work in these clothes made Babs and Ruth immediately quiz me if I had a 'heavy date' that night.

I just smiled and said nothing. But as the restaurant's maître d' escorted me down past the very swish Manhattan-style bar and into a dining room that looked like a design-magazine spread, all I could think was that my 'date' tonight would easily pass for my father. Vern was dressed in the same tweed jacket, tattersall shirt and knit tie he wore every day, and was nursing a small measure of whiskey.

'I bet that's Crown Royal,' I said as he stood up to greet me. He shook my hand shyly, then held my chair for me as I sat down.

'You want one yourself?'

'I was thinking about a gin Martini.'

'I used to specialize in gin Martinis. What kind of gin?'

'I'm not that picky.'

'Bombay's the best.'

He lifted a finger and a waiter showed up.

'Straight up, with olives?' Vern asked me. I nodded. He ordered the Martini.

'You're not having another?' I asked, knowing that I was venturing into tricky territory.

'I can't. Two drinks a night is my limit. Granted, sometimes I exceed that. But when I do . . .'

He opened his hands flatwards, like someone trying to ward off a deluge.

'Were you in AA and all that?' I asked.

'Oh, yes. Four years of AA. My sponsor still calls me regularly to see how I'm bearing up. He doesn't like the idea that I drink at all. They're all a bit doctrinaire and Jansenist, the AA. But as I had basically lost my career to the booze – and was also on the road to cirrhosis – I decided I could put up with all their Higher Power stuff. But Charlie – that's my sponsor – worries I'm going to backslide if I keep having the two every night.'

'Abstinence is an overrated virtue.'

'My thinking exactly – but only if you don't exceed the limits you've set for yourself. So . . . two drinks are better than no drinks. But three drinks . . .'

'You said you were teaching music back East. When did that start?'

'Around a year after I was finally allowed out of the hospital. But you don't want to hear about my little life . . .'

'Actually I do.'

'Because it's so messy?'

'Whose life isn't?'

'True.'

'I'm just interested . . .'

'Let's order first.'

He pointed to the menus that had been placed beside us. I opened mine and was shocked to discover that a main course cost anywhere between $28 and $42.

'We have to split this,' I said. 'It's far too expensive.'

'I just got a check in from the *Gramophone* yesterday. It will cover the entire evening – especially as the pound is still two-to-one to the Canadian dollar.'

'But I'm sure you could use that money for something more important than—'

'Let me be the judge of that.'

My Martini arrived. We ordered. I took a sip and shivered pleasantly as the super-chilled gin numbed the back of my throat. Opposite me, Vern started fingering his whiskey glass, clearly debating whether to order another one now or wait until the food arrived.

'Your wife . . . Jessica, wasn't it?' I asked.

'You have a good memory. Yeah, she was the ward sister in the hospital where I was . . . placed.'

Over the next hour and a half, I heard the second part of the Vernon Byrne story. As he talked, the narrative details took shape. The breakdown in London brought about by manic depression – but which was diagnosed wrongly as 'causal' rather than chemical. The three years of incarceration in a series of bleak Canadian hospitals. The electric shocks and mind-numbing cocktails of Librium which neutralized him, but also killed any ambition to ever re-attempt a concert career. The bland music-teacher job in a bland second-tier city. The nurse who wanted to mother him – and became a shrewish wife. The daughter he adored – but who, from an early age, was also showing signs of instability. The drinking that he and his wife engaged in – and the ferocious drunken fights that became a staple of their marriage. His wife finally running off with a local cop and never seeing their daughter again. Vern being determined to steer Lois out of the schizophrenia that had begun to claim her when she was eleven years old. The way this 'dementia praecox' (he used the actual clinical name) led Lois into attacking a teacher with a pair of scissors and then cutting her wrists after breaking a windowpane in the police station where she was first brought after the attack ('and she was only thirteen at the time'). Vern having no choice but to commit her. His escalating drinking. His leap from the car. The termination of his teaching job. Having to move back to Calgary. His mother taking him in – and in her own quiet, tough way, forcing him back into the land of the functioning. Him landing the job at the library. The gradual return to some sort of equilibrium – to the point where, when the doctors told him his daughter was never going to have a life again outside a supervised living facility, he managed to handle it. The way he made a point of flying East four times a year to spend four weekends with her. How, before she died, his mother made him promise that he would try to play the piano again. How . . .

When the bill arrived, Vern glanced at his watch and said that he felt shame for 'having spoiled a lovely dinner with all this talk about me'.

'I wanted to hear the story,' I countered, 'because you are an interesting man.'

He fingered the now-empty glass of Shiraz that he had ordered with his main course.

'No one has called me interesting in . . . well, not since my professor at the Royal College.'

'Well, you *are* interesting. Know that.'

The bill arrived and when I again offered to pay half of it, he said: 'After all that you had to listen to?'

We then crossed the street and entered Calgary's very spacious, very modern concert hall. It was obviously a big event as the lobby was buzzing and everyone seemed ever so slightly overdressed . . . the way people in cities with not much in the way of High Culture reach for the cocktail dress and the far-too-designer suit whenever they are about to

451

attend something that has been tagged 'serious'. Our seats were wonderful: sixth row, just off-center enough to give us a perfect view of the keyboard.

Then the house lights dimmed, the stage lights came up, and Angela Hewitt walked out on stage. She was a woman in her early fifties – not conventionally beautiful, but handsome in a sort of Simone de Beauvoir way, and dressed in a shiny royal-blue dress. But within moments of her settling herself behind the keyboard, waiting for the audience to fall completely silent, and raising her hands to play the first bars of Bach's *Goldberg Variations*, I wasn't thinking at all about her strange sartorial sense or the way she was probably the bookish, cerebral girl who never got a date in high school. Once Hewitt launched into the first meditative aria of Bach's extraordinarily dense and profound keyboard universe, she held me rapt. For the next seventy-five minutes – as she essayed the manifold variations of this massive work – I began to hear it as an encapsulation of the human emotional palate: from severe introspection, to giddy optimism, to careful cogitation, to middle-of-the-night despair, to ebullient dazzle, to the sad pervasive knowledge that life is but a collection of fleeting ephemera . . .

I had never heard a performance quite like this one – and was astonished by Hewitt's ability to shift emotional and dynamic gears so brilliantly, and weave Bach's complex and detailed musical variants into such a cohesively argued whole. I didn't move my eyes from her for the entire hour and fifteen minutes. When the final bars of the repeated aria drifted away into a resigned, plaintive silence there was a moment of complete, dense hush. Then the entire concert hall erupted. Everyone was immediately on their feet, cheering. When I looked over at Vern I could see that he was crying.

Once outside the hall I took Vern's arm and said: 'I cannot thank you enough for that.'

His response was a shy smile, a nod of the head, and a slight shift of his arm to free it from my grasp.

'Can I offer you a lift home?' he asked.

Vern's car was a ten-year-old Toyota Corolla – its color best described as rusted cream, its passenger seat thick with compact discs that he hastily dispatched to the back. He asked for my address, told me he knew the building and said nothing more all the way back there. I could have tried to make conversation. But the two times I stole a glance at him I could see that something had happened to him during that concert; that the sadness still so present in his eyes spoke volumes about so much which simply could not be articulated. When we reached my front door I again thanked him for a wonderful evening – and made a point of leaning over and giving him a peck on the cheek. I could see his shoulders tense as the kiss landed. Then, with a quiet 'See you in the morning', he waited for me to get out and drove off into the night.

I went upstairs. I sat down in my armchair, still dressed in my overcoat. I reflected on what I had just heard – and how grateful I was to Vern for having given me the opportunity to experience something so rich and luminous and forceful that – and it only now hit me – allowed me, for its entire seventy-five-minute duration, to vanish from the grief that had so wracked my life.

Of course, the moment I reflected on this was the moment it came rushing back. But *still*, Bach's long dark night of the pianistic soul had made me detach for a while. And I couldn't help but wonder – given all the children of his own that he lost – whether Bach himself hadn't found consolation in the contrapuntal immensity of this aria-and-variations.

The next morning, however, Emily loomed large over everything. I tried to bargain with the grief – to tell myself that I simply had to live with it. The problem was, I couldn't live with it. My daughter was forever gone. I couldn't reconcile myself to such an appalling reality – and yet that was the finite, inflexible heart of the matter. *There it is. What can you do about it? Nothing . . . except get through another day.*

I made coffee in my apartment while listening to the *Morning Show* on CBC Radio 2. The announcer, as always, was a mixture of cheeriness and erudition. At nine there was a break for international and provincial news – and the big story of the day was the disappearance of a local girl in the prairie town of Townsend, one hundred kilometers south of Calgary. It seems that Ivy MacIntyre, aged thirteen, had been heading to a medical appointment after school. Her part-time unemployed father, George, had been due to pick her up at a local dentist's office near the school but she never showed up there. Nor, as it turned out, had she actually arrived at school that day, though her father saw her off in the morning while her mother – who did the early shift at a local supermarket – was already at work. According to the CBC reporter, the RCMP were 'investigating all lines of inquiry' and had as yet to call this disappearance an abduction or something even more sinister.

I snapped off the radio. I didn't need – or want – to hear any more about this.

Later that morning, when I entered the staffroom during coffee break, Babs and Mrs Woods were having a most engaged conversation about the disappearance of Ivy MacIntyre.

'I heard that the father is a notorious drunk and that he'd attacked Ivy and her mom on two occasions,' Mrs Woods said.

'And there's an older son – Michael – who's eighteen and working the oilfields up at Fort McMurray. According to him, his sister was always worried about being alone with her dad, because . . .'

The door swung shut behind me and – upon seeing who it was – they instantly changed the subject. Later that morning I happened to pass Vern on my way out for lunch.

'Thank you again for such an amazing night,' I said.

His response was a diffident nod and then he walked right by me.

The next few days the media was full of Ivy MacIntyre.

Though everyone in the staffroom seemed to be preoccupied with the case – and all the newspapers regarded Ivy's suspicious disappearance as a commercial godsend – I was determined to block it out as much as possible.

A week went by. Vern sent me an email, asking if he could purchase a new edition of the *Grove Dictionary of Music and Musicians* – all twenty-nine volumes for an alarming $8,500. He wrote:

> *It is an essential reference tool, and one which no library should be without.*

I wrote back:

> *It's also a small fortune – and don't we already have an entire Grove's Dictionary on your floor?*

He wrote back:

> *Yes, we do have a Grove's but it's twenty years out of date. Could I convince you over brunch on Sunday to approve the purchase of the new edition?*

I didn't answer immediately, my reluctance having to do with the question of whether I really wanted to go out on another date with Vern. Had it taken him almost two weeks to get the courage up to ask me out again? If so, why on earth would I want to give him any hope of a future beyond an occasional concert or movie or dinner? The notion of an 'involvement' with Vern Byrne . . . well, I simply couldn't imagine it.

But this was the strident, defensive part of me talking. The other part – a little more rational and attune to the solitude in which I had decided to dwell – told me: *What's a brunch anyway, but a brunch? You have no contact with anyone outside of work. All right, that's your choice – but surely you can't live this way for ever, so why not accept the offer of company for a weekend afternoon?*

So I wrote back:

Brunch would be fine this Sunday . . . but only if you let me pay.

He wrote back:

Agreed, with reluctance. But let me choose the place. I'll pick you up at 12 noon.

That Sunday – like every Sunday – I got up early and dropped by the magazine shop around the corner from Caffé Beano that actually sold copies of the *Sunday New York Times* and now always had one put aside for me. I paid for the paper and brought it around to Beano where I drank a cappuccino and began to regret that I had agreed to this brunch, as the idea of having to make conversation with anyone outside of my workaday reality filled me with serious dread. Worse yet, having told me his story in full a few weeks ago, he might now be expecting to hear mine. But there was absolutely no way I'd ever share that with anyone. Anyway, what the hell was I doing going out to eat with this guy in the first place? It was a mistake, a stupid mistake. And if anyone at work learned about it . . .

I glanced at my watch. It was eleven-thirty a.m. With any luck I could catch him at home right before he left, and inform him that I just couldn't make it today. Scooping up my paper, I left the café and was back in my apartment within three minutes. Walking in the front door a thought struck me: *You don't have his phone number.* I grabbed my phone and dialed 411. 'Do you have the number of a V. Byrne, 29th Street NW in Calgary? . . . Yes, it's a residence . . . Yes, I would like to be connected, please . . .'

Then the number started to ring and ring and ring. No reply. No answerphone. I started pacing the floor of my apartment, nervous, frightened and simultaneously telling myself this was a wild overreaction. But this was how the grief often worked – the urge to sit down on a street, to blow up in a bar, to refuse to see anyone socially, to tell myself that seventy-five minutes of transcendent Bach would suddenly alleviate . . .

I got out of my sweat clothes and I dived into the shower. I dried off and threw on some clothes and ran a brush through my hair and put on my boots and my parka. The intercom rang. I grabbed my wallet and my keys and went downstairs.

Vern was standing by his elderly Corolla, trying to wear a grin on his face. He was dressed for the weekend: gray flannels, the usual tattersall shirt, a green crewneck jumper, one of those old-fashioned brown car coats, brown boots. He nodded shyly and held the car door open as I climbed inside.

The motor was running and the heater was on full blast, as it was minus fifteen today, even though it was still mid-March.

'Does winter ever end here?' I asked.

'Yes,' he said. 'In June.'

We drove off.

'Where are we eating?'

'You'll see.'

'That sounds mysterious.'

'It's a bit of a drive, but . . . I think you'll like it.'

We set off down 17th Avenue, turning right on 9, and then proceeded to the river, whereupon we crossed the Louise Bridge and connected to the highway system that led to the northern suburbs and beyond. During all this time we said nothing to each other – the dead space taken up by the Choral Concert program on CBC Radio 2. The presenter played excerpts from a new recording of Handel's *Esther* – specifically, one of the big tunes from the oratorio: 'My Heart is Inditing'.

'I only found out recently that Handel got the idea for the oratorio after seeing a play by Racine,' Vern said.

As attempts to make conversation go, it was . . .

'I never knew that,' I said.

Another dead zone of silence.

'Where are we going exactly?' I asked.

'Let me surprise you.'

Silence. Then, around three minutes later . . .

'Good weekend?' he asked.

'Low key. And you?'

'Wrote an article for the *Gramophone*.'

'On what?'

'A new recording of Handel's *Esther*.'

'You mean this recording . . . the one we're hearing now?'

'That's right.'

'Ah.'

Another silence. We turned off on the ramp leading to 16th Avenue NW, marked 'Banff'.

'We're not heading out of town, are we?' I asked.

'You'll see,' he said.

More silence. We continued along a gasoline alley, then past an artificial ski slope, marked 'Canada Ski Park'.

'That was the site of the ski jump when Calgary hosted the '84 Olympics.'

'I see.'

'Now there's skiing there around eight months a year . . . if you ski, that is.'

'I don't.'

'Nor do I.'

We pressed on. Within moments the city literally fell away. We were in open prairie – vast, endless plains, stretching to the limits of the horizon.

I suddenly felt a chill hit me; a chill that was undercut by a growing panic. It was the same panic that seized me on the bus ride north out of Montana when I made the mistake of looking up at all that epic grandeur and felt as if I was about to come unstuck.

I turned my eyes away from all that oceanic space laid out before us. I kneaded my hands together with such force that I felt as if I was trying to strangle my fingers. I felt my breathing become irregular. Next to me Vern could tell that something was seriously wrong.

'Jane, are you OK?'

'Where the hell are we going, Vern?'

'A nice place. A real nice place. But if, for some reason, all this is making you uncomfortable . . .'

I looked up in front of me and saw what we were heading for: the Rockies, now silhouetted on the horizon. Their fierce beauty – all jagged peaks, cliffed with snow that gleamed under harsh winter sunlight – was impossible to endure. I let out a stifled cry, put my head in my hands and started to weep. Immediately Vern pulled the car off the road. As soon as we reached a full stop, I threw open the door and began to bolt. I didn't run far – the cold put a quick end to my crazed reverie of escape. But after maybe twenty yards I did buckle down on my knees into the thick snow and pressed my gloved hands into my eyes and willed the world to go away.

Then I felt a pair of hands on my shoulders. Vern kept them there for a few moments, steadying me. Without saying a word, he slid them down to the sides of my arms and lifted me to my feet – and then got me back into the car.

'I'll take you home,' he said in a near-whisper.

'I don't want to go home. I want to . . .'

I fell silent. The motor hummed, the heater blasted warm air. I hung my head.

'Talk,' I said, finally completing the sentence. 'I want to talk. About what happened. That day.'

I stared up at Vern. He said nothing. He just nodded to me.

And I began to talk.

Seven

'I WAS FURIOUS at the world. I hadn't slept for several nights because Theo, my alleged "partner" – I hate that word, it's so PC, but what else to call him? – was on the verge of bankrupting me. And he'd run off with this absurd freak of a woman. I had several of their creditors chasing me for money. I was being threatened daily. I was talking to lawyers – and Theo was nowhere to be found. The thing was, my lawyer kept telling me to try to ignore all the vicious phone calls and my obsession that Theo's creditors would seize my apartment. My best friend Christy also said that I sounded seriously depressed and that I had to find something to help me sleep.

'She was right, of course. But I wouldn't accept that I was in a bad place. I kept telling myself: *I can handle it*, even though it was so apparent that I was coming apart.

'The next day . . . the day before it happened . . . the staff doctor at New England State actually called me. I've never admitted that to anyone until now. It seems that my department chairman had spoken with him and stated that he was worried about my mental health. Several colleagues and students had mentioned to him that I seemed to be tottering on the brink of something. The doctor was very direct with me and asked if I was overly anxious, suffering panic attacks, or not sleeping. The answer was "yes" to all the above. But I refused to admit this. Just as I told him, in a stupid knee-jerk sort of way, that I was just under a bit of strain due to "domestic difficulties" and that it was manageable.

' "Well, if your students and colleagues are making noises to the contrary," he said, "then the outward signs are showing

461

that you aren't handling things terribly well. Lack of sleep due to stress is a key cause of depression and also can lead to bad coordination which can put yourself and others in danger." He actually said that to me: "*put yourself and others in danger*". He then told me that he had a free appointment at the end of the afternoon.

' "There's nothing to be ashamed about here, Professor," he told me. "You're obviously in a dark wood. I would just like to help you out of it before it gets far darker."

'What was my reply to this? "I'll get back to you if I need you, sir." What complete arrogance on my part. Had I seen him that afternoon he would have given me something stronger that would truly knock me out. And I would have taken the pills that night and would have had the first eight hours of sleep in weeks. Which meant that my responses would have been far sharper than . . .'

I broke off and said nothing for what seemed like a few minutes. Vern just sat there, not making eye contact with me, staring out the windshield at the endless snow-covered prairie and the mountains to the west which I could not bear to lay eyes on.

'That will haunt me till the day I die . . . the fact that I was offered medical help which would have avoided the accident, but I turned it down. The next day, while making Emily breakfast, I actually had a five-second blackout – which my daughter registered, as she turned to me and said: "Mommy's tired. Mommy needs to go to bed."

'But instead of following my daughter's advice and spending the day with the covers over my head – advice that would have saved her life – I got us both dressed and dropped Emily at nursery school, then nodded off on the T and almost missed the stop for New England State. Once I had dragged myself off the train and into my office, I glanced at myself in the mirror and saw just how strained and netherworldly I looked. So I drank three large mugs of coffee and got through my lectures, constantly sensing that I was a bad actor inhabiting the body of this alleged professor of English, trying to sound erudite and engaged with her subject matter while simultaneously knowing that I was nothing less than a sham . . .

'And yes, at that moment I did realize just how depressed I was, how fast I was sinking. The faculty doctor was back on duty that afternoon – I know this because he phoned me again that day to see how I was. That's something I've also not told anybody, not even admitted to myself until now . . . the fact that he called me again and said I really needed to come in and see him.

' "I have to pick my daughter up at school now," I informed him. Know what his reply was? "Not in your current state. Call a parent you know whose child is also at the nursery. Tell him or her that you've got an emergency at work and get them to bring your daughter home. Then come in and see me straight away."

'Did I heed this advice? No. I just said: "I'm fine, Doctor." Then I put down the phone and grabbed my coat and hat and jumped the T back to Cambridge to pick up Emily.

'That was the other insane variable in that afternoon. I never picked my daughter up at school during the week, as I had office hours until five. But on this one day, the nanny had asked if she could have the afternoon off, as she had some appointment at a podiatrist about her bad feet.

'Had Julia been there that day . . . had I not given her the time off . . .'

I stopped speaking again and put my hand on the door handle of the car and was about to press it and throw the door open and run off into the absolute nothingness of the Alberta

463

plains. But I found myself thinking: *And then what? The story can't be avoided.*

I started speaking again.

' "Mommy, Mommy!" Emily said as she saw me in the doorway of the nursery. "Can we go get a treat?"

' "No problem, my love."

' "You tired, Mommy?"

' "Don't worry about it."

'And I helped her on with her coat and led her by the hand out the door.

' "I think there's a coffee shop near here that does great sundaes," I said. "But first you'll have to eat something nutritious . . . like a hamburger."

' "Are hamburgers good for you?"

' "They're better than ice-cream sundaes."

'Suddenly, in front of us, there was this commotion. An elderly woman – fat, heavy make-up, a stupid cigarette between her lips – was walking her terrier. The lead had broken and the terrier was running free, heading towards us. The woman was yelling its name. And then . . .

'What I told the police afterwards was that Emily, all wide-eyed, broke free of my grip and chased right after it. I lunged for my daughter, screaming at her to stop. But she was already off the curb . . .

'That's not the precise truth. Just as we saw the woman with the dog, I had another of those momentary blackouts I'd been suffering. It couldn't have been more than two seconds. But in that time, Emily went off the curb and . . .

'Suddenly I came to. And saw my daughter two steps behind the dog, and a taxi barreling around the corner. The cabbie was going too fast and didn't see Emily until . . .

'That's when I screamed my daughter's name. That's when I lunged for her.

'But the cab hit her directly – and the impact sent her flying.'

I put my fists in my eyes. *Black it out. Black it out.*

Eventually I pulled my fists away. I steadied myself. Vern sat there, hushed, silent.

'What happened next . . . I was screaming and scooping up my daughter from the ground where she lay crumpled, and the woman with the fucking dog was screaming, and the cabbie – who turned out to be Armenian – was hovering over us, hysterical, saying it wasn't his fault, he hadn't seen her . . . "*She suddenly there! She there! She there! She there!*" He kept repeating that, along with: "*No chance! No chance! I have no chance!*"

'Someone dialed 911. The cops came. The cabbie by this point was screaming at me to let him save her. "*I bring her back . . . I bring her back.*" But I kept holding her against me, my head buried in her still-warm body, her neck totally limp, no breathing, no reaction to all this madness around her. Nothing . . .

'One of the cops gently tried to get me to let go of her. But I shrieked at him to go away. Then there were more sirens. An ambulance. The paramedic somehow managed to separate me from Emily. When I was coerced into letting her go and I saw one of the ambulance guys checking for vital signs and looking up at one of the cops and shaking his head . . . that's when I lunged for the driver, screaming at him, calling him a murderer and . . .

'Two cops had to pull me off him. The cabbie was now so distraught that one of the paramedics had to hold him down. And then . . . *then* . . . I don't remember much of *then*. Emily was placed on a stretcher and put into the ambulance. One of the cops – a woman – sat in the back of the cop car with me as we raced after it. She had her arm around me so tightly I couldn't move, and told her colleague in the front seat to call for back-up when we reached the hospital.

' "Back-up" was a huge male nurse. He was waiting for me with a white-coated doctor. The doctor – a young guy – spoke quietly to me, and said they were going to give me something that would calm me down for a few hours. I somehow managed to promise I would stay calm. But as the woman cop helped me out of the car I made a break for it, screaming that I had to see Emily. That's when the male nurse grabbed me and got me into a wrestler's grip, and the doctor approached with a hypodermic and . . .

'When I awoke I discovered it was the next morning. I was in a bed – and I was being held down by restraints. A young nurse was on duty. She looked visibly pained when she saw I had come out of whatever they'd hit me with.

' "I'll be right back in a couple of minutes," she whispered. I sat there, staring up at the ceiling, telling myself: *This is not happening* . . . and knowing simultaneously that my world had just collapsed. When she returned some minutes later she was accompanied by a doctor – a quiet man in his mid-fifties – and a very sensible-looking woman also around the same age. He introduced himself as Dr Martin and said that the woman standing next to him was Mrs Potholm, and she would be my "social worker". *Social worker.* Thinking back on it, they must have a very strict protocol drawn up for breaking the news to people . . . especially parents. And they must have decided that mentioning the fact that you have been assigned a social worker before delivering the body blow will, in some way, prepare you for the horror of the news. It's like being told: "*In a moment you're about to be pushed off the ledge on the thirty-second floor*" – and then the shove happening. It's still a grotesque free-fall . . . but at least you're ready for it.

' "Ms Howard . . . Jane . . .' the doctor began, his voice just above a whisper. 'Emily was admitted here dead on arrival yesterday evening. An autopsy was carried out very early this morning – and the cause of death was severance of the spinal cord and massive cranial injury. I mention this to let you know that Emily died instantly. I doubt she suffered. I doubt . . ."

'But I didn't hear the rest of that sentence, as I turned away and started to howl. The social worker tried to speak with me, but I heard nothing. She tried to reason with me. I didn't want reason. I just wanted to howl.

'Then, *bam*, another injection in my arm . . . and I was gone again.

'It was night when I awoke – and my best friend Christy was seated at my side.

' "What are you doing here?" I whispered to her.

' "It seems you listed me as the person to get in touch with in the event of an emergency on your health insurance forms. So they called me and told me and I got the next plane to Boston and . . ."

'She started to cry. Tears cascading down her face. Trying to be brave for me and failing. I'd never seen Christy cry before – she was always too deliberately tough for that. But here she was, weeping and telling the nurse to get the damn restraints off my arms, then holding me as I let go and must have bawled my eyes out for around half an hour.

'Around an hour later – after a conversation with the social worker – they let me see Emily. She was in the morgue, but Mrs Potholm told me they'd move her to a "viewing room" where I could "spend as much time with her" as I liked.

'I remember walking down the corridor with Christy and Mrs Potholm to the "viewing room", and reaching the swing doors and my knees buckling and Christy holding me up and telling me: "You have to do this. There's no getting around it. But you will do it with me."

'And then Mrs Potholm held open the door and we went inside and . . .'

I paused and I looked up at Vern. He hadn't moved. Outside, snow was falling, whiting out visibility. The world had vanished.

I continued.

'She was on a small gurney, a sheet pulled up to her shoulders. Everyone says the dead look asleep. But I stared down at my wonderful daughter and all I could think was: *She's gone, she's never opening her eyes again and telling me she's afraid of the dark or wants me to read her a bedtime story or . . .*

'I stared down at Emily and could not escape the reality of what had happened. There was a huge blue contusion on her forehead, a deep gash on the side of her neck. And when I took her hands in mine they were ice. I thought I would fall apart again – but, at this moment, something came over me. Shock, I suppose you could call it . . . but it was deeper than shock. Trauma of the kind that simply sucks you into a vortex and . . .'

A deep, long, steadying breath.

'That night, I was released from the hospital under Christy's surveillance. We got back to my apartment and I walked into Emily's room and I sat down on her bed and . . .

'No, I didn't fall apart again. Trauma has its own strange stupor. I just sat there for around an hour. Christy was there beside me, saying nothing . . . because there was nothing to say. She did force me to eat something – and she did insist on me taking the pills that the hospital prescribed. After tucking me in, she herself collapsed on the sofa . . . because I don't think my wonderful friend had slept in over two days.

'But the pills did no good for me. I just lay in my bed, staring at the ceiling, knowing that all I could do now was die. That thought preoccupied me all night – especially as it was coupled with a horrendous instant replay of everything that had happened, and this insane growing belief that if I hurried back to the spot of the accident I could stop it. Turn time back completely and have my daughter hop off that mortuary gurney and come home to me . . .

'So, without thinking, I threw a robe on over my pajamas and grabbed my car keys and left the house. It was the middle of the night – and I drove right back to the place in Cambridge where it happened. Drove there, slammed on the brakes, got out, sat down on the pavement and . . .

'All I can remember after that is this sense of falling. Falling into . . . an abyss? A chasm without a bottom? I don't know. All I do know is that I sat in that spot for a long time . . . until some cops pulled up in a cruiser and tried to talk to me and when I said nothing, they called for back-up and . . .

'I was kept overnight in a psychiatric hospital for observation. They found my home number. They called Christy. She showed up and explained everything. According to the shrink who signed me over to her, it was very common for someone who'd lost a "loved one" in an accident to return to the scene in the hopes of . . .'

I broke off again.

Then: 'I'm not going to tell you much about the funeral. An old college friend of mine had become a Unitarian minister. She conducted it. There weren't many people there – some New England State colleagues, some Harvard people, the nanny, some people from the nursery, and the wife and daughter of the cabbie who'd hit Emily. They were crying even more than the rest of us. After the burial . . . you know, I've never once been back to my daughter's grave, I just couldn't . . . they gave Christy a letter from the family, saying how sorry they were. I never read it. Couldn't. But Christy talked to the wife. It seems the guy – his name was Mr Babula – had been so traumatized by what had happened that he quit

469

his job and was on Valium or something, unable to leave the house, unable to deal with . . .

'But he'd been driving too fast. The police told Christy that. And he'd already got two violations against him for speeding. And they were bringing charges. And . . .'

Another pause.

'During all this, an all-points bulletin went off for Emily's father. But he was nowhere to be found. We had the cops working on it. My lawyer. Even some of his so-called "business associates". Running from creditors had made him go to ground. Not a fucking word from him. Until . . .

'But I jump ahead. After the funeral my department chairman told me I should take as much "compassionate leave" as I wanted. I was back at work five days later. Everyone was stunned to see me – but I didn't know what else to do with myself. I was operating on some very spectral autopilot in which it was impossible to make sense of anything. Christy had returned to Oregon. I had closed the door of Emily's room and refused to go in there. I did my classes. I saw my students. I avoided my colleagues. I seemed to be functioning . . . even though my mind was increasingly preoccupied with the idea that I was living in this tunnel made of reinforced concrete. I could just about negotiate its narrow confines, but it was brutally limiting. There was no escaping it. There was no glimmer of light at the end of it. But – and this was the manic thing I kept telling myself – if I was just able to continue negotiating its confinement I would somehow be able to keep functioning . . .

'So, for around two weeks, I was an automaton twenty-four/seven. If anyone at the university asked me how I was doing I'd change the subject. I was doing how I was doing. I was coping. I was, privately, unhinged. But even I couldn't admit that yet.

'Then two things happened. My lawyer called me to say that Theo had resurfaced. He'd been lying low with his paramour in Morocco while their lawyer did some fancy footwork with the company that had taken away the movie they were selling. I didn't get all the details – I didn't want all the details – but the crux of the matter was that there were threats of all kinds of lawsuits by Theo and his bitch, Adrienne. Their legal guy had found some way of blocking the release of the film. The film company had deep pockets and agreed to clear all the debts that Theo and Adrienne had run up in exchange for no legal action . . . and, hey presto, they were in the clear.

'My lawyer said that he had actually talked with Theo who was "devastated" about what had happened to his daughter, and wanted to speak with me . . . but also didn't want to ring me directly. "That's courageous of him," I remember telling my lawyer, then adding: "Inform him that I never, *ever*, want to hear from him again."

'Theo must have taken him at his word – because I didn't hear from him. But ten days later, I was in a restaurant off Harvard Square having a meal. It was around eight – and this diner had become the place where I ate every meal, as I couldn't bear to do anything in my apartment except drink myself to sleep with the aid of Zopiclone and red wine. The waiters there were so used to me by now – and the fact that I always ordered a grilled cheese sandwich and coffee – that the food always showed up around five minutes after I sat down.

'But on the night in question, as the sandwich arrived, I looked up and saw Theo and Adrienne coming in. They didn't notice me at first, because I was in a booth in the back. Before I even could consider what I was doing, I threw some money down on the table, and grabbed my coat and the fork next to my plate. I walked straight towards Theo and Adrienne. They were waiting to be seated. Adrienne saw me first and actually said: "Jane! Oh, my God, we're so—"

'Before she could finish the sentence I took the fork and plunged it right into the side of her neck. She screamed, there was blood everywhere, I kept right on walking out the door, then dashed across the street to a taxi stand and was in a cab before anyone could stop me.

'I was home ten minutes later. I threw clothes in a bag. I grabbed the necessary documentation, including my two passports and some cash and traveler's checks. I tossed everything into my car. I started driving.

'Ten days later I drove into a snowbank in Montana. And . . .'

I fell silent again.

'End of story,' I said. 'Except the woman I stabbed didn't die and didn't press charges. And when I messed up my suicide . . . well, maybe living was the punishment I would have to endure for killing my daughter . . .'

Finally Vern spoke.

'You didn't kill your daughter.'

'Did you not listen to a word I just said?'

'You didn't kill your daughter.'

'All the advice I got, all the steps I could have taken to avoid disaster, what did I do . . . ?'

'You didn't kill her. That's all there is to it.'

'That's easy for you to say.'

'No, it's not. Because I still blame myself for losing my daughter. Even though . . .'

Silence. He put his hand on top of mine. I pulled it away.

'What are you doing here with me?' I said. 'I mean, do you really like damaged goods? Is that your kinky thing? Or do you actually think there's some sort of weird romantic future between us?'

472

As soon as this was out of my mouth I loathed myself for it. And I turned to him and instantly said: 'I'm sorry. I'm so stupid, so . . .'

I buried my head in his shoulder, but couldn't cry. He put an arm around me, but I could tell he was nervous about doing it, fearful about how I might react.

'You know,' he said quietly, 'even if I wanted "that", it could never be. The prostate cancer ended that part of my life . . . not that it had existed since my wife left me.'

'So what do you want from this?' I asked.

He disengaged himself from me. His eyes were red, rheumy. He pulled a handkerchief out of the pocket of his coat and wiped his face. Then he gripped the steering wheel and stared straight out at all that blowing snow.

'I want a whiskey,' he finally said.

Eight

WE WENT TO a bar in a strip mall. Like all strip malls, this one was grim. The fact that several inches of fresh snow had dappled it didn't lessen its ugliness. The bar was also ugly: a real beer-and-hockey joint which stank of urinated lager and male sweat. At least they weren't playing heavy metal music – though there was one of those massive televisions near the bar that was broadcasting a Calgary Flames game. On screen two guys from opposing teams had thrown off their helmets and were now doing their best to rip each other's ears off. All the patrons at the bar seemed to be enjoying the show – and were yelling encouragement to the pit-bull in the Flames uniform.

'Hey there, Vern,' the bartender said as we came in. The bartender was named Tommy. He looked like a biker and wore a T-shirt that exposed overripe biceps and a tattoo of the Canadian Maple Leaf intertwined with a crucifix.

'Nice place,' I said, following Vern into a booth and sliding in opposite him.

'That it is not,' Vern said. 'But it's local – and I can stagger home from here.'

Now this statement begged a question: *'Does having two drinks make you stagger . . . or do you come in here to break your two-drink rule?'* Over the next three hours I got an answer to that question, as Vern proceeded to drink me into an advanced stupor. After telling me in the car that he wanted a whiskey he drove me here in silence, saying absolutely nothing about all that I had told him. He plugged a CD into his sound system: a piano trio by Schumann; brooding, expressive, wintery music. We negotiated our way through the snow and back towards the city. I was grateful that he said nothing after everything I had said. There is a notion propagated in modern life that 'talking it out' will somehow make everything better. It's a lie. All talking does is articulate the agony. You have to get it out because you have to get it out. But it's not like vomiting up a toxic meal. You don't suddenly feel purged, scoured, cleansed and ready to start anew. All you feel is: *I've said it . . . and nothing has changed.*

So I was pleased to avoid extended soul searching with Vern. Maybe Vern himself had once been told by someone that his daughter's schizophrenia wasn't his fault and he too had decided otherwise. Or maybe my story had so appalled him that he just wanted to get drunk.

Whatever the reason, Vern started drinking seriously. Two shots disappeared within ten minutes of us sitting down. This seemed to steady him a bit. Then it was a double every thirty minutes. I matched him, drink for drink. It was an interesting experience, getting truly sloshed. Though I had often drunk myself to sleep in the recent past, this was different. From the hints dropped by Tommy the bartender – 'So it's going to be that sort of afternoon, Vern . . . How 'bout handing over your car keys for safekeeping?' – it was clear that this was not the first time my work colleague had gone on a binge here. I even posed that question to him – around the time round five showed up.

'So if you're into AA and all that, how do you explain an afternoon like this?'

'It's simple, really: every other month, when I sense the need to get drunk, I come in here and I get drunk. Tommy knows when I'm having one of those days and what to do when I get to the point where *I* don't know what to do. There was a time when I was blotto every day. Now I get smashed under controlled circumstances.'

Over the three hours we were in the bar, Vern did most of

the talking. The rye loosened him up considerably and he ranged over a wide variety of subjects, from interpretations of Mahler on record, to the lingering despair he felt about most things to do with the Central Public Library, to a brief mention of a woman he'd fallen in love with while he was at the Royal College of Music.

'Her name was Veronique. She was a cellist from Lyon. Brilliant and, to my eyes, very beautiful in a rather severe way. I once accompanied her in the Second Cello Sonata of Mendelssohn. And I sensed – from the hints she was dropping – that she was more than interested in me. God knows, I was smitten with her. But . . . I was just never good at that sort of thing.'

'By which you mean: seduction?'

'By which I mean: being normal.'

'Who's normal?'

'Oh, there are people who seem to get through life with a limited amount of difficulty; who know how to make their luck, to capitalize on their talents, to allow things to happen for them.'

'But the majority of people don't cut through life like it's very soft, malleable butter. It's always a brawl . . .'

'Especially against the one great force that none of us can counteract: death.'

'Does it scare you, death?'

'It's going to arrive, that's for sure. And I guess the one and only thing that perplexes me is the idea that I will be no more, that my entire story will vanish with me. No "me". How can that be?'

'"*No me*",' I said, repeating the phrase. 'A year ago that struck me as a very viable alternative.'

'And now?'

'Now . . . I have to live with myself, and all that that means.'

That was the only mention during the afternoon of all that had been articulated earlier that day. More drinks arrived. We kept talking. I felt the rye take hold of me – but I liked its alcoholic balm. I needed to get drunk for the same reason I needed to talk about 'that day': it had to be done. It was a necessity.

By keeping up a steady, but not rapid-fire pace of imbibing, neither of us pitched into incoherency until around five that afternoon . . . at which point Tommy phoned for two separate taxis (was he ensuring that we didn't wake up next to each other?) and helped each of us out of the bar and into the waiting vehicles. But around two hours before this, I made a momentary observation which – as it turned out – was to direct the course of events in my life for the next few months. Like so many events that manage to alter things for us, this one came about merely because I looked a certain way at a certain moment – glancing up at the television behind the bar just when . . .

'About time they nabbed that lying sonofabitch.'

That was Tommy the bartender staring up at the television. On the screen, George MacIntyre – the father of the missing thirteen-year-old girl, Ivy – was being led out of his very simple frame house. He was a man in his early forties – overweight, balding, with a wispy beard. He was dressed in a dirty T-shirt and pajama bottoms – the cops evidently deciding to arrest him while he was still in bed. But though I took in all the grubby details of his appearance – and the fact that he so seemed to fit the identikit portrait of a child molester – it was his eyes that really grabbed my attention. They were red from crying. But what I saw in them wasn't fear or guilt or denial; rather, it was anguish. The same anguish I caught in my own eyes on those occasions after Emily's death when I made the mistake of looking at myself in the mirror.

The eyes of someone who had also lost a child and now knew a sorrow beyond dreams. And at that precise moment, I knew: *that man did not kill his daughter.*

MacIntyre was now being perp-walked to a waiting cop car while dozens of reporters and paparazzi shouted questions and clicked camera shutters.

'As George MacIntyre was led away,' the CBC reporter said, 'he was heard shouting: "I would never hurt my daughter. Never." Since his daughter's disappearance he has made several dramatic public appeals for her safe return. MacIntyre, forty-two years old, is known to the police. His wife, Brenda, is very active in the local Assemblies of God church, and according to her pastor, Rev. Larry Coursen . . .'

The report cut to Larry Coursen. He was blond, square-jawed, with very good teeth, dressed in a light brown leather jacket and a dog collar, and oozing sanctimonious concern.

'This is an immensely sad day for Brenda MacIntyre, for all members of our Assembly of God congregation and, yes, for George MacIntyre too. What has happened is so tragic. We are praying very hard for Ivy's safe return – just as we are also praying that the light of our Lord Jesus Christ shines down upon her and also upon George MacIntyre.'

I pulled my glass towards me and threw back the dregs of rye.

'Praise the Lord,' I whispered under my breath. Vern heard me and favored me with a small smile.

Now onscreen was an RCMP officer named Floyd McKay. He explained that George MacIntyre had been transferred to Calgary for further investigation.

'Know what I heard this morning from one of the cops that drink here?' Tommy the bartender said to someone perched on a stool and drinking a Labatt's by the neck. 'That they found a "bloodied undergarment" under a pile of wood in

MacIntyre's workshop, and that's what led to his arrest this morning.'

'If I was the cops I'd castrate him,' the other guy said.

That's when I heard myself say: 'He didn't do it.'

Tommy the bartender glared at me.

'Did I hear you correctly?'

I met his gaze.

'You did,' I said. 'He didn't do it.'

'And how the hell do you know that?'

'I just do.'

'Even though they found his daughter's bloodstained panties hidden in his workshop?'

'That's hearsay. And I'm telling you, sir – the man is innocent.'

'And I'm telling you, ma'am, he's guilty as hell. And Vern . . . I don't know who your friend is, but I think all that Crown Royal you've both been drinking has clouded her judgment.'

'Think what you like,' I whispered under my breath. Vern held up his hand to me and gave me the sort of imploring look that let it be known I should now shut the hell up.

'I'm sorry if I offended you, sir,' I shouted to the bartender.

'Hey, just be grateful that Vern's a regular here. Otherwise you'd've been out on the street by now.'

Two more ryes later, the cabs arrived. I muttered a goodbye to Vern as I flopped across the back seat of my taxi. The driver asked me if I was going to be sick, and I assured him that I would keep the contents of my stomach within me until we got to my apartment, and he assured me he would deposit me in the minus-nineteen night air if I failed to make good on my promise.

I don't remember much after that, except tossing twenty dollars at the driver as I got out and somehow making my way upstairs. I unlocked my front door and fell face first on my bed. When I woke it was eleven the next morning. I felt as if my head had been cleaved by a very sharp instrument. I looked at the time and groaned. I was never late for work – and now I knew that, even if I wanted to make it in, I was too hungover. So I picked up my cellphone and called Mrs Woods and apologized profusely for only informing her now that I was out sick, but explained that I'd picked up some stomach bug and was up for most of the night.

'Something's obviously going around,' Mrs Woods said, 'because Vern Byrne also phoned in sick with the same complaint.'

Great hungover minds think alike.

I lolled in bed for another hour, thinking, thinking. As I replayed the insanity of that drinking session, it was clear to me that Vern had decided he was not the only person who needed to get drunk yesterday.

But the thoughts of this drinking contest – and its toxic aftermath – were soon overshadowed by a larger consideration: George MacIntyre. The way his eyes seemed to become haunted when faced with the specter of all those popping camera lights and shouted questions. The sense of resignation that seemed to dapple his face – as if this new fresh hell was nothing compared to that of his daughter's disappearance. A guilty man would have signaled his culpability by doing that Raskolnikov thing of self-incrimination. Something in his countenance would have given the game away. But MacIntyre simply looked crushed by all that had befallen him. He was a man who had lost hope, and who had now entered the ultimate Kafkaesque nightmare: being accused of killing his own daughter while simultaneously knowing that he was completely innocent . . .

And yet, from the little I'd heard in passing about the case, MacIntyre had a history of violent behavior. If it was true that he had beaten his wife and was considered dangerous by his son . . . of course, he'd be immediately regarded as the prime suspect in the case, though none of this could be publicized prior to his trial.

Then there was the fact that a bloody piece of underwear belonging to his daughter was allegedly (according to Tommy the bartender) found in his workshop. Why would he store that item of incredibly incriminating clothing there? Surely if he was the man behind her disappearance he would do everything in his power to hide evidence? Even if he was determined to have his guilt proclaimed by being 'found out', he wouldn't resort to something as lame as a pair of underwear in an obvious location. Self-denunciation – especially when something like infanticide is involved – would involve something leading directly to the body; a true sign of guilt, and one which would be quickly substantiated.

But the cops – needing to break the case as fast as possible – would jump on the bloody panties as proof that MacIntyre was guilty as hell (that is, if that bar-room rumor about this piece of evidence was even true). But until lab reports came back stating that the blood matched that of Ivy's . . .

Listen to you. Nancy goddamn Drew, with her Dostoevsky references and her hungover need to defend a much-touted sociopath. Talk about displacement activity . . .

But try as I did to put the case to one side, it continued to nag at me all day. Having finally hauled myself out of bed and into a penitential cold shower, followed by a further two-hour act of physical contrition at the gym, I found myself inextricably drawn to my local newspaper shop, where I bought the *Globe and Mail*, the *Calgary Herald* and the *Edmonton Journal* to get that day's journalistic take on George MacIntyre's arrest. I took my newspapers around the corner to Caffé Beano and started reading. The *Herald* had a full page on 'The Ivy MacIntyre Case' and noted that this was the third time in six years that an adolescent girl had gone missing from the Townsend area. In all of the previous cases, no traces of the vanished child had ever been found.

The *Herald* also noted that George MacIntyre was '*known to the police*' – that phrase again. It mentioned that he had a previous job driving long-haul trucks, but said little more because – as I was learning – the Canadian press wasn't like the American press when it came to reporting somebody under investigation for murder. No past misdeeds could be reported. No incriminating comments from neighbors or colleagues at work. The law stopped them from reporting, prior to a trial, anything but the basic facts of the case.

But the *Edmonton Journal* did carry a quote from the '*MacIntyre Family Minister*', Larry Coursen, saying that ' "*Ivy was one of God's little angels*" '. He also noted that, when he first met Brenda MacIntyre, she was in desperate need of healing. ' "*But when she accepted Jesus Christ as her Lord and Savior, the healing process began . . .*" '

Yeah, sure it did . . .

Within weeks of getting that telephone call from Jesus, Brenda was ' "*clean and sober*" '. She'd found a job in the local Safeway supermarket. She'd begun to ' "*take responsibility for her actions*" ' and had completely cleaned up the family home and had ' "*re-established her relationship with her children*" '. (What exactly did he mean by that?) But – as the Rev. Larry Coursen was quick to point out – there was an ' "*ongoing sadness in her life*" '.

No doubt this 'sadness' was her very unsaved, deadbeat husband George.

The *Herald*, meanwhile, had a quote from a local Townsend guy named Stu Pattison. He knew MacIntyre from a local hockey team they both played on, and said that he

' "*doted on Ivy and actually once went crazy in Townsend when some kids in a pickup drove her off the road while she was on a bicycle*" '.

I scribbled in my notebook the name Larry Coursen and that of Stu Pattison. I also noted the detail about MacIntyre driving long-haul trucks and placed a comment: '*Did she ever file a domestic abuse charge?*' next to an entry I made labeled: '*Brenda MacIntyre*'. Then I asked the woman behind the café counter for a pair of scissors and clipped all the articles I had just read. I folded them inside my notebook, walked up to Reid's stationers and bought some plain white paper, several files and a bottle of white glue. Down a little alleyway from Reid's was an internet café. I spent the next three hours there. Using assorted search engines I found out everything I could about George and Brenda MacIntyre and their two children, printing copious amounts of information along the way.

From the *Regina Leader-Post* in 2002 I learned that, in February of that year, MacIntyre had been arrested after manhandling a woman in a truck-stop bar. The woman didn't press charges – but it seems he also directly solicited sex from her and '*exposed himself to her*' while they were on the way back to his truck.

I read this paragraph again, trying to understand the narrative logic behind it. MacIntyre pulls into Regina and picks up some woman in a bar, then invites her back to his truck. He evidently didn't have to coerce her back – which meant that the manhandling charge just couldn't wash. She went willingly – but then, halfway there, he exposes himself to her? What the hell was that all about? If she had agreed to return to his vehicle for sex, why would he pull a stunt like that?

There was more. In an article in the local Townsend rag in May 2005, MacIntyre was found guilty of '*damaging private property after his daughter was forced off the road on her bicycle by a couple of adolescents in a car. Ivy wasn't injured in this incident* [the reporter pointed out] *but was nonetheless badly shaken up.*' This being a small town, she knew the two brothers who'd done it. When MacIntyre found out their names, he went over to their house in the middle of the night and, using a tire iron, proceeded to smash their pick-up. Their father ran out in the middle of this demolition job and MacIntyre threatened to flatten his head. The cops were called. MacIntyre spent the night in jail and ended up having to pay $3,000 in restitution.

In the same article, his then-employer, Dwane Poole, was quoted as saying that ' "*George MacIntyre was about the most talented guy with a lathe and a piece of wood that I'd ever come across*" ', but that he could turn ugly when crossed.

I read on, finding every published word I could about the case, printing over fifty pages of material, filling my notebook with names and places and dates and phrases that I was certain were pertinent to the case. By the time I got home it was late afternoon. I did something I had never done before: I plugged the television antenna cable into the wall socket and actually watched the news. The Ivy MacIntyre disappearance was the first item. A CBC reporter was standing outside the ' "*Criminal Investigation Unit of the RCMP in Calgary where George MacIntyre is still being questioned . . .*" ' but he had little else to say about the progress of the investigation.

But when I woke from a profoundly deep sleep at seven the next morning, there was a bombshell lead item on the CBC Radio news.

' "*A formal arraignment of Ivy's father George on charges of her abduction is scheduled to be brought today.*" '

Did this mean that the bloody undergarment had been found? And if so, did it prove conclusively that the blood was

Ivy MacIntyre's? And did the technicians also find DNA traces of her father on the same garment? And was his born-again wife really the saint she was being portrayed as? And was I the only damn person in the Province of Alberta who saw the look on George MacIntyre's face as he was being led off to jail and knew: the guy didn't do it?

Questions, questions . . . and why wasn't anybody posing them?

So, as soon as the news item was finished I made a decision: I was going to call in sick for the next two days . . . during which time I was going to crack this case. Crack it wide open.

As I decided this, another thought came to me: *You are seriously unhinged.*

Nine

Mrs Woods was far too understanding about my ongoing 'gastric flu'.

'I gather it's a horrible dose,' she said, 'and you really must look after yourself.'

'I feel bad about not being there,' I lied.

'Don't be,' she said. 'Illness is illness. Anyway, this is the first time all year you've ever been sick and you're always putting in extra hours and working weekends. Take the rest of the week off – and do get better.'

I actually felt fine. Maybe it was the restorative night's sleep that always follows a hangover. Or maybe it was a strange sense of direction. Ever since I had made the proper acquaintance of the Ivy MacIntyre case, some switch had clicked in my brain. It wasn't the switch that suddenly erased all memory, all pain. No, this was a mechanism which simply pushed me deeper and deeper into the bizarre narration that was this case. It was like losing yourself in a movie, yet one in which I had no idea whatsoever what the ending would be . . . if, that is, there was even to be an ending.

Still . . . *to work*.

I called Avis and arranged to pick up in a couple of hours. Then I used my cellphone and called Information for Townsend, Alberta. I was in luck. All the numbers I sought were listed – with the exception of that for George and Brenda MacIntyre, which (according to the operator) had recently been changed to unlisted. I then began to make a series of calls, starting with Dwane Poole. He was a soft-spoken man with what I sensed was a natural graciousness. I explained that I was Nancy Lloyd (a name I simply made up), a reporter with the *Vancouver Sun*, and that I was coming to Townsend that afternoon and was wondering if I could have a half-hour of his time.

'I kind of feel talked out about all this,' he said.

'I can appreciate that,' I said, 'but I have serious doubts about the "rush to judgment" element in this case. I think George MacIntyre is being hanged, drawn and quartered before all the evidence is in.'

'I thought that too,' he said, 'until that piece of clothing was found in his shop. Now everyone's saying that the DNA and blood match up . . .'

'Would two-thirty p.m. be OK?'

'I guess so,' he said, sounding reluctant but not wanting to come across as impolite.

I then called the Rev. Larry Coursen and got his answering machine. So I left a message, telling him that Nancy Lloyd from the *Vancouver Sun* called, and might he be around today or tomorrow for an interview? Of course I knew I was taking a risk by giving him the name of the paper. If he was conscientious about such things, he could easily call them and discover he was dealing with a fraud. But I was banking on the fact that he had been so besieged by requests from the media that he would simply accept this one on face value . . . especially as I had also gone to the precaution of making certain that Coursen had yet to be interviewed by anyone from the *Sun*.

I rang the school where Ivy MacIntyre was a student and asked to speak to the principal. When I explained who I was, I was put on to a deputy named Mrs Missy Schulder. She told me that the school had made a decision not to engage in any interviews with the press.

'We have nothing to say about this,' she told me.

'Did you yourself know Ivy?' I asked.

'Of course I know Ivy,' she said. 'I was her home-room teacher for two years. Nice girl. Liked the dad too – even if he did have his angry side.'

'But did he ever turn that anger against his daughter?'

'What you trying to get me to say here?' she asked.

'Nothing, ma'am . . . and this is totally off the record.'

'That's what they all say.'

'Well, totally off the record between us: I don't think he did it.'

'And what makes you say that, Ms . . . ?'

'Lloyd. Nancy Lloyd. And the reason I'm saying that is because I know damn well a guilty man wouldn't keep a bloodstained article of clothing around his workshop.'

'I'm with you there,' she said in a low excited hush. 'Let me tell you something else, Ms Lloyd. I never liked the wife. And ever since she got religion . . . well, "insufferable" is about the mildest word I can use to describe her. George may have been from a low-rent background, and he may have had a lot of "anger issues", and also never got on with his boy, Michael . . . who I always thought was a bit of a punk anyway . . .'

'Why's that?'

'He was always hanging with biker types, got into a lot of drugs, gave his dad a lot of lip. George, from what I heard, got real furious with Michael when he discovered he was dealing crystal meth, and Brenda, the wife, defended her "poor little victimized boy" and sent him off to her people. And Michael did get himself straightened out and is driving trucks cross-country. But if I was a journalist nosing around this case, I'd look long and hard at the wife. She was always trailer trash.

'You know, her mother had done time as a prostitute in Winnipeg – what a place to be a working girl. And she had this father who'd beaten her older brother so senseless after an argument that the kid was in a coma for a week and was never completely right again after that. Her dad did seven years in prison for that little incident.

'But the big rumor about Brenda, and one that came out of Red Deer – the town where she grew up – is that, at thirteen, she'd fallen pregnant after being raped by her father. The pregnancy was terminated. No charges were ever brought against him. And three years after this, she met George MacIntyre. He was twenty-four – and was driving trucks at this time. He'd made the mistake of eyeing Brenda up in a café in Red Deer frequented by long-distance drivers. They ended up "doing it" in the back of his pick-up. And, wouldn't you know it, she fell pregnant.'

So George MacIntyre, from a young age, had a habit of picking up women whenever he stopped while driving, and using the sleeping area behind his cab as the romantic spot in which to bed them.

Now why did he do the right thing by Brenda and marry her – and how did she track him down after she discovered herself with child? According to Missy Schulder, the couple lived in Red Deer for six years, during which time Ivy was also born. Then MacIntyre lost his job, due to excessive drinking. So the family moved to Townsend where he was offered the chance to apprentice as a carpenter to an old family friend named Dwane Poole. And then things started going really wrong.

I scribbled all this down as she spewed it forth – and felt that giddy high a real journalist must feel when they bump into the motherload of sources.

'Can you elaborate a little more on that?' I asked.

'I actually think I've said enough.'

'One final thing: the other two local girls who went missing . . .'

'You mean, Hildy Krebs and Mimi Pullinger?'

489

I wrote those names down.

'That's right,' I said, trying to sound knowledgeable. 'Hildy and Mimi.'

'Well, Hildy disappeared in 2002 and Mimi in 2005. They were both a little older than Ivy when they vanished. Fifteen, sixteen years old. The thing was, they were both the sort of girls who were always landing themselves in deep doo-doo. Hildy got herself up the spout at fourteen and then lost the baby early due to a drug overdose. And Mimi was thrown out of school twice for sniffing glue in the ladies, then ran off for a bit with a biker . . .'

'Sounds like a quiet little town you have there.'

'Now don't go writing anything like that in your paper. Townsend is, by and large, a pretty OK place. Everywhere's got white trash. We just have white trash that does dumb stuff which lands us all in the papers and has snoopy reporters like you digging for dirt . . . no offense meant, *of course.*'

I decided Missy Schulder was pretty damn good news – and someone who probably relished her role as the town cynic.

'Any chance you might want to meet up with me for a coffee when I'm down in Townsend?'

'Hell, no,' she said. 'I mean, I've got to live here, right? And if I'm seen with some Nosey Parker, well, I'll never hear the end of it, now, will I? But two tips. Since you're from Vancouver, you might want to ask around the flop houses off East Hastings. Rumor has it that both Hildy and Mimi have gone to ground there. Junkies. And my second ten-cent bit of wisdom of the morning is to repeat what I said to you earlier: follow the wife. She's the evil one in the story . . . but if you quote me on that . . .'

'Fear not, it won't happen,' I told her.

After the call I went to the local cybercafé and looked up all I could find about Hildy Krebs and Mimi Pullinger.

490

Everything Missy Schulder told me was on the money – all the trouble into which they landed themselves, the idiot boy-friends, the two disappearances three years apart which were not connected at the time, but which had now come back into focus courtesy of Ivy MacIntyre.

I printed all the material on the two missing girls and wondered if their parents might be amenable to a visit by a fraudulent *Vancouver Sun* journalist. Then I Googled everything I could find on Michael MacIntyre. Nothing of interest. But even if he was legally allowed to come out and say that, as much as he hated his father, George couldn't harm his daughter . . . well, would that change anything? Of course not. In a case like this, everyone was so wrapped up in the need for closure – for finding the bogeyman and seeing him punished – that they were willing to construct a narrative which served their purposes. And this narrative essentially revolved around the idea that George MacIntyre was the killer amongst them.

On the way south to Townsend, the local Calgary CBC station talked about the investigation which was continuing both in Calgary – where Mr MacIntyre was still being held – and in Townsend. No doubt a team of RCMP forensic specialists were now inspecting every fiber in every corner of George's workshop.

Yes, go ahead and micro-examine every damn corner of it. And while you're at it, why not follow the advice of Missy Schulder – someone who actually knows the human territory here – and cherchez la femme.

That is certainly what I was planning to do if Brenda MacIntyre would see me.

The road south edged its way through Calgary's endless urban sprawl. Then, suddenly, it all fell away and I was in open country. Though part of me wanted to look up and see what exactly I was passing through, I knew that this could be, at the very least, unsettling . . . especially after the business with Vern the other day. But it's amazing how you can limit your peripheral vision when necessary and simply focus your eyes on the roll of the tarmacadam in front of you.

I did finally look up when I got to Townsend. It was a blink-twice-you-miss-it sort of place: a gasoline alley with the requisite monocultural crap (Tim Horton's, an outpost of the Red Lobster, a Burger King), augmented by a short Main Street of undistinguished concrete buildings and one or two red-brick hold-overs from the 1950s. There was a bank. There was a supermarket. There was a shop that sold outdoor stuff. There was an old-style Mom and Pop restaurant. There was a sad-looking used bookstore, largely specializing in blockbuster paperbacks (but still, it *was* a bookstore). There was a bar. I thought about doing that old reporter thing of going into the local saloon and trying to strike up a conversation with the proprietor, in the hopes of eliciting some insights or useful information. But small towns have their own internal bush telegraphs and I didn't want word to get out too fast about me being here. Best to not announce myself to the world.

Dwane Poole lived on a side street not far from the ugly breezeblock high school which Ivy attended. His was a simple ranch house on a half-acre lot, with an extended detached garage taking up most of the available garden space. I heard the whirr of a rotary saw from the garage, so I approached its door. It was open. Poole was inside, wearing clear goggles as he fed a large piece of finished timber into the circular saw. He pushed the wood through, cutting it cleanly, then looked up and saw me.

'You Nancy?' he asked, whipping off his goggles. He was a thin, diminutive man in his late fifties, wearing a wool check shirt, baggy jeans and round wire-rimmed glasses. I could easily imagine him, thirty years earlier, passing the bong around a crash pad while wearing a tie-dyed T-shirt. Now he came across as quiet, reserved, with a strong streak of shyness. His workshop was a masterpiece of organization: all the tools immaculately arranged, stacks of finished cabinets on one wall (the craftsmanship was impressive), drawings, design plans and a large wooden desk filling another wall. Behind the desk was a picture of Dwane with a young man attired in the uniform of the Canadian Armed Forces.

'Thank you for seeing me on such short notice,' I said, accepting his outstretched hand.

'You're about the fifth journalist who's beaten a path to this door,' he said.

'I won't take up too much of your time.'

He moved towards his office area, where there was a drip machine of coffee brewing.

'You're in luck,' he said. 'I just made a fresh pot.'

'Is that your son?' I asked, pointing to the photograph I had spied moments earlier.

'Yes, that's David. He's out in Afghanistan now. Stationed with the Canadian NATO Forces near Kandahar.'

'That must be a source of pride and worry,' I said, trying to choose my words carefully.

'More of the latter,' he said. 'I don't really know what we're doing over there. But I'm not a politician and my boy did sign up for a tour of duty, so I suppose he has to accept the risks that come with the job.'

He poured me a mug of coffee and motioned for me to sit down on a simple wooden stool opposite his desk. I pulled out my notebook and pen. He himself perched on the edge of the desk and, from the outset, looked like he regretted agreeing to this interview in the first place.

'You know, George might have been the most talented carpenter I'd ever seen. When I was apprenticing – around

493

forty years ago – every skill was hard won and I really had to work at getting the principals down right. But George walked into this workshop and, within an hour, he was using a lathe as if he was born to it. And his eye when it came to understanding the intricacies of how to cut against the grain . . . like I said, he was a total natural.'

'Did he talk much about the problems he had at home?'

'For the first six months he was all business when he came through that door. He was here to learn a craft, a trade – and he was very determined. He was also, at this point, on benefit – but the provincial government was also paying him what's called a Skills Re-Training stipend to work with me. It wasn't much – around two hundred dollars a week – and I sensed money was very tight at home, especially as the wife wasn't yet working. But, as I said, he kept a tight rein of all that – until he came in one morning with a gash over one eye. I asked him what had happened. He told me Brenda had been drunk and got into a real bad fight with Ivy, roaring at the girl and slapping her across the face. When George tried to pull Ivy away Brenda grabbed an iron and caught him right above the eye. He had to drive himself to a local hospital, get five stitches and – this was a big mistake – cover for Brenda by telling the doctor on duty that he'd gotten the gash in a bar fight. That went on his medical records – and was used against him after Brenda's arrest, especially as there was another incident when she punched him in the nose and broke it. Again he told the doctors that it was a drunken brawl – and these two recorded "bar brawls" have ended up now as further evidence that he has a violent temper.'

'You say, "further evidence". Were there other violent incidents besides those two?'

It's a fact that he did punch her once in the stomach – but, according to George, that was only after she had pulled his hair and tried to throw a pot of boiling water on him, which he dodged just in time. Anyway, after throwing the punch, she doubled over and hit her head on a kitchen counter. Ivy came running into the room and saw her mother concussed, so she ran into her room, locked the door and dialed 911. The police came and arrested her dad.'

'But didn't he explain to them what had happened?'

'Brenda also had her side of the story – how he'd gotten furious with her for being such a bad housekeeper and slugged her.'

'Surely the cops also interviewed Ivy and she confirmed that her mother had attacked George in the past,' I said.

'Ivy was totally intimidated by her mother. She always threatened her with all sorts of bad stuff – like being sent away to an institution for disturbed children – if she ratted on her. Anyway, she already had a reputation as something of a wild child so it would have been her word against her mother's. And since George was already exposed as a liar because of what he told the doctor . . .'

He went quiet and stared down into his coffee.

'Word has it that he still hasn't confessed to Ivy's death,' he said, 'that he's holding on to his story.'

'Do you believe him?'

'Part of me does – because he so loved her. But they had their terrible moments together. Like I was his biggest supporter. But when he was boozing we were in Jekyll and Hyde territory. I had great hopes that we were going to be partners together. We had three big jobs lined up – but he either showed up for work so hungover that he couldn't function, or he'd not show up at all. Believe me, I pleaded with George to clean up his act – even told him to take two months off to get sober. George didn't want to know. Eventually, one morning he walked in here so loaded and crazy that he actually picked up a two-by-four and told me he was going to kill me.'

'What happened?'

'My wife came in while this stand-off was going on and had no choice but to call the police. I managed to make a dash out of the workshop. He started smashing up some cabinets we were working on. But here's the intriguing thing: he only smashed those that he himself had built. Then he collapsed in a heap on the floor and started crying. I mean, bawling like he was the saddest, loneliest man on earth . . . which, at that moment, maybe he was. The police showed up. I told them I didn't want to press charges, but they still took him off for "psychological evaluation" and that was another mark against him.

'He was released two days later and wrote me this long sad letter, telling me how he was going to sober up and how he hated himself for turning against me. I wrote back, saying that, of course, I accepted his apology and thought he was a brilliantly talented carpenter – but we could no longer work together. It was just out of the question. I never heard from him again. And then Ivy went missing . . .'

'How about the son, Michael?'

'I never liked him. Sullen, self-important kid – and like a lot of self-important people, not that bright. I know he tangled frequently with George and that George once knocked him down when Michael sassed him. Another black mark against George – though I gathered he only slugged Michael after the kid got caught dealing crystal meth. As you can gather it was one big happy family.'

'You still haven't said whether or not you think George did it.'

Another long stare into his coffee.

'Will I be quoted on this?'

'Not if you don't want to be.'

'I don't. Everything instinctually tells me he would never have hurt Ivy. But I know how he turned against me. And I also know that, once he had nine beers in him, he was capable of extreme craziness. Then there's the fact that he had that undergarment of hers in his workshop. So, anything is possible here. *Anything*. That's about as conclusive as I'm going to get.'

I asked him if there was anyone else I should speak to.

'I guess there's Larry Coursen – but I don't like holy rollers who are as smooth as a Vegas croupier, if you take my meaning.'

'Nice metaphor. Maybe I'll steal it.'

'Just as long as you don't say you got it from me.'

'Anyone else worth chatting with?' I asked.

He shook his head.

'You ask around town, everyone will tell you that George is guilty as hell . . . especially as the wife is now in good with God. But I have doubt. A lot of doubt.'

Before I left I thanked Dwane for his time and asked for directions to the MacIntyres' house.

'It's just two streets over from here,' he said. 'You'll see all the TV vans out front. I think the ghouls are waiting for the moment when Ivy's body is discovered so they can get Brenda's hysterical reaction.'

'When a mother loses a child . . .' I heard myself saying, then lowered my head.

'Tell me about it. Every day my boy is in Afghanistan, I think about that. About how . . . *if* . . . I'd cope.'

He stared back into his coffee.

'I think I've said a little too much.'

When I left Dwane I drove immediately over to the MacIntyre residence. As he said, it was easy to find. There were five large television vans parked outside – and assorted camera and sound men lounging around, smoking cigarettes, drinking coffee in paper cups, looking bored. Behind them was a run-down split-level house. It needed a new roof, new siding, new steps up to its front door. There was laundry hanging rigid with cold on a clothesline. It had the prerequisite rusted-out car perched on the front lawn. It reminded me of one of those houses you see in Appalachia or any rednecked corner of North America which immediately spoke of social deprivation and bad education and a no-hope view of life. Poor George MacIntyre didn't have a chance. Everything Dwane told me – like Missy Schulder before him – painted a picture of a man who was in a domestic hell without respite. I could only think about my own personal situation – with my parents, and then with Theo – where I too felt a certain helplessness; a sense that I was with people who just didn't play fair. George MacIntyre raged against others and drank. I raged against others and used the delusion of being in control of things as a way of denying my depression. George MacIntyre lost a child. I lost a child. Though the details of our stories were wildly different, we shared the same underlying fury at the inequity of others. And it killed the most important thing in both our lives.

I drove around Townsend for another half-hour. I passed by the school again. I noted that none of the houses were substantial or venerable, that this was a community with no visible signs of wealth. I stopped in the Mom and Pop restaurant for a cup of coffee. I sat at the lunch counter and tried to start a conversation with the hard-faced woman who was serving me.

'Sad about the MacIntyre girl, isn't it?' I said.

'Uh huh,' she replied, half-regarding me warily.

'Did you know her or the family?'

'Everybody knows the MacIntyres.'

'Were they good neighbors?'

'You're a reporter, right?'

'Maybe.'

'That's not a definitive answer.'

'Yes, I'm a reporter.'

'Well, now that I know that, I've got nothing more to say to you.'

'I'm just doing my job,' I said.

'And I'm doing mine – which is running my restaurant and not answering your questions. George MacIntyre's got enough problems on his hands right now . . .'

'That's sort of an answer, isn't it?'

'You trying to twist my words?'

'No – but I sense from what you just said that you aren't of the opinion that MacIntyre is evil incarnate.'

'I'm not carrying on this conversation.'

'Was he as bad as the papers made him out to be?'

'You tell me. You're on their side.'

'I'm on nobody's side.'

Behind us came a voice.

'Brenda MacIntyre is a saintly woman.'

The owner of this voice was a woman in her early forties – plump, dressed in the brown polyester uniform that workers at Safeway were forced to wear. When I caught sight of the uniform I immediately remembered that Brenda MacIntyre wore one of these as well.

'Are you a member of her church?' I asked.

'She's Assemblies, I'm Church of Christ. But we're both people who have been touched by the Lord. And I know that Brenda is really suffering right now – but she has her faith which is sustaining her.'

From behind the counter came the voice of the boss.

'I think you've said plenty, Louise. And I think we're going to ask this visitor to finish her coffee and leave us in peace.'

499

'I was just trying to help,' Louise said.

'You were very helpful,' I said.

'And you owe me one dollar twenty-five for the coffee,' the boss said.

As I left the restaurant my cellphone started to ring.

'Nancy Lloyd?' said a voice I was already familiar with courtesy of many television and radio interviews. 'It's Reverend Larry Coursen here. Might you be in Townsend now?'

How did he know that . . . or was he just surmising?

'Actually I am.'

'Well, it's a truly busy day – and not just because of poor dear Ivy MacIntyre. But I could spare you fifteen minutes if you came by the church right now.'

'I appreciate that,' I said, then quickly wrote down the directions he gave me.

I didn't need them – as the Assemblies of God church was located at the far end of the gasoline alley. It was modest-sized, built in an International House of Pancakes red-brick style. There was a large billboard-sized poster to the right of the main entrance, showing two very well-scrubbed, very white parents in their mid-thirties, their arms around two very well-scrubbed, very white children (a boy and a girl, naturally), both around nine or ten years old. I felt that same aching sadness that always hit me whenever I saw any tableau – either real or staged – of parents and children. This time, however, the sorrow was undercut by the 'Kodak moment' cuteness of the family and the mawkishness of the words blazoned above this picture: '*All Families Are Miraculously Healed at Townsend Assemblies of God!*'

You mean, the way the MacIntyre family was 'miraculously healed'?

I parked in the capacious car park – its ability to handle a large number of vehicles an indication of either Coursen's success as a pastor or a very false sense of optimism. There was a large new Land Rover Discovery parked to the side of the church. I sensed it must be Coursen's as he advertised it with a vanity license plate on which were embossed two words: '*Preacher Man*'. The front doors of the church were open. I wandered inside. The vestibule had more blown-up life-sized photographs of the sort of happy parishioners who looked like they also modeled part-time for the Land's End catalog. There were slogans on all of them: '*Divine Love Conquers All!*' . . . '*At Townsend Assemblies We Are All One!*' . . . and finally, just one word: '*Praise!*' There were also donation boxes, above which were further slogans: '*It Feels Great to Tithe!*' and '*He is Always There for You!*' I had never visited any Eastern European countries during the era of Communism – I was far too young – but I imagined this was a miniature version of the exhortations that were plastered in all public places, reminding the subservient citizenry that '*the Five Year Program is the Only Way Forward*'.

I doubted, however, if any Eastern European apparatchik dressed liked Larry Coursen. He must have heard me come in, as he emerged from the main body of the church into the vestibule. He was wearing a chocolate-brown cardigan, a purple shirt with a clerical collar, slightly flared blue jeans and (just to remind everyone we were in Alberta) highly polished black cowboy boots. He was in his early forties, with thick blond hair somewhat coiffed and – as I had noted on the television – very white teeth. His voice was sonorous, calming.

'Nancy, what a pleasure . . .' he said, extending his hand.

'I appreciate your time, Reverend.'

'*Larry*, please.'

'OK, Larry . . .'

'And you're with the *Vancouver Sun*?'

'That's right.'

'A fine newspaper. You from BC yourself?'

'No, back East.'

'Whereabouts?'

'Ontario.'

'Whereabouts?'

'Dundas,' I said, pulling a name out of a hat, as I had read a recent newspaper story about a well-known Canadian rock singer turned ace photographer who grew up in Dundas.

'Dundas! No kidding. I did some of my early pastoral work in Dundas!'

Oh, great . . .

'Do you know the Assemblies church on King and Sydenham Streets . . . ?' he continued.

'Of course I know it. Passed it many times.'

'Right near the local branch of the Bay.'

'That's it. It's a rather modern building . . .'

'All Assemblies churches are. We are a rather new faith in Canada. Come on in – I'll show you where we worship.'

As he held open the door into the church I felt a wave of fear. *How insane to choose a small town as your false place of residence. Why didn't you say Toronto or Montreal – a big city where anonymity rules?*

But, at least, he seemed to have bought it . . .

The main body of the church itself looked like it had been styled after a sports stadium, albeit on a smaller scale, with banked seating all padded in white Naugahyde and a pulpit on a thrust stage. It was surrounded by spotlights. There was a garish white organ with gold-painted pipes and a choir loft which appeared to have room for one hundred voices.

'It's very impressive,' I said. 'And it also looks like it's tailor made for televangelism.'

My tone was neutral, not sneering. But Coursen smiled tightly, trying to weigh what I meant by that.

'If you mean by "televangelism", spreading the Gospel through electronic means, then yes – it is something towards which we as a church are definitely aiming. Of course, we are a small town in Canada. But you know Oral Roberts began his ministry in a small church in Tulsa, Oklahoma – and look how his "vision" expanded into his own nationally broadcast program and his very own university. Now do understand: my ambitions are not *personal* ones. Rather they are *communal* – in that Townsend Assemblies of God is a very close community with great spiritual aspirations when it comes to spreading the Good News that is the Gospel of Jesus Christ.'

'How many do you have in your congregation?'

'Well over two hundred very dedicated souls – which may not seem like a grand figure, but is still, if I may say so, impressive for a town of five thousand. You show me another church in Townsend that has five percent of the population.'

He motioned for me to sit down on one of the Naugahyde benches. He positioned himself relatively close to me.

'Might I ask your faith affiliation?' he said.

'I don't have one.'

'I see. And why is that?'

'I'm not a believer, I suppose.'

He nodded and gave me the sort of smile that was somewhere between avuncular and sympathetic.

'For many people faith is the hardest thing in the world. "The Great Leap" and all that. But it is also the greatest gift you can receive. With it comes Life Ever After and a wonderful community of souls to support you while on Earth.'

I took out my pen and notepad.

'Is that a hint I should get off this subject?' he asked.

'I just don't want to take up too much of your time.'

'Very good response,' he said, 'even if it evades the subject. Were you raised in any faith, Nancy?'

'My dad was nothing, my mom a Unitarian – which, I suppose, from where you sit, is the equivalent of nothing.'

'Well, Unitarians don't really believe in Divine Revelation, or the Paradise to Come, or even the Prevalence of Miracles . . . so, quite honestly, it's hard to know what Unitarians get from their religion.'

'It's a faith not based on certainty, but on doubt.'

'Can faith and doubt be neighbors?'

'Aren't they *always* neighbors? You can't have faith without doubt.'

'Well, I would argue otherwise. Faith negates doubt. Faith provides you with the sustenance needed to face life's challenges. Faith provides definitive answers to the biggest questions facing us. And don't you think there is a huge amount of comfort to be gleaned from that?'

'If you need definitive answers, yes.'

'We all need definitive answers,' he said.

'That's your point of view, not mine.'

'So you can live with ongoing doubt, no matter how painful that doubt might prove to be?'

'Perhaps it would be more painful to profess faith when you have none.'

A small smile from Larry Coursen. He was enjoying this banter, especially as he could see it was making me uncomfortable.

'We all have faith, Nancy. And we all have the power within us to remake ourselves anew. It's simply a matter of giving yourself over to the Greatest Gift we can receive while we are alive.'

'Did Brenda MacIntyre remake herself anew?'

504

Another smile from the Reverend.

'Yes, Brenda herself had a magnificent transformation. When she first came to me she was a woman in crisis. Angry, hostile, alcohol-dependent, enraged at the world . . .'

'Violent?' I asked.

'I think she would be the first to admit she was raised in a violent family, that she married a violent man, and therefore was well acquainted with violent behavior.'

'But was she herself violent?'

'Describe what you mean by "violent".'

'Physically attacking her children . . .'

'I'm sure she smacked her children when they were naughty. But attacking George? I think you have it backwards. It was he who attacked her repeatedly.'

'Even though several people I interviewed informed me that George MacIntyre told them he'd been violently attacked by your parishioner?'

His lips tightened as I said the words 'your parishioner'. He didn't like that expression at all.

'And who might these people be?' he asked.

'I can't reveal sources.'

'Well, I can *definitively* reveal the fact that I know Brenda MacIntyre's soul – because, in the course of accepting Jesus as Her Lord and Savior, she revealed unto me all her sins . . . sins that have now been washed clean. And I can *definitively* state that she was never violent towards her violent and tragic husband.'

'Was Ivy MacIntyre also washed clean of her sins?' I asked.

'Ivy was in the process of accepting the gift of redemption when she disappeared.'

'By which you mean . . . ?'

'Brenda had brought her to church several times. She was beginning to make friends with parishioners of her own age.

505

She had seen me on several occasions, during which we had several long private talks.'

'And these talks concerned . . . ?'

'The trouble in her life. Her acceptance of sin as a way of living. Her weakness when it came to boys and drugs.'

'She'd already lost her virginity at thirteen?'

'I never said that.'

'Then what did you mean by "trouble with boys"?'

'Just that. She had trouble with boys.'

'And as regards drugs . . . ?'

'She admitted to me that she had smoked pot.'

'That's not wholly unusual for many thirteen-year-olds.'

'Are you saying you approve of the idea of teenagers smoking pot?'

'No, what I'm saying is: it's not a shocking revelation that a thirteen-year-old girl had tried it.'

'Did you try it when you were thirteen?'

'No – I was sixteen.'

'Did you like it enough to continue smoking it?'

'Actually, no.'

'Well, Ivy did like it . . .'

'Then I stand corrected.'

'I suppose you do,' he said.

'So Ivy had yet to be "saved"?'

'I am sure that, if she were to leave this life now, she would be with God in Heaven. Because right before she disappeared she did accept Jesus as Her Lord and Savior.'

'You didn't say that before.'

'You didn't ask me that before.'

'I'm asking it now.'

'Yes, in one of our last private talks, she finally did become born again.'

'Which means she's in paradise now.'

'She's not dead,' he said.

'How can you be so sure?'

'I can't be sure. I simply have *faith* that she is alive.'

'In most cases of disappearance, if the child isn't found within forty-eight hours, it's foul play . . . and the person who has abducted the child usually resorts to homicide.'

'There are two things different about this case. The first is that Ivy is not a child, she's an adolescent. And adolescents – if they disappear – often end up on the street somewhere . . .'

'Like Hildy Krebs and Mimi Pullinger?'

'Exactly.'

'You know they are on the street?'

'I have to surmise that they have drifted into a bad life.'

'But if Ivy had been saved before she disappeared, why then did she end up on the street?'

'If she *is*, in fact, on the street. People backslide, Nancy. They give in to their most base instincts and make mistakes.'

'Do you think George MacIntyre actually harmed his daughter?'

'The evidence points to his guilt. Just as there was a history of physical abuse by him in the MacIntyre household.'

'All perpetrated by George MacIntyre?'

'That's what I was led to believe.'

'But never by Brenda MacIntyre?'

'You evidently have your suspicions that Brenda was not telling the truth.'

'Yes – I do have my suspicions.'

'And why is that?'

'Because of things that people have told me.'

'Such as . . . ?'

'Such as the fact that she assaulted George on several occasions, that she was violent with Ivy, that—'

'All lies,' he said, his voice quiet but definitive.

'How do you know that?'

'Because I am very good at sniffing out lies . . . and liars.'

'Is your nose that infallible?'

'I am not the Pope,' he said. 'But I do understand the complexities of human nature. Just as I know when someone is not telling the truth . . . or is telling me they are something they are not.'

He looked at me directly as he said this – and that's when I realized he had me figured out.

'But getting back to George MacIntyre . . .' I said.

'No, let's get back to King and Sydenham Streets in Dundas,' he said. 'I mentioned that's where the Assemblies of God church was in Dundas. You said: "Of course I know it. Passed it many times." The fact is, the Assemblies of God church is not on King and Sydenham. Just as there is no branch of the Bay in the town.'

'I was just playing along,' I said, knowing that I sounded completely unconvincing.

'Just as you were "playing along" about being a reporter on the *Vancouver Sun*?'

He favored me with a big smile and continued talking.

'There is no Nancy Lloyd on the *Vancouver Sun*. I know this because when you called me I called the newspaper. Given the big media attention surrounding this case it's best to check out everyone's bona fides. Yours turned out to be false ones. Which, in turn, makes me wonder: Who you are and why are you so interested in this case?'

I stood up.

'I apologize for deceiving you.'

'You still haven't answered my questions.'

'Who I am doesn't matter.'

'Oh, but it does matter. Because it's clear to me that, though you might not be certifiably disturbed, you are nonetheless a woman in a very troubled place in her life. *Very troubled indeed* . . . to the point where I might even call you damaged. That's why I agreed to see you, even though I knew you were lying to me . . . because I wanted to see who exactly was this damaged person and why was she so *involved* in Ivy MacIntyre's disappearance?'

'I have my reasons,' I said, glancing at the nearest exit.

'I'm sure you do,' he said. 'Fear not, I am not going to stop you from leaving here. I am not angry at you. On the contrary I feel desperately sad for you. Sad because it's so evident that you are harboring an anger and a grief that has turned you against yourself and against the world. And sad because you are, I'm sure, alone and without love . . . and yet you reject He who loves you more than anyone else. And that is God. But to you, God doesn't exist. To you God is a fraud . . . even though it's you yourself who has committed the fraud here today.'

'Again I apologize. If you'll let me, I'll just go now and never bother you again.'

'But I'd rather you bother me. Just as I'd rather you admit to me that you are willing to open your heart to God's love and let Him heal your grief.'

'He won't do that,' I said.

'How can you be so sure?'

'I have my reasons.'

'You sound so definite.'

'I am.'

'Now I am certainly not a Catholic – but I did once learn in theology school about Pascal's Wager. You know about that?'

I shook my head.

'Pascal – a French theologian – stated that, even though we couldn't be certain about God's existence, weren't we better off accepting it? After all, Nancy – or whatever your name is –

if you were to get down on your knees right now next to me and let me bring you to Jesus, then the gift of Eternal Life would be yours. Think about that – Life Hereafter. Death Defeated. Not only that, but all your sins would be washed clean. Now give me one – *just one* – good reason why you shouldn't accept the Greatest Gift You Will Ever Receive.'

I finally met his gaze.

'Because it's all ridiculous,' I said.

And then I turned and fled.

Ten

IDIOT, IDIOT, IDIOT.

This was my line of thought all the way back to Calgary. How could I have been so stupid, so naive, to think that His Holiness wouldn't have checked up on me? The guy was a hyper-ambitious televangelist-in-waiting. As such, he was very protective of his image. So naturally he was going to make a phone call to verify that Nancy Lloyd was who she said she was.

What made this entire incident five times worse was the fact that Coursen was no slouch when it came to targeting other people's weaknesses. The bastard read me like an open goddamn book – and knew exactly what buttons to push to make me squirm.

'*On the contrary I feel desperately sad for you. Sad because it's so evident that you are harboring an anger and a grief that has turned you against yourself and against the world. And sad because you are, I'm sure, alone and without love . . . and yet you reject He who loves you more than anyone else.*'

If *He* loved me, none of this would have ever happened. But to say that would have been to engage in a dialog about Emily – and that would have been manna from heaven for an evangelist like Coursen. *The Bereaved Mother Searching for Healing*. As it turned out he still caught me out in a major lie and so brilliantly turned the tables on me that he left me feeling as if I was completely crazy . . . which perhaps was the case.

Idiot, idiot, idiot. Getting obsessed about the persecution of a sad loser who might have been framed, but who – given all the conflicting evidence surrounding the case – might also be very guilty.

And now I wondered if Coursen had managed to write down the license plate on my car and had contacted the cops who, in turn, had contacted Avis Rent-a-Car who, in turn, had informed them that the car had been rented to a certain Jane Howard of . . .

Idiot, idiot, idiot . . .

But maybe he'd do the Christian thing and let the whole matter drop. Maybe . . . just maybe . . . I'd get away with it.

That night, back home in my little apartment, I couldn't sleep. When I decided that the night was lost, I walked down 17th Avenue to an all-night internet café and Googled everything I could about the Rev. Larry Coursen. Most of the articles were connected with the Ivy MacIntyre case, but I did find the Townsend Assemblies of God official website, which had many glossy pictures of Coursen leading services, laying healing hands on wheelchair-bound parishioners and posing with his wife Bonnie – a very blonde, rather plump woman – and their two daughters, Heather and Katie. Under this photograph was the caption: '*Family Is All!*' There was also a biographical sketch of Coursen, talking about how he had been raised on the '*Plains of Saskatchewan*', attended the Liberty Bible College in Virginia, then returned home to Canada to '*begin his ministry*'. After brief stints at Assemblies of God churches in Dundas and Toronto, '*he was personally chosen to create a new ministry in Townsend, Alberta. Starting with only ten parishioners, the dynamic, inspirational leadership of Larry Coursen has resulted in a twenty-fold increase in membership and a Major Spiritual Impact in this corner of the Canadian West.*'

From Toronto to Townsend. The powers that be in the hierarchy of his church must have decided he needed to be sent out to pasture. Or maybe they considered him just a little too ambitious too young, and thought a nowhere parish would teach him some necessary humility.

I printed off all the articles on Coursen, then spent the next two hours continuing to Google everything else to do with the Ivy MacIntyre case – trying to fill any further gaps I had in my knowledge. All my pre-dawn research turned up little that was new, bar those details on Coursen and the discovery that the Regina woman who had accused George MacIntyre of sexual abuse also had a previous conviction for prostitution. Her name was Chrissy Ely – and, according to the *Regina Journal*, she later rescinded her accusation against him, saying it was all a misunderstanding. (Now why wasn't that more widely reported – and what made her have this volte-face?)

By the time I left the internet café it was nearly seven a.m. I gathered up all my printed papers. I zipped up my parka. I stepped out into the cold and, head down against the wind, pushed my way home, determined to finally get some sleep.

But as I approached the doorway of my apartment building I saw an unwelcome presence outside: a police car. Part of me wondered if I should execute a crisp about-face and get the hell out of there. Another part of me knew: *There's no escaping this.* There were two uniformed officers in the car. They both got out as I approached.

'Jane Howard?' the first one said to me.

I nodded, wondering how they knew it was me. I could see them sizing me up, gauging whether I was going to try and do a runner or struggle or . . .

'This is not an arrest, Ms Howard,' the second one said as they moved to either side of me, effectively hemming me in. 'However, you are wanted for questioning as regards an incident yesterday in Townsend. You can refuse to submit to questioning now, but that will entail one of us remaining with you at your apartment while we secure a court order to have you formally questioned by the RCMP. You can also request legal counsel be present during the questioning. That will also entail you being held by us until your counsel – or one appointed for you by the province – arrives. Or you can simply expedite matters by coming with us now.'

Did I really have much choice in the matter? I wanted it all behind me, so I told them: 'I'll come now.'

'That's the smart decision,' the first cop said, lightly taking my arm and escorting me to their waiting patrol car.

They drove me to an unmarked office block on the edge of the Central Business District. We plunged into an underground car park, pulling in near an elevator. The policemen hadn't spoken to me during the drive from my apartment. Once we came to a stop, the cop who wasn't driving got out and opened the door for me. We waited for the other cop to get out. He punched a code onto a keypad. A door clicked open. Lightly touching my arm, the other cop informed me I should move forward.

Up we rode four flights. When we reached this floor, I was directed to turn right, then left. We came to a set of steel doors. Another code was punched into a keypad. Another click. I was ushered inside a small room with a steel table and three chairs. There was a mirror on one wall. I'd seen enough cop shows on television to know this was one of those mirrors which allowed people on the other side to observe the proceedings.

'Have a seat,' the first cop said. 'Sergeant Clark will be in to see you in a moment.'

I sat down.

'Can I get you anything? Water? Coffee?'

'Black coffee with one sugar would be great,' I said, also thinking: *I can't imagine they always treat criminals this way.* Maybe they'd decided I wasn't a criminal, just a loon.

The door shut behind the cop. I took off my parka and attempted to slump into the steel-backed chair, the completely sleepless night suddenly hitting me. But these chairs were designed to keep their occupants rigid and upright. Even though I was profoundly tired, I did have to reflect on the fact that I had landed myself in a police station . . . an act of profound stupidity on my part.

The door opened again. A man in his early fifties came in. He was tall and had the build of an ageing football player. His suit was gray, his tie an indifferent collection of stripes. And he was holding a steaming plastic cup.

'Ms Howard? Sergeant William Clark of the RCMP. Here's your coffee.'

'Thank you,' I said, accepting it.

'I'm not planning to detain you here, as long as the matter at hand can be resolved quickly . . . which, in turn, will depend on the answers you give me.'

'I'll help you in any way I can, sir.'

He studied me as I said that, gauging my sincerity, then nodded his approval. During the drive over to what I now knew was a federal police building, I had made the decision to come clean with the cops. I would talk to them directly. I would not make excuses. I would tell them an approximation of the truth – because, after all, what is the actual truth in any situation like this? Sipping my weak black coffee – and ruminating again on the thought that a policeman actually offered it to me – I decided: *They've had a complaint from His Holiness and they've had to investigate it. If I tell them what they want to know – as the Sergeant informed me – they might just be done with me in an hour or two.*

He asked me to confirm my full name, my address, my date of birth, my place of birth . . .

'So you're American?' he asked. I explained the Canadian passport – and how long I had been resident in the country. I sensed he knew all this already, but wanted to see how I would respond to his questions.

'This is not a formal interview,' he said. 'You're not under arrest. But we need to know why you were impersonating a newspaper reporter to gain access to individuals associated with the Ivy MacIntyre case.'

'Because I became obsessed with it.'

'And why did you become so obsessed with it?'

'Because I lost my only child in January last year.'

I articulated that sentence flatly, without emotion. Sergeant Clark looked down into a folder open on the table. I glanced over and saw there were clippings about Emily's death on the top of the pile. He too had used Google to find out about me.

'In the wake of your daughter's death, did you suffer from any psychological breakdown?'

'I'm sure you have all that in the file,' I replied.

He said nothing, but again looked down at his papers. Had he run a check on me already and found out that my accident was on a national police database down South? No doubt about it. No doubt at all.

'Now, I am given to understand that you hold a doctorate from Harvard and a very responsible job at the Central Public Library here in Calgary. I only spoke a few minutes ago with your boss, Mrs Woods.'

'Did you tell her why I was being held by the police?'

'Yes, I did – even though, I need to reiterate, you are not being held by us.'

That's the end of my job then.

'I did explain to Mrs Woods that what you had done wasn't criminal, but could become so were you to repeat such behavior again.'

'I won't repeat it.'

'I'm glad to hear that. Speaking directly, the Public Prosecutor could – were we to approach him – make a case against you for impersonation, for perverting the course of

516

justice and for wasting police time. We've expended a good half-day on all this; time that could be better used trying to track down the individual or individuals responsible for Ivy MacIntyre's disappearance.'

I hung my head, feeling nothing but shame.

'Given that, I do recognize there are extenuating circumstances here. You should know that Mrs Woods robustly defended you – and said that, under the circumstances, you were coping well with the psychological damage that, I know, accompanies the loss of a child.

'That said, you did "interview" Rev. Coursen under false pretenses – and the *Vancouver Sun* is also most displeased with having been falsely represented by you. So I need to first ask you this, Ms Howard: What did you hope to get out of your "interviews" with Rev. Coursen and Dwane Poole and everyone else you spoke to in Townsend?'

'I don't know,' I said. 'Maybe I was thinking, if I could solve the case . . .'

'You'd somehow bring your daughter back to life?'

'I never thought that. I just became a little too focused on the details of Ivy's disappearance – and kept wondering if there might be another side to the story. It was, I see now, a displacement activity. So I want to apologize to you, Sergeant, for any time I've wasted. Just as I plan to write Rev. Coursen to say just how sorry I am.'

'Let me ask you this, Ms Howard – do you yourself have any thoughts about the case?'

Careful here. If you enthusiastically begin to talk about how he should really check out all the talk about Brenda's violent streak, he'll probably decide you're still very much obsessed with it all.

Then again, if you say nothing . . .

'One thing did stick with me. Dwane Poole stated that

George MacIntyre informed him that his injuries requiring hospital treatment didn't happen in a bar brawl, but were the direct cause of an attack by his wife, Brenda.'

'We got the same information from MacIntyre himself. And, of course, we investigated it. It's his word against hers – and the medical records at the hospital show that he reported his injuries as received in a bar fight.'

'Did he also talk about how Brenda was violent towards Ivy?'

'Again it's a "he said, she said" situation. Police work is never infallible, but we wouldn't have charged him with Ivy's disappearance unless we were certain we had a case against him . . . which we do. I mention all this because, I sense, that you still have your doubts about his guilt. Which, as a member of the public, you are entitled to have – as long as those doubts do not interfere with an ongoing investigation. Do you understand what I am saying here, Ms Howard?'

'You have my assurances I will stay out of all this in the future.'

'I accept those assurances. And given the circumstances of your case, I want to be humane about all this. But do understand: if you make further contact with any of the people associated with this case – or if, for that matter, you're seen snooping around Townsend again – you will be prosecuted. I hope it doesn't have to come to all that.'

I was allowed to leave half an hour later – a uniformed officer actually giving me a lift back to my apartment. When I returned there was a message on my cellphone from Geraldine Woods, asking me to phone her. I did as instructed. She was pleasant yet direct on the phone.

'Now whatever about the police phoning me up and reporting your interference into an ongoing criminal investigation, there is the fact that you lied to me about the reason for your absence from work this week. Would you like to explain this to me, please?'

I rolled out the same apologies I had given the Sergeant – and again pleaded emotional distress.

She heard me out and said: 'I'm willing to let this ride the one time – out of actual respect for you and the fact that you're doing such a brilliant job for us. So please don't make me fire you, Jane. And please report back to work on Monday without fail.'

After this conversation I did the one thing I could do under the circumstances: I crawled beneath the covers of my bed and passed out until around midnight. When I awoke I felt that momentary rejuvenation that comes with having slept for twelve hours without interruption, followed by the usual nightmarish déjà vu that I had now accepted as a facet of every morning. But as I showered and made coffee and listened to the all-night concert on CBC Radio 2, another thought came to me: *Say there was a similar instance of three girls disappearing from another small town in Canada?*

Before I knew it I was dressed and back at the all-night internet café. The guy behind the counter grumbled a 'Hello' as I came in – no doubt categorizing me as another of his weirdo night-time clients. I bought a bad instant coffee, slid in front of a monitor and went to work.

Eight hours later, I'd come up with very little. Kids went missing all the time in Canada. The web was full of page after page of desperate postings by parents with details about their vanished children. But most of these were runaways and, with a couple of gruesome exceptions, the adolescents were usually traced to down-at-heel squats in the grimmer corners of every major city in the country.

One item did interest me: the story of an eleven-year-old girl who went missing near Hamilton, Ontario and was then

519

found ten days later deposited on her parents' doorstep, babbling about having been abducted and sexually molested. The article from the *Hamilton Daily Record* spoke about '*police investigations*' into her disappearance and accusations, and then, in a later article, about how a '*trusted family counselor*' had been investigated by the local constabulary. No charges, however, were brought against him. The girl, meanwhile, had been admitted to a psychiatric facility, suffering from post-traumatic stress.

At least they got her back, I thought as I printed the article and added it to my burgeoning file of Ivy MacIntyre-related clippings.

As I was paying off the charges for eight hours of internet use – a bargain at twelve bucks – my cellphone rang. Much to my surprise I found myself talking to Vern. He sounded hesitant and tense.

'Thought I should check in, see how things were going,' he said.

'Did you hear what happened?'

'You mean, about the . . . uhm . . . police?'

'The RCMP, to be specific about it.'

'Yeah, I heard.'

'Marlene Tucker, no doubt, heard it from Geraldine Woods who passed it on to . . .'

A nervous cough from Vern.

'Well, you know how small things can get talked about around here,' he said. 'You got time for a cup of coffee this morning?'

'Something on your mind, Vern?'

'No . . . just . . . uhm . . . like to see you, if it's not too early or anything like that.

'I've been up for hours. You know Caffé Beano?'

We agreed to meet there in half an hour.

Though Calgary wasn't exactly New York when it came to style, Caffé Beano still had a clientele who dressed as if this was SoHo. So when Vern showed up – in his chocolate-brown anorak and his matching chocolate-brown flat corduroy cap and his gray polyester trousers – eyes did turn towards him, and I suddenly regretted arranging our rendezvous here, because I could also sense his unease at being so out of place amidst the black leather jackets and designer shades, and the fifteen varieties of java on sale.

He sat down nervously at my table.

'They serve just regular black coffee here?' he said.

'They sure do,' I said. After sorting him out with a mug I sat down opposite him.

'So . . .' I said.

'So . . .' he said.

'That was quite a drinking session last Sunday.'

'That's one of the reasons I'm here. I felt pretty damn awful about getting so smashed in front of you.'

'I wasn't exactly being abstemious either,' I said.

'I know, but . . . I hate when I do that.'

'Then don't do it.'

'I need to do it from time to time.'

'Then don't feel bad about it. I didn't.'

'You sure?'

'Absolutely.'

'This week, when I found out about your . . . uhm . . . problems with the . . . uhm . . . law, I couldn't help but think . . . uhm . . . maybe if I hadn't gotten you into that marathon drinking session . . .'

'You mean, because I saw George MacIntyre on the TV in the bar?'

'That's right.'

'You're blaming yourself for *that*?'

'Well . . .'

'Jesus . . . and I thought I was the Guilt Queen here.'

'Are you OK now?'

'I wasn't *not* OK before. I just got this thing into my head that the police were holding the wrong man.'

'Were they?'

'You want to know?'

'Of course.'

'Really?'

'I said that, yes.'

Before pausing for breath I started talking. I must have talked straight through without stopping for the next forty-five minutes. I couldn't shut myself up. As I worked my way through the entire Ivy MacIntyre case – raising the questions I had about who exactly was guilty here and whether there had been a terrible miscarriage of justice – I kept digging and digging into my file of papers on the case. It was only much later that day – when I recalled this monologue and my cross-examination-style presentation of the case for and against George MacIntyre – that I shuddered at the thought of how damn unhinged I sounded . . . and how Vern just sat there, looking a little stunned at my soliloquy, conscious of the stares I was receiving from other café patrons who were just a little appalled to hear this woman defend what the vast majority of the public considered the indefensible . . . but which, according to the rules of Canadian politeness, they weren't going to contradict out loud. (Tattooed bartenders operated according to a different set of rules than the latte drinkers at Caffé Beano.)

When I finally finished Vern just sat there, appearing simultaneously shell-shocked and too embarrassed to admit that he felt shell-shocked.

'Well, come on, Vern,' I said, still on a manic high from my

Perry Mason monologue. 'Tell me I'm full of shit, or talking out of my ass, or just . . .'

'Jane, *please*,' he hissed, quickly tapping my hand. 'There's no need to . . .'

'What?' I said, my voice still raised. 'Articulate the thing no one wants to admit? . . . That they've tried and convicted a man without fully weighing all the other evidence?'

Silence. Vern glanced around and could see all the eyes in the café on us.

'I've got to go,' he said. Then, thanking me for the coffee, he left.

But I followed him right out onto the street.

'Have I said the wrong thing?' I asked him as he was trying to get into his car. 'Did I embarrass you in there?'

He shut his car door and turned back towards me.

'I'm going to tell you what my AA sponsor told me when I was coming off a binge. You can continue to convince yourself this sort of behavior is normal and skid off the edge of the cliff. Or you can stop it and save yourself.'

It was the first time I ever heard Vern become stern with me – and it was clear that he was uncomfortable with such paternal directness. Especially as my reaction was shameful.

'The difference between us, Vern, is that I'm not a drunk.'

Having landed that one on him, I turned and went upstairs to my apartment and collapsed into my armchair and thought to myself: *You are a drunk. Only what's intoxicating you all the time isn't booze, but anger. The sort of anger brought about by grief. The sort of anger which refuses to resolve itself and finds displacement in . . .*

But this bout of self-recrimination was superseded by another thought: the newspapers! So I was back down at the magazine shop around the corner from Caffé Beano, buying the *Globe and Mail*, the *National Post*, the *Calgary Herald*, the *Edmonton Telegraph* . . . every Canadian paper they sold there, including the *Vancouver Sun*.

'You really want all of these?' the guy asked me as he rang them up.

'Any problem with that?' I asked.

'It's your money,' he said.

Back at the apartment, I tore through them all, hoping that somewhere I'd find an article raising a shadow of doubt on the guilt of George MacIntyre. But everyone was adhering to the law and just reporting the basic facts of the case. While flipping through the *Globe and Mail* I noticed a column – about an incest trial in Thunder Bay – by Charlotte Plainfield. She was a star journalist, well known in Canada as someone who frequently took up cases of child abuse and malfeasant criminal behavior. Without stopping to think I clipped out Plainfield's article, grabbed my MacIntyre case file and hot-tailed it back to the internet café.

'You again?' grunted the clerk before handing me a password to one of the terminals. There, over the next two hours, I composed a very lengthy letter to Plainfield in defense of George MacIntyre, citing the interviews and research I had done, together with the doubts raised by the conflicting testimony, urging her to find that prostitute in Regina who had retracted the charges against him, and to generally re-examine the case. Fortunately the *Globe and Mail* listed her email address at the bottom of her article, so I didn't have to search the net for it. And when I hit the print button to make a copy of my email for my files I saw that I had written over ten pages.

On Monday I returned to work. The first order of business was to pay a visit to Geraldine Woods and again apologize in person. But when I came into her office I could see that something was terribly wrong . . . or, more to the point, that I was in serious trouble.

'I'm glad you came to see me straight away, Jane,' she said, 'because I was planning to ask you to come by here as soon as you arrived.'

'What's happened?' I asked.

'You mean, you don't know what's happened? You're so out of touch with your actions that you didn't realize that by sending that very long and frankly unstable email to Charlotte Plainfield . . .'

Idiot, idiot, idiot.

'If I could try and explain . . .' I started to say.

She raised up her hand.

'That won't be necessary – as a decision has already been taken about this matter.'

'But surely before firing me, you can, at least, let me defend—'

'We're not firing you, Jane. We're putting you on Health Leave. Three months' fully paid Health Leave, to be exact . . . and if, during that time, you agree to see a state psychiatrist and agree to the course of treatment he or she recommends, you will be welcomed back here once you have been given the all-clear.'

'And if I don't agree?'

'Please don't go down that road, Jane. We do like you here. We all know what you have gone through, what you still have to deal with every day. There are people here who are actually pulling for you. I wish you'd see that.'

Then she picked up the phone on her desk.

'Now I have to do something official here – which is to call Sergeant Clark and tell him you're here. When Charlotte Plainfield contacted him about your email, it wasn't to register a complaint; rather, to raise some of the points you made. He then asked to see a copy of it – and that was that.'

'This isn't fair,' I said. 'I simply wrote a well-known journalist with my ideas about the case . . .'

'After impersonating a journalist and wasting police time. Come on, Jane. Sergeant Clark warned you to stay clear of all this. And I told you the same thing. Everybody's not just been fair; they've bent the rules to keep you out of trouble. You're not getting shown the door. And Sergeant Clark told me he isn't formally charging you with anything.'

'Then why does he need to see me?'

'He'll explain that.'

She dialed a number, then turned around and spoke quietly into the phone. After a minute or so she hung up.

'He said he could send someone around in a police car to collect you,' she told me, 'but as their headquarters are located just behind us he thought you might find it less embarrassing if you just walked over there.'

How Canadian.

'That's very trusting of him.'

'I don't think he considers you a security risk, Jane.'

Just a flake.

'He'll explain about the psychiatrist and the program they will want you to follow. Please listen to him and please do as he asks. Also, I hope you'll remember you can always call me if you want to talk anything over. And Ruth Fowler wanted you to know that she would very much like to see you when and if you are willing.'

'Tell her "thank you",' I said, my voice weak. I had suddenly been hit by a wave of tiredness and wondered if I could take any more of this excessive decency.

'Would you do one favor for me, please?' I said.

'Of course.'

'Would you tell Vern "sorry" for me. He'll understand.'

Geraldine Woods looked at me as if she was very intrigued, but also sensed it was best not to delve any further.

'Of course I'll do that,' she said.

At that precise moment the phone rang. Mrs Woods answered it.

'Geraldine Woods . . . Oh, hello, Sergeant . . . Yes, yes, of course I'll tell her . . . Is it something serious . . . ?'

Her face turned the color of chalk.

'Oh, God, that's dreadful . . . When did this happen? . . . I see . . . Absolutely, absolutely . . . Leave it with me . . . I'm so . . . Well, I actually don't know what to say, Sergeant.'

She put down the phone. She didn't turn towards me for a good minute, trying to take in what she had just been told. Finally she said: 'That was Sergeant Clark. He has to cancel his appointment with you. Something has happened.'

'Something bad?' I asked.

'Very bad. George MacIntyre hanged himself in his cell this morning.'

Eleven

BY THE END of the day the story was everywhere. It was the lead item on all the national news programs in Canada. It was the cover story on the afternoon edition of the local tabloid, the *Calgary Sun*: '*MacIntyre Hangs Himself*' was blazoned across the front page, followed by the sub-headline: '*Accused of His Daughter's Death He Leaves Note Saying He Can't Take It Anymore*'. All the afternoon radio programs also made it their big piece of breaking news. Every inch and minute of coverage concentrated on one salient notion: that MacIntyre hanged himself to escape justice.

One psychologist interviewed on CBC Radio talked about how a guilty individual can live for weeks, months, even years, denying the fact that he is culpable for the heinous crime he committed, and then the moment arises when they have to confront themselves face on. 'That's when the urge to take your own life – to essentially become your own judge and executioner – becomes immense. The dawn of reality for a sociopath is the dawn either of self-destruction or of some sort of redemption. Sadly, in the case of George MacIntyre his confrontation with the enormity of what he had done proved too much to bear.'

A senior RCMP inspector held a news conference, in which the facts of MacIntyre's suicide were officially recounted. He'd not been on twenty-four-hour suicide watch because, upon his arrest, he had none of the telltale signs of someone on the verge of killing himself. On the contrary, he'd been so adamant about his own innocence. 'Having said that, we did follow all procedures and protocols when it came to ensuring his safety. Sadly these failed him – and I take full responsibility for that.'

Rare as it was to see someone in authority actually take responsibility for a catastrophe (and yes, George MacIntyre's suicide was just that), I still couldn't fathom how they could have missed what I saw so clearly in his eyes the first time I caught a glimpse of him on the television: the haunted features of a man who was in the throes of a downward spiral. *He'd been accused of killing his child, for Christ's sake . . .* Did they really expect him to take all that on the chin? Who could withstand such torment? And why the hell didn't they protect him against himself? (Because, no doubt, part of them believed he deserved the self-inflicted fate.)

I myself was in deep shock about all this. George MacIntyre had been my cause, a certain *raison d'être*. But without him to fight for . . .

Oh, will you listen to yourself, sounding like the truly disturbed and pathetic sad case that you are. You and your wacko theories. The evidence – though not watertight – still pointed to his supreme guilt. Accept it – and now get it behind you.

This line of argument was also put forward by Officer Sheila Rivers, a direct, hard-edged member of the RCMP who stepped in for Sergeant Clark when it came to formally cautioning me.

After Geraldine Woods had received the call from Clark, telling him about MacIntyre's suicide, he also informed her that I still had to report to the RCMP's offices – and they would be expecting me in a half-hour or 'a warrant will be put out for her arrest'.

I was at their headquarters ten minutes later. The uniformed receptionist seemed to be expecting me. She hit a button and spoke into a phone, then told me: 'Officer Rivers will be with you in a moment.'

Officer Sheila Rivers was in her late thirties: tall, angular, with short black hair and a rapid-fire way of speaking. She was dressed in a simple black pants suit and a white shirt. She could have passed for a businesswoman, had it not been for the holster and gun clearly visible beneath her suit coat.

'Jane Howard?'

I nodded and accepted her extended hand.

'We'll do this downstairs,' she said, pointing towards a door across the lobby from the reception area. She punched in a code on the external keypad. We were in an identikit version of the same room in which Sergeant Clark had interviewed me.

'This shouldn't take too long,' she said. 'As you have probably heard, it's a crazy day around here.'

She opened my file – and explained that I could have legal counsel present for this 'process'. I told her that wasn't needed – and she gave me a document in which I waived my right to have such counsel present. I signed it. Then she formally said that it had been decided to place me under something called 'Alternative Measures'. She explained that, under both provincial and federal law, these 'measures' were not looked upon as a criminal charge; that, though it would remain on 'the system', it could 'not be construed as a misdemeanor or felony – which means that if you travel outside of the country and are asked a question on a visa application about whether or not you have a criminal record the answer can be a definitive "No".'

She then read through the 'Alternative Measures' – in which it was explained that, having been 'involved in activities that wasted police time and also hindered an ongoing criminal investigation', I hereby was being cautioned that any further such actions on my behalf which were perceived to 'involve police action' would result in charges being preferred against me. I also agreed to voluntarily enter a program of psychological counseling, to be administered by the Health Board of

Alberta – to submit myself to all medical and psychological examinations demanded of me by the board, and to agree to whatever program of therapy they deemed appropriate for me.

I had a few objections about this clause.

'Say they decide I need electro-shock therapy?' I asked.

'There is a small-print clause here saying you can refuse to accept said therapies if you consider them detrimental to you.'

'And I bet there's also a small-print clause allowing them to override my objections.'

'In my experience, the province isn't in the habit of letting people they classify as unstable roam the streets. They consider you nothing more than a nuisance – and one who can be helped through more conventional means. My advice to you, Ms Howard, is to accept the terms of the Alternative Measures, see the psychiatrist for however long it is mandated, take the pills they give you and get this behind you. I've read your file. You're not a misfit and you are certainly no dummy. So cut yourself a break – and play by the rules of the Alternative Measures. MacIntyre is dead. The case is closed now. Move on from it.'

But that afternoon I was back at the internet café, watching all those newscasts online, reading every damn column inch that had been written on MacIntyre's suicide. Halfway through this media binge, my cellphone rang. A woman introduced herself as Dr Maeve Collins and said that she was the psychiatrist assigned to my case. She was wondering if I might be able to come in and see her tomorrow at three p.m.

'No problem,' I told her, and took down the address of her office in Kensington.

As soon as I hung up I returned to the CBC website and resumed watching their rolling twenty-four-hour news service. On screen the Rev. Larry Coursen was being interviewed. He was wearing an expression that could best be described as

Piously Pained. He was pictured in front of his church, talking to a phalanx of reporters.

'This is a terrible time for Brenda and her dear son, Michael. First the loss of Ivy, now George. I can only hope that George is in a better place today and that the pain and anguish of his life have been replaced by Eternal Peace. I've been asked to speak for the family – and to ask that you respect their privacy at this moment of intense loss for them. Brenda will make a formal statement to the press in the coming days, but for the moment she just wanted me to express to you her infinite sorrow and her belief that George is with Jesus.'

One of the reporters asked: 'Any thoughts, Reverend, on whether Ivy MacIntyre will now be found alive?'

'Tragically one must assume that she is dead. Why else would George MacIntyre take his life if she was, verily, alive?'

Hang on, you told me . . .

And I started racing through the files I always carted with me, the files with everything on the case, until I found my notes of my 'interview' with him.

'*She's not dead,*' he told me.

And I replied: '*How can you be so sure?*'

And he said: '*I just am.*'

Why were you so certain of that?

And now . . . was it only because MacIntyre killed himself that you changed your mind?

Another reporter tossed out a new question.

'The police have been very close-lipped on all this, but – presuming, as you said, that Ivy must now be considered dead – do you think MacIntyre left any clue as to where her body might be found?'

There was an involuntary moment when Coursen's lips almost worked their way into a smile. He caught it before it was noticeable. But *I* noticed it – perhaps because I had the facility, courtesy of the internet and the stop/start feature attached to this broadcast, to replay the moment over and over again. The sides of his mouth began to curve outwards – the hint of an inward grin wiped off his face before it could become discernible to anyone. Anyone, that is, but me. Then again, I was playing it back non-stop. Was the bastard laughing at us? Laughing because he knew . . . ?

I replayed that moment four times over.

'. . . do you think MacIntyre left any clue as to where her body might be found?' the journalist asked Coursen.

And then there was, unmistakably, that involuntary, one-eighth-of-a-second smile which crossed Coursen's face . . . followed by his answer: 'I'm certain he didn't.'

How can you be so certain, mister? What gives you the right to make an incontestable statement like that? Why are you telling us it's a foregone conclusion *that he didn't leave a hint where the body could be found? Because MacIntyre didn't do it? And because you know who did do it?*

The interview ended. The news broadcast rolled on. We were back in the CBC News Studio. The talking head looked at the camera and said: 'In other news, a terrible crash east of Dundas near Hamilton claimed the life of a family of six today . . .'

East of Dundas near Hamilton . . .

Why did the mention of those two placenames suddenly trigger a déjà-vu moment in my brain?

Dundas . . . Hamilton . . . Dundas . . . Hamilton. . . .

Got it.

I reopened the file and scanned again the notes of my interview with Coursen. When he'd asked me where I'd grown up, I'd said: 'Dundas,' pulling the name out of nowhere. And his reply?

'*Dundas! No kidding. I did some of my early pastoral work in*

Dundas! Do you know the Assemblies church on King and Sydenham . . . ?'

Of course he caught me out on that. But . . .

The Assemblies church in Dundas . . .

And Dundas is near Hamilton. And in my burgeoning file, there is . . .

A clipping from the *Hamilton Daily Record* about the disappearance four years ago of an eleven-year-old girl. Her name – I hadn't noticed it before – was Kelly Franklin. And the *Hamilton Daily Record* article spoke about '*police investigations*' into her disappearance, and then, in a later article, about how a '*trusted family counselor*' had been investigated by the local constabulary. No charges, however, were brought against him. The girl, meanwhile, had been admitted to a psychiatric facility, suffering from post-traumatic stress.

Kelly Franklin, Kelly Franklin. I Googled her name. Around two dozen stories surrounding her disappearance and mysterious return. Many police investigations. Suspicions about someone known to the family. And then this, in a later *Toronto Star* article, which I hadn't bothered to open the first time around:

'Kelly's parents, Michelle and Morgan Franklin, are devout Christians and say that their religious faith sustained them through the ten days when Kelly went missing. Once-time members of the Assemblies of God church in Dundas, they are now stalwarts of the Life Tabernacle in Hamilton.'

The Assemblies of God church in Dundas. How's that for happenstance. And why did they leave the church?

The article continued:

'In the wake of Kelly's return, the Franklins and the police have remained very tight-lipped about what they know about her alleged abductor. Though rumors have been rife in both Dundas

and Hamilton as to the name of this individual, there is another school of local thought that Kelly was so traumatized by what happened that she couldn't identify her abductor, and/or that the Franklins have been paid a substantial sum for their silence.'

But who would pay them such a large sum? What organization would be willing to hand over a big settlement in order to keep their name out of the press – especially as their name would be linked to a child's disappearance?

I Googled Dundas Assemblies of God church. Up popped their website – all smiling faces and words of praise. I found the link for '*Dundas Assemblies History*' – and there, in their list of former pastors, was the Rev. Larry Coursen, with his dates of service: December 2002–May 2004. A short tenure. And when did Kelly Franklin go missing? April 2nd 2004. And when did Larry Coursen get dispatched to Townsend? I dug back into my file and found this detail listed on a printout from the Townsend Assemblies website: June 2004.

So Coursen parted company with the Dundas Assemblies not long after Kelly Franklin went missing . . . or perhaps right after she showed up alive again. But then this wall of silence enveloped the case, during which time, Coursen was conveniently dispatched to a nowhere town in the Alberta badlands.

I typed in '*Telephone Directory Information*' for a Franklin, M. in Hamilton, Ontario. There were three. I scribbled down their numbers, then dug out my cellphone and started calling.

'Is this Kelly's mom?' I asked on the first try.

'Wrong number,' the voice on the other end said – and hung up.

But the second number hit the jackpot.

'Is this Kelly's mom?' I asked.

'Who's this?'

The voice was loud, raspy.

'My name's Nancy Lloyd. I'm a journalist with the *Vancouver Sun*.'

'I ain't talking to no reporters. All that was years ago.'

'I'm aware of that – and I genuinely apologize for bothering you at home. It's just . . . I'm certain you've read all about Ivy MacIntyre's disappearance . . .'

'I've got nothing to say about all that either.'

'I understand. However, I do note that you and your family were once members of the Dundas Assemblies of God church. Did you know that Ivy MacIntyre's family were members of an Assemblies of God church in Alberta, and that your former pastor – Larry Coursen – is now their pastor out here?'

'I'm not talking about him,' she said, sounding angry.

'Why not?'

'Because that was the deal.'

'What deal?'

'Now you've made me shoot my mouth off.'

'Did someone – some *organization* – do a deal with you to say nothing about Larry Coursen?'

'I ain't answering no more of your questions.'

'How much did they pay for your silence?'

'That's my business,' she said. The line went dead.

I sat there, my head reeling. Coursen had abducted Kelly Franklin. Then he either let her go or . . . might she have escaped his clutches? Then what? She's so traumatized by whatever he did to her during those ten days that she can't identify him? Or she identifies him and he has a solid alibi? Or she returns home and retreats into herself, to the point where she has to be institutionalized and can't identify her captor? No, scratch that last idea. She must have been able to point the finger at Coursen. Perhaps when she told her parents, their first reaction was to phone the Assemblies of God big boys – who moved in quickly to dampen down the scandal and ensure that their pastor didn't get his face on every front page in North America.

And was Kelly Franklin still institutionalized all these years later?

Another quick Google and I came up with the following *Hamilton Daily Record* item: '*Abducted Girl Falls Foul of the Law Again*'.

It was dated September 23rd, 2007 and stated that Kelly Franklin, '*the girl who was mysteriously abducted three years ago*', had been arrested at a local Woolworths for sniffing glue and becoming sick thereafter. The story recounted how Franklin, aged fourteen, already had a rap sheet for shoplifting, aggravated assault of a woman police officer and vagrancy. When she walked into the Woolworths in Hamilton she found the aisle which sold epoxy glue, opened four tubes into a plastic bag, then proceeded to place the bag over her mouth and inhale deeply. She was at this for several minutes before staff found her, delirious and incoherent. The police were called, but she became violently ill and started to choke on her own vomit. Fortunately the assistant manager at Woolworths knew CPR and managed to clear her esophagus and avoid asphyxiation. She was rushed to a local hospital where she was reported to be in a stable condition.

A subsequent article – dated six weeks after this one – noted a court hearing where Kelly Franklin was sentenced to be detained in an institution for young offenders '*until it was determined that she was no longer a danger to the community or herself*'.

There was nothing further on her after this, leading me to surmise that she was still incarcerated.

You son of a bitch, Coursen. You destroy that girl's life and get your church to pay her family hush money. Then you get transferred out west and two girls go missing in the very town in which you operate and your church does nothing. Maybe because – as I quickly discovered through further use of a search engine – their families weren't affiliated with Townsend Assemblies. Then, when Ivy MacIntyre goes missing, you frame her poor fool of a father, a man who couldn't control his temper or his boozing, and therefore was an easy target. The perfect fall guy.

I gripped the sides of the computer table, trying to keep my rage and distress in check. I wanted to call Sergeant Clark and reveal everything I had just discovered. To do so, however, would be to risk getting picked up for breach of my Alternative Measures. Best to say nothing right now. Best to . . .

I checked my watch. It was just four p.m. I called the local car-rental place and asked them if they had any vehicles ready to be borrowed. They told me they could fix me up with a Corolla in fifteen minutes. I paid for the many hours I had spent online. I said goodbye to the slacker dude who was still absorbed in some goth website. As I headed towards the door his response to me was: 'Happy trails.'

I doubted this trail would lead to anything happy.

Half an hour later I was edging my way through the usual rush-hour automotive crawl. The days were getting longer now so I had light with me during the hour it took to edge my way out of all those endless sub-developments and hit open country. I played the drive-time program on CBC Radio 2 – and clicked the radio off when the hourly news rolled around at five and six p.m. I wanted to hear no more about the case. I just wanted to get to Townsend and then . . .

Well, I really didn't have a clue what I was going to do next. Drive up to Coursen's house, knock on the door and confront him with the fact that I knew about his antics with Kelly Franklin back East and was going to expose him to the world? He'd be on to Sergeant Clark in an instant. Then the Franklins, bound by the hush money they'd been paid by the church, wouldn't be able to finger Coursen. And I'd end up with a criminal record for, yet again, wasting police time.

No – confronting Coursen was definitely out. But tailing him and seeing what he did with his time outside of church . . . well, that might yield something.

The problem was, how to follow him and not be seen? In a small town someone from outside the community, driving around in a car which (damn it) had a big Avis sticker across its trunk would be immediately spotted. Given that I already had a bit of notoriety in the local restaurant and with Coursen himself . . .

So I had no plan, no idea what I was even looking for. All I knew was that I had to find a way of getting to tag along on any 'errand' Coursen might be making in the vicinity.

Why was I so certain that he would be making such errands? Just instinct, along with the growing notion that if he kept Kelly Franklin alive after abducting her . . .

Yes, but she was released – or, more likely, got away – after ten days. Why would Coursen keep Ivy alive for three weeks?

Then again, what did he say to you last week during your interview?

'She's not dead.'

Unless he had taken care of that bit of business in the wake of George's suicide. After all, what was his comment on the afternoon news?

'Tragically one must assume that she is dead.'

Because you've rendered her so?

I reached Townsend by seven and drove straight over to Coursen's church. A stroke of luck. The parking lot was full and the church lights were on. From the shouting and roaring coming from within they were probably handling snakes and talking in tongues. A sign near the church entrance advertised this: *'Monday Miracles Tonight at 7 p.m.!'*

539

There was certainly another 'miracle' awaiting me. Larry Coursen's Land Rover – immediately identifiable thanks to its *Preacher Man* vanity plate – was parked in its usual place. No one was in the lot so I was able to drive over to it and peer inside. Nothing unusual about it, except that the passenger seat in the front was filled with old newspapers and empty paper cups from McDonald's and Burger King. The back seat had DVD boxes scattered everywhere. I could make out the cover that adorned all the DVD cases: a big smiling Larry Coursen, his hands raised heavenwards, above which was the title: *'Everyday Miracles With Larry Coursen!'* I tested the door and discovered it was unlocked. This was Small-Town Canada – and in Small-Town Canada everyone left their doors open. Immediately I went around to the hatchback trunk and pressed the handle. It too opened and I saw that there were two dirty blankets. I also noted that this vehicle didn't have an enclosed trunk; rather, a canvas awning was pulled across the roof of the cargo area. Suddenly an insane idea clouded my head. Were you to stow away inside, you wouldn't be locked in. You could simply detach the awning and escape. Without further thinking, I decided to pursue this.

I closed the trunk door and returned to my rented vehicle. I was about to leave it in a corner of the lot but then realized that this was not a very bright idea. Once the parking lot emptied after the Monday Miracles show, my rental would be left behind. Coursen or one of his staff might wonder why this one car remained. And upon seeing the Avis rental sticker on its trunk . . .

Well, the rental car could be easily traced, resulting in me being picked up by the local sheriff.

So I drove out of the parking lot and down onto Main Street. There was a medium-sized supermarket at the far end of the street. It was open until ten p.m. I gambled on the fact that the local law wouldn't snoop around this parking lot after hours and left it in a corner far away from the street. I checked my watch. It was 7:45 p.m. The Monday Miracles had to continue for another hour at least – and I would need a good fifteen minutes to walk back to the church. It was cold tonight – minus twelve according to the dashboard digital readout. I pulled on a wool-knit hat and kept my head bowed low as I hiked back up to Townsend Assemblies of God. But the streets were empty. I passed no one. I checked my watch again as I reached the church. 8:04 p.m. From inside the church came the electrified voice of Larry Coursen: 'We know you're there, Jesus! We know you're right inside this church, filling us with love!'

This last word was pronounced with an extended wail. It was followed by shrieks and howls from the congregation. I glanced around the parking lot. Not another person was in sight. Under cover of all that high volume of religiosity I walked quickly to Coursen's vehicle. I pressed the handle. I grabbed the blankets that had been stuffed into the back of the trunk space. They smelled old, musty – and were cold to the touch. I slid into the trunk, then had to work at lying flat while reaching out with my left hand and attempting to slam the trunk door behind me. It took three tries – but, after watching it nearly catch twice, I yanked extra hard and the trunk slammed closed. I was in. As the awning was covering me, I was also in darkness. I had to shift around a great deal to find a fetal position that was even moderately comfortable. When this was achieved I reached into my jacket pocket and turned off my cellphone. Then I checked the time again. 8:12 p.m. It wasn't just dark in the car, it was also cold. I pulled on my gloves. I zipped my jacket right up to my neck. I covered myself with the thin, putrid blankets. I waited.

An hour went by, during which time I found myself frequently thinking: *What possessed you to pull such a deranged stunt?* At least twice in that first hour, I was on the verge of disengaging the awning, climbing over the back seat, out a side door and vanishing into the night. But just when the cold and the dark and the fear were about to defeat me I heard voices outside and cars starting up. *Too late, too late. You're stuck now.*

I checked my watch again. 9:14 p.m. But no sign of the Preacher Man. Cars continued to leave the lot. Then at 9:43 p.m., there were footsteps outside, followed by voices.

'The thing is, Carl,' Larry Coursen said, 'if Brenda keeps phoning me day and night, someone's gonna put two and two together. I mean, every time I walk into the door of my house Bonnie is ripping me a new asshole, telling me she's gonna expose me blah, blah, blah. The denial thing – the line that Brenda is so suffering she keeps having to call me – will only go so far. So you've got to go talk to Brenda again and make it clear that silence is golden here, that she doesn't want trouble from me. Tell her, once things calm down, I'll be around again. You cool with that?'

'I'm cool, brother,' the other voice said.

'And next month, once all this has blown over, we can look into getting the parish to buy you that GMC Acadia you've been after – for pastoral purposes, naturally.'

'Yeah, naturally.'

And they both laughed.

Jesus Christ, Coursen had been screwing Brenda. This subplot didn't exactly astonish me – I'd wondered to myself on several occasions whether there was a romantic link between them. But to hear Coursen speak about it in such a blatantly cynical way to one of his henchmen . . . well, it seriously unsettled me, perhaps because I was stuffed in a corner of the trunk of his car, shivering with the cold. *'Make*

542

it clear that silence is golden here, that she doesn't want trouble from me.' If he found me stowed away in his vehicle, how would he ensure my silence?

The front car door opened. I held my breath, hoping my teeth – slightly chattering with the cold – wouldn't be discernible. I heard Coursen slide into the driver's seat and fumble for his keys. Then there was the sound of an engine turning over and the whoosh of air as the heater was turned on full blast. From the speakers situated around the car came this voice – a super-smooth baritone speaking in a deeply motivational way about Optimizing the Whole You.

'Now today we're going to look at "Saying No to the Negative". Wherever you are right now – right this very instant – I want you to say, out loud, right now: "I AM SAYING NO TO THE NEGATIVE!"'

And Larry Coursen did just that. Saying no to the negative he put the car into gear and drove off.

We didn't travel far – maybe four, five minutes maximum. En route the motivational CD continued to play, exhorting its listener to: 'Treat the negative like a cancer – and one which you can stop from metastasizing.'

'I want you to say that now out loud: "The Negative is a Cancer – and I won't let that cancer eat me up."'

Yet again Larry Coursen did as demanded. Having asserted that the Negative is, verily, a Cancer, he braked to a halt. The engine cut out. The heat – which had hardly kicked in as yet – died. A car door slammed. And then he did the unthinkable: with a telltale *beep-beep* he locked the car and also primed the inside burglar alarm.

I knew that *beep-beep* sound because my old VW had the same kind of alarm system. Once primed, any upward movement inside the car itself would trigger it. I was certain that we had pulled up in front of Coursen's house, given how short a distance we had traveled from the church. The fact that he had electronically set the car alarm could only mean one thing: He was going in for the night, leaving me to freeze while crammed like a balled-up fetus in his trunk.

Idiot, idiot, idiot.

I started to cry – for the stupidity of my actions, for the way I had again shot myself in the foot with a machine-gun, for the fact that my mental state was still calamitous, for the realization that my grief for Emily hadn't dissipated one bit in the fifteen months since the accident.

I must have cried for a good ten minutes. When this wave of anguish finally burnt off, I decided that I would simply jump up and release the awning, then clamber over the back seat, open a door and hightail it down the street. It would take Coursen a good minute to react to the alarm – and I would be far away at this point.

And then what? Back to my sad little life. Back to the days doing work that I found only marginally interesting. Back to the small apartment – and the empty evenings. Back to everything I did in order to distract myself from the deep-rooted sadness that I simply couldn't shake. Back to the realization: *You are simply marking time.*

So why abandon ship now? Why run off when you might just find out . . .

You know what you're going to find out? That Coursen drives his car between his home and his church . . . and that you are going to be stuck here until some point tomorrow when he leaves the car unlocked and you can hopefully hightail it out of here and not get apprehended by the law or by Coursen and his henchman . . .

This internal debate was overshadowed by a far larger concern: I urgently needed to pee. For around an hour I had tried to ignore the pain in my bladder and the sense that I was about to burst. Now I knew I was courting renal failure if I didn't do something about it instantly. So I pulled one of the blankets off me, folded it several times over, somehow managed to pull down my jeans and underwear, then shoved the blanket behind me and let go.

It was all ferociously grubby and depressing but the relief was enormous. When I was finished I folded the now-sodden blanket one more time and carefully shoved it to a far corner of the trunk. Then I pulled up my jeans, rezipped my parka and wondered if I would be able to make it through the night without succumbing to frostbite.

A small blessing arrived: sleep. I nodded off for what seemed like minutes. But when I awoke and checked my watch it was 2:43 a.m. We were on the move again. That's what had jolted me awake: the *beep-beep* sound of the car alarm being disengaged, the driver's door opening and closing, the engine turning over, the heat coming on full blast and the God-awful motivational CD blaring as Coursen drove us off.

We were on the road for over an hour and a half, a long drive during which Coursen repeated platitudinous catch-phrases about 'The Need to Assert Me', 'The Way Forward Without Fear' and 'I Can Master Anything and Any Situation'. The motivational speaker unnerved me as he tried to convince his audience that 'Everything Can be Overcome if you Want to Overcome It'. His smoothie-smoothie voice was cloying and infuriating. I switched him off. I listened to the road.

For around forty minutes, the road seemed well-paved, with few bumps or changes of gradient. From what I could also discern we were the only car out here tonight, one or two roaring trucks (or, at least, I presumed they were trucks) breaking the aural loneliness.

But then we took a sharp right turn and the road changed. Suddenly we were driving along something half-paved and jolting. Every forward movement of the car seemed to throw me up against the back wall of the trunk – and I could only hope that Coursen didn't wonder what load was in the back causing all this commotion. But the CD was still blaring its motivational bromides and the heat was on full blast and the grind of the tires on the rocky road so constant that it must have blotted out the shake, rattle and roll of my body in the trunk.

On and on we drove. I glanced repeatedly at my watch as ten minutes went by, then fifteen, then . . .

We slowed down and came to a complete halt. The engine died. The door opened, but there was a pause as Coursen seemed to be getting something out of the glove compartment of the car. Then the door slammed shut and I could hear his footsteps walking away from the vehicle. This time he did not, thankfully, trigger the car alarm.

Once the sound of the footsteps had died away I waited a good five minutes before daring to reach up and hit the system that spun away the canvas roof of the trunk. Getting up took some work. I had been cramped in this space for over eight hours and every joint in my body felt as if it had been glued tight. But the relief of actually being able to move again was counterbalanced by sheer unadulterated fear. Fear of where we were. Fear of what I might find. Fear of what Coursen might do to me if he found me . . .

I inched my way up from the trunk and looked out through the car windows. A landscape pitch black, bar one low light in the immediate distance. I pulled myself head first over the back seat – there was no other way to negotiate it – breaking my fall with my hands. Then I straightened myself up and – as slowly and quietly as possible – I opened one of the back passenger doors. I got out, but didn't close it behind me. A boreal wind immediately hit me. Movement was difficult – my body felt rigid – and the darkness was all enveloping. But I forced myself to walk slowly towards the light in the distance. I couldn't see the ground beneath my feet. I had no idea what I was heading for; if I was traversing the edge of a cliff, a body of water, a path that would suddenly give way, sending me into free fall.

All there was up ahead was the light. Step by step, I inched my way towards it.

As I drew nearer, I could vaguely discern the outline of a structure. With every footstep the structure came into sharper silhouette. It was a shack. The light was inside the shack. And from within the shack was the sound of a male voice – Coursen's voice – panting and heaving and simultaneously shouting stuff.

I was now maybe ten yards from the shack. There was a door directly in front of me and a small window to the left of it. I crouched down and headed for the window. Reaching it I sat below it, listening now to Coursen's rhythmic breathing and the moans of a female voice.

I dared to raise my head and glance through the window. What I saw was . . . unspeakable. A girl – maybe twelve, thirteen years old – was positioned on a filthy mattress, naked from the waist down. A shackle, attached to a chain, was around her left ankle. Coursen, his trousers pulled down, was on top of her, thrusting in and out of her while berating her at the top of his voice. I sat down again, not knowing what to do next. That's when I put my hand out and discovered a shovel that had been left against this side of the house. My hands were drenched with sweat as I touched it, my heart going insane in my chest. I felt for the handle of the shovel. It was long, substantial. I carefully got myself into a crouching position. I grabbed the shovel with two hands. From inside the shack Coursen's rant was getting louder, the girl's cries even more frightened, extreme. Still hunched down I inched my way nearer to the door. It was closed, but looked flimsy. One, two, three, and . . .

I kicked the door in and came rushing towards Coursen, screaming. He jumped up, startled. That's when I caught him in the stomach with the shovel. He doubled over and I brought the shovel down on the top of his head. He reeled away from the blow, stumbled a few paces, then fell to his knees, not moving, blood cascading down his face.

On the mattress the girl was howling like a wounded animal. I dropped the shovel and went over to comfort her, but she shrieked when I tried to put my arms around her.

'It's OK, it's OK,' I said, even though I knew that all this was the antithesis of OK. The girl was filthy, the lower half of her body covered in bruises and cuts. There were open sores around her lips, embedded dirt in her fingernails. The shackle on her leg had cut deep into her skin and looked septic, as if gangrene had set in. To the left of the mattress was a bucket from which came a distinct fecal smell. Her hair was matted, her scalp scabby. But it was her eyes that really frightened me. They were hollow, sunken, devoid of any emotion except horror.

'Ivy MacIntyre?' I whispered.

She gave a tentative nod. I nodded back, then looked over at Coursen. He had slumped to the floor. I grabbed the shovel again. I approached him, raising it above me, ready to strike again if he dared move. But he was half-conscious – and judging from the bemused look on his face, seriously concussed. When I prodded him with the shovel there was only a groan as a response. His trousers were still down around his ankles. I reached into one pocket and found his car keys and a big chain with around ten keys attached to it. I pulled them both out, prodded him again with the shovel and saw that, stuck into the inside pocket of his leather jacket, was a gun. I reached for it, pulled it out, my hand shaking as I held its flat cold handle. I put it inside my own pocket, then returned to Ivy. She was curled up on the mattress, shaking. I went to work with the keys, trying each one in the lock attached to the shackle. The eighth one opened it. As I carefully lifted the shackle off her the extent of the damage done to her ankle became apparent. The iron mangle had eaten into her flesh. There was exposed bone beneath the septic wound.

Before turning my attention again to Ivy I moved towards Coursen, the shackle in my hand. En route, I pulled hard, testing the strength of the chain. It was attached by another shackle to an iron beam located across a corner of the barn. It seemed to be able to withstand a considerable amount of weight – and I tried not to think about how often she had struggled against its medieval restraint. Now Coursen was about to get a taste of his own monstrousness, as I attached the shackle to one of his ankles, locked it, then slapped him hard across the face to rouse him. His eyes opened momentarily. He seemed to be semi-cognizant of where he was. I leaned down and whispered in his ear three words: 'Praise the Lord.'

Then I stood up and kicked him hard in the crotch.

This time he let out an agonized groan. I scoured around the floor and found a filthy pair of track pants that had been left near the mattress. Ivy resisted at first when I tried to help her into them, but I kept whispering to her that she was going to be all right, that it was all over now. I managed to get the track pants on her, then tried to raise her to her feet. But the septic ankle gave way and she howled with pain. So I heaved her over my shoulder, expecting to buckle with the strain, but she was so thin, so emaciated, that she seemed to weigh nothing at all. Without stopping to look back at Coursen I moved towards the door. The absolute darkness of the countryside meant that I had to walk with immense care towards a car whose outline was barely visible. It took over five minutes to find it. By the time we reached it I could hear Coursen in the distance, now screaming.

He was back in the land of the fully conscious. And he was going nowhere now.

When we reached the car there was a tricky moment when I had to lean Ivy up against the side as I opened the passenger door. Some weight was put on her ankle and she almost pitched forward from the pain.

'Sorry, sorry,' I said as I kept her upright with one hand and opened the door with another. Then I carefully maneuvered her into the passenger seat and lowered it, so it resembled a makeshift bed. Instinctually she curled back up into a ball and started to shudder.

I shut her door, then raced around to the driver's seat. The car started on the first turn of the ignition. As my hands clutched the steering wheel they began to shake so hard I had to squeeze the wheel tightly to bring the shudder under control. I turned on the lights, put the car in gear, reversed and, peering over the lights, steered it back onto the dirt track. We bumped along for fifteen minutes, Ivy saying nothing, me trying to keep the shock of everything that had just happened at bay. When there was a final bump and we hit tarmacadam, I remembered that Coursen had turned right here. So I knew I would have to turn left. But before I did I dug out my cellphone and a card that was in my wallet. A card with Sergeant Clark's coordinates on it. His cell number was the last one listed. I dialed it. The phone must have rung nine times before he picked it up – and from the grogginess in his voice it was clear that I had woken him.

'Sergeant, it's Jane Howard.'

'Who?'

'Jane Howard.'

'Jesus Christ, do you know what time it is?'

'Four-thirty-one exactly. And you need to get into your car now and meet me in Townsend.'

'What?'

'I'm around ninety minutes from Townsend, so get into your car now. You're going to meet me in front of the Townsend Assemblies of God church.'

Now he was fully awake.

'You have really crossed the line now,' he said. 'Do you have any idea what sort of trouble is in store—'

'I want you there,' I continued, ignoring him. 'And I want an ambulance there as well.'

'Why? So they can cart you away?'

'I've got Ivy MacIntyre.'

A silence. Then: 'You're talking bullshit.'

'You want me to drive her all the way to you in Calgary?'

'Seriously?'

'Seriously.'

'You're insane.'

'You've got it in one, Sergeant. I am insane.'

Twelve

TWO DAYS LATER, I left the country. And Sergeant Clark even drove me to the airport – to ensure, as he put it, that I was 'packed off out of town'.

But I'm getting ahead of myself here . . .

Townsend.

The road was empty and I arrived there in ninety minutes, stopping once at the only service station en route to avoid running out of gas and to buy several liters of water. As I paid for everything, the woman behind the counter – she couldn't have been more than twenty – gave me the once-over and said: 'You don't mind me saying so, you look like you've had one rough night.'

I managed a crazed smile and said: 'You have no idea.'

Then I went back to the car. Ivy was still curled up in a ball, her thumb in her mouth. I sat down beside her and opened a liter of water and told her she had to drink it. It didn't take much coaxing. I lifted her head up and held the bottle as she gulped half a liter down without pause. The water seemed to revive her a bit. When she pushed the bottle away, she then immediately took my hands and pulled it back towards her, downing the remaining half-liter with great urgency.

Then we were off again, a passing road sign informing us we were one hundred and fifty kilometers outside of Townsend.

'Once we're there you'll be with people who will look after you, make you better,' I said.

'You promise?'

The voice was small, hushed – but at least there was a voice there.

'I promise,' I said.

'What's your name?'

'Eleanor,' I lied. 'And what's your name?'

'I told you already: Ivy.'

I smiled.

'I know exactly who you are,' I said.

She fell silent. Then, ten minutes later, she suddenly said: 'He killed the other girls.'

'He told you this?' I said, trying not to sound shocked.

She nodded.

'Was he talking about Hildy and Mimi?'

She nodded again.

'Did he say where he buried them?' I asked.

'There's a basement under the shed. He told me I was going there as well once he was done with me.'

She fell silent again. Then, around five minutes before we reached Townsend she said: 'I've got to talk to my daddy first thing. I know he's been so worried about me.'

I bit down on my lip and said nothing.

Light was perforating the blackened night as we crossed the town line. Upon turning down a side street towards Townsend Assemblies of God I saw what was awaiting us: two cop cars, an unmarked vehicle, an ambulance. I pulled into the parking lot – and Clark approached us. He was accompanied by Officer Rivers. Clark looked at me with hardened professional skepticism as I got out of the car. I just nodded to both of them, then opened the passenger door. As Clark and Rivers peered inside, Ivy simply looked up at them. I could see what they were seeing – the haunted eyes, the cuts and abrasions, the virulent sores around her lips, the ankle wound that was possibly gangrenous. Rivers put her hand to her mouth. Even Clark – Mr Professional Tough Guy – looked shaken, then immediately waved the medical people over.

Five minutes later, Clark was driving me back from where I

had just come, a police car with two officers trailing us. Sunrise meant I could now discern the terrain through which I had already traveled. It was a two-lane blacktop traversing the loneliest stretch of geographic infinity I'd ever seen – bare flat plains which seemed to extend beyond all limits and enveloped you in that most terrifying of scenic prospects: a measureless void without boundaries. On my way back to Townsend I'd made a point of checking the odometer at that exact moment when I turned off the dirt path and back onto this paved road. So I could now tell Sergeant Clark that we'd find a turning off to the right exactly 153 km from the Townsend Assemblies of God church. As I mentioned this I touched my jacket pocket and felt a hard metal object contained within.

'In all the confusion and excitement back there I forgot to give you something,' I said. Then I pulled out Coursen's gun.

'Jesus Christ,' Clark said, relieving me of it, weighing it in his right hand (while steering with his left), checking that the safety was on, then telling me to open the glove compartment and find a plastic evidence bag. There were around a dozen such bags in there, along with surgical gloves and other forensic debris. He asked me to hold open the bag as he dumped the gun into it. Afterwards he popped the lid of a storage compartment between the two seats and lay the gun inside it.

'I think you'd best tell me exactly what happened,' he said. 'And I want to know everything, minute by minute.'

I did as asked. Clark didn't interrupt me until I got to the end of it all.

'And Ivy definitely confirmed that Coursen told her the bodies are in the basement?' he asked.

'I'm afraid so.'

He shook his head and said nothing for a while.

'So he's mangled and waiting for us.'

'You bet.'

'If we've got him for Ivy and Hildy and Mimi and can now reveal him to be the guy behind that hushed-up abduction in Dundas, what else might he have done over the years?'

'I'm sure the two of you will have a lot to talk about.'

Before we reached the dirt track I informed Clark of something that had been formulating in my mind all the way back to Townsend.

'When this story breaks in a few hours,' I said, 'it will be huge. And you must agree to one thing – in fact, I'm going to go so far as to say this is a non-negotiable demand.'

'Nothing's "non-negotiable" when it comes to a major murder investigation,' he said. 'But go on, tell me what it is.'

'I am to remain completely out of it.'

'You serious?'

'Completely. I want no one to know about my role in all this.'

'That's going to be difficult.'

'Find a way to make it not difficult, Sergeant. It's the only thing I ask of you.'

He thought this over for a few moments.

'You know what you're turning down by choosing to remain out of the story?'

'Yeah – instant celebrity . . . the idea of which fills me with horror.'

'Even though it might also mean a fantastic amount of recognition? Hell, word gets out what you did, you'll be offered book contracts, deals for the movie rights, not to mention a trip to Ottawa to get some bravery medal from the Governor General. But to hell with the glory . . . think of the money.'

'I have thought of that. Just as I have thought about how every damn journalist would fashion the story around my . . .'

'Loss?' he asked, finishing the sentence for me.

'That's right.'

'Well . . . human interest and all that.'

'No – good copy and all that. And I want no part of it, Sergeant. You take the glory, just leave me my anonymity.'

'I'll have to talk to my chief about this. But I think he'll be sympathetic.'

We hit the one hundred and fifty-third kilometer of the drive – and there, as I had gauged, was a blink-once-you-miss-it track.

'This is the right turn,' I said.

'Good thing you clocked it,' Sergeant Clark said. 'Who'd even notice this?'

'I sense that was the point.'

'It's going to be very interesting to discover how Coursen found this place – who rented it to him etc.'

'As I said before: I'm sure the two of you will have many long conversations.'

But as it turned out I was completely wrong on that score – as the Rev. Larry Coursen had one more final surprise in store for us.

Police sedans do not handle well on unpaved roads. For the next twenty minutes we were tossed like peanuts along the dirt track. Clark didn't like this one bit and his face became seriously peeved.

'Should have taken Coursen's goddamn Land Rover . . . except that would have been tampering with evidence.'

'Almost there, I think,' I said as the shack came into view.

By day it looked even more tumbledown, more forlorn and grim than I had seen the night before. We drove right up to its front door. The marked police car pulled right up by us. Clark conferred with the two uniformed officers, then turned to me and said: 'Your role in all this is now finished. So if you wouldn't mind waiting in the car . . .'

I wanted to object; to say that, at the very least, I deserved to see Coursen taken into justice. But I was too tired, too wound tight, to argue. So I leaned against Clark's car as he signaled for the two officers to draw their weapons. He, in turn, drew his own gun. Then, positioning themselves on either side of the door, they waited while Clark also stood to one side and shouted: 'Police! Do not move!'

No reply.

'Coursen, this is the RCMP. We are coming inside. Do you understand?'

No reply.

The cops glanced at each other. Crouching down, Clark ran to the window. When he raised his head up to the pane what he saw made him turn white. He charged back towards the other cops, yelling at one of them to call for medical back-up as he ran into the shack. The uniformed cop dashed to the squad car and got on the radio, while his partner went inside. Disobeying orders I walked towards the shack. When I got to the doorway I saw Coursen. He was still attached to the shackle – but he was lying face up on the mattress where he had raped Ivy. His throat had been slashed and there was blood everywhere. The knife which had caused this fatal wound was still half-clutched in his right hand.

'Oh, Jesus,' I said. Clark knelt down by the body to check for vital signs, then stood up and came charging towards me.

'Did you know he had a knife?' he said, his voice raised, the stress so clearly showing.

'Of course I didn't know—'

'You found the gun—'

'Because it was sticking out of his pocket. The knife must have been—'

'You should have checked, you should have—'

'I'm not a goddamn cop,' I yelled back, my brain also reeling at the splatter canvas that was now Larry Coursen. 'So don't tell me I should have been doing your job when—'

'Oh, fuck off,' he said. 'Just fuck right off.'

Several hours later, en route back to Calgary, Clark apologized for that comment.

'I think I was a little out of line back there,' he said.

'Is that an expression of regret?'

'Yes, it is.'

'You know something, Sergeant, for a Canadian you're particularly foul mouthed.'

'Blame my dad. A Detroit auto worker who headed across the border to Windsor when he met my mom and was offered a half-share in her dad's GM dealership.'

'So you're a compatriot.'

'Only temperamentally.'

'Apology accepted then.'

'Thank you. Now when we get to Calgary, we're going to need to get you to make a statement. But I want my Inspector present for this – and he's out of town until tomorrow – so how about letting the Province of Alberta spring for a hotel for you tonight?'

'You could hold me in a cell overnight.'

'This will be a slightly higher class of accommodation – and it also means your privacy will be protected, just in case somebody got wind that you might be associated with the case . . . though once you've had a night's sleep I am going to try to convince you to let the RCMP "announce" your role in all this.'

'Don't bother.'

'Being proclaimed a hero might do you some good.'

'It also might do me some harm. No thanks.'

'Sleep on it.'

'My mind is fully made up on this one.'

'Sleep on it.'

They checked me into the Hyatt that was located downtown. A woman police officer named Sharon Bradley brought me to my room, then said that if there was anything I wanted from my apartment she would send a colleague over there straight away. I gave her my apartment key and asked for a clean set of clothes, pajamas, the volume of *Paris Review Interviews* I was reading, my portable radio and my pills.

'The pills are crucial,' I said. Though I was now so tired that I was certain I could sleep through an air raid, I still didn't know if everything I'd absorbed in the last twenty-four hours would play havoc with my psyche and deny me eight very necessary hours of sleep. The pills, on the other hand, would ensure the oblivion I craved.

The hotel room was clean and modern and rather stylish. I stripped off my dank, filthy clothes and filled the bathtub with very hot water and the bath salts provided. Then I lowered myself in the tub and sat there for nearly an hour. There was a lot to wash away.

A knock on the door finally roused me out of this watery cocoon. I pulled on a hotel bathrobe and answered it. Officer Bradley handed me a black plastic bag containing everything I had requested. I thanked her, then pulled on the pajamas, downed the necessary pills, pulled down the blinds, hit the lights and surrendered to sleep – even though it was only six at night.

The pills did their magic and, combined with the sleepless night I had just spent, put me down for almost twelve hours. When I woke, the fact that I hadn't eaten for around thirty-six hours hit me. I ordered a very large breakfast from room service and turned on the television just in time to catch the six a.m. news on the CBC. The discovery of Ivy MacIntyre was the lead story – and it was reported that she was in a serious but stable condition at Foothills Hospital in Calgary.

A reporter on the scene talked about how she had been admitted suffering from malnutrition, dehydration, septicemia and severe physical abuse – and that a statement by the attending doctor would be released later in the day.

Then they switched over to a press conference with the chief of the RCMP in Alberta, in which he explained the circumstances by which Ivy MacIntyre had been discovered; about how an individual who wishes to remain nameless but was 'clearly obsessed with this case' acted on a hunch and followed the Rev. Larry Coursen to an abandoned shed off Route 2 around one hundred kilometers from Townsend whereupon . . .

I clicked off the television. I couldn't watch any more.

I ate the room-service breakfast, and I tossed the morning edition of the *Calgary Herald* that accompanied it (*'IVY FOUND ALIVE'* screamed the front page) into the circular bin beneath the desk. I had a shower and changed into clean clothes and opened my volume of *Paris Review Interviews* and waited.

At nine a.m. there was a knock on the door. A new woman police officer was there.

'Sergeant Clark would like to see you now at headquarters. Can you be ready in five minutes?'

On the way downstairs, we didn't take the main guest elevators. Instead we were escorted to a rear freight elevator and brought down to a service entrance on the ground floor. An unmarked car was awaiting us and took me and the woman officer the few short blocks to RCMP headquarters. This time we plunged again into its underground parking lot and I was brought upstairs by elevator.

Inside the interview room on the fourth floor was Sergeant Clark and a man in his early sixties who introduced himself as

Inspector Laughlin. He had the sort of leathery face one associated with elderly ranchers and that somewhat distanced, detached manner which was Pure West. He stood up and took my hands in his large paws.

'Miss Howard . . .'

A pause. Then: 'Well done.'

And that, thankfully, was the only note of congratulations sounded for the next two hours.

Sergeant Clark took over.

'We've been very firm in all public announcements to the press that the person who led us to Ivy MacIntyre wishes to remain anonymous – and this, of course, has created a media feeding frenzy. But only Inspector Laughlin, Officer Rivers and the two officers who accompanied us to the shack know of your identity – and we plan to keep it that way.

'Now, we are aware that certain people at your place of employment might have known about your "interest" in the Ivy MacIntyre case – and I have already personally spoken with Geraldine Woods late yesterday evening. I explained that I was entrusting her with a piece of highly classified information, and asked if she could keep a confidence. I then explained, as simply as possible, that you had been "greatly resourceful" to us in the search for Ivy MacIntyre, but that – for assorted personal reasons – you did not want your identity revealed to the public. She was most understanding and also assured me that she would never reveal anything. You've worked with her. Do you believe her?'

'Unlike most everyone else at the library she's not a gossip. And she is pretty honorable.'

'That was my impression – especially as she pointed out to me that it might be best to invent a story about you having left the country several days before Ivy was discovered.'

Personally, I couldn't see Marlene or Ruth buying this – but I also sensed that Geraldine, in her own quiet forceful way, might make it clear to them that she would not entertain any discussion of the matter, especially if . . .

'I think you should let her inform the staff that I had a nervous breakdown and was dispatched back to a hospital in the States for treatment.'

'Do you really want your colleagues to think that?'

'I was heading for one before all this – and they all knew it. So . . . yes, by all means. Anything to cover my tracks.'

Clark looked to Inspector Laughlin for advice. His reply was a curt assenting nod.

'Consider it done then,' he said.

'Have they found the bodies in the cellar?' I asked.

'The forensic teams began excavation this morning.'

'And Ivy? I heard on the news she was classified as "Serious".'

'She's not in danger of dying. She is in danger of losing her foot, though the doctors are doing everything to save it. She hasn't been interviewed by us as yet – and won't be until her condition considerably improves. But she keeps asking for the woman who found her . . . and for her father.'

I was going to say something like: '*You got that all wrong, didn't you?*' but Inspector Laughlin pre-empted me.

'A bad miscarriage of justice took place,' he said. 'Nothing more. Nothing less. We will have to deal with the consequences of all that.'

'And Brenda?' I asked.

'You mean, you didn't see her everywhere on the television this morning?' Clark asked.

'No. I avoided all that.'

'Lucky you. She played the overjoyed mother and grieving widow at the same time.'

'She's now grieving for two men – as she was also involved with Coursen.'

'How do you know?'

I recounted the conversation I had heard between Coursen and his henchman, Carl, while sandwiched in his trunk.

'You didn't mention this yesterday,' Clark said.

'There was a lot going on.'

'Point taken. But just to ensure that you didn't forget anything else – and to have an official transcript of your version of events – I'd like to take you through the entire story again. We're going to videotape it – but don't worry, this will never be made public. And Inspector Laughlin's going to sit with us, if that's all fine with you.'

'I'll do whatever's asked.'

Another curt acknowledging nod from Inspector Laughlin.

For the next hour I retold everything. As I spoke I could hear myself functioning not just as a witness, but also as the weaver of a tale. Courtesy of a night's sleep and even a single day's critical distance, I knew that this version – though completely similar to the narrative I spoke yesterday while driving back to the shack with Sergeant Clark – still had a more polished feel to it. I had never been able to talk about Emily's death until that moment in Vern's car. But this story came easily. Because it was a story I could live with. Because it was a story with an ending that wasn't awful.

Clark rarely interrupted me as I spoke. Laughlin stared straight at me, his gaze level, unwavering. Only once did I see his face contort – when I spoke about the string of scatalogical abuse Coursen leveled at Ivy as he raped her. Even this hardened cop found that aspect of the story unspeakable.

When I was finished, Clark thanked me and said that I might as well have another night's sleep in a decent hotel courtesy of the Province of Alberta. 'It's the least we owe you,' he said . . . but I sensed this offer of a free room was a ruse to politely keep me under surveillance while the coroner confirmed that Coursen had died by his own hand.

'And while you're killing time in the hotel room,' Clark said, 'you might want to think about where you intend to spend your three months of paid sick leave. The sooner you are out of Canada the better.'

As I stood up to leave, Laughlin and Clark both got to their feet. A final handshake from each of them. A final quiet nod from Laughlin – and I was handed over to the woman police officer and escorted back, through the same clandestine sequence of underground parking lots and freight elevators, to the Hyatt.

There was an internet facility in my room and I checked my bank account. I had more than enough to live on for several months in a cheap corner of Europe. Only a week earlier, I had read an article in the *New York Times* travel supplement about how Berlin was the only affordable capital city left on the Continent. As it turned out, Lufthansa had a daily flight from Calgary to Frankfurt, with onward connections to Berlin. They even had a last-minute standby fare for just under $1,000. Not a bargain, but bearable. I called them up and reserved it for the following night.

Clark called me at five-thirty that evening to check in.

'Any news from the coroner?' I asked.

There was an embarrassed silence on the other end, then Clark said that the Calgary medical examiner had conclusively reached the decision that Coursen had cut his own throat and had died from massive hemorrhaging of blood.

'Meanwhile they have found two sets of bones in the basement – so it looks like everything he told Ivy was absolutely true. We now have every police force in the country with missing girls on the books inundating us. We're going to spend years sifting through the other cases.'

'And I'm going to spend the next few months in Berlin.'

'Lucky you. When are you flying?'

'Tomorrow, actually.'

'I'm pleased to hear that, as there is now all sorts of media speculation about the "Lone Vigilante" – that's what the *Calgary Sun* called you, but they are a rag – who saved Ivy. Already the press are giving us a very hard time about refusing to name you. We keep saying that we are just respecting your wishes – and with every statement we make the pressure grows. So . . . yeah, getting out of here tomorrow is a very good idea. And just to absolutely ensure that your exit is completely trouble-free I'll pick you up at noon at the hotel, get you to your apartment to pack, then have you at the airport by three for the five p.m. flight.'

'How do you know what time the Frankfurt flight leaves?'

'Simple – I looked it up while talking to you.'

Another good night's sleep. Another clandestine exit from the hotel, only this time into a car driven by Sergeant Clark. He got me back to my apartment and told me I had half an hour to pack. The time constraint focused the mind, but I owned so little in the way of clothes that I had my bag packed within minutes. All my bills – the rent, the utilities, the cellphone – were paid directly from my bank account. My salary would continue to roll in, at least for a while. I would continue to keep the cellphone off. No one knew my private email address, bar my banker back in Boston, and the professional address I used at the library would remain untouched during my absence. I was free to disappear again, slipping away under the radar.

Certainly that was Clark's intention as well. At the airport he drove me into a special secure corner of the terminal, where I was privately checked in and passed through security, then accompanied by a member of the airport staff to a small lounge off the departures area. There was a bar there and Clark, who had insisted on accompanying me through these various formalities, opened up the fridge and said: 'Can I buy you a beer?'

He returned to the sofa and handed me a bottle of Labatt's.

'Was all this clandestine stuff necessary?' I asked.

'Probably not – but at noon today the *Calgary Sun* offered a ten-thousand-dollar reward to anyone who could name the "Lone Vigilante", so why take chances? Anyway, I think you merit a stylish send-off – and I also want to make certain you're packed off out of town.'

He clinked his bottle against mine.

'How're you feeling, Professor?'

'Tired – despite the two nights in a good hotel.'

'Don't be surprised if all this comes back and bites you in the ass in a couple of days. You don't shake off everything you've seen overnight.'

'I'll keep that in mind.'

'Still, when the dark stuff hits, keep in mind that old line about how if you save one life you save the world.'

'Sergeant,' I said, 'that's bullshit – and you know it.'

He looked momentarily taken aback by this, then shrugged and took another slug of beer.

'So much for my stab at profundity.'

'Save it for the next "Lone Vigilante".'

'Or maybe I'll try the line out again when you're back in town . . . if you'd like to hear it again.'

'You never know,' I said.

But I actually did know. I wouldn't be coming back to Calgary again.

Clark, however, was right about the return of the dark stuff. It happened a few nights after I landed in Berlin. I was staying in a cheap hotel near Mitte. I was still fighting jet lag. I was coping with the isolation of being in a strange, shadowy city with no command of the *sprache*. Jolting awake at four a.m. on my third night there all I could see in my mind's eye was Coursen's blooded neck, his clothes drenched in gore, his eyes frozen but reflecting the crazed fear of his last moments. He was beyond monstrous – and I couldn't even begin to fathom the way he could do such appalling harm and simultaneously get through the day, ministering to others, acting smugly self-righteous, listening to his motivational tapes. And at that four a.m. juncture – when Coursen's slashed and hemorrhaging throat filled my head – all I could think was: *This is an image that will never quite leave me.*

The next day the weather was clement, sunny – so I decided to walk off my nocturnal phantoms with a long hike down Unter den Linden. I turned left at the Brandenburg Gate, and then happened upon two acres of gray stone slabs. This was the Holocaust Memorial. Walking into it was an unsettling experience, as the slabs were laid out like sarcophagi in a cemetery. The deeper you walked into their labyrinth-like formation, the more they engulfed you. After fifteen steps into its epicenter you were entombed by it all – gray block upon gray block, removing all peripheral vision, all sky, all sense of anything beyond the absolute unyielding prospect of immutable slabs of rock, determined to bury you.

It was overwhelming, this memorial to a horror that was beyond words. It said everything by not trying to say anything. Its creator understood that a grief – whether collective or individual – is entombing. And how do you excavate yourself from a tomb?

I had no idea. But again, I worked at getting through the days.

Berlin improved once I discovered Prenzlauer Berg. It was a reconstructed quarter just north of Mitte; a place of nineteenth-century burgher sensibilities updated for the new century, and in a once-divided city remaking itself. Prenzlauer Berg was a place of young families – and that was hard. But on the bulletin board in its very excellent English-language bookshop, the St George, I saw an ad for a small studio apartment. I paid it a visit. It was just 15 square meters of living space, but off Kollwitzplatz – the best address in the district – and tastefully furnished in a simple bleached-wood style. The landlord was willing to rent it to me on a three-month basis, renewable thereafter. I didn't have to buy anything for it bar sheets and towels. I signed up for an intensive language course at the Goethe-Institut. I spent six hours a day mastering umlauts and the dative case – and met a quiet Swedish artist named Johann. He'd come to Berlin on a fellowship to learn the language and to paint. Much to my surprise we drifted into a fling: nothing serious (he told me he had a girlfriend back home) and, through mutual agreement, pleasantly circumscribed. We went out two, maybe three nights a week together. We got cheap seats for the Berlin Phil or the Komische Oper. We went to jazz joints that didn't have a cover charge. We saw movies at the cool little kino in an alley off Hackescher Markt. And then we would spend the night together in my fold-out (but still double-sized) bed.

It was strange – almost impossible – at first to reconnect to that arena called physical intimacy. When Johann first made a move, my initial reaction was to flee. But fortunately that reaction was internalized and was supplanted by a far simpler thought: I wanted to have sex again.

Johann was decent, tender, and a little distant . . . which, truth be told, suited me fine. I liked being held by him. I liked being taken by him, and I liked taking him. We rarely talked about things that mattered to us – though I did hear about his authoritarian semi-aristocratic father who wanted him to join the family law firm, but still half-subsidized his attempts to be an abstract painter. The fact was, he did have talent and the Ellsworth Kelly-style color studies he showed me demonstrated actual promise. But as he himself admitted, he had just enough of a trust fund to ruin him – and he preferred mooching in bars and cafés to getting down to the serious business of mastering his craft. He rarely asked me much about myself – and when he once commented, early on, that I seemed to be in the throes of an ongoing sadness, I just shrugged and said: 'We all have our stuff.'

And my stuff was something I simply didn't want to discuss.

Nor did I want to go near anything to do with the press – though a week after I landed in Berlin I passed a newspaper kiosk and saw that, on the front page of a particularly low-rent tabloid, there was a grainy photograph of Coursen with the headline: 'Das Monstrum der Rockies!' In the future, I averted my eyes whenever passing any news-stand.

But between intensive German, and my nights with Johann, and the fact that I could always fill a free evening with a concert, a film, a play, the time in Berlin passed easily. There was a playground on one corner of Kollwitzplatz and that had to be avoided. So too did a dinner with some German friends of Johann's. When he mentioned that it was at the home of a couple with a five-year-old daughter I begged off.

'I'm not that keen on young children either,' he said. 'But do what you want.'

That was the beginning of the end of things with Johann – not that it ever progressed beyond a pleasant enough convenience for both of us. He announced one day that he was returning to Stockholm in a week's time. Jutta – the woman he'd been with for three years, a diplomat's daughter, well-heeled – was missing him. And his father had offered to buy them an apartment if he would return to his long-abandoned law studies.

'I suppose I'll be a part-time painter now,' he said, sounding a little sheepish.

'I'm certain you'll have a very good life.'

'And what will you do now?'

'Return to the States – and find a use for the dative case.'

Beyond such facetiousness, I knew that I had to be doing something with my life. There was a part of me that couldn't function without a sense of direction, of ambition, of some sort of purpose to the day. As I found out in those early months in Calgary, to drift meant to retreat deeper into myself. Even taking German classes now struck me as treading water. Maybe I just wasn't good at playing the bohemian card. Or maybe, deep at heart, I was simply frightened of standing still for any longer. Whatever the reason, I knew that Dr Goodchild was right all those many months ago in Calgary: What choice did I have in life but to go back to work?

So, around a week before I made the decision to head home ('*home*' – it was the first time I had used that word in years), I sent an email to my old contact, Margaret Noonan, at the Harvard Placement Office – explaining that, due to a 'personal tragedy', I had left the academic world for the last while, but was now thinking how much I missed standing up in front of a class and talking about literature. And I was just wondering if she might know of any teaching job that had opened up for the fall.

A day later I had a reply – and one which began with Noonan saying she had, of course, learned about my 'personal tragedy' and could only express her 'immense regret' at my 'terrible loss', but was pleased to hear that I was ready to 're-enter the world'.

Re-enter the world? Perhaps – but with everything changed. Changed utterly.

She also said my luck was with me. Did I know Colby College in Maine? A top-twenty liberal-arts college, lovely rural location, smart students. A two-year post had just opened up there, a faculty member having just been offered a big job at Cornell. And though I'd be in competition with around eight other candidates, she was pretty certain they would like my credentials. Was I interested? I emailed back, saying yes indeed. Five days later I was told I had a job interview in a week's time.

So I threw away my fixed-date ticket back to Calgary and bought a one-way fare to Boston. I closed up my apartment and said goodbye to Johann. We had one valedictory night together in bed. In the morning, as he left, he simply said: 'I enjoyed our time together.' Then he kissed me on the head and was gone. En route to the airport my taxi was diverted around the Brandenburg Gate and I passed the Holocaust Memorial for one last time. Today – after days of early spring sleet – the sun had cracked the gloomy dome of the Berlin sky. It was actually balmy. So balmy that a trio of adolescents had decided to use three of the Memorial's slabs as makeshift sun beds. I wasn't offended by this. Rather I found it strangely affirming. What I see as a metaphor for all the granitic grief in the world you see as a tanning opportunity. Life – even at its most excruciating – is never more than a few steps away from all its inherent absurdity.

Later that day, as the plane dipped and began its approach to Boston, I felt nothing but dread, wondering how, *if*, I could handle being there. I rented a car at the airport and drove straight up to Waterville, Maine. The college had arranged a hotel for the night. The chairman of the department – a young live wire named Tad Morrow – took me out to dinner. He'd liked my book. He liked my credentials. He liked the fact that I could talk a good game about recent novels and movies, and had even tried being a librarian for a while. And I actually found him good news – very convincing about the college's attributes and the pleasures of living in Maine, while also explaining that, up here, you were cut off from big-league academia.

'I can live with that,' I told him – and the next day, despite fighting jet lag, I nailed the interview. So much so that, when I returned to Boston that night and checked into a hotel called the Onyx near North Station, there was a message awaiting me from Margaret Noonan. I had been the last candidate to be interviewed and I actually had the job, starting this September.

'The chairman did indicate that the post could go tenure track, especially if you publish another book in the meantime. I have here in my notes that you were, at one time, working on a biography of Sinclair Lewis. Might you think about going back to it?'

'I might.'

So there it was: a job offer, a motivation to return to that world.

I was still flagging from the flight – but the management of the hotel had put a complimentary bottle of wine in my room, and I celebrated with a few glasses of Australian red. Then, around midnight, too wired to go to sleep, I called a number I had so wanted to call for so many months, but just couldn't.

I could hear Christy's sharp intake of breath as I said hello.

'Oh, my God,' she said. 'Where are you? *How* are you?'

'That's a rather long story,' I said. 'But the short answer is: I'm in Boston and I'm . . . OK, I guess.'

'I've only tried to make contact with you around six hundred times . . .'

'I know, I know. And I hope you know why that was impossible for me.'

572

'I did know about Montana and your flight north to Calgary. Half a dozen times I was ready to jump into my car, drive over and arrive unannounced . . . but Barry always advised me against it.'

'Who's Barry?'

'Barry Edwards is a town planner here in Eugene. In fact, he is *the* town planner for Eugene, Oregon. And he also happens to have been my husband for the past six months.'

'Now that's news.'

'Yes, it certainly came as a surprise to me as well.'

'Happy?'

She laughed.

'Like you I don't do happy. But . . . well, it's actually not bad. And I've got some other news as well – and I'd rather tell you straight out than later. I'm pregnant.'

'That's . . . wonderful,' I said. 'When are you due?'

'In sixteen weeks. And I find it difficult telling you all this.'

'But you just did. And I'm glad you did now, rather than when I come out to see you.'

'Now *that's* news. Do you have an ETA?'

'That depends on your schedule.'

'My schedule remains what it was. I teach on Tuesday and Thursdays. I lock myself away from three to six all other days to try to inch my craft forward a bit – my usual prolific output of a poem every ten months, if I'm lucky. But . . . *you* . . . I need to know more about you.'

'I'll tell all on Friday. I'm going to Calgary in two days to close down my life there. I'm pretty sure I can fly on to Portland.'

'What brings you back to Boston?'

'You'll get the whole *spiel* on Friday.'

'You're not planning to see Theo while you're around Cambridge?'

'Jesus Christ, no. I haven't been in contact since I had an incident with himself and his lover in a diner off Harvard Square.'

'Yes, I did hear about that . . .'

'I figured you probably did. The world is sometimes too damn small.'

'Well, I know for a fact that Theo wants to talk to you.'

'And how do you know this?'

'Because he's called me every couple of months, wondering if I had any further news of your whereabouts. On two occasions he was rather drunk and very teary. Talking about how Adrienne had dropped him, and how not an hour went by when he didn't think about Emily and you, and how he wished—'

'I don't want to hear any more of this.'

'I don't blame you. So . . . Friday then. Email me the flight details. I'll be there.'

'I'm really pleased with all your news, Christy. All of it.'

'Who would have thought? Me who always said I'd run a mile from all this.'

'Life does have this habit of upending all our dogmas.'

'I am so glad you called.'

'I'm glad too.'

Afterwards I put my head in my hands. Theo. In all the months since Emily's death I'd tried to suppress my rage against him. In one session after my botched suicide Dr Ireland told me that, at some point in the future, I would have to find a way of detaching myself from the hatred I felt for him.

'I'm not saying you have to forgive him,' she told me. 'That might be impossible – and if it proves so, there it is. But what you will have to do is stop hating him. Because hate is ultimately toxic to yourself. You can't win with hate. It goes nowhere, it solves nothing and, sadly, it can't turn back time.

One of these days – and it might be years from now – you're going to have to drop it. But that might take a long time.'

Too damn true – because all I could still feel was contempt and fury.

I told Mr Alkan the same thing when I met him the next day. He seemed genuinely pleased to see me – and, in his own quiet, hesitant way, asked me how I was bearing up.

'Some days are tolerable, some aren't. The nature of the beast, I guess . . .'

'Before we get on to other things I must tell you that your . . . "ex-partner" I suppose is the official term for him . . . Mr Theo Morgan . . . has been in touch with me on a regular basis, attempting to re-initiate contact with you. Naturally I followed your instructions to the word and never contacted you about this. But . . . how can I put this? . . . he fell apart on the phone and seemed disconsolate about his break-up with you and . . . uhm . . .'

'The death of our child?' I asked.

'Quite. There are around half a dozen letters from him here for you, sent over the past year or so.'

'I don't want to read them.'

'Then they will remain here until you're ready . . .'

'Burn them, throw them out.'

'Perhaps you will think differently in time.'

'No, I won't. It's exactly how I felt when I asked you to sell the apartment.'

'Yes, you did ask me to sell the apartment, Ms Howard – just as you also directed me, quite clearly, to hand over the insurance settlement to a charity for bereaved parents. But apropos the apartment . . . when you signed over power of attorney to me, you simultaneously signed a document giving me free rein over what I could do with your estate. So, I'm afraid, I breached your directive – as your apartment in

Somerville is being rented to a very nice visiting Professor of French at Tufts. He's paying two thousand a month – and after tax and running costs, you've been netting around twelve hundred a month, all earning interest in an account I set up for you. Not a fortune, but . . .'

I was going to say something whiny like: '*I did tell you to sell the damn thing.*' But I knew it would sound . . . well, *whiny*. Something else struck me: All those months ago, when I was in the darkest wood I could imagine, my need to shed everything was, without question, colored by the fact that I could think of no other solution than to leave the world.

But now . . . *now* . . . well, it's somewhat graceless to admit this, but I was rather glad he had held on to the apartment for me.

'Thank you for thinking clearly for me when I simply couldn't.'

'It's what I'm paid to do. But yes, I did arrange the entire insurance payment to create a fund in Emily's name with the Samaritans—'

I held up my hand.

'Some other time, OK?' I said.

'Fine. But there is one other thing that has to be discussed. The cemetery called around two months ago, asking if you were going to commission a headstone for Emily's grave.'

I knew this was coming – as I also knew that Mr Alkan would be sent a 'reminder' from the powers that be at this 'place of rest' (as they called it in their scuzzy brochures), wondering when I'd fork up the several thousand dollars for the requisite marble slab.

We're all selling something in this life . . .

'Can you give me a pad and pen, please?' I asked.

He pushed both forward. I picked up the pen and wrote:

Emily Howard Morgan
July 24, 2003–January 18, 2007
Beloved Daughter

Then I pushed the pad back towards him.

'Can you take care of this?' I asked.

'Of course. And if you would like to go out and view the site . . . ?'

'I just . . . can't. It's just too soon.'

I felt immense guilt about this – the fact that I still couldn't bring myself to visit my daughter's grave. But as much as I tried to talk myself out of this decision, a voice inside my head uttered two words: *Not yet.* There will be a time, somewhere in the future, when, perhaps, I can stand above where she is buried and not fall apart. But that's not possible right now.

'No problem,' Alkan said. 'I'll take care of everything.'

After this meeting I went to an internet café and booked myself on a flight to Portland, Oregon, with a two-day stopover in Calgary. I also wrote an email to Geraldine Woods, thanking her for all her decency and kindness towards me. Though part of me felt badly about not going in to see her and my other colleagues while in town, I also sensed it was better this way. I wanted to travel under the radar – to pay off what few bills I owed, ship my books back south to Maine, redirect my mail, call the realtor and ask her to terminate my tenancy of the apartment, close down my bank account: all that endgame-in-a-place stuff.

Upon reaching Calgary at lunchtime the next day all this was achieved in a matter of hours. I even went to Caffé Beano for a valedictory cappuccino – and asked one of the baristas behind the counter if I could borrow the phone to make a local call.

I dialed the number for the Central Public Library. Just in case Ruth Fowler was answering the switchboard late this afternoon I put on a terrible English accent and asked to be put through to Vernon Byrne. He answered on the third ring, announcing his name in that hesitant, I-really-don't-do-public-conversations manner of his.

'Vern, it's me.'

A long silence. I broke it.

'Are you still angry at me?'

'I was never angry at you,' he said.

'If I were you, I would have been.'

'Where are you right now?'

'Calgary – but please, don't tell anyone else that.'

'Your secret is good with me. Anyway, you know I talk to nobody around here.'

'Any chance of a drink tonight?'

'I'm hearing András Schiff play Beethoven – and the concert's long since sold out, otherwise I'd say come along. But I have the day off tomorrow. You free?'

'I'm free.'

The next morning he was outside my apartment building at ten. He was, as always, dressed in that brown car coat and flat corduroy cap (which he probably wore to the beach – if, that is, he ever went to the beach). He greeted me with his usual tentative nod of the head.

'You have to be anywhere today?' he asked as I closed the car door behind me.

'Actually, no. My books are packed up, my suitcase ready. I've got a flight out tomorrow morning at eleven. Other than that . . .'

'How about a drive?' he asked.

'Out of town?'

He caught the worry in my voice.

'That's what I was thinking – but not south. We don't have to head down there.'

South meant Townsend and the badlands. *We don't have to head down there.* Was this Vern's way of dropping a hint that he was on to me?

'I was thinking northwest – if that was OK with you?'

'I think I can do that now.'

We headed off, CBC Radio 2 (as always) playing on the radio. There was an uncomfortable minute or so when we didn't seem to be able to say anything to each other.

Then: 'I want to apologize,' I said.

'For what?'

'For calling you a drunk.'

'Why apologize for an observation that is truthful? I'm a drunk.'

'It was still a lousy thing to say.'

'It didn't bother me.'

'Well, it bothered me.'

A pause. Then he asked: 'Have you been following the news about Ivy MacIntyre?'

'I gave up on news a few months ago.'

'Then you missed all the big stuff. Seems that Brenda MacIntyre was having a big fling with Coursen, not knowing that it was he who was holding her daughter. She's gone into hiding since then, public opinion having completely turned against her.'

'How's the girl?'

'The doctors actually managed to save her foot. Otherwise she's been sent to some rehabilitation place outside of Toronto where they deal with children who have been through severe trauma. I know all this because every day there's been something on the case in the *Herald* and on the news. The press can't get enough of it.'

'I'm sure.'

'There's no question that Brenda's going to be declared an

unfit mother and Ivy – when she's ready – will be found foster parents.'

'And how did the police and the press deal with the fact that they so demonized George MacIntyre?'

'A major *mea culpa* from the RCMP, an editorial in the *Herald* apologizing for rushing to judgement, and the province has just announced compensation in the form of a two-million-dollar trust for Ivy MacIntyre.'

'That's not going to bring her father back,' I said. Once again I saw her lying face down in the car, telling me how desperate she was to see her daddy.

'According to the press she still keeps asking to meet the woman who rescued her. And the press keep upping the reward for the person who will come forward and reveal themselves as her savior. So far around fifty different women have said it was them.'

'Evidently there are a lot of "Lone Vigilantes" out there.'

'Seems to be,' he said quietly. Then, with his eyes never once deviating from the road up ahead, he added: 'But I know it was you.'

I fought off a half-smile. I failed. Vern's eyes veered over towards me to catch this. The radio played on. And the matter was not raised again.

We reached that juncture in Calgary geography where the city drops away and the plains reassert dominance of the landscape.

'Where are we heading exactly?' I asked.

You'll see,' he said.

For the next ninety minutes, as we drove steadily north, I kept my head lowered and avoided looking out the window – because as we gained altitude the badlands were soon encumbered by the jagged, epic silhouettes of the Rockies. Once or twice I caught their stern grandeur out of a corner of my eye – and I had to turn away. It was still too hard to look at such beauty.

Vern knew this, so he kept up a reasonably steady stream of chat, asking about my forthcoming return to the college classroom and quizzing me intensely about every good concert I had heard in Berlin.

'There were no bad concerts,' I said. 'Because it's Berlin.'

'I'd like to find a way of getting over there.'

'You should, Vern. Because sitting in the Philharmonie, listening to that orchestra, would make you happy.'

'Happy,' he said, trying out the word as if it was a foreign one he had hardly uttered before and wasn't quite sure how it sounded. 'Maybe one day . . .'

'Yeah, maybe one day.'

We passed a town called Canmore, a suburban sprawl dwarfed by mountains. We entered Banff National Park. My ears popped as the road gained further altitude. We ignored the turnoff to Banff. I chanced another glance out the window and again instantly turned away. The road narrowed. We skipped the exit to Lake Louise and the Icefields Highway towards Jasper. Instead we continued our western progress, soon crossing the border into British Columbia and passing an old railroad town called Field.

It was here that Vern finally signaled a turn off the road: a blink-once-you-miss-it turn. The road suddenly became as narrow as a country lane. It plunged us past a rushing stream and then down a long corridor of densely packed Douglas firs. They towered above us, taking away the sky.

'Not too much longer now,' he said.

But it was still another ten minutes before we came to a halt. As the car bumped along the half-paved road, as this forest primeval closed in around us, all I could feel was mounting panic: *I can't go on, I won't go on.*

581

But we kept going on . . . until, suddenly, the road ended. This was it. Nowhere else to drive beyond here. Vern parked the car and got out. When I stayed rooted to my seat he came around to my side of the vehicle and opened the door for me.

'Come on,' he said.

'I don't think I can—'

'Don't think,' he said, interrupting me. 'Just get out of the car.'

Fear. It's always there, isn't it? Endlessly ruining your sleep and holding you hostage and taunting you with the knowledge that, like everyone else who has ever done time on this planet, you are so scared of so much.

But to give in to fear is to . . .

Stay sitting in this car, I guess.

Go on, be brave, shoot crap, take a swing at it – and every other bromide you care to mention. They're all telling you the same thing: *You have to get out of the damn car.*

So I did just that.

Vern took my arm and guided me a few steps to my immediate right. My head was bowed, my eyes half-shut. I kept focusing on the ground, the paved parking area giving way to a dirt path bordered by deep grass.

We stopped. I thought: *If I about-face now, I'll be able to make it back to the car and not have to see anything.*

But Vern, reading my thoughts, touched my arm again and said: 'Look up, Jane. Look up.'

I took a deep steadying breath. I felt a shudder come over me. I held it in check. After a moment I finally did look up.

And what I saw in front of me was . . .

A lake. Absolutely still, serene and, yes, emerald. The lake stretched towards a definable horizon – a vast meadow that, in turn, ran right into a wall of mountains. It was a peerless day in the West. A hard, blue sky, empty of clouds. A sun that, though initially harsh to the eye, bathed everything in a honeyed glow. Its glare forced me to lower my head, but then I raised it up again. The lake was one of topology's more fortuitous accidents. It occupied center stage in an amphitheater of glacial peaks, many still dense with snow. It was a scenic vista of such scope, such complete purity, that I blinked and felt tears. I had been able to look at the lake. It meant everything. It meant nothing. But I *had* looked up. I had seen the lake. And that was something, I suppose.

'Thank you,' I said to Vern, my voice a whisper. He did something unexpected. He took my hand. We said nothing for several minutes. I turned my gaze from the lake to the sky. And somewhere in the messy filing cabinet that is my brain came a remembrance of a particular sleepless night some months past. Up with grief and the sense that I was now living in a fathomless world. Surfing the net, trying to murder the hours until first light – and suddenly deciding to Google the word 'uncertainty'. And what did I find? Well, among other things, there were several pages on a German mathematical physicist named Werner Heisenberg, the father of the Uncertainty Principle who posited the idea that, in physics, 'there is no way of knowing where a moving particle is given its detail' . . . and 'thereby, by extension, we can never predict where it will go'.

That's destiny, I told myself after reading this. *A random dispatch of particles which brings you to places you never imagined finding yourself. After all, uncertainty governs every moment of human existence.*

But staring now at that deep blue western sky and seeing it reflected in the lake, a second quote came back to me from that web page. It was the notion, put forward by another physicist, that space was a field of linear operations. Heisenberg – ever the pragmatist – would have none of it.

And what was his famous retort?

Suddenly I heard myself saying out loud: 'Space is blue and birds fly through it.'

'Sorry?' Vern said, trying to make sense of this non-sequitur.

I looked at him and smiled. And said again: 'Space is blue and birds fly through it.'

Vernon Byrne thought this one over.

'Can't argue with that,' he finally said.

And we kept looking at the lake.